Harvey

A novel by David Tarrant

ISBN : 9780992857943

First Published 2016
Shadows Books & Media Publishing
Torridon House
East the Water
Bideford
Devon
EX39 4HF

ISBN: 978-0-9928579-4-3

HARVEY

Website: www.shadowsmedia.co.uk
Email: shadowsbooks@aol.com
Telephone: 01237 700901

Ronald (Harvey) Bright dropped out of school in the mid Sixties causing consternation in his family. Following experimentation with illicit drugs and a long spell in hospital he gets married. Following the birth of his son he rejoins society and gets a job.

Harvey loses both parents but is often haunted by his mother in various guises.

His ineptitude in the bedroom leads to the failure of his marriage but help is at hand. His son leaves him with two grandchildren of the same age, from different mothers, mild mannered Amber and the coarse fiery Verna.

During his work in a Social Security office Harvey meets the formidable Herbert Crowe, an out of control beast of a man, with a soft centre. Crowe plays a major part in a custody battle with Verna who is in league with feeble Robin Lewis.

Lewis has many dark secrets, including a cache of pornography destined to be his downfall.

Harvey is a black comedy complete with flights of fancy and genuine emotion.

Acknowledgements

Stephen Millen - my friend and true support. Willie Gray & Justin (Mustard) Gokgol Mark Tarrant - for techy stuff

South African Wayne - for spending a day of your holiday unraveling my computer

Trevor Mosely Tarrant - for being the brother to me that Theo was to Vincent Elena lionnidi & Giannis lionnidis of The Tudor Inn, Gouvia, Corfu John Glenville-Dowling - for the many laughs Kindle Direct Publishing - for the opportunity Nikki Brownson - who made the whole thing possible Shadows Books/Shadowsmedia & again Nikki Brownson. Bex Tarrant - for being the daughter every man wishes for.

Darren Tarrant - for being solid and sensible

In Memory of (Scottish) Charlie Campbell RIP

I hope to meet Kate Moss (Fashion icon) before I die

Contents

Chapter One

"Goodbye Grandad" cried Nicki, "Bye-bye Grandad" yelled Bernadette, "Love You" they screamed together. "Love you two, too" was the reply, less audibly "you little buggers" and with a cheery wave Ronald Verity Bright reversed his old Vauxhall Senator out of the drive. He glanced over his shoulder to acknowledge more shrieks and viewed the 'little buggers' with Mrs Kitson waving frantically. Engaging his James Brown cassette he gave one final wave, blew a kiss to each of the seven-year-olds and was gone. Singing at the top of his voice 'I feel good dododadoo....' en route from Hampshire to Gatwick Airport, 9 am, bags of time.

Ronald Bright, known by all as Harvey, considered himself a lucky man. He had not an enemy in the world and his only weaknesses were pretty members of the opposite sex and strong drink, neither of which he had held for some time. Now, having sorted out several pressing matters, he was destined for a whole two weeks on his own, in the sun.

Many Years Earlier - The Beginning

Born in Northern Hampshire, England in 1947, of good stock to a lifelong cricket fanatic, young Ronald was adorned with the middle name of Verity, after one of his father's heroes. Although he was the apple of his more than a little weird father's eye, to his mother, RV was a 'little shite'. He had cost her a head-turning figure and produced nothing except an endless source of noise and laundry, neither of which she tolerated gladly.

Apart from free milk and a few extra ration coupons, Mrs B could see nothing in the future of parenthood and instructed Mr Bright to seek his carnal satisfaction elsewhere. She had no further intentions for her 'front bottom' to be anything but the most private of private parts and most certainly a one-way street. "You know I love you dear, but one of the girls from the village is better suited for that sort of thing," she told him, adding a note of caution. "But no scandal and certainly no more brats".

To avoid the need to chase girls, which he was entirely unsuited and to avoid scandal, Bright senior settled for the occasional wank. As time passed the places he chose to take the matter in hand were invariably public. He was extremely lucky to have avoided recognition, let alone a scandal and a prison stretch. Masturbation, he had deduced, was kind of boring unless there was an element of risk or even an occasional implement attached. Finally he was chased, and nearly caught, from the rambling cross-country course of Winthorpe Secondary Modern School for Girls. Wearing only a cricket pads, a keepers glove on his working hand and a Donald Duck mask concealing his identity, he just managed to outrun the burly Games Mistress. It was then he decided that public performances were not his forte. This left 'The Winthorpe Wanker' one of the Hampshire Police Force's unsolved cases and the girls of the school extremely grateful to have the cross-country cancelled until further notice.

Following his narrow escape, Mr B contented himself with the odd tweak of the Willie while sniffing from a small bottle of linseed oil in his potting shed. He would sometimes tie items of cricket memorabilia to personal parts and pendulum them to and fro. Getting enormous pleasure when he was able to hit his own backside with the spikes of a swinging boot. The Brights also employed a local girl to help with RV, who offered to perform the odd 'wristy' for a shilling. During her time with them she had amassed more than an average Scout Troup could expect during Bob-a-Job Week. Fortunately, for all concerned, Mr B's urges dwindled following an unsuccessful experiment with a soldering iron that left third-degree burns requiring treatment at Odstock Special Burns Unit in Salisbury. It was hard to explain and harder to believe that a can of lighter fuel had soaked his trousers while he was sleeping with a lit cigaret in an ashtray on his knee. But there was only one injured party so no great enquiry. Staff did notice, however, in all his time both as an inpatient and later an outpatient that Mr B was never once seen smoking.

Moving on.

RV was shipped off to school at the earliest opportunity. The first school was selected by Mrs B because it was far enough away to make Boarding compulsory and visiting limited. This school was followed by one that Mr B approved as it had produced some better than average cricketers over the years and was not renowned for anything more than the odd rash of buggery.

In his first year class of his second school, there was another R Bright and an identifiable nickname for the two was essential. It was evident that RV was blessed with a natural intellect whereas RB was as thick as two short planks. So it evolved that RV was anointed by his peers as 'Very' and RB was lumbered with the unfortunate handle of 'Not-so' which irritated the brute greatly. Masters and staff, however, referred to them as RV and RB so the 'Very' tag was dropped and replaced by 'Harvey'. Much to his angst, no change was deemed necessary for Not-so.

Harvey received the start of a good education and he also had that certain something that everybody liked which made him popular with peers and staff to a man. Bearing the name of a great cricketer, the Verity part of young Harvey felt obliged to give the game a go. But he had to admit he was not a natural and much to his father's disappointment he never made the school team and never troubled a willow tree again.

An aside

Not-so, however, looked on the game of cricket as the perfect way of getting back at his tormentors and stormed in when bowling. On delivery he hurled the leather clad lethal weapon at the batsmen in an attempt to inflict serious injury. He also had the knack when batting, to place many a hard hit shot between the fielders eyebrows while notching up a fair number of runs. As his list of victims grew his fame spread and he was looked on favourably by both county and national scouts. When a visiting Fred Trueman suggested that the lad aim the occasional ball at the stumps he was surprised to be told by the youngster to 'Fuck off you bow-legged bastard and mind yer own'. These and other words of wisdom were enough to ensure no county would touch the lad with a barge pole and he was destined to spend his working life bent double harvesting watercress in all weathers. His sport was kept within the confines of village cricket where he was greatly feared, even by his own team, as his enthusiasm for breaking bones even extended to them during net practice.

He did get to Lords in a village final. Although he scored one of the fasted fifties in history and recorded a haul of five wickets, he will be remembered most for chasing an umpire back to the pavilion after being no-balled three times in succession. The unseemly behaviour that followed in the Long Room with the Umpire's rear end and a stump earned Not-so a six-month stretch in Winchester Prison and a life ban from any form of cricket. His status at the watercress farm was however significantly enhanced.

If his son's lack of expertise at cricket disappointed Mr B, it was nothing to the devastation he felt when the teenager joined the great unwashed, turned on, tuned in and dropped out. Harvey prefered to be a child of the sixties to a possible Captain of Industry or leader of the Ninetie. He found the serious business of enjoying himself, as with most of his undertakings, came to him naturally and he excelled in this new-found freedom. Also, as fortune would have it, Harvey, by courtesy of birth year, missed the Mods and Rocker era and the later Skinhead violence, neither of which would have suited his nature.

Chapter Two

Cass

Catherine 'Cass' Palmer was an orphan by the age of eight, losing both parents in a road traffic accident from which she was the only survivor. She went to live with her Uncle Samuel and Aunt Amy Mears, in a small earthy smelling flat above their fruit and vegetable shop in Middlesex. The pair were her Mother's brother and sister who had never been married but stepped into the parental breach following the accident. While they were considered locally as being a bit odd, their charge always appeared well cared for with impeccable manners. Albeit a mite shabby she was never the subject of concern from any quarter.

Sam was at first attentative and often took Cass to the wholesalers and the market where he would give her healthy treats of luscious grapes, satsumas and the like. He often played little games with her like letting her put her hand in his pocket to feel the carrot grow, which made her giggle. This became tiresome as she grew older and he began touching her to the extent that she was unhappy or even frightened to be alone with him. Cass also began to wonder, and worry, why between the three of them they only ever used two beds or sometimes just one. She never mentioned this at home and was too confused or even ashamed to tell her closest friends, and there were never visitors to the flat. As she grew from the deep slumbers of childhood she would sometimes awake to find a warm hand retracting from her nightdress. Sam or Amy would laugh as if enjoying a game.

Shortly before her 15th birthday, Cass awoke to find Sam standing over her and realised this time there was no game. She leaped up and screamed for Amy to help. As she rushed into the room, the mousy spinster delivered a forceful slap across the young girl's face and gripped her wrists pulling her forward over the bed. Her ankles were pulled in the opposite direction until she was spread eagled with her face down. She sobbed and pleaded while Sam forced her legs apart and made his entry salivating and gasping

15

with the effort and excitement of the struggle. He withdrew clumsily and the pain began immediately. She felt as if she was burning and she tried to scream or even cry out but only succeeded in swallowing the salty combination of her own tears and mucus. It had not taken long, but afterwards the soft coos and caresses of Amy were not enough, nothing could take away the shame and hurt to her body and heart.

The next day Cass slipped away without a word and taking nothing. She came across Harvey on his way to St Ives in Cornwall after a hard weekend of guard baiting at the American airbase in Ruislip. Despite the guards' instructions to 'Get away from the gate Bud', and the big dogs on the other side of the fence. Both guard and demonstrator knew no harm could be inflicted with the worlds' press watching. It was 1966 and the Hippy Revolution was beginning.

Cass adored Harvey, who looked good in his tie-dye cheesecloth shirt and multi-coloured flares, which in common with his peers were rarely changed and washed even less. He spoke well but could turn on the Jaggeresque speak of the day and look part stoned whenever the need or opportunity arose. When he was actually stoned he was amusing beyond words and his accent would slip from LSE modern to USA drawl to Hampshire crawl. Or as she put it,'from Elvis to Reg without passing go'. When she was stoned she forgot everything except the moment, but was always sick after it had passed.

Cass was to learn he was not too good in the sack but what did that matter? He always found somewhere to stay or squat that was safe and dry and it was never too long before it was party time. Love-ins were generally overrated as the hash and booze made most male genitalia point at their shoes rather than their hairstyles and their attitudes less than lethargic. This left the gyrating girls open to abuse from sly pretenders and over-agers who only came along at weekends. This could include the celebrity rock stars and DJ's of the day who fancied a bit of young. Do you want to be in my gang, now then now then, everybody's gone to the moon. Cass and Victoria, another refugee from family 'life', preferred not to tune in too often and enjoyed finding their amusement in each other. After all, there was only so much sick flavoured sex one could take.

As the decade progressed, the substances became more available and varied and the experiences wilder than the worst nightmare or better than the best dream. Everybody was invincible as in Jimi's 'Purple Haze' and on the verge of destruction at the same time. Leading lights in the arts, music and fringes of the political worlds were at it or advocating it, so the trend was to 'keep on doing it'. LSD had not been banned and it featured on many early evening TV shows. In a Tonight show, a presenter was given a tab at the start of the programme and his 'progress' monitored during the show. The Southern TV channels whose areas covered Salisbury Plain even showed soldiers who had been spiked and sent on manoeuvres. Hilarious when they were trying to hide in trees but not so cool when they were attempting to shoot each other. City dogs were getting high by licking spit off the sidewalks and kids were getting a buzz from sniffing any bank note that passed through their hands, crazy days.

Even at his wildest, Harvey was never heartless and was a good provider. True he may wander off but would always return like the trappers of old, sometimes days or perhaps a week or two later. Some of his gifts were collectors items if they had had the mind or motivation. An acorn from John and Yoko in Trafalgar Square. ('Man you should have seen them'), a few rough note sheets from William Burroughs ('he probably thinks he lit up with them anyway') and Larry Adler's harmonica case to name a few. Whatever he returned with, may it be incredible or incredibly stupid, he never returned empty handed and always found a buyer. Sometimes she would go with him but, although it would be an experience in itself to meet the like of Allen Ginsburg or the prophets of Timothy Leary. The endless non-speak and semi-stoned twilight world was not for her and anyway while he was away there was always Victoria.

The sixties were preparing for the seventies and the scene was not so much to be enjoyed but endured. It was inevitable as the experiments went on that there would be casualties, from the unknown to the infamous. From the lonely confines of a Charing Cross station toilet cubicle to the facedown isolation of a luxury swimming pool in the millionaire belt of Sussex. Deaths were occurring that the release of a million butterflies could not stop. Harvey came back to earth, or at least down to it, with a great reluctance and considerable pain. While Neil Armstrong was taking giant leaps for mankind Harvey was making leaps of his own. Following a low flying accident with the assistance of illegal substances, but without an aircraft, Harvey sustained a severe back injury and lost a great deal of the Summer of '69.

It was Sharkey that nearly did for Harvey by introducing him to speedball while he was still in the time drop of an acid trip. The height of the building and proximity of the ground did not help much either. At least he lived, followed by a long term of hospitalisation which left him with a limp and slight stoop. Also he developed a reduction in his existing somewhat limited sexual competence. Sharkey made a better landing but his head and torso came to rest on different sides of a metal fence and he was no more.

The time apart was to blame for another event and nature's way of addressing a balance of one out one in. Conception had taken place in the Physical Medicine Ward of Harvey's hospital in Winchester. While one of the auxiliary nurses, Olivia Kitson, was preparing scrambled eggs in the small kitchen of the outbuildings. The ever friendly Mrs Kitson looked on all her long-term patients as family and Harvey was one of her favourites so she was happy to make herself scarce on Cass's visit. The conception owed much to Cass's ingenuity and a loose fitting kaftan from Kaftan East rather than Harvey' chair bound speedy ejaculation. She was missing him and wanting him so leapt on him at the earliest opportunity, but he had literally made a right mess of it. Alas, the seed was planted.

Chapter Three

When he finally emerged from his plaster bed in the Winchester Hospital the much reformed Harvey vowed to make things right with his father, who promptly died, and his mother, who went insane. He also promised to live up to his responsibilities towards Cass, who had been confirmed as an expectant mother.

The death of Mr B had been a shock to all and had he not been the deceased, it would have been to him also. The little and large things in life would now remain undone. The hard fact of the matter was these unfinished deeds were mainly financial that left Mrs B poor in status and mental well-being. All that could be sold was sold and finally enough was raised to keep her unsatisfactorily institutionalised for the rest of her unhappy days.

Harvey had not ever been close to either parent but visited his mother once she was settled in the Hampshire Home for the Frail and Infirm. Due to the previous owners passion for chestnut, hazel and filbert nut production the home had already acquired the local nickname of The Nuthouse. That was now more appropriate than ever. On sunny days beds were moved to the open windows, chairs were wheeled to the terrace and Zimmer-frames of all varieties were shooed in the direction. Here the smell of stale urine was carried on the wind as lazy staff could play cards and drink in the shade. They took turns to observe their charges, with minimum effort, while the wind did their cleaning duties. After a few sunny days, the pink closed-eyed inmates started to turn brown and the terrace resembled a coconut shy thus enhancing the home's nickname further.

As he strolled up the tree lined drive, Harvey was filled with mixed feelings of dread, love and reconciliation. He was greeted by the sight of a confused, virtually unrecognisable old lady who was in no mood to receive the person whom she now perceived as the root of the family misfortune. Surrounded by a gaggle of old toothless crones, Mrs B lifted her heavy skirt and pulled down her oversized bloomers while screaming 'This place is full of cunts, and here is another one'. She emphasised her outburst with wild gyrations of the hips and motions of the tongue that would not be out of place in a Swedish movie of the day. Harvey fled to more chants of what he would remember as 'The Cunts Chorus' as her ever helpful fellow inmates joined in with the deafening libretto. He was never to see his mother alive again although he would dream and visualise her often.

Mother's visit behind him, Harvey started to plan for the wedding of Ronald Verity Bright to Miss Catherine Palmer. The wedding party would not include any member of the Bright or Palmer households. Missing also were Victoria Manson (overdose - accidental!), and Roy Plummer (cells - unintentional) who were to be the sole guests and witnesses, after all this was the age of dis-convention.

After being advised by the Registrar that legalities currently outweighed dis-convention and that, no matter who, two witnesses equals one wedding. So Harvey raced to the nearest pub to explain his plight. He returned accompanied by The landlord of The Dog And Duck, Les and his good lady Wife Doris. They agreed to be witnesses as long as the ceremony did not flow into the lunchtime rush at the pub. On being summoned to the wedding, Doris, who was always one for an occasion, plucked a couple of carnations from her bar display as buttonholes for her and Les. She noticed, however, despite being dressed in matching beige trousers and brown velvet jackets, the happy couple were bereft of flowers and she rushed back to her ageing display. She duly installed the blooms in each jacket, fussing and flicking at the falling petals from the past the sell by date carnations. Following the ceremony, it was only natural to offer a bite and a drink and they returned to The Dog And Duck in plenty of time.

Little known to the newly-weds. The last time the pub had experienced a rush of any sort was when an unexploded bomb from World War II had been discovered in the cellar and announced by a pale-faced Les. Apart from Incontinent Kev, who declared 'we wondered where that fucker went', a general stampede from the Dog And Duck ensued. The pub was closed for two days while the Bomb was disarmed with remarkable ease, as it turned out to be a stray British one.

As his clientele was dispersed around the towns' hostelries, Les reasoned it would take a week to get back to normal because it would be natural for his competitors to exploit their windfall of new customers. But when the majority of displaced drinkers found their inherent acid stomachs improving Les's pipes and Doris's cuisine were under scrutiny in the bars around the town. As doctors and chemist visits declined so did Les's locals. Incontinent Kev became the lonesome regular, slighted by the 'musical chairs' that greeted his entrance to the other pubs. He was pleased when Doris had a small brass plate engraved 'Kev's Place' set in the bar. Here, she was able to circulate three seat pads (one in use, one in the washing machine and one in the dryer). To the comfort of all and give reassuring blasts of Haze Air Freshener as required. Fortunately, these were the days when pubs were hosted by retired Winco's, RSM's or Plod. They could get reasonable accommodation on site plus supplement their pensions, by selling drinks to those whom they considered mates. Les was ex-Navy and was quite happy to scale down his High Street operation to accommodate passing trade, a fortunate clause meant if sales dropped so did his rent. This would suit them until they had had enough and were eligible for that beautiful little Council bungalow just out of town. Also, they were happy to cater for the passing trade rather than face the same old faces who thought they were entitled to dictate procedure. Now it was only those from foreign parts who would rue the day they fancied a quick pie and pint at The Dog And Duck. The High Street would bring no more to cries of "ow my bleeding guts" and the area was saved from a botulism epidemic. Les survived the cooking by claiming he could not face a pie since his Navy days, but never expanded on the subject.

The drink and bite led to an afternoon lock-in, an evening meal and a stopover that lasted several months until a proper place could be found. During the evening, dwelling on his own married life, Les was only too happy to give Harvey (or the poor fucker) the benefit of his advice and the contents of several glasses. Doris furnished Cass with endless gems of wisdom but no alcohol, having noted the not inconsiderable bulge in the beige.

"Strange about Victoria" slurred Harvey as they finally got to bed. "Never thought she did much stuff normally, is she going to be alright?" "Yes strange, no she doesn't generally, and yes she is. Now go to sleep before I lump you one" grunted the new Mrs Bright, with all the skill of a hardened professional, doing Doris proud.

With no further encouragement needed Harvey was pleased to fall asleep. He had drunk too much and although he had eaten, in an attempt to soak up the booze, he was not feeling too well. As he drifted off to sleep the old bed span faster and at will. Dreamland afforded no respite either. Here he was presented with visions of his mother on a whirling flying carpet gesticulating frantically. One second she would be far away and the next in his face zooming within inches causing him to duck. Here she hovered and performed her version of The Haka with all the venom of an All Black at Twickenham. He noticed she was completely naked. Fortunately, this was a silent dream so he could not hear the mouthed obscenities. The newly acquired tattoo of four large letters vertical down her spine left him in no doubt as to her message. Freud would have been in his element.

Strange indeed mused the bride as she lay next to her sleeping husband, who had taken on the mantle of a mad dog having a seizure. Why on earth had Victoria acted so out of character? After all, nothing was going to change that much!

Chapter Four

Change arrived at 3 am Tuesday 3rd March 1970, in the form of a 7lb 4 oz, fighting fit bundle of male-hood. He was fully equipped in all quarters, and blessed with the wail of an alley-cat on steroids.

Fortunately, Harvey had run into Roy Plummer only two weeks earlier, while looking for a place to stay. He had been privileged to witness one of the small daily whimsies that pockmarked Roy's life. Roy for reasons best known to him, was walking a young Maltese dog of about eight months, very fluffy and puppy noisy. Outside a Baker's Shop was a small girl whose Mother was inside buying the girl a treat. She had just completed her first day in a new class at school and had been moved after much badgering by the mother who disliked most things in life. She hated the girls old class because the male teacher was too young (and probably sexually active). The class also contained a few gipsy types and a recent influx of brown and coloured children and the mother thought her delicate daughter would be happier in a less of a 'melting pot' environment.

Roy, of course, was unaware of this when the puppy pushed his nose into the girl's crotch and made her giggle. 'He touched my you-know' she told Roy. "Don't tell your Mother?" Said Roy. "Ok, what's its name?" "Mr Fuckface" said Roy "and it's him, he is all boy," he said helpfully as he moved on slowly, letting the dog sniff at will. They were only feet away as the mother appeared from the shop. She offered the pastry to the girl who was still gazing admiringly at the puppy. "How is your new teacher?" asked mother. "He is cute and all boy said the girl" "What" cried the mother, fearing a flush coming on. "What's his name?" "Mr Fuckface and he touched my you-know" The mother felt faint. "Oops, sorry he told me not to tell you that" "Who did, Mr Fuc....your teacher?" "No, silly. The man with him." "What man? There were two of them? Where were the other children when this happened?" "Oh mother, that is two things for me to say now, no three, ok right. The man who had the strap lead thingy, you know on a collar Mr Fuckface wore, a nice red one with study things on. Of course there were two of them, Mr Fuckface would not be safe on his own and umm oh yes, the other children were at home I expect, their Mummies collected them." The mother grabbed the child, dropping the pastry in the process, and marched off unsure if to go to the Police, Social Services or the School. The puppy returned to his paper wrapped reward, now on the pavement.

"Hey Dude" Roy hailed a chuckling Harvey. "Hi man, still choking the chicken that is the life I see," said Harvey. "Ah quit the Hippy Speak Man, whazzup?" Roy was off to Mexico for England's defence of The World Cup (round ball) and offered the use of his flat on the spot. Thanks to an inheritance, and his lifestyle, Roy was able to loan his flat to whoever needed it most. He looked on it more as an investment than a home, making him an early Hippy capitalist and, of course, popular. "But that's months away yet man" said Harvey, hoping the offer was for now not then. "A long way to go, dude, on you initiative and fuck all else" replied Roy in his usual cheery optimistic way that always got him by. "Anyway man, the pad is yours until at least late August or more. I plan to pay homage to Che while I'm down that way" he grinned, revealing a T-shirt with 'that' picture of the great Marxist. "Man, there is so much to take in down there I could be months away. I will probably, wear my thumb out hitching, my dick out humping and, of course, there is always, The Green Grass of Home. Not to mention a particular kind of gold, hey make that years." "Years in jail maybe," said Harvey "and mind those Bolivian bastards don't blow your balls off" he cautioned. "They wouldn't dare man, we are the holders of the cup after all, and when they get over the shock of us retaining it we who make it there will be Gods." Harvey envied his friend's look at life but somehow knew he would make it. "What's the dog called Man?" Asked Harvey. "Spiffy," said Roy "why?" "Oh nothing, tell me more about the pad". Arrangements were made there and then as Roy was off in two days and was happy not to have to close down the apartment, notify utilities, etc. Harvey shot back to the pub to break the news to Cass and of course Doris.

Doris insisted on an inspection, but even she agreed that it was fine and for the best. Viewing some of the drug paraphernalia she had enquired if Roy was a Doctor and somehow formed the opinion that he was. Les thought the flat 'smashing' and offered to help with anything as long as it avoided the rush hours at the pub. More importantly he also offered them a return to the D&D if it was ever needed. After all he enjoyed his late night chats with Harvey, and

Cass occupying Doris gave him more free time than he had ever known. Still time moves on and so did the Bright's with so much gratitude in their hearts to their new found and generous friends.

The flat was above a bookshop selling new but mostly old books, limited and first editions a speciality. The accommodation was deceptively spacious, remarkably clean and most importantly, very close to the hospital. It reminded Cass a little of Sam and Amy's making her feel ill at ease in one of the bedrooms and although it was the warmest, they settled on the front one as theirs. A large draughty bay window looked down on the street and was always a useful time waster as they watched people scurry by, cross the road or browse the shop below. People could be very interesting when they thought they were unobserved.

To Cass, the smell of old books were indistinguishable from the vegetable smells of years past but she had little time to dwell on the matter. Within two days, she experienced a very quick but painful labour/delivery after which she felt deflated and confused. While loving their son and heir with all her heart, she somehow felt the same pangs of pain and shame that Sam had brought upon her some four years earlier. She knew it was not the same and she was not thinking rationally, but she could not accept the difference as a form of depression crept over her and this time she could not escape to her life. Harvey, her friend, saviour and mentor of that time was now so absorbed in parenthood he failed to notice the sparkle that was slowly draining from her. Oh help, oh shit. He had also started his weird contortions during his fitful sleep which kept waking her and giving more time for her black thoughts.

During the night, Harvey's mother would appear in varying guises of unpleasantness throwing his sleep into turmoil and his/their bed into a less than a restful place. The first night above the bookshop she appeared as a librarian and put books in rows at the foot of the bed. The books were held in place and indexed by white painted blocks with large red letters indicating authors surnames. The letters of C, N, T and U, however, were placed together and not in alphabetical order spelling out a somewhat familiar message to Harvey.

During the day, Harvey was on cloud nine and did not limp for several days despite the cold, wet weather and for those early weeks of March 1970 to him it was high Summer.

The summer actual sped along with young Ronnie taking most of their time. Bobby Moore and his squad dominated the news and Moore even more when arrested in Colombia on shoplifting charges. The team failed to retain the Cup, losing to their old adversaries, West Germany, in the quarterfinals in Mexico. All too soon it was over and one day unannounced Roy was back. Tanned and looking like an Amazonian he was full of football but mostly telling tales of cocaine, superb grass and mighty shags, all three he offered Cass, in no particular order, but none was accepted.

Roy had amazingly brought back enough illegal gear to open a small pharmacy. He could have made a lot of money but preferred to ingest consistently and was, of course, very generous to his growing list of friends. Harvey joined him in a bit of blow but baulked at heavier stuff. Aping a BBC Newscaster he said, "I mean, it is alright for you youngsters, in moderation, of course......but I'm a responsible parent and must set an example, what?" It was a cop out he knew, but nobody pushed him on it and deep down he was pleased to be out of the scene. Cass was not sure if she was pleased, proud or even disappointed at Harvey's resolve, but she did not have too long to ponder. On his travels, Roy had picked up and returned with Victoria and there was much to catch up on. Cass felt her depression lift for the first time since the birth.

Reunited with Roy and Victoria the Brights decided on a naming ceremony for the young Bright. All had been referring to him as Ronnie. He had that round innocent look of Ronnie Wood of The Small Faces, but of course, it was his father's real name too.

Whether it was the dying embers of their rebellion or the hopes of a new one they decided on Savernake Forest as the venue for the deed.

Friends old and new descended on a small glade in the forest, a good decade and a half before Michael Ryan would debase the spot by commencing his bloody massacre. Cass wanted to name the child after his grandfathers who had both left space in the world for the young master to fill. Roy cynically remarked this was fortunate as it was the name on the child's Birth Certificate. One of the side-effects of his over indulgence was the need to comment on everything. So it was with horns and shells being blown, that the babe was held aloft, firstly by the absent wedding witnesses, Roy and Victoria and then the slightly confused witnesses actual, Les and Doris. The babe was then passed hand to hand through the assembled 'tribe' each taking a turn to bless the sky, trees and whatever came to mind or in view. As the last of the tribe presented the unperturbed child to his mother, she declared to the expectant ensemble. "In love we are gathered, and in love we proudly name Ronald Reginald to be known as Ronnie."

"Kray," said Roy.

"Sorry?" enquired Les

"They forgot Charlie" mused Roy again.

"Charlie?" asked Les.

"Kray" repeated Roy.

Les was becoming confused by his surroundings and Roy's incoherence. Looking first at Roy's hand rolled joint with suspicion and then his own tailor-made Capstan Full Strenght, of which he took an almighty drag before stubbing it out. "Kray" continued Roy helpfully, though beginning to sound like a mating Magpie. He passed his smoke to Les, who unconsciously took another mighty drag. "Kray, Kray, K R A Y, Kray get it?" "Fuck off," said Les with feeling as he turned to Doris for support. "Kray, Reginald, Ronald" she began as if to a five- year old. "Don't you fucking start?" He said with a strange new courage. "REGGIE AND RONNIE" she boomed. Recognition dawned. "Oh, I err, sorry," he spluttered, adding "err we shouldn't be here you know, I didn't know they were involved with err ...."

"Will you shut u...."

She did not continue as she noticed the tree opposite had suddenly sprouted legs - blue uniformed ones to be precise. Then in turn a blue uniformed body topped off by one of those strange helmets that would need an extremely odd shaped head to fill. Doris watched open mouthed as trees all around were reproducing the phenomenon. The tribe instinctively tried to scatter as Wiltshire's finest closed in. Roy would probably have made it if he hadn't returned to snatch his joint from Les and swallow it lit.

"Manners of a fucking ape" giggled Les, who had been taking more than a few drags. "Whoop, whoop and fucking whoop" he shouted as he pranced around with legs apart and half bent at the knee. Trying simultaneously to beat his chest and scratch either his armpits or balls or both he collapsed in a giggling heap where he lay until apprehended.

"Say nothing, nuffing, say nothing, nuffing right" repeated Roy, who was the only one saying anything. Before long they had been rounded up and bundled unceremoniously into J4 Black Maria's' and headed in a convoy to Marlborough. In the Police station and to the background of Roy's mantra, tobacco pouches and cigarettes were investigated and prescribed medications verified. Most of the tribe had gone through this experience countless times, only Les and Doris found it a little traumatic and decided to follow Roy's advice. Nothing was found and only Roy was detained as he insisted on speaking to a lawyer. The Duty Sergeant later allowed him to go to the toilet unaccompanied in the hopes that he may run away, which he promptly did. He later claimed a daring and dashing escape to anybody who would listen, which were not many.

On his release, Les was more reticent than earlier and looked around before speaking to Doris in lowered tones "You see, this is how you're treated when you mix with the underworld. We could be targeted now, I seen it on TV. The Police will not trust us and THEY won't like us trying to get on the inside. Or they will use us to cover for them and we will be in court all the time with dodgy briefs and all. I had no idea, oh dear, what will the brewery say, I bet they are calling 'em now, Oh My God, no chance of that little council bung......" "HOWARD LESLIE PRICE," said Doris, in an address that Les knew meant trouble, whether outside a Police Station or not, "WILL YOU PLEASE SHUT THE FUCK UP! She endorsed this with the point of a well-honed elbow to the ribs, with twice as much force than was really necessary. There the matter rested never to be mentioned again. As Les was doubled over, Roy ran past "Say, nothing...." "Fuck off" wheezed Les defiantly.

After an interview with Social Services, and an unnecessary medical check for the baby, the Brights were also sent on their way. Not being offered and then firmly declined assistance back to their transport the mixed bag trooped off to the bus stop hoping for the best. Surveying the band of bohemians who were and always would be their friends, Harvey was in reflective mood. "We can't go on like this Cass, I am going to learn to drive, find us somewhere permanent to live and err ..... get a job!" She sighed resignedly, so this is how it's going to be, she thought and shivered involuntary inside as her soul started to pack.

Fate conspired on this occasion as the party were trekking back to Savernake Forest. Across the county line Mrs Bright was becoming restless. Passing the unattended medicine trolley, on her way to the toilet, she helped herself to a handful of coloured pills, especially liking the wobbly green ones. She then knocked them back like a navvy would a pack of KP nuts. As the staff were dozing, drinking or watching television in the restroom, the old lady made her way to the top floor and threw herself from an open balcony. With a trajectory that would have assured an Olympic Gold Medal in diving , she launched herself into the night. She began to enjoy herself for the first time in years as the night air caressed her body. The polyester nightdress shrink-wrapped her spindly body and she landed without a sound, except for the twig like snapping of her neck. By the time, the grossly negligent staff found her missing four hours had elapsed. When they later found her dew sodden body they were all blaming each other, and claiming to have been on pressing business elsewhere.

The Coroner was scathing in his remarks about the management of the home and certain members of staff in particular. All were willing to testify as to their co-workers' negligence. The door to the balcony, for example, had been unlocked and undetected for weeks despite being signed off as secure. This only came to light when a decorator suddenly realised he still had both keys for the door. This was weeks after he had finished his work repainting the bed scratches from the summer. Wholesale dismissals of management and staff led to a general overall of the home which by now had been re-nicknamed 'The Nutcracker Suite' by the local wags.

Compensation was duly offered and accepted, without the need of further court appearances or the much-offered help of 'ambulance chasing' law firms. Harvey was suffering an understandable guilt trip, and trusted his small circle of friends as advisers. He also needed instant cash like of yesterday. All he wanted really was a home for his family that he could claim was an indirect inheritance from his Mother.

Chapter Five

The small chalk-cob thatched cottage was built in authentic Hampshire tradition. It was set in a small garden with a fabulous view, on the outskirts of Marsden, and filled the bill for a home of their own.

The nearby town of Chandlers Bottom was known locally as 'Chuffers'. It was a major rail junction and had the ability to chuff along despite world events. It proved perfect for most needs. Primarily a sensible Morris 1000 Traveller estate car, in light blue with oak trim, and finally/eventually the ever important licence to drive it. Harvey never took to driving naturally. Many stories could be told of his exploits, but it is easier to say that Harold Wilson had the same problem with telling the truth. Harvey's driving was much like his lovemaking - he got there eventually.

Now, to complete the set he promised Cass, he needed a place of employment to drive to. He knew that the legacy from his mother's demise was more than he deserved. He felt that, now gone, he had spent it wisely for his family and now needed a fresh supply.

Being a Social Security Scrounger for many years, Harvey naturally gravitated towards the benefits section of The Department of Social Security. It was his first time at Chandlers Bottom office but he was about to stumble upon his vocation in life. He attended his assessment and was greeted by the manager, Fred Alexander, who Harvey took an instant liking to. A large loopy man with a kindly face and gentle mannerisms listened as Harvey outlined his needs and entitlements. Harvey by now was an old hand at these assessment sessions and it became instantly apparent to the manager that he knew his stuff. He quoted chapter and verse on his entitlements and the system in general. Towards the end of the session the kindly manager, who had mostly listened without comment, presented Harvey with a form he was not at all familiar with - a job application. A long time vacancy at the office was still unfilled, despite the hard times nobody aspired to a career in Social Services. But this time the manager was confident that (with the right training and himself as mentor) he had just interviewed the right candidate. With some small adjustments to his work schedule, juggling some dates and generally working a fast one Fred Alexander appointed Harvey on the spot.

In October 1970 790 couples of the Unification Church were married by their leader, Sun Myung Moon, in a mass ceremony in Seoul, South Korea. In Chandlers Bottom an even more memorable event occurred, for the first time in his life, Harvey began work.

Fred Alexander's judgement had served him well as Harvey used his previously unexploited talents. Coupled with his natural intellect and affability soon saw him through to managing the A-E clients.

As he progressed through the ranks it was without animosity from his colleagues. Mostly old-timers they were ticking off the days to their 60th Birthday and an inflation-linked Civil Service Pension. Basically going through the motions until the great day arrived they were content. The fact that some still had over ten years to go did not hasten them towards promotion, aka responsibility. The whole complement of staff was fourteen in total when they all attended. With proper terms and conditions, generous holidays and a sick scheme open to abuse, this was very rare. They were only divided by minor points on their incremental scale, and it was easy for Harvey to float to the top without bruising any egos.

Before long he was treating them all to cream cakes in celebration at becoming an Assistant Manager, albeit one of three.

What had really pleased Fred was the way his Junior Assistant dealt with the clients and how they in turn responded to him. It must be nearly two years since raised voices had been heard he mused. As for the Police he could not remember their last visit, whereas pre-Bright they were more frequent visitors than the tea lady.

The secret, of course, was that Harvey had been there and understood what the clients were after. Instead of challenging their claims or looking for inconsistencies and telling them what they were not entitled to he would explain how he had dealt with his own circumstances. He would more than often rip up their claims and with their permission work with them on a new one. Here, he would extol the virtues of what could be legally declared over that which could be challenged. With all the benefits then available the claimants were finding themselves better off. Ok, they may have had less in their pocket, but rent, gas, electric and food were not a problem.Travel was also becoming increasingly available to them. They readily accepted Harvey's suggestions that a Summer on the coast may be more preferable to one stuck on a council estate. Some preferred his other ideas of acquiring an old bus or ambulance to live and move around in. "Don't get carried away and tax or insure it" he warned. "As long as it is your home, you can more or less do what you want and if they take it away from you, hooray. They have to house you there and then". Thus several problems moved along taking their claims with them. Some people at District level smelled a rat. Auditors and Special Investigations could not find any deeds worth pursuing. They gave up, as there were more pressing problems elsewhere, and Fred Alexander was content.

Far from content was Cass. It was now 1975, with nerve-ends jangling she finally exploded. "It's no fucking good, I can't put up with this any longer or any more" she wailed. "I love you Harvey and always will but I, I yes, I, don't have a life any longer, it all belongs to HIM" indicating Ronnie playing in the garden. "You, you are too good for him, to him anyway, and you are a better parent than me because you want to be and I don't". She was starting to lose it and those annoying clicks began in her neck, but she continued. "You are, you know what I mean, TOO GOOD. Too good for me, too good for my crap, too good for me to hurt you, that you don't deserve. I need my space, my life and decent sex. You are not too good at that, in fact, fucking useless and, and, and ..... I love Victoria" she slumped to the floor, exhausted. It had been five years, not a bad half-decade, give or take a bit on both sides. Harvey had been 'bringing home the bacon', Cass was mixing Motherhood with her business of sale-able Hippy art and crafts and young Ronnie was a pain in the ass ready for school.

Harvey reflected, they lived relatively well on his increasing salary and Cass's work was becoming quite lucrative. They had no rent or mortgage, but he realised it was not what they were originally about, and, of course, she was that bit younger. Things had been changing for some time, maybe since the birth, hmmm!

He was extremely conservative in matters of the bedroom where he become even more inept. Cass, on the other hand, had taken on the dominant role with relish . She would force herself on him, trying all kinds of established and experimental forms of arousal. Only to have her efforts thwarted once she climbed aboard. As time wore on, creams and gel aids were replaced by those of a more personal, feminine type resembling more martial arts than marital aids. The bathroom became an arsenal of spiky or misshapen dildos, some manual, some mechanical, battery and even mains varieties. Again supported by various creams that made cleaning one's teeth in the dark an absolute nightmare. Harvey became accustomed to loud buzzing sounds emanating from behind closed doors or even under the bedclothes but drew the line when she tried to invigorate his privates with one of her whirling weapons. His father would have turned in his grave, had he not had a larger than life erection. She was changing in front of his eyes but only when he sat and mulled it over did he really see the change. He suspected that one day an old friend, or even a new prophet, on their way to somewhere would end up bedding her when he was not around. This, however, started to look unlikely as most all recent visitors were odd looking women with an inclination towards facial hair, bovver boots and mud. So it had been with some relief, he reflected, when Victoria Manson walked into his office. She was after cash, of course, on her way to the Summer Solstice at Stonehenge that now hosted free festivals. Harvey was pleased to see somebody normal and took her home to Cass, who was delighted.

Although they had lost regular contact with the tribe as a mass, they were never short of visitors or groups of old friends. They were often treated as a stop-over for Stonehenge, Savernake or New Forests, the beach and all points South and West. Harvey, was of late, viewed as a bit of a cross-over working for the establishment as he did, but they did bone him for inside information on benefits. He in turn was happy to give advice and the address of the nearest Department of Social Services, ensuring this was not Chandlers Bottom. Cass attracted greater favour from guests with her back to the land approach to handicrafts. Though she failed to mention the capitalistic side to her venture.

So as Harvey returned to work and Minnie Ripperton trilled away on his radio and up the charts he whistled along with the birds. 'Loving you is easy 'cause you're beautiful, making love to you is all I want to do .....' Back at the house the same radio show was playing. Minnie sang with the same feeling, but her audience were less involved with the chorus as Victoria made love to, and walked away with Cass.

Across the water, at the same time in June 1975, in LeHavre, Claudette Golan was offering her very first sounds to the world.

Fred had been a gem and allowed Harvey to couple two weeks special leave to his annual entitlement. This would give him six weeks to sort out his domestic situation and if that was not enough 'throw a stress sickie' he had been told. Harvey said if he couldn't do it in that time he never would, so he had a mission. He also reasoned that the office could do without another long-term sickie, and Fred was sure Harvey would sort things to the benefit of all. He had also vowed to be available for any severe cases.

Harvey knew that he could go straight on to state benefits and not be much worse off financially. Ronnie had started school now so what would Harvey do with his days? He also enjoyed his job and owed it to Fred to find a solution. Short term, Gwendoline Orchard from Hope Cottage stepped forward. Gwen had two children at the school and would be able to take Ronnie to and fro and look after him until Harvey got home. She also stated that school holidays would not be a problem 'What is one more?' It was agreed that Harvey would need to take time for the odd bout of sickness as Ronnie would need that but, with fingers crossed, he was pretty robust.

A small payment was agreed and Harvey arranged for additional milk and provisions to be delivered, these were quietly received and much appreciated. But .... this could only last until the end of November. Gwen's husband, Keith, was to move the family to Milton Keynes where he had been promoted to a more senior position in the new telephone exchange. Still it was a much-appreciated breathing space. Harvey was able to return to work with leave in hand. This would give Ronnie a good start and who knows what will turn up?

Cass turned up one day at the office. The reason was divorce, Cass wanted it to be amicable but soon, 'a quickie' she said. The term still brought flashbacks to Harvey. 'You must Harvey, you will find someone else and may not know where I am, I am not coming back to you so we should do this - for you." Then the custody arrangements, 'it is only fair for you to have the formal agreement and I know you will not ever deny me. Harvey, we are friends and always will be. I'll keep in touch of course ....'

Fred, Gwen and colleagues also urged Harvey to take the divorce route for his and Ronnie's sake. Nobody cared much about Cass's thoughts or logic, but Harvey finally decided to do it for her, naming Roy as a correspondent. 'Yeh man, I always wanted to fuck her and did so many times in my sleep, sort of the same s'pose, so yeah, no problem.' 'I fucked Vicky Manson too, can I help her as well?' November was approaching fast so it would be one less thing to do.

They attended the divorce hearing together, no solicitors or agenda. It was clinical to the extreme, with around 15 - 20 other couples to hear their names read out and the Decree Nisi was granted. If neither party complained and nothing emerged in the next six weeks, the Decree Absolute would be in the post, almost easier than getting married.

Now to the Judge's Chambers for the small matter of the future of Master R, R Bright, custody and welfare to the fore.

His Honour Judge Garfield-Bull did not like divorce cases, if he had to put up with his lot then why should others be able to duck out and fuck off at will. He could hear a hundred in a week and the only good thing about it was he only got home on the weekends.

His brood had fled at the earliest opportunity and were now only a drain on the purse, whereas the lovely Virginia was becoming less Golden by the day. She resembled the Viking lady in the film What's New Pussycat - only less endearing, but His Honour knew she was his for life and by God it felt like a life sentence.

His Father-in-Law would have him blackballed at The Lodge if he even suspected a hint of divorce and without a Lodge a Mason could not survive and what Judge ever progressed without the backing of a good Lodge.

With the height and bearing of his former Rugby days still evident, the love of Port polishing his complexion and single malt whiskey bruising his temperament the Judge was quite unappreciative of most trivia that appeared before him. He also loathed modern women and 'round ball' football.

The Judge's Chambers were a more personal setting with all sitting around a large conference table with His Honour of course at the head. Harvey and Cass sat together with empty chairs either side, presumably for solicitors. A Clerk, Court Official and a transcriber took the other seats.

Dressed in his gown and wig, Judge Garfield-Bull advised they had the freedom to speak their piece if they desired and he would ask them to clarify anything that was not clear. Cass cleared her throat, "Hmmph, Ladies first then." he huffed.

She told the Judge that she was not cut out to be a parent and needed to live her life unshackled by parental duties or responsibilities. She went on, amid raised eyebrows and flushed cheeks, that she was not prepared to give her life away, that Harvey was a good and responsible person and parent. She knew he would provide their son with the best he could manage and that she had already begun her new life. She intended to spend her time with her lover who was an old and beautiful friend.

"And where is 'this beautiful friend', um Palmer, today when you need him?" inquired the Judge with a hint of bias. "Her Your Honour, and it is not Mr Palmer, that was a thing" replied Cass hopefully helpful. "A 'thing' by Jove I think it was a young woman. What do you mean Herr? Herr, who is the wretched fellow a German, ?" asked His Honour, instantly regretting his persistence. "Her, she, Victoria - my lover, is a woman - Your Honour, and is not here today. She is training a girls football team in preparation for a tour," spat back Cass, scoring one for the sisters.

Judge Garfield-Bull was on his feet before she had finished speaking. "Bah," he bellowed. "Custody to Mr Bright, no restrictions or recommendations, and no comment. Bah". With a flourish of his gold and platinum fountain pen across all the relevant papers he was gone without another word, although the odd Bah could be heard from the corridor.

Back in his Robing Room, Judge Garfield-Bull removed his wig with a sigh. He plucked the efforts of the day lovingly from the tight curls before placing it in the purpose made velvet lined box. The gown was removed with all the aplomb of a Matador facing the penultimate charge and then given the same attention as the wig. As he bent to remove his suspenders he wondered what made people behave like that, lovely thing too. "Bah' he bellowed to nobody in particular, and the world in general. "Bah, Bah, Bah and Bloody Round-ball to boot, Bah."

Chapter Six

The stresses and strains of recent events had for some reason caused Harvey's back to act up in sympathy. With reluctance, he had to resort to taking pain killers which in turn made him constipated. Constipation led to piles, which in turn were painful, itchy and a bloody nuisance.

One evening he was working late to catch up and his piles were at their worse. He looked up to see Fred staring at him in sympathy. "You look in pain M'Boy, don't over do things eh. We don't want you poorly. Can I help with anything?" he enquired.

Harvey explained his problem and was surprised by the reply. "Rockets" exclaimed Fred. Harvey looked puzzled. "Anusol Suppositories my dear Harvey. Marvellous little things, like white rockets they are. Just stick your foot on the side of the bath, preferably after a bath. Locate the entry point and pop it in, slippery little bugger will find his own way from there, and by this time tomorrow the problem will be solved." he described with evident authority. "Knocks all the creams in the world into a cocked hat, especially if you let rip before he finds his location" he chuckled, looking at his watch. "The French take all their medicines that way, strange folk, imagine using throat lozenges or eye drops," he chuckled, checking his watch again. "Do you know that most Americans write 'Jai Presque mange un suppositoire ici' in their postcards home from Paris" "What?" " Oh sorry Dear Boy, roughly 'I nearly ate a suppository here'. He checked his watch again, "Brown &Winslow (pharmacy) is still open so leave all this for another day and go and relieve Mafeking."

Harvey took the advice and thanked his mentor before rushing to Brown & Winslow for a pack of rockets. He located them quickly as they were on a promotional end of aisle position as a 'Manager's Special Deal'. He must have a problem, a good sense of humour or is managing an epidemic thought, Harvey.

He had been in the shop a good deal recently but had not noticed the assistant on duty before, and, of course, she was a lady. There was a vague sense of recognition to her, however.

Harvey, already embarrassed by his purchase, grabbed the first thing to hand to accompany his rockets - a pair of tweezers, may be handy one day.

"You don't need them together dear, they may be slippery when warm but are quite simple to use on their own" smiled the assistant. They both laughed, each probably envisaging a different image.

The penny dropped, "Mrs Kitson" exclaimed Harvey, staring into the kindly face of the Auxiliary Nurse from Winchester and years past. "My word it's Harvey, or is it Mr Bright now. How are you?" she asked "of course apart from these" she added, putting the Rockets in a bag and the tweezers on the shelf behind her. "I never thought I would see you walking so well, it must have been the haircut that did it."

The shop was now empty and they were able to exchange the circumstances that led to this unexpected reunion.

Olivia Kitson had been a victim of cutbacks. When hospital beds are left empty for fiscal reasons the idea is that those who maintain them are surplus to requirements, auxiliaries were the first to go. Cleaners could be trained up to make beds and nurses trained down to feed and wash, good economics.

Olivia had been forced to look elsewhere, much to Harvey's relief this did not include a certain nursing home. At present, she was only covering for sick leave at the pharmacy, who called her in from time to time, but this was ending in a few more days, then back to the agency.

Olivia was at that 'certain age' as the French would call it, that covers anyone who is not young, beautiful or sexually active to those dressed forever in widow's weeds. She was however blessed with a friendly jovial manner that cross all divides. She now lived locally with her husband Bill, who had to leave the docks due to a lung disorder which was a combination of too much smoking and certain cargo that would later be banned from British soil.

After his long stay in the hospital, Harvey knew Olivia long enough to offer her a job. "Forget the Agency, I know you and know you will be the best thing to happen for Ronnie, and me of course, please say you will."

The arrangement continued happily and uncomplicated for most of Ronnie's school years. Olivia assumed the role of surrogate Grandmother and Housemaid/Cook until poor Bill was in need of more care than they were. Hospices were a growing venture at that time and the Countess of Brecknock was not a household name. So Olivia was needed to assist Bill with all his needs and functions, 'Til Death Do Us Part.'

By the time Olivia left, Ronnie had become a teenager and was happy to cope when Dad was not around. Harvey employed agency folk to clean and launder for them and he and Ronnie both enjoyed experimenting in the kitchen. After a bout of eating each other's mistakes they became quite good but they both agreed though that they missed the smell of fresh bread that used to greet them when they got home.

Olivia's presence was also missed by both who, unknowingly were starting to agitate each other but she had always managed to find a balance without interfering.

Cass was little or no help, she thought it was time Ronnie began to find his own way and would actively encourage him to take to the road. This made her infrequent visits something of an annoyance as she tried to sway her son towards her preference of body piercing and artwork. One day Harvey returned home to find Ronnie with a pink Mohican haircut and an earring. He could do nothing about the hair but threatened to bite the stud out if it was not voluntary flushed down the toilet. If there was, is such an animal as, a typical teenager Ronnie had developed all the essentials. He could sulk with the best for no reason, cut those who loved him dead with a single glance. He could also be generally obnoxious when the mood decided, or his friends were around to impress.

Deep down they loved each other but were getting to the stage of protecting their own space and outgrowing each other. Cass's infrequent and unwanted visits irritated and the typical teenage syndrome developed with hormones to match.

Crystal Baker-Bromley could not be described as typical, and at age thirty was most certainly not a teenager but had an excess of hormone activity, that would have shamed an alley cat, was in abundance. 'Trouble' was a very apt description of Crystal and while never typical she certainly was topical. When the chips were down and a label was needed, the word 'slapper' was made for her.

As one delivery boy to her office told his mates, "Fucking Hell, she is dirty and hot but she has a whore's hole, you know, one big enough to hide in." This led to a procession of large dicked drivers, whose penises resembled a banana looking at the sun, volunteering for that office run.

She would shag anything and her exploits in numerous Social Security offices in London and Home Counties were legendary. She would always gain a new position within the service, albeit a different town, by her excellent qualifications and impeccable references. All of the latter given by previous Managers' who had bedded her and later found she was too hot to handle.

Unfortunately, Fred was recruiting after losing one of his team of long-term sick people. The retiree promptly held a dinner dance as her retirement party and was dancing the night away long after others had flagged.

Chandlers Bottom was far enough away to have not heard the Crystal stories and Fred received her transfer application with a happy heart. Her experience took her over and above any outside applicant, which was the criterion for internal appointments. As with most of his dealings, when Fred knew what he wanted, the interview was a formality, her bearing, good looks, charm and sensible shoes could only prove an asset to the department.

Chapter Seven

Harvey had coped with the last lonely decade well, which only surprised him. The over-riding factor was the well-being, welfare and development of his son. With Olivia's unprecedented input, this had been managed above and beyond expectations. Perhaps more than a little of his own welfare had suffered in place, but that was parenthood and life.

He remained Assistant Manager and the other two were phased out. Maggie's Law said 'if you have three people in Public Service doing a job, get rid of one. Then look at the other two and keep the best on new terms if you can get them'. Harvey had survived, with terms and conditions intact due to one of his colleagues retiring and the other getting a sickie at the right time. Fred was pleased and relieved and had had a small hand in spreading Maggie's Law to the scared ears of those wanting to jump ship, an early retirement and sick leave were much appreciated.

Transfers were exempt from Maggie's Law as it was known there was no hiding place and all would be reviewed eventually.

The years had come and gone without any memorable personal happenings. The world stage saw 'Evil Empires' an 'Iron Lady', Local Riots and World Famine. Had he still been an activist Harvey would have been at the forefront of something or other but now was obliviously lazy of events.

Odd members of the tribe kept in touch but, apart from Roy, he was not really close to anybody and quietly happy with the status quo. Roy as usual was exploiting all he could on his journey through life and really should be the subject of a book if he could only remember all that stuff.

For company, Harvey had begun to drink quite heavily and was well known at the local. The current description of drinking was to 'have' or 'sink a foo' and Harvey sank enough 'foos' to fill a Chinese

Battleship. He nearly always appeared in control and hoped this was the case but knew deep down the opposite was true.

He had found, however, that being a single father had a certain kudos as it was a bit unusual. Without trying, he had a certain amount of pulling power with unattached females and the less unattached barmaids of the area. His dalliances never amounted to much as his conquests found that their unbridled passions were nearly all wasted. Most blamed themselves for failing to arouse or engineer an evening of sexual magnitude. They would leave feeling deflated. Some blamed themselves for selling him too much ale and crept away to waiting husbands. The 'slave driver' Landlord at the pub was cited as the reason for being late home, then they would seek permission to climb aboard and give sleepy hubby a happy ending to the day.

None of Harvey's 'conquests' was aggrieved enough to be in the remotest unfriendly towards him, and still enjoyed his company. If he was honest with himself, he much preferred the flirting to the deed but he couldn't help taking that one step too far.

After each of his failures had made a modestly moist departure Harvey would drift into another alcohol induced attempt at sleep. His mother would then glide into his room, straighten his bedclothes, plump his pillow, smooth his hair and ever so gently whisper 'Cunt' in his ear. This never failed to jolt him awake as if a massive electric shock of Old Sparky proportions had passed through his body.

Where the father failed the son excelled. Ronnie had more than his share of good looks, a personality that would never have a crisis and a dick to die for. The latter he was not afraid of using. He was aware of Harvey' exploits as had witnessed many a lady taking the shadows homeward. He was never to know that his father had a diploma in sexual ineptitude. In early 1987 Ronnie followed his mother's lead and wandered off. Also like his mother, he spent a long time in bed with women of all shapes, sizes and denominations. Harvey had recognised the signs his son was emitting and did not stand in his way - how could he? It had been a long way they had traveled together but now found it hard to live together and each deserved their break. Harvey gave him his extensive knowledge of life on the road and his favourite Kerouac book, On The Road, with every other page concealing a pound or five-pound note. He also gave ignored advice on safe sex and illicit drugs. Whatever the current name for tetrahydrocannabinol imbibing was had already made an impression on the fledgling. Harvey hoped and maybe prayed that the interest would not drift to the killing fields of harder stuff. Harvey warned, and was heeded, on the use of crack cocaine which once used became the orchestrator of one's life and in a lot of cases - death.

Chapter Eight

Crystal Baker-Bromley had watched Harvey from afar. This one puzzled her, the girls at work appeared to adore him and would do anything he asked. Although most were either much married or the other side of attractive he treated all flirtatious with equality as if charmed by their attention, even hers! She had noticed a few occasions when she was sure that he must be a stud. The first being when she spotted Harvey in a huddle in the pub with Brigit from S – Z. Later she had seen his old car misted up inside at a local, condom littered beauty spot. A week later the new barmaid at The Swinging Sign, Claire, was getting the treatment. This time, she witnessed him driving Claire towards the beauty spot after closing time and wondered how many discarded Durex were his. She noticed with amusement the next day that a silver and clear closed back ladies sandal, with studded strap and 6-inch heels, as worn by Claire was on display in the front of his car. The semi-lethal heel was embedded in the car radio, toe down so she presumed Clare was a straddler. The shoe was being used to house a plastic drinking cup, and the radio was destined to play Radio Solent for the rest of its days. Later she saw him again in The Swinging Sign with both Claire and Brigit, drinking and laughing together like old buddies, hmm?

Crystal had not been sexually rested since her arrival. Discretely The Sign Boys band at the pub could just manage a joint effort between sets on a Friday. Digger Daley, with his muscular physic and mutton chops sideburns, could work up a slight sweat on a Wednesday, whilst Mrs Digger was at Bingo. Then Barry from Office Supplies, could perk up a tea break when staples were low. Had they conferred, The Sign Boys may have wondered how she fitted them all in at once. Barry may have thought for the first time ever that his huge dick was subsiding as it seemed to rattle inside. Digger, meanwhile, knew his JCB bucket had produced smaller holes in the Hampshire soil. But for all this, Crystal had not had a good seeing to for a while. The last time she had been ridden home hard was by an over enthusiastic group of jockeys after the

Hennessy Gold Cup at Newbury. In fairness they should have been cautioned for excessive use of the whip. Now for some strange reason she thought Ronald Verity Bright was the man up to the task and for some even more bizarre reason he was.

With is back continually agitating Harvey had signed on with Dr Hope in Chandlers Bottom and was now on a permanent pain killer. He had been assured it was non-addictive and if rested occasionally the drug could be stopped should something better come along, or the condition improve. One unfortunate side effect was erectile dysfunction, but Harvey had laughed and assured Dr Hope that he knew all about that already. The doctor partially registered this comment as he was in dire need to stick his head out of the window and partake in one of his eighty a day cigarettes. With Harvey gone, and this accomplished, the comment came back to him and he started to rummage through his papers.

Sipping the head off a pint in 'The Sign' later, Harvey was surprised to see Doctor Hope approaching. "Sorry Doctor, I'll just have the one" he lied, thinking about his medication. "Crap and you know it" smiled the doctor as he lit a fresh cigarette from the one he was smoking, "Now buy me a Sherry, I may have news for you."

Sherry in one hand and a cigarette in the other, Dr Hope explained his reason for seeking out Harvey. "Friend of mine works for a drug company in Kent, funny name, German or Swiss, but anyway based in Sandwich. They are half way through testing a new drug, all very hush hush, and five years in, one of the human testers ups and dies, daft bugger. Nothing related to the drug, his wife accidentally pushed him off a balcony on holiday, horny bugger was trying to rear end her." Harvey looked confused. "Don't worry all will come clear" wheezed the doctor. "This drug has all the components to treat angina and other heart problems". He held up his hand, "I know you are ok on that score, let me finish please, I need to get home tonight. Well, it turns out that it is only moderately successful in that area, but chemists are funny buggers and like to test or at least try their own inventions. Before long some of the chemists are walking around with a totem pole in their trousers, they had actually stumbled upon what they think is a cure for erectile dysfunction for all ages. They started tests with the usual mixed bunch and the results were immediately phenomenal. Those testing the drug perked up in more ways than one. Cheered up immensely, one old Vicar even started to breed again. The filled in their weekly results forms and, had it been one case, the lab would have thought it a matter of boasting. But all sent the same responses and all had a request to reduce the dose as sitting in public places was becoming an embarrassment. Those on the placebo remained as miserable as ever." He paused to light up again. "So here they are with this red hot product on their hands with fortunes to be made and in need of a new tester without advertising why. You, my dear chap fill the bill to the T. You have a history of um, you know, you are the same age as the late tester and, no history of heart problems, or blood pressure issues. You are on medication which can only help prove their case if the drug helps you. The only problem is I cannot guarantee if you will be given the drug or a placebo. Testers are not meant to know, but as the last one had a horny demise one can assume he had the real deal. Are you up for me putting you forward, like I say, all hush, hush, and they have reduced the amount of the dose. You don't take it every day and carry on in all other regards as you do now, only thing is their blasted log, but you must be used to paperwork by now -eh? What do you say."

There was only one answer "YES" and Doctor Hope would later be happy with his no fuss Finders Fee.

Harvey attended the laboratory in Sandwich where he was treated like minor Royalty. The company being grateful to find a discreet volunteer who quite readily fitted into their programme. He was given a full medical examination and specimens were taken for analysis.

He was then given the grand tour and a brief history of the drug. He was told that they hoped to release it with a clean bill of health in the UK by 1991. This would be after all Government Agencies etc, had considered the evidence, side effects and unbiased testing.

They were hoping for a worldwide release soon after and their big dream was to open over the counter sales, with the right promotion they were sitting on a gold mine. In reality, they thought that the drug would be regulated to those with medical needs. Indeed in the UK, Maggie's Law would not like the general public enjoying themselves. The country was already awash with unwanted pregnancies and miners with too much time on their hands.

When he saw the drug Harvey was surprised to find it a small purple tablet not much larger than an aspirin. It was sectioned into quarters that resembled one of those pie charts political programmes used to show divides of one sort or another. He would be required to take one tablet a week, a quarter at a time, he could freely upgrade to two-quarters but would never be issued with more tablets than the weekly allowance. His doctor, Doctor Hope would be entrusted with the administration, his medical well-being and receiving his daily log in weekly instalments. Then it was a short matter of waiting for his specimen results before he took his first dose.

Harvey could not wait to try the drug when it arrived. Suddenly he was randy as a rabbit as the blood rushed to his penis. His usual 'have another drink' philosophy did not calm the swelling as he walked around ogling everything in a skirt and he felt genuinely sorry for those who had started on a stronger dose. His habitually dormant member was in a constant state of readiness and displayed a vein pattern that resembled an All Major Routes map of the United Kingdom. Early into his programme he decided to take his dose only in even amounts every two days or when there was a promise of sexual activity. Dr Hope agreed this was probably for the best.

Crystal Baker-Bromley did not know there had been a transformation, but her basic animal instincts detected a powerful chemistry when Harvey was close. She longed for the opportunity to exploit her primeval senses to the full.

It was thanks to modern technology when this chance presented itself on Friday 12th June 1987. The office had been party to joining the electronic super highway many years hence. But, Luddite Fred had been a little remiss when it came to disposing of files and had maintained an unofficial archive 'just in case'. This had now become manic in size, costly to maintain, never used and a complete embarrassment. Harvey finally got Fred to agree to dispose of it before it was discovered. Best intentions held little water, especially with the great handbag of Whitehall. The disposal was quite a responsibility. Not only was the information highly confidential, it was probably illegal under the Data Protection Act, so the managers' undertook to shred it themselves.

With the office shredder going full pelt, it should have been a menial task but nevertheless manageable for them to accomplish in a working day. All was going swimmingly until Fred's cases were up for the chop. Then it was 'did I ever tell you about this one?' 'My word, I'd forgotten about him' 'I wonder whatever happened to them?"

The list was endless and almost all accompanied by an anecdote from Fred's extensive memory, but he was no fool.

"Did I tell you about the penny pyramid at 'The Sign'?" he asked, Harvey shook his head and awaited another tale.

"No, well it was huge. Made out of pre-decimal penny's, 12 to a shilling, 240 to the pound and there was about £50 of it. Well at Christmas, Dudley, the then landlord before Salty, sold tickets, bob-a-go. Guess the total of the pyramid, or nearest penny, and win the ticket money. The amount from the pyramid in turn would go to a charity nominated by the Mayor, who agreed to push over the pyramid a week before Christmas."

He paused for breath. "Dudley asked for volunteers to count the money and two readily stepped forward. Unfortunately, they were coin collectors and what should have taken a couple of hours dragged on for a second day. Each coin was examined as they looked for rare one. Edward III being a particular favourite as he was only King for a year. Dudley got fed up, kicked the buggers out, and he and Wacker Payne finished the job in no time."

Fred sensed Harvey was tiring. "My point dear Harvey is it is impossible for me to pass one of these files without taking a peek so I am withdrawing my labour."

He instructed Harvey to take Miss Baker-Bromley to lunch and sweet talk her into helping him in the afternoon while he (Fred) took over the desk. Not an especially attractive task after the pubs closed on a Friday afternoon. "It will help me keep my hand in" he groaned. "Tell her it must be cleared today though Harvey. If it means working on. I will have to arrange some lieu time or something, and it must stay between the three of us, or....", he made sawing motion across his throat, no more needed to be said.

"Don't worry Boss" Harvey assured him, "if she can't stay on I'll not push it. I'm a free man if it takes until dawn considers it done! Those District Audit Boys will never know. Oh just make sure you don't put the alarm on when you go, ok?" "What would I do without you?" was Fred's relieved reply.

Harvey approached Miss Baker-Bromley at around 11.30, with the proposition of lunch, followed by an unspecified mundane task, that could be a bit dusty. He had half expected some form of protest or even an outright refusal, but none was forthcoming. The only condition she levied was that she be permitted to leave the office immediately to fulfill a prior commitment.

She would meet him in The Lamb around 12.45, rather than The Sign, as she had been told their Friday Fish'n'Chips were second to none. He agreed, 'Head Office' may not have been pleased to hear that public officials were making up their own rules or even the reasons for it but needs must etc The sooner the job was done and dusted the better.

Harvey thought he had emphasised the 'dusted' or dusty part of the operation but when Crystal walked or was it glided into the crowded pub there was an audible gasp. The busy lunchtime trade of The Lamb had rarely seen such beauty personified and gawped as chips slid from plates.

She was certainly not dressed for manual labour. Gone was the M&S suit of the morning, replaced by a flimsy white blouse that revealed a strapless bra, which in turn presented the raised and darkened image of her nipples beneath. A silk scarf was loosely draped around her neck in a casual swirl that would take a supermodel years to perfect. All this was put in the shade by the figure hugging mid-length skirt with a strategically placed slit in the oriental style, that positively oozed sexuality coupled with class, and no visible panty line.

"Where have you been?" croaked Harvey, trying not to shake. "It's five to, I should discipline you for being late." "Oooh, yes" she purred.

He had been standing side on to the bar, watching for her to arrive. After her stunning entrance, a sudden movement in his underwear made it prudent for him to face front immediately. She had not been slow to notice that there could be more than one outstanding matter that needed attention this afternoon.

Lunch had been fun and the food was excellent but Harvey had problems dealing with the stirring in his loins. He sat bolt upright as possible, blaming his back injury. He pushed his backside hard into the seat and hoped that his jacket would disguise the coiled spring that was pushing against his zipper.

There was no chance of hiding his predicament from his companion, who was flattered and amused by the development. "How did you learn about the fish lunch?" he asked innocently. "Oh, I know some sailors" she joked, and so it went on. She put a double entendre to the most innocent remark and touched him at every opportunity. Once she made a great play of brushing crumbs from his lap, ensuring that a well-placed thumb happened to lightly prod his area of concern. If she had any doubt that he was aroused, there was none now. She giggled, if she had prodded harder it would have broken her thumb or burst free and attacked her - had he wanted he could have used it to play pool.

"Yur, yu, yrr, err your nail" he spluttered, indicating her right middle finger. Though perfectly manicured it was childishly short in comparison with the sensuous talons of her other digits. "What about it?" "Have you broken it?" He blushed, "I hope we don't have any more of those this afternoon" he spluttered on. "No, I like to keep it short for special occasions" she replied. "Really, what special circumstances necessitate a short finger nail then?" he teased innocently, wondering what was happening here. "You'll see - if you are lucky" Crystal replied, almost threateningly, and then continued with a giggle, "well not exactly see..." She then exploded with a husky, contagious, full-bodied laugh, that he picked up on and it spread around the bar. Soon everybody was in on the laugh but only she knew the joke.

"If he doesn't slip her on like a well-oiled seaboot zafternoon, then my cocks a kipper" mused the Landlord. "Best dead cert since Shergar, no more bets please" he grinned.

They returned to the office and went straight to the archive. As he shut the door, she was at him, taking a small leap she locked her legs around his waist. With her hands around his neck, she simultaneously ran each hand through his hair and clung on like python with her legs. She closed her mouth over his and forcing her tongue between his teeth she found his tongue and engaged in full battle.

To say he had been caught unawares was a slight understatement. Harvey had expected some flirting and maybe some contact but never had he anticipated an onslaught.

His heart was pounding, and the pressure on his back was almost unbearable, but this paled into insignificance, compared to the pressure of his erection against his zip.

He lifted his hands to her bottom to take some of the weight of his failing back and the slit of the skirt draped over his arms. The ends of his fingers and tops of his thumbs contacted warm, soft and very wet flesh, as he had thought, she was not hindered by underwear. Feeling this contact she went into overdrive and shifted to enable both thumbs to enter her. This accomplished, she appeared to develop an extra limb as she opened his trousers and lowered them along with his pants. Now released, his guided missile hit its long-awaited target.

Never before had he been so forceful or brutal and, although he ejaculated with total commitment, he was nowhere near done and she knew it. He felt her eagle-like talons around his buttocks. Then the unusual experience of his anus being penetrated, and suddenly, he realised the significance of the short nail. As her finger explored his rectum and he ejaculated again, was it the drug or her? In his life, this was unprecedented.

When it seemed, he might be flailing she fell to her knees and took him into her throat until he was fully prepared to continue. She was in her ecstasy, this was what she needed right enough and she was getting what she wanted too.

Up and down the wall they went. First him against the shiny government green gloss then her. As her skin touched the cold hard surface she exploded again and again and he continued to issue sperm like the draught at The Swinging Sign. On and on they went until neither could give or take anymore as they slid to a dusty, sweaty and very sticky halt on the floor by the shredder.

Their union had been all-consuming, to the exclusion of any surroundings, but now, as they sat recovering, they were aware that the shredder was screaming at them. In their passion, the machine had been switched on and had spent the last twenty minutes devouring or digesting all that they knocked its way.

All of Fred's files, including binders, several pens, markers and rubber stamps were all reduced to hamster bedding. The ceaseless omnipotent machine finally baulked and began to protest about the stapler that was jammed against the cutters. Before its final scream Harvey leapt up and switched the beast off and surveyed the damage.

Remarkably, apart from mangled shredder blades and small items of office supplies, there was little amiss. It was exceedingly messy but as Crystal got to her feet, they could see that there was nothing left to do but clear up. As it was the second Friday of the month, the cleaners were scheduled to expect more than the usual spit and wipe and it was office practice to ditch unwanted papers on that day. All in all - mission accomplished!

Harvey was straightening himself as the door burst in. "What are you two doing in .... oh my word" Fred sputtered. "What? Oh, my word." "The bloody stapler fell in, we tried to stop it mid-programme, but it kept on going. I'm afraid it's had it. I am sorry we were doing so well. But at least we managed to finish." Harvey blurted out, not daring to look at Crystal, who had made at least three double meanings from his explanation, and was on the verge of a giggle fit.

"Well? I'll say you did well, exceptionally well and in good time too, the office is still open. It's all done, well the .." hand across the throat motion.." err that has been done, the rest is just noise. Talking of which, you must have been going at it like maniacs.." "We were that," they said in unison, but again not daring to look at each other, "That's why I came in, I thought you were trying to kill each other".

"Well," the manager was starting to overuse the metaphor, "neither of you can go to the desk like that. I don't want Nosy Parkers asking questions so get yourselves off. I'll see to things here, make sure nothing for the cleaners to complain about. Oh and thank you both, I certainly couldn't have matched your performance ...." He stopped as they found this was too much to hold back and erupted in laughter as they burst from the room.

They went straight to the chalk cob cottage. Here they spent the whole weekend together, mainly in bed. They never made love once - they fucked, screwed and shagged many times, but love or even a hint of it never entered the ring or even made the dressing room.

Miss Baker-Bromley could have fallen in love had she had time, but she was too busy enjoying the sport. After nearly two decades of nymphomania she had enjoyed every mentionable and unmentionable kind of sexual depravity. Two abortions and a near full-term stillbirth had somewhat corrupted her purity and ladies parts but for once she thought 'This is it'.

She had found a man with brains as well as balls, the thought had crossed her mind that he may be trying to fuck her to death, but she reasoned what will be will be. Her raison d'être was nearly fait accompli.

She did not know that the events of that weekend were the culmination of a lifetime of sexual ineptitude. She did not know about a decade of celibacy and the introduction of a certain little purple pill or she would never have asked him to marry her. Had she known that probably the chances of Harvey ever repeating such recent feats was as likely as a mouse surviving a lightning strike she would never have asked him to marry her. Had she known about the tests, she would never have asked him to marry her, but she did not know, and she did ask and he did accept.

Harvey was in shock at his recent transformation but he was able to keep it up in more ways than one. He was not entirely enamoured with the wandering finger and was glad that at least the target area was now rocket free. He was also concerned that his performance was entirely due to the little purple pill if it were then he was a sham.

He filed an extremely watered down version of events in his log and waited to see Dr Hope's reactions. "Let's go outside for a stroll," said the doctor, reaching for his cigarettes. Once clear of the building he started to talk in a wheezy whisper. "Now My Boy, allowing for some gross exaggeration and a lively imagination, I must say that your story is remarkable. You have come from the shadows to the spotlight in a matter of weeks and you appear in rude health to boot. This pill is going to revolutionise the world." "But Doctor, I have agreed to marry a lady based on a sham, what do I do if the supply dries up?" he pitifully asked. "Now then, if this is the partner in your report she is firstly no lady, secondly she cannot expect this kind of performance every night, surely? Buy her a jackhammer for a wedding present" he joked. "Seriously though My Boy, most marriages are a sham, sit in my chair for a day and you will learn. Your sham, as you call it, is no shame, you can't tell her without breaching your contract. Believe me, they would sue your ass off if you did. So don't worry, you have five years and if it is pronounced safe for the general public you will be on it for life. If it is deemed unsafe, you will have at least a five-year weaning programme. You are guaranteed ten years on the stuff. When you have been married for ten years you will be lucky if you can spell sex let alone partake with the same person, Ok My Boy?"

After a moment's thought, he continued, "Try without for one week if you want, don't tell me when, just do a 'normal' report or claim a cold or something." Lighting yet another cigaret he patted Harvey reassuringly on the shoulder and hurried back to his surgery where his appointments were backing up.

Crystal had not entirely moved into the cottage but did spend most nights there. For a while, they made love before falling asleep in awkward places as lovers do. The novelty of waking up with a crook in her neck soon began to wear off for Crystal. The fucking finger up the ass became an unwanted invasion to Harvey - postillion indeed, more like having your kidneys removed via your ear.

As he decided to rest the pill, his recently acquired impetus diminished, as he feared. He claimed his back was spoiling his performance and resumed the programme with a double dose. Alas too late, a girl's needs are many and varied, Crystal's being more many and varied than most.

Within three weeks, Digger was helping out again on Wednesdays with Trevor, Nigel and Chris from The Sign Boys lending a hand the following week. By Harvey's 40th Birthday all but Barry 'The Stapler' had resumed regular duties. Extra portions were served up to the engineer sent to fix the shredder, so often a new shredder was considered. The salesmen from three shredder companies experienced sweaty quickies in the shredder room then the new shredder delivery men had a quick two's up in the back of their box Luton van. Even the aged scrap man and his cross-eyed son were tipped a quickie each, again in the shredder room, as they collected the doomed machine. She missed the commissioning engineer who disappointingly just turned on the machine before leaving, but Barry's stapler had proved a worthy tool.

By the time Fred called him in to discuss some discrepancies in Crystal's performance, and warn him against 'poking the payroll', the wedding date had been set. Fred's words of criticism and wisdom remained unsaid. "Well my word, good luck to you err, surprise eh? I hope all goes well for you" he tried to enthuse, with fingers tightly crossed behind his back

They decided on 20th August for the wedding, with a growing apprehension they kept from each other. Being a Friday would let them have a week on the south coast before returning to the cottage for a long weekend. This would enable them to tackle the Bank Holiday traffic in reverse. Then for some restful home time and Mr and Mrs would float into work on the Tuesday, all good plans of mice and men!

Harvey's 40th had not been a bad party and, with all the drinks they had consumed, it was not surprising that Harvey and Crystal had fallen asleep in separate rooms. He in their room, she on top of an unclaimed pile of coats. As the guests were friends and colleagues of Harvey's for many years, Crystal and the coats remained unclaimed for the night.

"You had better come" Crystal croaked from the bedroom doorway. Harvey sat up, his head thumping. "What, from here?" he managed to jest. "The door, front door." she said curtly, ignoring the joke. " Some person, err people, ouch my head - you sort it out, I need a douse." as she stomped to the bathroom.

When she went down to the lounge Crystal was in a slightly better mood for a nanosecond or two.

Harvey stood, "This is my son Ronnie and err..." "Amber," said Ronnie, smiling disarmingly. "Amber" continued Harvey. "Typical, he would be late for his own funeral, this one. You missed the party, but at least you didn't forget" "Forget?" "My Birthday ...." "Oh no, course not, get you something later," was the unconvincing reply.

Introductions and niceties were completed over a breakfast of coffee and Alka-Seltzers. "Dad, err Harvey, do you think we can stay over for a whi...." NO" said Crystal. Ronnie continued as if not hearing, "It's just that we saw a doctor and he said Amber was anaemic or something. He said she needed rest away from the road for a couple of weeks or so if that is ok?" "NO," said Crystal again, all heart.

"Anaemic?" enquired Harvey, half suspecting the answer. "Pregnant, pleeeese oh please no!" Crystal guessed correctly.

They moved in and Crystal never stayed over anymore before the wedding, but she had plenty of extra-curricular activities to keep a girl busy.

The lunch time wedding went ahead as planned, it was a Registry Office job again, although with a few more guests in attendance, but with less atmosphere than the first, if that was possible. The witnesses were Ronnie and, at the last minute! Brigit stood in for a sickly Amber.

An informal wedding breakfast followed at the cottage. Olivia Kitson organised catering and flowers and continually fussed around Ronnie and of course Amber. Crystal received very little attention for a Bride and noticed.

Fred and some of the staff were a bit tongue-tied having heard certain rumours about Crystal, and the small group of neighbours hardly knew her.

Friends and other acquaintances of both parties were either not asked or declined on some lame excuses.

Crystal looked stunning of course, but today she appeared to be issuing more venom than charm which just added to the less than convivial atmosphere that hung over the proceedings.

Fred stood as unofficial Best Man and made a humorous speech about office romance and other such rubbish, ending with maybe a serious message in disguise. "Remember Mrs Bright" he winked openly, "you can always beat him up when you get him home, but in the office, although you chose not to say earlier, you will obey him. Ha ha..." Others politely joined in the merriment and raised their glasses in the traditional toast.

"Regroup" cried Fred and with handshakes and kisses all round he led the team back to face the delights of Friday afternoon in the office. Eventually and equally prematurely the other guests took their lead from a neighbour claiming children to collect and were all gone.

Olivia stayed to organise and mainly carry out the clean-up operation and she too was gone. She apologised that she too would be away the next week and would not be able to check on Ronnie and Amber. "They will be fine," said Harvey, fingers crossed behind his back. "They better be!" Said Crystal in an attempt at humour, but emphasised her remark with a threatening finger that made Harvey wince.

Later in the lounge, Harvey implored his son to keep the place tidy while they were away. In the kitchen, Crystal told a frightened Amber to 'Fuck off before we get back if you know what is good for you.' Amber thankfully had obtained contact arrangements from Olivia 'just in case dear' which she now intended to use, hallelujah!

The week away was a total disaster, the weather changed from warm sunshine to cold and overcast with rain threatened. Nights were cold.

Crystal began her period en-route and complained all the way. Once they arrived they fled to their room and ignored goodwill greetings and a bottle of champagne, thoughtfully provided by 'Fred and the A-Team'.

Given time without distraction, they soon found they had very little in common and it was evident to both that an error of epic proportions had been made.

By Tuesday, they had taken to going for separate walks. Harvey's led to a bar, coincidentally named Harvey's. Here he would sit surrounded by images of white rabbits and James Stewart. He started to contemplate, over a large glass of Gordon's gin and iced water, or two.

Crystal, on the other hand, had taken the beach road where she found the young deckchair attendant had boundless time and energy to expend - bloody period.

One evening Harvey returned to the hotel to find Crystal rummaging in the cleaners cupboard. When he enquired what she was after he was told she wanted one of those sponge scouring pads, you know, green and yellow. "There is one by the loo," he said helpfully. "A clean one stupid, do you want us to get a disease? Do you want sex or not?" Feeling the gin nudging in the right direction he thought he did. "Then find one she snapped" and went to the room.

Confused again, Harvey was relieved to see the cupboard was logically thought out and found a new pack of pads quickly. He removed one and returned to the room where he found Crystal brandishing a pair of scissors. She grabbed the pad and quartered it with the scissors. "Trick I learned from the hookers who used the Hackney Office," she said, "one of many." Harvey was not surprised at that but still a bit intrigued. She took one square and inserted it into her vagina.

"As long as you are not bleeding too heavy this will staunch the blood and enable regular sex." she explained. "After all, a girl cannot give up everything because of her gender eh?"

Harvey was not sure but was soon taking part in an unsatisfactory union. He was convinced something was amiss and couldn't put his all into it. She was a bit annoyed at being found out rummaging before she could go to the deckchair boy but hey ho, sex is sex. This time however, Harvey was starting to bore her so she reverted to another Hackney tip and they both groaned in dissatisfaction.

Needless to say, this was his portion for the week and as he compiled his log for Doctor Hope the other three-quarters of the pad were being put to a more satisfying use.

The trip home was uneventful, but the homecoming was worse than expected. Amber had indeed taken to her heels and had been accommodated by Olivia. "You just get back there when Mr Harvey is home, he is a good man and I can't see that floozy sticking around long" she had advised.

With Amber gone, Ronnie had used everything to cook or eat with and not cleared up anything and the place was a mess. Harvey's chastisement efforts were met with indifference and contempt, from Crystal, and a shrug from Ronnie. He claimed they had arrived a day early and he had no chance to clean up.

Crystal declined to move anything but the basics into her new home. Within six days of returning to work, the marriage was over. On the seventh day, Crystal accepted the immediate transfer to a destination known only to her and Fred.

She shot back to the cottage to grab her few things. One other thing she grabbed belonged to young Ronnie. A dick like that could not be ignored whatever or whoever it was attached to. Anyway, it was a quick one before they both left to go their separate ways.

Harvey was not too disappointed about Crystal's departure although he felt somewhat stupid. He knew however he would recover and resume life, a little wiser but much as before. He was also not too surprised to find Ronnie's 'Sorry Pops - see you' note that he had left on the kitchen table.

He would have preferred to wish his son Bon Voyage and say goodbye to Amber, but after the mess and all, AMEN. A new day tomorrow, must ring those contract cleaners.

True to form, Harvey's mother, of course, would not desert her son when he was down and visited as soon as he fell asleep. On this occasion her middle finger had acquired a strange bulbous growth. This glowed in the dark and threw large shadows and luminous letters at the walls each spelling out a familiar four-letter word of her repertoire. Still glowing it crept under his bedclothes and stayed there flashing as he sat bolt upright grasping the mattress with all his might until it was gone. He knew the intended target and decided to sit on this sensitive spot until he was sure she would not return.

Following this experience it took nearly a bottle of Beefeater Gin, several Piriton tablets and a large swig of Night Nurse to calm him down and let sleep return, "Thank you Mother" he mumbled. "My pleasure, cunt," she cackled like a crone down the chimney, as he threw up in the grate.

Chapter Nine

As with most of Harvey's life, apart from his time as a reactionary, the outside world and it's chatter remained only of mild interest, and no more than white noise.

As his time that would never return ticked by Presidents and Popes were shot and survived. Superpowers invaded small countries and Islam became a word even young children had heard. A radical Pope mysteriously died in his sleep. Even John Lennon and Elvis Presley proved to be immortal The man bouncing across the moon's surface, in the year of his son's birth, was now being challenged as a Hollywood invention. Freddie Starr ate my hamster, the Chanel Tunnel was originally dug by Brandy Smugglers and a London Bus was pictured on the moon. A Peanut Farmer was replaced by an Actor, miners became statistics, riots and punks abounded.

Chuffers suffered little from beggars and homeless in the streets and chuffed along as normal. All that appeared to come into Harvey's view were the ever growing unemployed with their demands on his office, and, eventually, Amber.

Amber returned cautiously, as Summer nights became Autumn evenings. She was hoping Ronnie was still around to give some help and support without any aggro'. She found the help and support without any aggro' but without the presence of Ronnie.

Harvey was pleased to see Amber and was not going to turn her away if she wanted to stay for a while, which she did and did. The pregnancy was much further advanced than Harvey had thought and her small frame portrayed. She confirmed she was in the last two months or less of confinement. Early January was the expected time of arrival, or ETA as Houston were fond of using.

She moved in with what she was carrying or wearing and with a smile of gratitude and disarmament. Using his fingers for counters, Harvey worked out she did not really have a clue of the date and that she must be the most ill-prepared mother to be in the modern world and probably beyond. This did not appear to bother her. In her short life, being prepared was for Boy Scouts and wusses, Amber ambled.

Amber, however, proved an asset, giving him something to take his mind off recent events. She provided nourishing meals at regular times and when he faltered, put him to bed in the Recovery Position. The latter being once or twice a week as he found, post Crystal, he needed to be plastered to fulfil his obligations to the little purple pill.

Harvey had misread Dr Hope's instructions a bit. It was his health that was being monitored primarily. His sex life or at least erection on tap needed recording, of course, and was a bonus to the shareholders, but not compulsory. Average for his age was twice a month - not every two days.

Harvey's antics made right for later advertising if the 'Fathers' Little Helper' ever became an over the counter drug of choice. Like Newt Gingrich, King of Capitol Hill was to say, "Tell the people want they want and then give it to them." Or sell it - in the case of a little purple pill.

Amber knew nothing of the tests or reasons for heavy drinking but just got on with it. Harvey in return provided the essentials she would need in the weeks to come. He would commission Olivia to get the rest nearer the time, if they guessed it right.

Harvey also gave Amber support and little compliments to boost her self-confidence when her hormones and bathroom mirror were at their cruelest and unbalanced. He became fond of her in a Fatherly way and missed her when she visited 'somebody' over Christmas.

She returned on New Years Day, The Year of The Reader she had heard on the radio. She missed the meaning but thought Harvey would know. He probably would have, had he not been in a drunken stupor in the back garden. His arm was draped in the small fish pond, where he had fallen the night before.

Capillary Action, or Reaction, had syphoned water from the pond via his sleeve soaking most of his clothing to the skin, but at least he was alive. A face down experience a few inches either way would have seen him drowned.

Despite her condition and his much later embarrassment, she managed to get him inside and undressed from his sodden clothes. She was also able to dry him of sorts and wrap him in his large fluffy dressing gown before putting him to rest on the sofa. Next she managed a roaring fire and within an hour he was full of apologies and starting to think the year was already too long.

"My Dad did it all the time," she told him, as she sat in front of the fire leaning back on the sofa. He lay shame-faced and ill but a good listener, well most captive audiences are. "Now he forgets how he was and wants to be Mr Nice Guy. You are different, you ARE Mr Nice, drunk or sober. So what? You get pissed, who does that hurt? Bet you never hurt anybody who didn't deserve it, or even if they did. Or give a 'friendly slap' that knocked you backwards, I saw Mom go full circle on a 'friendly' that split her lip."

He was about to say he had never slapped the deserved or undeserved, but he couldn't string it together before she continued. "Trouble was we were based at Greenham Common, USAF, too much free time, drink, lecturns of cocaine, local girls under the wire, you name it. Trouble was when Mom and I were over his wings were clipped a bit and he was supposed to play the family, man. He was based there more or less permanently. Usually, single men had that domain, but some career people like him provided stability." Harvey nodded, thankful for the lack of required input as she continued. "Trouble was Mom would not leave him be when he had been drinking, snorting or whatever, or was just in one humdinger of a mood. God I could see it coming, but she kept nagging and bothering then the fireworks would begin and get worse as I got older. They shipped us out short notice the last time,. He avoided a Courts Marshall because she would not give evidence against him or file for divorce, wants his pension I think." She paused, but only to poke the fire. "They live Stateside again now and he has a new girlfriend, my age, and it is Mom that drinks now, crazeee or what? Anyways, I split, I got dual nationality through Mom, she' a Brit but you'd never know. I got a scholarship to University College Oxford, like Bill Clinton..." "Who?" enquired Harvey, pleased he was contributing something. "Our Governor, next President, my Dad says. Anyways, I met your Ronnie and left with him, couldn't grasp it anyway so I was going to drop out and along he came, all good looks and charm. Very much like you really. You're funny when you are shit-faced, like Dudley Moore in Arthur, except you don't spit, you ever take drugs, Harvey?" "What? no, err never, harrumph." "Good, where was I?"

It didn't seem to bother her she was talking non-stop she liked talking to him. "Harvey, where was I." "Dudley Moore" he stated with some effort. "Ah yes, thank you for keeping up. I was a bit scared of you early on, but Olivia swears by you as a sound guy. Ronnie said you were a bit of a sex maniac and liked a drink so what? You are an old softie really and I mean that in a good way..." she reached up planted a platonic kiss on his sweaty forehead, ".... and I wish you were my Pops." He smiled down at her and wished the same as they drifted asleep.

He woke in time to help her into the ambulance, with the bag he had helped her pack weeks ago, this must be one of her last guesstimated days.

It was only a short trip to the hospital but, by the time the ambulance pulled into the emergency bay it was carrying an extra passenger. Nicolette was a healthy baby, with Amber's frail beauty and Ronnie's dark eyes - a born heartbreaker.

Overcrowding at the Maternity Unit coupled with Amber's good health and resolve saw her back at the cottage within two days.

She took to motherhood as she took to most tasks, she had her routines and the baby. She still found time however for Harvey and his quirks.

It was a leap year and on 29th February Amber was very pensive as Harvey stumbled from drawer to drawer looking for a Nurofen Plus for his hangover. "I thought I had some Resolve here too" he mumbled. "That you certainly need," she said with unusual force.

"Sorry was I noisy when I came in? Did I wake Nicki or something?" he inquired, sensing a fragile atmosphere. "Or are you building up to ask me to marry you?" he tried humour. "What?" "It's Leap Year Day, and that's what spinsters of the parish do in this country today, well historically, so?" "Oh! Err grief, God no!" "Good, I couldn't have anyway, still bruised from the last one, been there, done that, didn't like it' he joked. She realised what she had just said, "Oh God sorry, I didn't mean ...." "No worries, not exactly the catch of the day. That's ok, it was me coming in then?" "No, well you didn't exactly come in, you know?" "Oh no, not the fish pond again?" he groaned as she nodded. "You should leave me - really." "You know if it was warmer and you were not face down in the water, I may have been tempted". She wagged a playful finger. " but it's not that really, although it does scare me to leave you when you keep doing that. Nurofen top right, Resolve left a bit, right, got them. Really though, should you drink so much on a Sunday when you have to work - oh no, now you will be late!"

He grinned through the pain, "Day off, sorry forgot to tell you." He swallowed some pills. "That should fix it – well maybe after a laydown. Hey" the penny dropped, "leave, what did you mean, leave?"

She explained that her father was over mixing some unfinished business with a European experience for his girlfriend. He had tracked her through friends of friends of mutual standing. He had expressed a wish to meet up and see his new Granddaughter. He indicated he had a small gift that would help with her future, and some friends, who would pay for a live in gopher - house sitter who were away most of the time, leaving her with time to plan or Amblelize.

She appreciated more than could she say, or ever repay, Harvey's help and support but thought best if she moved on. Ronnie was obviously now in the past and would only complicate things if he showed up, so go girl go. "I have dreaded telling you and feel like I am cheating on you but I hope you understand, not sure I really do, or maybe I should ask you to marry me."

Harvey laughed through his sadness, he assured her he knew what she meant. He told her, if needed, she could return at any time, without the Vicar or a ring.

After tears and hugs all round he got her a taxi to the station after not considering driving himself.

Quiet and unassuming as she was, Amber was strong and determined. With a few quid 'borrowed' from Harvey, she bundled up Nicki and was gone with promises of keeping in touch.

As she made her way to the taxi, "don't come out, you are still pissed". He watched them go and they reminded him of North

American Indians, or Native Americans as they are now called by those who think they know best. Amber striding on with the little papoose staring back at him he wondered what would become of them. Would Nicki ever be turned around to face the future and good fortune or would she always be facing back?

As the driver helped her in she turned and waved and worked Nicki as a puppet to do the same, Harvey lamely waved back wondering if he would ever see them again and under what condition? When the taxi departed his eyes brimmed with tears as he went in search of gin and a little purple pill.

"What do you mean Grannie?" wailed Cass down the line. "I'm not old enough, how's Ronnie and who the hell is Amber?" "He's not here mate, Amber is his girlfriend, they came last year on my birthday. He buggered off about a month later (not mentioning the wedding), not seen him since. Then Amber comes back, gives birth and leaves a bit later" he summarised. "He knows she was pregnant but doesn't know anymore and probably doesn't want to. You realise he is 18 tomorrow?" "You are dim sometimes, why do you think I'm ringing? I thought he and Verna were heading your way, at least they said so in October" she bomb shelled. "Verna" it was Harvey's turn to wail." who is Verna?"

-

"C'mon Harvey, you'll enjoy it. Ok, you don't know everybody but you soon will. The more, the merrier, and less we all have to do. It won't hurt your back I promise, c'mon Harvey, we haven't got together for ages."

It was Roy acting as a recruitment officer for another old friend, Mike Brindley. Mike had developed a successful building company which was riding high and prospects were endless - if you didn't possess a crystal ball. As a mini progression, diversification, or tax fiddle, as Roy called it, Mike had joined forces with a like-minded Spaniard. They built an apartment block between Malaga and Fuengirola on the Costa Del Sol in Southern Spain.

The apartments would be let to holidaymakers. Used by family and friends or lent rent free to oil the wheels of commerce, when contracts were up for tender. Roy, Mike and several others were going over just before Easter to clean and add final touches prior to the first lets due in early April. "We spread out to start with. As each apartment becomes finished, we have less available to live in so by the end of the week it should be fucking cozy unless somebody dies." Roy explained. "Mike's wife and a friend are taking over from us so we don't have to bother about the last two apartments, except for clearing away the hash, porn and condoms" he laughed.

Having shared a Winter with a pregnancy and awaiting his divorce, Harvey considered it would be good to get away, even if there was a bit of work attached. It would only be light work of the brain dead type. He would have to spin it by Fred, but that should not be a problem. His monthly check up would not be a problem, as it would have to be moved to one side of Easter or the other. He decided he would have the check before he left if possible.

"Ok, I'll come" he submitted. "Great, I can't wait. Only thing is...." "I knew it" Harvey sighed. "No nothing untoward" Roy assured," we are making our own ways there, but it couldn't be simpler if you are traveling light, as Cliff would sing." "Cliff?" "Richard" "Oh" "Bet you didn't know it was Number One when that first bit of the M1 opened." "Eh?" "Never mind. Get a flight on 28th or 29th so you don't pay Easter prices. Mike and I are driving down with the door entry bits, tools, decent bacon and a bit of hash, we plan to be there early Monday. I'll send directions and a bit of the system to stick in your pocket." "Eh?" "Well it is not strictly importable, due to some disputed patent or other and we don't want them all in the van. Anyway, it is tiny and nobody will pick it up, tell you what, stick it in a fag packet ok? So I'll send you directions as we can't meet all the flights. It couldn't be easier, though. Fly to Malaga, out the front of the airport, cross the road, get the train. It's a single track so if the train is going left don't get on it or you'll be heading for the Malaga slums. So your back is to the airport and the train goes right, quite an experience, it is a wooden rattling thing that hurtles along. Buy a ticket from the conductor and get off at Los Boliches, next to last stop, if you get to Fuengirola your a prat, go back one. Off the train, down the steps, sea to your right 200 - 300 metres, near the Hotel Angela, Sunny Beach Apartments, see you there. Oh only bring traveling Pesetas and a few quid, I'll explain when we are there, better to buy in bulk". Then he was gone, true Roy style.

Directions duly arrived and arrangements were made. He would fly out on 29th and return on 5th. He would carry only a small amount of cash as directed but would take his cash card and flexible friend, just in case.

"Good idea," said Dr Hope after he had finished his examination and scanned the log. "Nice time of year and all. You know, these little pills have worked wonders for you, your heart rate is healthy, your blood pressure is fine. The Cholesterol that everybody is talking about is around three which is nearly excellent. If your understated alcohol intake is to be believed, I think you have single-handedly sorted out Brewers Droop. Now you have stopped acting like a rutting stag, your logs are becoming more predictable and I think you are living the life of a man ten to fifteen years your junior. Good for you, see you when you get back. I will not give you two pills, with Gibraltar a bit sensitive at present we don't need you inseminating half of Spain." All good plans of mice and men.

"Hi Dad" it was 1.29 on the alarm clock, it was 29th March. Harvey had been in a fitful pre-flight sleep when a tattoo beaten on the front door caused him to rise and blink into the darkness beneath his window.

"It's 1.29" he growled. "You're late, your Mother said you were on your way five months ago. Amber and the baby, YOUR ......" "Sssshhhh" hissed Ronnie, but not in consideration for the neighbours. Harvey let him in.

"Ronnie, it's nice to see you, of course, why you choose 1.29 to descend on me I don't know. Listen I have a flight to Spain in a few hours, and after last time, I'm not leaving you here again on your own..." "You're a bit picky Dad, you said it was 1.29 five minutes ago" observed Ronnie. "Anyway, I am not on my own, meet Verna, Verna meet Harvey."

Where Amber had been quite unassuming with the bearing of a Coolie, Verna was brash, in your face Northern Irish of the hardened variety. With fiery red hair and the durability of a galvanised water tank. She could not have been more of a contrast to Amber even if The Good Lord wanted. When she spoke it was brash and harsh.

Each sentence, and sometimes each word, Verna said was prefixed with an obscenity. She stressed or emphasised everything. She used a small pool of words all of which should not be whispered within a mile of a church. If she ever knew what whispering was.

"Hiya, how the feck are yooze? Fuck you, Ronnie, he's not a fecking all like you said. Mind you those fucking pants need a stitch, I'm fecking sure his wee man was waving at me just then." This was followed by a laugh that could stop lightening.

What Verna did have in common with Amber, was that it appeared that at any moment she was about to become a mother.

The baby was to be Ronnie's, but he would have not known about it had he not gone back on the road in September. Verna was heading home and they would have missed each other. After Crystal had given him the rogering of his life, Ronnie found himself in Wales and met Verna heading for the ferry.

It appeared, given the brief history picked up while Verna was in the toilet, that Ronnie was flitting between both girls at the same time. Neither were aware of the other, even now. Harvey was sorely tempted to spill the beans. However, having seen a friendly version of Verna, he was scared of what could be unleashed.

Both girls, or even any girls, had equal standing with Ronnie the young buck. He had only decided to devote more time to Amber because of the pregnancy and medical warnings. He did not know, as he and Amber were seeking shelter from Harvey, that Verna was discovering she was also with child. It had been a prolific year for Ronnie. (Nobody would ever know about the female foetus he had fertilised in September and Crystal had terminated in November.)

Ronnie and Verna had met up with Cass and some of her friends, but neither could remember where, who and when. A motorway or nuclear protest was being organised by large muddy women.

A small fourteen-year-old from the Newbury area was also present and developing tunnelling as a peaceful form of protest. This was years before the Newbury Bye-pass would spring him and his ilk to the front pages, but for now he was with his muddy Mum.

They had not discussed the pregnancy with his mother. As far as Ronnie knew, Cass was unaware of her eligibility to enter a Glamorous Grandmother competition twice over. Harvey wished he had her number.

Ronnie had no interest in his first child and Verna had no intention of keeping her baby. She explained to Harvey

"Certainfeckinglynot" (she needed a section in the Oxford English Dictionary to herself). "My Father wouldn't fecking like it one fecking bit." she said seriously. "Why ever not?" asked Harvey, as the trap was sprung. "Because he's a fucking priest" she cackled wickedly. "Ow feck, now I've fucking pissed me pants" she laughed, heading back to the toilet.

"I can't stand much more of this," Harvey thought without daring to utter it.

Verna returned, holding the crotch of her pedal pushers down a bit to dry. "We only need a few effing days Harvey me fucking darling. When the wee baby pops out the Frankilins will fly over and pick him up" she said, without passion or emotion. "After dropping us a few shillings for our trouble, they'll be back in Eire before you can say Fingerfuckingroller"

Harvey could not picture himself ever saying such a thing. But, if it meant this dreadful creature would return to the planet from whence she came, he would indeed begin practising.

Any thoughts he had on illegal adoption Harvey countermanded silently. A couple of gay cannibals would provide a better future for a child than this evil bitch, he reasoned.

Against his better judgement he left them to it and escaped to Fuengirola - now why couldn't she say it like that?

As he was pulling away, he was horrified to see her running after him. "Wait" she hollered. Harvey was sure the car shook from the verbal onslaught. He rolled down his window.

She thrust £5 in his hand. "Be a love Harvey, we lost some Brothers in Gibraltar, can you pop along and lay some flowers at 'The' gas station. The World has to see what murdering bastards you Brits are" she spat.

He drove way with no promises made.

Chapter Ten

The Malaga flight and directions were perfect and there were no problems with his illicit fag packet.

Even Roy's description of the train as 'a Rattler' was right as this metal and wood contraption hurtled its way along the coast. It barely crept through some stages as the incline grew, only to launch itself at horrendous speed through other bits. The conductor somehow made it from carriage to carriage mainly ignoring Spanish types and concentrating on the tourist and gypsy money. The tourists were however spared the well-shod boot in the backside reserved solely for the odd gypsy who dared to cross his path. He also appeared adept at fumbling for change for disembarking passengers who had made their destinations and had to rush from the train.

After a few inclines, Harvey realised that he had missed the essential part of this railway. Normal trains did not do hills but The Rattler first threw itself down inclines and the momentum took it up the other side. Pure genius, pure Toytown.

Sunny Beach Apartments were easily found and had been well cited. It appeared at present to be the hub of activity as shops, restaurants and bars were being slotted around.

He had been told to have a drink at the Hill Street Blues Cafe bar and wait to be found. He was not alone long, as soon as he mentioned Mike's name he was directed to a table where four men were enjoying pints of San Miguel in the shade. Introductions were made(and forgotten as with all mass introductions) and instructions given to 'tab' everything.

Mike and Roy had arrived earlier and were now off on an errand. The next train from Malaga deposited four more volunteers who Harvey recognised from his flight. Roy and Mike pulled up in an old VW Hippy Trail Camper. Laughter, smiles and beer were the order of the day with a work plan starting Tuesday, proper planning.

The original four Harvey had met were family/friends of Mikes wife and had been here a week. They had been installing the wiring for the door entry system making the rest of the job simple, they were returning home later that day leaving seven guys in two apartments with the final fix and cleaning duties.

Mike delegated Roy to show the newcomers their apartment. The new four would take the place of the departing four, Harvey would room with Roy and Mike. Their apartment was sea facing, pleasantly furnished and spacious. They certainly would not be overcrowding the place.

This would really be a prime site as the area grew. Across the road was the glorious beach (sunny of course). An easy walk along the beach, sea on the left, took you along the Paseo Maritimo to the heart of Fuengirola.

Back in the bar Mike let Roy explain the setup. Hill Street was their base, for food and drinks, they would tab everything and settle at the end. 'Eat and drink what you want and we all pay an equal share at the end, it will not be horrendous so don't be shy" he instructed. The departing four had enjoyed the hospitality and it had cost less than £50 each for their week.

With regard to money, Roy advised Mike had a deal with his Spanish mate who was awash with unexplainable amounts of the local currency. At a reasonable exchange rate, with no commission. All they had to do was ask and he would provide all the cash they needed, including their tab at The Hill. On departure, each would be given their bill in English money and a Building Society account number in the UK where they could deposit their dues.

Harvey was given a Bradford & Bingley account for his deposit and wondered how many accounts the mystery man had. Ah well, Maggie was all for a bit of enterprise. Twin tower action of the future saw such loop-holes well and truly plugged, but for now innocence prevailed.

Hill Street Blues, Hill Street or just The Hill was their favourite haunt and was run by two brothers Marco and Mario. They were happy to go along with the weekly tab 'cash in hand'.

The brothers were half Italian and half Scottish, brought up in Glasgow by their Italian PoW Father Enzo and their Scottish

Mother Maura, now sadly gone. Her presence, however, was still there in the broad Glaswegian spoken by the brothers.

Marco was the much older brother and referred to Mario as 'my little poof'. Their Father lived at the back of the bar, as a watchdog at night, and in a white plastic chair out front playing dominoes during the day. Enzo yearned to return to Sorrento now his wife was gone and was soon to do this accompanied by Mario.

Marco had three sons by his Scottish wife Mollie, Enzo (12), Mario (10) and Marco (7) were already part of the family firm, waiting table and other duties. Harvey liked this family's and he hoped that their industry would be rewarded as the tourist was awaited.

Parts of the area was already busy as English holiday makers sought some early sun on their Easter break. Open All Hours, Happy Hour, Two for One, All Day Breakfast and Sunday Roast A-Frame signs fought for pavement room in front of every establishment. The competition was rife and 'An Ode to a Spanish Bar Owner' was displayed on the wall behind every bar. Viva Espania.

The Magnificent Seven screwed boxes to walls, connected wires, tested intercoms, cleaned, washed polished and shone each apartment methodically through the day. Working well together and enjoying each others company the time flew. It was unchallenging and refreshing at the same time and thoughts of illegal adoptions et al. faded away on a wind of Mr Sheen, Pledge and Domestos to the accompaniment of terrific music piped through the building.

Strangely enough, Marco had stumbled upon a Canadian radio station that seemed to know what they liked and was the backdrop to all they did, like a movie soundtrack.

By early Thursday morning, the work was complete, leaving only a bit in their apartments for the girls to do, but they would ensure this would be minimal.

They enjoyed their evenings in The Hill but with nothing to get up for on Good Friday they decided to venture out.

After an excellent meal and a few 'Sannys' the team tried the local nightclub, Whispers, first. It was pleasant enough and took its name from George Michael's song Careless Whispers which happened to be a favourite of the owner, another Scot.

Unfortunately the owner was also the DJ and played the song every time a group of four or more came down the stairs to the club. "Fuck me, I like a bit of George but how many more times?" Roy commented.

There was an awful smell of bad drains about the place. As another group entered Roy shouted to the owner/DJ "Smells like George's ass in here mate. Do you think somebody's had a careless whisper or silent fart?" The owner left his little booth and explained the problem was in hand with the authorities, he was using gallons of Jeyes Fluid in the interim.

"Stuart" Harvey called, having glimpsed the owner for the first time. "Surprised the let you back in Spain" "What?" "Stuart Christie, c'mon, I'd know you anywhere, still planning to blow up Franco, or are you full-time Secret Service now?" He laughed. Roy started to take an interest "Hey fuck me, come to think about it" he said. "Ok, so you lost the bouffant but ......" insisted Harvey. "Time to go, lads," said the owner gruffly and, unsmilingly, had them removed without explanation.

"They say he is gay you know," said Roy. "Stuart?" asked Harvey. "No, twat-head, George," said Roy. Adding, "probably why his ass is smelling the place out." "By the way, I don't think that was Stuart.' said Harvey. "Twat, me too." agreed Roy. They moved on unperturbed, in body and conversation.

They took the sea walk to town using a couple of bars to top up the levels and add a little to the drains. Roy noted a girlie bar en route but nobody paid him any attention. They settled on The London Underground in Fuengirola for the remainder of the night. The music was good, the bar was fast and furious and the drains were good. The establishment had made good use of space, smart lighting and the use of mirror walls made it look gigantic and crowded.

After a few more drinks, Harvey became confused and held a long meaningful conversation with himself. Roy was on the pull now but with the average age around 20 he had a little luck.

The group started to divide and slope off in different directions. After one more fruitless trawl of the female clientele, Roy was restless and told Harvey he was going to the girlie bar they had passed, they were sure to get a result. Harvey had rested the little purple pill for a spell. He knew his result would probably be a home goal without it so made his excuses.

As the warm night air hit him, he started to wobble in the direction (sea on right) of the apartments. Being a mite unsteady and a bit vague on the Spanish laws about urinating in a public place Harvey hailed a passing taxi. As it pulled along side Harvey went to climb in the back but the front door popped open so he jumped in next to the driver. They exchanged 'Ola' greetings.

"Hill Street Blues Cafe Bar, munching grasses pleeees." Harvey spluttered. He cursed himself for not checking his financial situation or checking the price before accepting the ride. He hoped The Hill would come to his rescue if necessary.

He also hoped they missed the few potholes he had seen before as his bladder was nearly beyond its tolerance. The young driver noticed Harvey pulling at his waist and fumbling in his pocket. "You Anglaise?" he asked, as they sped past the girlie bar where Roy and the others were entering. Harvey nodded, finding it weird not having the steering wheel in front of him.

"You like me?" the driver inquired. "Very much, saved my life, thanks for stopping." The driver lifted his right hand from the gear stick but retained the grip like pose. "You like?" he asked his passenger, pretending to lick and swallow the space above his hand. "An ice cream? No thank you, I really need a pee," he pointed to his groin, "you know?" "You, me" continued the driver, repeating the action. Then without slowing one iota he made a circle with his left thumb and forefinger which he penetrated with his right forefinger backwards and forwards. "Ah, you like bum fuck?" he asked encouragingly. Harvey got the message. "God no, oh no" he cried. "No no not at all, misunderstanding, sorry and all that" he felt sick.

The driver was not happy, "What's the matter with me, eh?" he almost screamed. "Nothing, really, your nice it's just that, I'm err, you know...." tried Harvey, but he was already receiving backhand slaps. "But you think I am don't you?" screamed the driver. "Give me money, the same for a suck or I'll ...." he had no need to complete his threat. "Here" Harvey threw all the cash he had been trying to count at him and as the car slowed he leapt from the car, landing on all fours in the street (sea on right).

The taxi sped away and did a manic handbrake turn at the next junction. For a moment it looked as if the driver intended to race back, head on to the crouched figure. Harvey waited, hardly able to breath, as the driver delivered a stream of indistinguishable insults before disappearing with a squeal of tyres.

Harvey stayed crouched on the ground but was shaken back to life by the sound of another car approaching from behind. Getting to his feet he was pleased to have survived his ordeal and more glad to see he was at the rear of the Hotel Angela and, therefore, close to Hill Street and the apartment.

He decided that after his tribulation another drink was in order but first, a must deserved piss behind a wheelie bin and bugger the bye-laws (but not the taxi drivers).

Much sobered but ragged from his adventure, Harvey approached the bar that he was happy to see lit up.

As he grew closer, he could see Enzo in an argument with a group of young men, possibly tourists, who were obviously 'in drink'.

They had come upon the old man clearing the front of the bar and piling the plastic seats prior to retiring for the night. They had started to tease, then taunt and demand drinks. One guy had helped himself to a can from the glass-fronted fridge. Enzo would not stand for such behaviour and was all for teaching them a thing or two.

Harvey's head had cleared and he could see that the shoving game, now in progress, was getting out of hand. Mob rule would soon take over what little restraint they had and would be replaced by the red mist of violence. The alcohol was still active in Harvey's system and his adrenalin was already up and ready which gave him the necessary sharpness and courage for action.

"Marco, Mario, Roy, quick!" he shouted to nobody. "C'mon lads, Yeeeaaaagh, let's have 'em", he bellowed to his invisible comrades, waving them on.

It was sufficient for the youths, they had only wanted a bit of fun initially, certainly not a battle, and certainly not with this maniac charging towards them. They turned and fled the scene, leaving the unpaid can untouched behind them. They were five in all and happy to get away unscathed, bloody mad Spaniards.

"Harvey, Harvey mya friend" cried Enzo, also relieved to be out of the situation. "Mya friend, didda you see them? Sixa maybe seven," he exaggerated. " You a were magnifica." He hugged his rescuer, "Mamma Mia, eight maybe ten" he expanded. "I musta tell Marco, you were terrifico, a dozen," he lied,"single handed, what ta man, a lion among asses, my ero."

"It was nothing Enzo, err you ok, you hurt your leg, you're limping, Enzo, you Ok?" Harvey asked the old warrior. "It's a ok Harvey, Iya aha shi ta myself" he squirmed. "Sit down Enzo, let's get you sorted out, want a drink?" "Iya can't sit Harvey, I really shi ta myself" "Oh yes, of course."

By the time Marco had been contacted Harvey had helped the old man out and they were taking a drink together, Harvey's dishevelled appearance only added to Enzo's tale. Now, according to Enzo, Harvey had seen off half the males of the region. Single-handed, without a thought or consideration for his own safety and regardless that they had been armed to the teeth. Although they accepted his more modest version of events, Harvey had won a place in the hearts of Ercolanese family forever.

On Saturday the weather, that had been sweltering when they worked, changed to that of a grey English Summer.

Marco suggested and then arranged a minibus to Gibraltar. Mike's transport was not suitable as it could draw unwanted attention. Also, the bus came with a driver who was known, and experienced, in the tricky border crossing. Any excuse to delay traffic to and from 'The Rock' was deemed, as fair play by the Spanish and the recent IRA killings that Verna spoke of was a good reason to be difficult, but they made it ok and almost unhindered.

They were each photographed as they disembarked the mini-bus, but if this were a security measure it was a marketable one. As they returned, they found their faces looking out of ashtrays and key ring souvenirs, which of course they bought.

Although it was not altogether a warm day, Marco had insisted they all traveled without a jacket. He led them to a leather shop where he knew the turbaned owner. Here they purchased leather jackets at a good price. The scam was to wear them back, labels attached, thus providing Marco with a lucrative earner from a friend in Torremolinos. He would sell them on as new at the much higher Spanish rates, but at a price still attractive to tourists.

After a pub lunch of Shepherds Pie and too many real ales, Marco led the group to a shop, Here he bought trays of Heinz Tomato Ketchup and Daddies Brown Sauce. To be under armed back to the bus and later to be enjoyed by Marco's English Breakfast customers, as they soaked up the authentic local atmosphere.

An enjoyable trip ended with Rugby songs on the bus to the accompaniment of hissing from the opening of cans. Marco had already confiscated the jackets which were resting safely in the back.

The remaining time was marred by rain mirrored the Bank Holiday weather back home. It did not rain in The Hill Street Blues Bar and the time passed too quickly. Harvey, of course, remained the Hero of the week. Enzo would repeat his tale, without prompting, whenever the mood took him.

Harvey was offered a lift with Mike and Roy but with the situation at home unresolved he declined. He also had an appointment with Dr Hope in a couple of days.

Harvey had refrained from taking his purple triangle each day and there had been no stirring in the loins. He was a bit relieved that he had not been in a position that required participation. He left alone with his modest bill for Messrs B&B and promised to return when able.

The return flight was routine, pleasant and landed on time at 1900hrs. By the time he had boarded the courtesy bus to the long stay car park it was dark. Harvey noted with irony that it was a bit warmer than the previous evening in Spain.

The bus pulled into the car park and started to stop as requested by returning passengers at the little blue and yellow shelters.

A large group stood to get off at stop 1F. As they were fussing over their luggage, gathering their children and losing their tempers

Harvey glanced out of the window. In the artificial light, he noticed a large Afro-Caribean man a couple of ranks across. He appeared to be having difficulty pushing an awkwardly shaped object onto the rear seat of his car.

From his vantage point, Harvey observed the struggle the large man was having. As he used his tummy as an extra thrusting tool Harvey mused, if this fine specimen was having trouble, what hope for us mere mortals.

An argument was breaking out with the alighting passengers over identical luggage. As they sorted the dispute Harvey glanced back to the black man and with delight noticed a pair of legs (white) protruding from the car with an ankle placed on either shoulder.

It became obvious that the ebony Adonis was not having trouble and the only struggle was one of manifest pleasure. Harvey grinned and was about to alert a fellow passenger when he caught the driver's eye in the rear view mirror. He gave a wicked wink and motioned silence with a finger to his lips. "This could be good," Harvey thought and sat quietly.

He did not have to wait long as the 1Fs, finally sorted, moved off to locate their vehicles. The driver turned the large spotlights on top of the bus towards the performers. When he was sure, they were in the catchment area he turned both lights on and gave three large blasts on his air horns as they were bathed in light brighter than a day.

Undeterred our hero carried on with the task, he raised a hand in recognition and waved it above his head as if doffing a large hat. Startled '1Fs' looked on as he presented them with a broad ear to ear grin. Even from his distance, Harvey was able to see the sparkle in the black's eyes, indicating pure enjoyment.

Harvey was impressed and chuckled. He then grimaced. He noticed that the other (white) half of the union was wearing the sort of sensible shoes favoured by a particularly estranged wife, and he shuddered.

Had he been able to look closer he may have shuddered some more. He would not have needed to wait the statutory two years for a divorce on grounds of desertion. It was indeed Crystal polishing the rear seat with her rear end.

By coincidence she had just returned from an Easter break in Dublin. Here she had caused an Easter Uprising of her own, albeit, apart from the odd slap, peaceful. She was now getting acquainted with the large gentleman who had rubbed legs with her on the short flight and helped her with her bag.

Harvey retrieved his car and drove slowly by 1F on his way to the exit. There was no sign of the entertainment or a fond farewell. This time he did not have the advantage of the higher up coach window to spy from.

To suggest that Crystal was saying her farewells would, however, have been a misrepresentation. The only oral activity on her part was receptive and she was too well bred to speak with her mouth full.

Had he strained his ear, though, Harvey may have heard her partner as he was almost howling, either with ecstasy or pain. For once she had forgotten to trim a rather important finger nail.

The drive back was uneventful, the M25 was slow but moving. The M3 was crowded in the opposite direction.

Back at Marsden, Harvey turned into the unmade parking space in his garden with apprehension, coupled with dread. After the last time, what awaited him inside he could only guess.

He made the conscious decision that if Verna were still here he would cancel the remainder of his holiday and return to work in the morning. Alas, this would not be necessary, or even possible.

He slowly opened the door and was staring at a scene from Apocalypse Now. Not the part where the nice Martin Sheen was tracking Marlon Brando but when he found him.

Harvey walked through the door into his, yes it was his, cottage. He felt that he was the nice Mr Sheen in that boat looking up at the red river banks with small fires and destruction everywhere.

In the middle of this mayhem was Ronnie holding a frail looking baby who was filthy, hungry and screaming. "What the hell?" Harvey was lost for words. Ronnie's were not freely forthcoming either but a picture started to emerge.

Verna had given birth at home, unaided and almost as soon as he had departed for Spain, to a little girl.

The Franklins arrived but insisted they wanted a boy, there had been a fight between them and Verna. Not only verbal, but the full on version, with things flying around the room, lots of punchings, biting, etc.,

Fortunately for the Franklins, Verna was weakened by the birth and they were able to escape to lick their wounds.

Next she had turned on Ronnie, throwing what had not already been thrown, or was intact enough to throw again. She then took whatever cash she could find and fled into the night.

This had been two days ago or so Ronnie thought. She had not returned and nobody had cleaned up the house or given any proper attention to the child.

"You are useless at times Ronnie, honestly. You can't treat babies like this, she needs medical attention and quickly or else..."

Words failed him again. He bent to pick up the child, who was released without resistance. He looked down at her, she stopped screaming and looked back. Harvey could detect some of Cass's features and an unmistakable crop of red hair, what to do?

He wrapped the baby in a large soft towel and then put her appropriately in his large Moses laundry basket.

The Accident & Emergency Unit at the hospital was quiet and Harvey was given time to tell his sorry tale. Remarkably there were no real problems, a little dehydrated and hungry but a night in the ward with some TLC would soon cure that. Would he need to contact anybody, the authorities, Police, who?

They assured Harvey that the child had not been abused or injured and, unfortunately, was not a unique case now or in history.

Now she was here things could be attended to at a proper time and pace, thank God he had not taken the road trip option. The mother's location and welfare were a concern as she could be the one in dire need of attention. Harvey doubted this, from what he had seen of Verna. Although she had given birth a week ago and taken part in one, maybe two, violent struggles, he was convinced she was blessed with a hardness that could withstand earthquakes.

Harvey was told he could do nothing more at the hospital tonight. Go home and have a good night of sleep he was advised. Some chance, he had to instill a sense of responsibility into his son, by force if necessary and try to untangle this unholy mess.

When he got back to the cottage, he was greeted by all the lights blazing from the windows. At least Ronnie had begun preparations. If he gave a hand they could discuss the matter as they worked, then sleep on it, and awake at least to clean house and a problem shared.

No chance. All that greeted him was a note pinned to the door saying "Sorry" and a trail of odd socks Ronnie had dropped as he fled to who knows where.

Harvey's heart sank, it had only been a few hours since the entertainment at Gatwick, but he felt years older. He made his way to the bedroom, this had obviously been the epicentre of Verna's onslaught on Ronnie.

Harvey rolled the bedding up, hopefully catching all the shards of mirror glass and assorted ornaments before placing it on the floor. He then retrieved his old sleeping bag from above the airing cupboard laid it on his bed and accepted the invitation to climb in.

The traveling, home events and worries had exhausted him, but tomorrow was another day, the baby was safe and there was no need to rush.

One step at a time, organise a clean up, get food, go to the doctor go to the hospital, seek advice.............zzzzzzzzzzzzzz.Sleep came eventually.

His mother flew into the room on a large smiling Afro-Caribbean. She was wearing sensible shoes and a fluffy white towel. This, fortunately, hid most of her body and that awful tattoo. Alas she exposed an enormous amount of red hair under her arms, which she had part braided. She hovered in the bedroom for a while then took a trip around the cottage chased by broken mirrors and an umbilical cord, that had a large spotlight attached. The procession returned to his room where her beaming unconventional mode of transport emitted a loud "blooooooop blooooooop".

She alighted with several identical suitcases, and a signpost bearing the legend 1F, that she threw around the room several times until satisfied. She tiptoed ever so quietly to Harvey's side where she straightened his bedclothes, plumped his pillow, smoothed his hair and then bellowed "CUNT" in his ear and was gone.

After a fitful night Harvey arose to survey the cottage in the cold light of day, which was actually quite warm. This made him think about Spain and he thought about ringing Mike or Roy, to see if they could assemble the cleaning squad for one last bash. He then realised, of course, they would be somewhere en route. Again it hit him how soon things had turned sour, but life goes on, shit happens – nobody died.

Harvey rang the hospital and was relieved to hear the little one had spent a good night. She had slept through until 6 am, been changed and fed then was asleep again. The doctors had yet to do their rounds and they were treating her like a princess. Really she would be no problem until the end of the week. He could visit anytime, but there was no pressure, she wouldn't know. This was good up to a point but what to do next?

He contacted his contract cleaner again and explained his predicament. Harvey was fortunate to find a sympathetic ear. "Spain you say, a nice bloody homecoming that was eh? Teenage party, yes tell me all about it, I got twins boys that age, bleeding nightmare. You leave it to us, mate, may cost a bit extra, but you are a regular so...oh if they find any dope they will flush it down the toilet ok. Well, that's what they tell me!"

They could call in an hour or so, quiet week, make yourself scarce, leave the key in the usual place, etc. All would be normal by six, promise, he was advised.

Harvey had to see his doctor later and also decided to see his friend, manager and mentor, Fred. Fred gratefully accepted an invitation to lunch at The Sign.

-

Across many miles of sea and land, on the small island of Malta, thirteen-year-old Claudette Golan and her mother were also seeking sanctuary amongst friends.

Chapter Eleven

Dr Hope was wafting smoke out of the window as Harvey entered. "You look well," he told Harvey. "Any action?" Harvey handed over his log.

After a quick scan the doctor laughed. "Ha, ha you out buggered the buggers." "Eh?" Harvey sometimes wondered what else the good doctor smoked. "I shouldn't really tell you, but I had lunch with my friend from Sandwich, a sandwich lunch, ha ha. Well, he told me, they have been jiggling the testers around. Some on the real stuff have been given the placebo and those on the placebo given the real deal. A bit of a double blind test they have to do. Probably been a few disappointments and many surprises in the trouser department over the last couple of weeks eh?" "Yes, well probably suits me at the moment" Harvey replied and went on to tell Dr Hope about his homecoming.

"Two things my boy, firstly on the test, they have enough now to sail through on a clean bill of health and are just a bit concerned about some blood pressure issues. I believe they will release 'a take at will' instruction soon to those with no ill side effects, like you. So you have one pill to use as and when, when used you come back to me for another, after a quick check over and simplified report." "Oh, good. Err, and secondly?" "What, oh yes.. the baby. Well, if it turns out that you want to be Guardian or something I am sure I can help smooth a few bumps, let me know."

'Guardian' Harvey thought. He hadn't thought about that. He thanked the doctor and left with a strange feeling, maybe relief, maybe something else. He called the hospital, from the phone box opposite the surgery, noting whispers of blue smoke curling from Dr Hope's window. "The baby is fine" he was told. He explained he had just returned from holiday and had a few things to do, he promised to call later and was told that was ok, no worries.

Fred was waiting at The Sign. "Pint?" He greeted Harvey, who nodded. He was pleased to see his Assistant but sorry to hear his news, especially as he had something exciting to impart.

"God, I feel high," said Harvey, unable to shake the strange feeling he acquired at the doctors. "Not sure what you mean mate, but probably stress, too much happening too soon, think I'm about to add to it now" Fred replied, concerned. They ordered a Ploughman's Lunch each as Fred explained.

The modernising of the department that brought Harvey and Crystal together was forging on apace.

Fred had been offered a good deal if he would accept early retirement. After deducing that the next offer would not, most likely, be anywhere near as good but with the same outcome he had agreed to go.

He would be leaving at the end of May, earlier really as he had some leave to take. Harvey would be offered the post in charge but under an Area Supremo rather than a full Branch Manager. It was a deal but not a very generous one. Harvey would not have an assistant, forthcoming vacancies would not be filled (natural wastage sounded a bit like ethnic cleansing) and he would only be given a small hike in his salary.

They chatted over the pros and cons of the change. Both knew this would eventually lead to the office closing or at least amalgamating with another. "Get what you can, Harvey, they will creep up on you one day," Fred told him. "Fuck Thatcher!" Harvey exclaimed. "Not her fault old chap, can't stop progress, not even the Great Handbag of Whitehall can do that" Fred replied, typically without a hint of bitterness. "Mind you" he continued, "I wouldn't have minded when we were both younger, Cecil Parkinson said she had nice legs and I think he could judge a woman. Bloody Clarke was probably sniffing around as well, trying to juggle his mother and daughter conquests to fit her in no doubt. Have to watch out now though, those teeth look a bit ragged."

They laughed and chatted together before returning to Harvey's latest domestic crisis.

"Charlie" exclaimed the elder. "Who's Charlie?" Harvey enquired, why did everybody speak in riddles? "Charlotte, my wife's second cousin's daughter, or something, never sure. Sweet girl, calls me uncle, makes life simpler. She is staying with us at the moment, was a registered childminder, is an absolute pearl, adores kids and babies - well say no more." he enthused. "Come meet her now, I took the afternoon off, I thought we might have a few. Say let's have one more, I'm driving." Fred ordered and Harvey paid.

While Fred was getting the car from the office Harvey rushed to the Bradford & Bingley to settle his debt. Nobody wore bowler hats or offered a problem with his transaction, sorted.

Fred was waiting, a bit away from the pub. "You know this could be a Godsend all around, see what you think. If you are serious about this Guardian thing, this could be just the ticket. I think if you are serious I'm bloody sure between us we know all the right people to smooth out all the bumps, with the paperwork, etc."

"Smoothed out bumps, where have I heard that before? Harvey muttered more to himself, feeling strange again.

"Belt up, oh and sorry about Herbert Crowe," said Fred, then continued. "Hmm, I'd forgotten about him, ah well, what will be....""Right, have you belted up? Clunk klick every trip, as Jimmy Saville tells us - can't argue with Jim. Now don't interrupt and I will have enough time to explain on the way, OK?"

Harvey settled back as Fred drove. Charlie, he explained, was at a crisis stage in her life having broken with her long-term boyfriend with whom she had lived. Now she had nowhere to live and no job after burning her bridges with the chap who was also her employer. She was the eldest child of five and impaired by a deformed foot that required a built up shoe and drained her teenage confidence. When the time came for college or work she had chosen to stay home to look after her much younger brothers and sister. When some years later even the youngest had outgrown the need of her assistance. Charlie took courses on childminding and landed a job at an upmarket Nursery School and also moonlighted with some of the parents as a babysitter, damned good she was too. One day she met Brian a building contractor carrying out work at the school. A whirlwind romance ensued and his business was riding high. He stole her away to deal with his ever growing needs in the small company office and later his bedroom. For a while things were good, then Charlie noticed she was chasing the money owed more than doing anything else. When a large builder went to the wall, he owed

Brian a small fortune. Brian smashed a few things and then picked a softer target - Charlie. Of course he was all apologetic after but she became very wary of him as his moods changed frequently. He was also around more and frustrated at kicking his heels so much. He started going to the gymnasium and developed a real hard body on top of his natural physique. When another contractor slipped into the night with several items of Brian's plant and materials and owing him a substantial amount, Charlie was in for another hiding. This time it really hurt, he grovelled and pleaded as he drove her to A&E but this time she could not forgive and forget. "She would not press charges but would not return either and that is the tale to date, and here we are, Du habite Fred" he concluded.

Charlie was delightful and Harvey fell for her at once. He guessed she was about twenty-five, or put another way, fifteen years his junior. No, twenty-five sounded better. She was pretty with blonde hair that she chose to wear in a swirl of loose curls. She was a jot under average height, slim with, to him, a disabling personality, careful Harvey!

She wore long baggy pants that covered her shoes and he detected only the slightest limp as her bottom wobbled nicely when she walked. "Slappy Bum Day" he chuckled, "Heck am I high?" She did not make out what he had said, thankfully, but smiled all the same.

She had heard about Harvey from Uncle Fred and was now pleased to meet him. She liked his looks, his manners and the way he spoke. She put his little giggles down to maybe shyness or nerves, which was charming, and she decided he was a man you could trust.

His concern for the baby would have melted the heart of most women and she was not surprised to hear herself offering help and like now.

At the hospital, the child was presented to them in a much better condition than Harvey had seen her last night. Her blue eyes appeared much bigger and her hair seemed to have sprouted like fresh grass after a Summer rain, except that it was fiery red. She greeted them with a cross-eyed smile that the unaffected would have diagnosed as the wind.

Harvey looked at Charlie whose eyes were brimming with tears, as he felt one roll down his own cheek.

They agreed if it were at all possible they would work between them to give her the best start they were able to give. The baby was to stay in care for nearly a month, with daily visits from Harvey and Charlie.

Faithful to their words, Fred and Dr Hope had indeed smoothed out the bumps and Social Workers Harvey knew professionally were extremely helpful. Charlie's qualifications and experience were also known and considered icing on the cake.

As they were collecting the baby from the hospital, they were asked if a name had been chosen as she needed registering ASAP. "I like Charlotte," said Charlie, adding hastily "if that is not too egotistical." "Yes it is," said the nurse, "we have called her Bernadette or Bernie." The child tried to turn. " You see, that Bernadette Devlin - McAliskey has been on telly a lot lately and every time she hears her voice little Bernie here responds in some way. We noticed and started to call her Bernie, but you do what you want." Charlie made Bernie give a small wave to the nurses as they left for home.

 Formalities such as pay and conditions were mutually agreed, Charlie would be self-employed and live in the second bedroom, all found. She shared with Bernie for the first eight weeks and then the baby was moved, to the small warm, adjoining bedroom that proved an excellent Nursery.

The child accepted everything as if appreciating all that had been done for her. To an experienced hand like Charlie, she never posed a problem and in turn, she excelled in her role as a poorly paid Mary Poppins.

This gave Harvey the time he needed to succeed Fred at the office and knuckle down to the reorganisation. It was different in many ways, but the remote Manager proved to be a little lazy and would go along with most things if there was no grief attached.

1988 was passing as do most years without pain, there were ups and downs, of course, and the odd surprise.

One surprise was a call out of the blue from Crystal, very business like. To paraphrase: She wanted a quickie divorce and had a friendly solicitor who would handle everything. Just sign the papers he sends, agree to everything and please send him the Marriage Certificate, it will cost you nothing, I promise.

Harvey was surprised and quietly pleased that Charlie appeared happy when his divorce was finalised in November. Crystal, true to her word, had handled everything and at no cost to him.

Charlie found that she was getting fond of this lovely man with whom she stayed. He was kind and all the other things she had liked from their first meeting. She even started to get a little ping when he came home, why not?

Harvey continued his testing role but had had no reaction in that quarter for some time. He thought that he may be being fed a placebo, or perhaps he was just content. Dr Hope found the latest logs just boring, but made no comment.

Amber called by soon after, with baby Nicki who looked well. She was smaller in stature than her younger sister, within ounces of her weight and not an inch longer/taller. She retained her jet black hair, and eyes, making Amber look a lot paler in comparison. Amber looked well and not at all surprised or concerned that Ronnie had deceived her throughout their brief relationship. She was also immediately happy to meet Charlie.

Amber was quite taken with the little girl sharing the sofa with her own, and baby talk abounded. While the two prodded and squeezed each other the elder girls bonded.

Amber explained that she was to meet her father later. He and Lulu were going to stop over at her employers on the way back to the States, from yet another holiday."He seems to have cleaned up good" Amber explained. "He used some of his influence and has landed a good security job for Uncle Sam. He gets a humongous salary which he mainly spends on Lulu. He is generous to Mom and doesn't drink anymore. He may even give me some more dosh." She blushed as her intended joke made her sound mercenary.

"Go for it girl," enthused Charlie. "What will you do when you guys meet up?" she continued, surprised by her slip towards the American vernacular. "Not sure really. Pops liked seeing Nicki, but I got the impression Lulu, do you believe anybody is called Lulu? will not want cozy nights around the fire. I guess I'll see them through the day or something."

"I forgot to ask," said Harvey, "how are you getting about?" "I forgot too, Pops sorted me out my little Ford Fiesta last time. He got it licensed and insured and everything, whizzed me through my test too."

"Well done, and your stately pile is where exactly?" "Stately pile?" "House" Charlie helped. "Oh, interesting, yeh well, not far from Greenham, there are still USAF links. Not sure of all the ins and outs but that is where I am and where Pops will stay, why?" "Not far then," said Harvey. "Go meet Pops and Lulu as planned with Nicki and bring her back tomorrow." He suggested and continued ad lib. "Or I can meet you or something. We can take care of her and you can enjoy their visit, what do you think Charlie?" "We can" she laughed.

Next day Amber arrived after lunch, very grateful. "Lulu doesn't do diapers " she laughed. The time passed pleasantly hitch free. Charlie was Charlie efficient, the babes enjoyed each other and Harvey glowed.

Amber was two full days away but had been in touch with contact numbers if needed. When she returned to collect Nicki, Harvey made coffee and Charlie itched to hear the news of Amber's meeting.

Pops had to go to Germany on business and would leave Lulu briefly to her own devices in Paris. Here she would be content walking the West Bank/Left Bank, and not bothered about spending - so much!

When he was done in Germany, they would return to the UK, where they would stay for Christmas/New Year. They planned to spend the Festive Week in a swanky London hotel and asked Amber to join them.

Lulu was a Bimbo and not bothered either way if Amber joined them, providing she was not a burden on her Chester, Amber's father. Lulu also had no time for living, breathing shitty babies. She did not want Chester getting all 'Grandpappyfied' and diverting his attention from her silicone enhanced babies.

Harvey was annoyed by this apparent selfish behaviour and wished Amber had told Lulu and Pops where to get off. Harvey being Harvey decided to keep his own council. Instead, he and Charlie invited them to spend Christmas in the cottage. No pressure, "or maybe you'd like the swanky hotel and leave Nicki here." he joked.

He was taken aback when she too readily, albeit gratefully, accepted the latter option. After she had gone, Charlie shrugged off the surprise outcome, "What does one more matter?" was her typical response ala Gwen Orchard.

Christmas turned out to be a nightmare. Both children contracted a bout of gastroenteritis making them really poorly.

Dr Hope was reluctantly summoned on Christmas Eve. As he was admitted a small motorbike puttered by unnoticed. "They don't need hospitalisation, yet," he tried to cheer them up after his examination. "It will not be easy for a couple of days. I can't give them anything to help that you don't already have, but if they get worse call me, no matter when," he told them.

On the good doctors orders, they were only fed tepid boiled water to prevent dehydration. This provided no nourishment, but even a spoonful of anything caused projectile vomiting. This made the babes scared and they screamed and screamed for love, nourishment and all the other reasons that sick little girls scream.

They alternated care, cleaning and cuddle duties, treating both the same. What didn't come out of one end spewed from the other? The wheelie bin was full to overflowing with foul-smelling black bags and the washing machine would never work so hard again.

Harvey and Charlie had managed to exchange non-committal Christmas Gifts, both wishing for the nerve to be more expressive. Neither wanted to ruin the status quo or at least destroy the slowly developing bond between them. This was pondered when the gifts were being wrapped in opposite ends of the cottage, but gastroenteritis changed that.

Harvey returned from the bin as Charlie was emptying the washing machine, "Listen" he said, she looked up puzzled. "I don't hear anything" "Exactly." The little sisters were finally over their illness and were sleeping.

Harvey and Charlie were exhausted. "Well done Mr Bin," she said, "Same to you Mrs Machine" he replied as they moved towards a congratulatory hug. They fell to the couch in a congratulatory embrace, this became a tired but passionate clinch and eventually led to a tired but soft and sensual intercourse.

Harvey carried Charlie to his bed where they slept the sleep of the untroubled.

In the morning, the girls were nearly as good as new and hungry as wolves. Charlie heard them both burping and carried them down to the small kitchen.

Seating them in their baby seats she worried what to give them and decided to mix a little apple purée with some oats. Doctor Hope had warned about over feeding them when they first showed signs of recovery so she made the meal into a game.

They squealed with delight as Charlie played aeroplanes with the spoons making them guess who was going to receive and who was going to have their nose buzzed. The game ended with both girls happy if not full and they were chomping on their bottles of boiled water when Charlie noticed a face straining at the window.

It had to be Verna. Harvey had described her often enough but forewarned was not always forearmed. Verna saw she had been spotted and indicated that Charlie comes to the door.

Charlie decided to open the window a smidgin. "Hello, can I help?" "Hum, Hiya, I'm looking for Ronnie Bright, is he home at all?" Verna enquired. "He's moved" lied Charlie. "What about the old Fuc..., the father, Harvey." "Who?" Charlie was getting uncomfortable. "The old man, Ronnie's Da', it's his friggin house, so it is" Verna was finding social graces difficult. ""Oh, that's who I thought you meant, sorry he moved away, I don't know about any son." This was getting harder by the second. "Youse live here then?" Verna enjoyed asking questions at kitchen windows. "Yes just me and err my husband" replied Charlie, crossing her fingers. "You sure?" "Err, yes, what do you mean sure?" "What about the frigginn kids? Jaizus, how could you forget them? I heard them from the Fuc.. Err from the road, they twins or something?" "Ha, oh yes I see, ha ha silly me. Yes, twins, Rachel and Rebecca, nine months old now." Charlie countered, feeling faint and thinking 'Please go before I faint, please God let Harvey stay upstairs'

She stood and was about to carry the dishes to the sink. "You hurt your leg" Verna wasn't budging. "Yes, no, I was born with it, just an inconvenience really" who is this bitch? "I bet, bet you were joshed at school, I remembers a gimpy at my school, the Nuns made her do games regardless, friggin hilarious .... Ah well, can't chew the fat all day, I'll have to think on, see ya." "Bye, good luck." Charlie sighed and lied for the umpteenth time.

She reached to close the window but Verna stopped her, "Do you like kids?" she asked mischievously. "Yes very much, don't you?" "A little but I couldn't eat a whole one." Without waiting for a response, but with a revolting cackle, was away to the road.

Charlie watched in horror as Verna reached the hedge and walked straight into Amber. After cursory glances and a short exchange both girls carried on their way. Charlie shook from head to toe, a noise distracted her and she laughed to see the little ones wearing their breakfast dishes on their heads.

Harvey had felt Charlie leave his side but had fallen asleep again, in a happy glow that didn't last. He was busy trying to prevent his mother from putting a half hitch in his erect penis when Verna's once heard but not forgotten tones gallopeded up the stairs.

He was shaken to full alert, although his penis was now inverted. He strained to hear the conversation below. From what he could gather, Charlie was putting on a convincing act as a little mother and Verna was swallowing it, albeit with barbed and crude comments.

Why this conversation was taking place Harvey had no idea and pinched himself to make sure it was not a part of his dream. He crept to the head of the stairs ensuring he distributed his weight so the old cottage would not betray him. His happiness of-of the night and joy of a new day were quickly being erased and replaced by a strange dark foreboding.

When he heard Verna cackle her way up the garden he cautiously descended the stairs to the kitchen. He took the shaking Charlie in his arms and asked "Why?" "Because I love you ... and them." as she pointed to the porridge coated duo.

Amber tapped on the back door "Amber" said Charlie, and she was admitted by the entwined couple. "Good Christmas?" she asked, with a knowing look that exceeded her years. "Yes," they replied together, all thoughts of sick babies and Irish demons forgotten for the moment, as they greeted her and laughed at the 'twins'.

"Was that who I think it was in the garden?" Amber asked. "Verna," said Harvey. "My God, what a beast." Charlie added. She went on to explain the short encounter while mother and surrogate parents cleaned up the babes, who were now well and truly bonded.

"What did you say to each other just then?" Charlie was keen to know, "she never said who she was" she added. "Nor to me, I kinda guessed who she was, Harvey once described her to me." "He should do that for a living," said Charlie. "She asked if I lived here. So I kinda told her I was the Nanny. She muttered something about getting a life then told me to lift my tits to meet my horizons. Or something like that, I think that's it really, and oh that awful Godforsaken laugh. Reminded me of The Exorcist "your mother sucks cocks in hell" "she blushed. "Mine probably does," said Harvey without thinking.

Amber also appeared able to spin a yarn when needed. She and Charlie, like the two babes, seemed to like each other as the tale of Christmas was told. "Oh no, and there was I being spoilt. Pops was trying a bit too hard to please Daughter and Girlfriend. We both ended up spoilt, look."

She waved an expensive bracelet under their noses, "from Koln, Cologne, Germany." "Nice," they said together. "Look, guys, I got fed up of being spoilt so I cut. I missed Nicki and wanted to spend a bit with you if that is ok. My bloody car boiled up in the village and did something, it is at Potters. God knows how long, ha. Now that you told me about your Christmas I want us to have a good coming of the new year, ok?" They both nodded agreement. "Only thing is the sleeping arrangement...... " she didn't finish as plastic bowls were frizbeed in her direction.

They would have a New Years Eve get together of who they could muster at short notice, for a dignified, don't wake the children, entry to 1989.

"We must get some supplies" Charlie kept slipping into TV American mode. "What day is it?" "Don't know or care?" said a chilled Harvey. "Thursday" replied Amber with confidence.

97

"That means New Years Eve is two days away," said Charlie. More to herself than anyone, as she thumbed the calendar "so we can rest today and go shopping tomorrow, Friday, who is Herbert Crowe, is it a Birthday?"

Harvey crashed out of tranquility, "Friday, Herbert Crowe" he groaned. "Like I said, who is Herbert Crowe?" "Manager's privilege your Uncle Fred called it. Noblesse oblige and all that crap, a legacy from Uncle Fred." He half explained half wailed. "I have to go in tomorrow, Herbert Crowe. Oh my God!" "Harvey, who is Herbert Crowe,?" they asked again and together. "This could take some time he said."

Herbert Crowe.

Herbert Crowe was a strange sort of character, the likes of which is rarely encountered by average folks on a day to day basis. Occasionally, one comes across a person who amazes or appals them, disgusts or scares them. One that a prayer is offered to on high, to be spared on a bus, in a bar, in a queue or wherever. This may or not be Herbert Crowe, but one would risk jumping into speeding traffic to avoid a second meeting.

He lived with his sister, Maude, in an old railway carriage that had come to rest miles from any form of rails and intended as a Home Guard position in The Second World War. Maybe Hitler would be confused enough by finding something like this in the woods, to surrender without further ado, who knows?

Jeremiah Crowe claimed it as a home for his wife and young family when he was demobbed without a bean or job. During the war, Jeremiah was a bit of a war hero, the stupid sort you sent in first, or hid behind. After the war he had little purpose, and a violent temper made him virtually unemployable.

Though both parents were now long departed Herbert and Maude remained in residence in the woods.

The carriage had very little home comforts. This did not prevent Herbert growing to a massive 6ft 4 inches in his stocking feet. He forbade Maude, as had his father, from leaving the confines of the carriage unless it was to tend the vegetables and chickens or dig fresh latrines. She in turn followed her father's habit of telling Herbert to "stop masturbating with your mouth open" at meal times. Neither knew what this meant and assumed it was a form of Grace.

Herbert provided food for the table in true hunter-gatherer style. and whatever necessities were somehow acquired. Maude had no concept of money or indeed things in general. Where Herbert was large, she was small and mousy relying on him for everything. When he went on one of his many escapades, she would loyally sit by the window for days until he returned. Should the day came when he did not return, she would die from neglect, starvation and a broken heart.

Herbert Crowe dressed perennially in a lilac jacket, lumberjack shirt and maroon trousers, all extremely ill fitting. His preferred mode of transport was an old Massey Furgeson tractor of some gone by era. This was thrown erratically around Chuffers without consideration, to keep it going he would pull up at any farm and just fill up. He had an overbearing presence with a smell to match. He drank copiously and his behaviour went far beyond any reasonable interpretation of decency. The only chinks in his armour were his genuine love of children and small animals. He also suffered with Asthma, which could bring him to his knees if he had a bad enough attack.

He had favourite catchphrases which included "Never mind her hairy legs, whop it up her dung bucket." "I've seen em come and I've seen em go. With their fingers up their hairy holes." (a bit too close for comfort for Harvey this one). Also, for inexplicable reasons he would bellow "Romsey Abbey" at all and sundry.

When he delivered one of his set pieces, or something amused him, Herbert Crowe would screw up his nut brown and weathered face to allow tears of mirth flow unabated from his bright blue eyes. When he laughed, it was a horrible bellow like an animal in pain, emphasised by his enormous shoulders shaking up and down. His right fist would burrow into the side of his large hooked nose and as he wheezed for breath, his left fist would pound the surface of whatever was closest. Plates would jump from tables, glasses from bars and pictures from walls. Nothing was normal in the presence of Herbert Crowe, fortunately like most rare creatures he was rarely sighted at large.

When spotted, tales of Herbert Crowe's escapades would become the day's topic in the area he was seen. Legends that became more embellished with each telling were recounted by those who knew to those who were learning. Among those known to be true was the time he was chased by a Police patrol car on his tractor, equipped with full ploughing tackle, he was also well and truly drunk. As the car came alongside, he swung into a field, set the tractor on full lock and jumped clear. Only the quick reverse action of the qualified advanced driver prevented the car from being cut in half.

On another occasion, he had been advised that his local pub, The Fox, was holding a private party for The Ramsden-Marden Hunt and would he mind spending the tenner he was offered elsewhere on this one occasion. He did not mind spending it in The Lamb but when in drink, he started to mind and, decided to visit The Fox. He presented himself dressed as a fox toting a 12 bore shotgun. He had carefully removed the shot from the cartridges and replaced it with rock salt in both barrels. "Ahem," he announced from outside, "I've come for some revenge." Laughter ensued from inside as he found the door locked, but not for long, as he poked the weapon through the letter box and fired. Needless to say, the meal was destroyed and many a backside stung for days, leaving a few hunt members not wishing to ride.

He should by rights have been locked up for life for these or any one of a dozen dastardly deeds, but Herbert Crowe had never been brought to book for anything. He was apprehended on some minor misdemeanours for which he received small fines that were never paid.

In short Herbert Crowe was a mystery man, out of control, who terrified almost all those he met. Nobody knew too much about him, apart from hearsay, but he knew an awful lot about them.

Despite his larger than life presence, Herbert Crowe could, when he chose to, be quieter than a mouse as he stole into the night. His creeping around and feral instincts, always observing while unobserved, served him well as both a Police informer and an accomplished blackmailer.

Only Crowe was aware of a particular high-ranking Police Officer's preference for young men of Eastern European origin. He had an obsession with their feet and footwear as well as their flesh. The young men had no idea of his identity or rank but Herbert Crowe knew and it served him well.

Everybody knew Crowe was fond of children and used his resources to raise funds or champion children's causes. One charitable side to him was very unconventional. It involved whisking young men from the area to the red light districts of Southampton, Swindon and Bristol. He thought it appropriate to be instrument in their 'first official shagging,' Crowe would commandeer a fleet of taxis to the 'lucky' chosen area. Here he paced the area ensuring all were satisfied. Where the money came from was only rumoured. True that prostitutes and cabbies alike were terrified and never charged the full rate for their respective rides and those seconded were also subsidised by those who had not been chosen. All this added to Herbert Crowe's gratification or pleasure as he would burst in on his young charges as they were in the act. After he would whoop with enjoyment for all he was worth. If he could not get in he would urinate through the letter box and reap equal pleasure.

Harvey then explained the significance of the coming Friday.

Fred Alexander had reached an agreement with Herbert Crowe that he should present himself on the last Friday of each year at the benefits office. He would be admitted through the back door by the manager. They would discuss his past twelve months income and estimate his and Maude's needs for the coming year. A figure would then be agreed upon as their entitlement that he would draw until the next meeting. Fred would then find the appropriate benefits to match the agreed sum. Highly irregular but how else could you deal with the beast? Far better than having him around day after day terrorising the staff and all he met until he got what he wanted.

This was the only bit of Fred's legacy that Harvey would have to sort out eventually, but it would serve for the coming year until he could find a way around it. In short, Herbert Crowe frightened the life out of him and Harvey was not going to be on the receiving end of the 12 bore, with or without salt. If the Police, the courts and the rest of Officialdom would not take him on why should Harvey?

Prior to, 'The Alexander Accord' as Harvey had christened the arrangement Herbert Crowe was a regular visitor, with outrageous demands. The police were regularly called upon and extended periods of staff sick leave followed. Any change to the existing arrangement was to be given considerable thought but not now. If the change was to be forced The Area Supremo or Harvey's successor would have to do it, and fuck his luck.

Chapter Twelve

Friday loomed large and Herbert Crowe loomed larger as Harvey let him in the back door. Something was obviously amusing him, his huge shoulders were heaving as he lowered his bulk into the offered chair. "Ha ha, haaagh," he bellowed. "Well Mr Bright, ha ha. Seen that wife of yours lately? Not the dyke, tuther one, the good shagger with the shafting finger nail. Ha Haaagh, you can't half pick 'em. Now you gone and got two more, younguns too eh? Haaagh!"

He thumped the desk causing all the pens to jump from the desk tidy. "Ha! I've seen 'em come and I......" "Enough" Harvey was on his feet. "Enough!" He repeated. "We are here to discuss ...." "Touchy subject eh? Only kidding, you gotta larf eh?"

Harvey could not be bothered haggling with this manic oaf, or with listening to his barely concealed lies regarding income. He just agreed to carry over the previous amount then got him to sign 12 declarations, eleven of which were post dated. He rose and prepared to show him out. "Don't fuck about next time Mr Bright, Registry Office is crap. They'll give you Romsey Abbey for sure, especially if you marries 'em both. Probably get a discount, haaagh!"

Herbert Crowe then limped off, exaggerating what Harvey presumed was his imitation of Charlie's walk, the bastard. As he was closing the door, Harvey witnessed the Butcher Shop delivery bike flying over the wall into the yard next door. "What a brute, thank The Lord that's over for another year" he was just in time to hear the begining of "Never mind her hairy legs......" before returning to his office.

He raised his glass of Beefeater London Dry in a silent toast to Fred and 'the Alexander Accord'.

While Harvey was dealing with Herbert Crowe, the girls were trying to put a guest list together for New Year. Amber was easy, she had no friends and her family were a no, no. Christmas had been enough. Charlie was similarly placed with friends and her family would prove awkward. They had disapproved of her living with Brian and now there was Harvey, it was going to be so difficult, she decided not to bother. Down to Harvey's friends then, Uncle Fred was committed but suggested Olivia. They knew that Bill Kitson was fading fast now and no way could they even think to burden Olivia further.

Amber remembered the wedding being sparsely attended and thought Harvey probably wouldn't want the office group around over the holiday. "Let's just ask his two wives and leave them to it, while we go to the pub," suggested Amber mischievously.

They both giggled, although Charlie would have preferred not to have been reminded that he had already been married twice before. "Just us then" they agreed and went to break the news to Harvey, and prepare a shopping list.

As they passed the Butchers, they witnessed a bit of a rumpus involving a large scruffy man in a lilac jacket with two of the Butcher's assistants. The delivery driver from the Cantonese takeaway was also taking part. The driver was remonstrating about a flying bicycle hitting his van. A string of obscenities issued from the large man who was enjoying himself, whereas the Butcher's assistants were not. One was covered in blood, not from a belated animal, but his own squashed nose. His colleague was desperately trying to release himself from a suffocating headlock that the large man had on him. All the time he was telling the little Chinese his thoughts on immigration in general and 'slant-eyed bastards' in particular.

Harvey's powers of description were again up to the mark. Charlie and Amber spotted the lilac jacket and mouthed "Herbert Crowe" to each other as they tried to scurry past. He, however, spotted them and collected up assistant one and waved him at them as if he was a prize Christmas turkey. "Haaa Haaa" he cried with glee. "Never mind her gammy leg, whop it up her dung bucket, aaagh," pleased by his slight variation. He then lost interest in his sport and threw the two assistants at the retreating Chinese and went off in pursuit of something more challenging.

Harvey was not in the least disappointed with the guest list as they explained their efforts to him. They noticed he was somewhat detached from the conversation but having seen Herbert Crowe outside they could understand why. He also carried a strong smell of juniper about him, but they did manage to cobble together a shopping list, before leaving him to his own devices.

Amber waited outside Lafferty's store minding the children. Charlie fought her way round inside, ticking nibbles and treats off her list that would be consumed in front of the TV, as they celebrated the coming of 1989.

"Hya Nanny, how you doin?" Amber physically jumped and she span round to meet Verna's hard glare. "And where is that fucking lying gimpy bitch? Of all the friggin nerve, trying to pass my own wee little darling off as a twin of her ugly fucking brat."

Amber instinctively stood in front of Bernie. "As if I wouldn't know me, own wee child, God love her, and she is the image of her Da', the fecking shite, so she is." Verna then lunged forward, grabbed Nicki and prepared to run.

"Boo!" It was Charlie's turn to jump. There before her was her former boyfriend-lover, Brian Golding, looking fit, well, relaxed and gorgeous. "It must be Christmas, New Year and my Birthday rolled into one meeting you" he charmed. "It is, and you say the same thing every year, you are so predictable," she scoffed very unconvincingly, as she fluttered inside. "How about a Birthday kiss?" he purred, but withdrew immediately. "Sorry that was insensitive of me, how are you? You look great, and I've really missed you." She had to be firm, for her own sake if nothing else she knew, but this was going to be hard. "So you say but you never missed me when the fists were flying did you, everyone hit home I remember." He looked physically shaken by the comeback, shaken, shocked and shamed by one sentence. "I know I was wrong, unforgivable, but it is not incurable believe me I've taken advice. I had therapy and now I am enrolled on an anger management course, all tax deductible ...." he tried to lighten things a bit. "I don't blame you one bit for leaving, but really you left the old me......well not the old me because we had fun eh? It was a sort of a middle me a very stressed me, still unforgivable I know but....." She interrupted, "I'm pleased for you, I never wished you harm, but, well that's it really, that was then this is now. If you want to be friends, fine. If not, I can live with that too."

She was being very brave and almost started to believe herself. He presented her with another earth moving smile. "Does that mean that friends can have a drink together or is that too...." He stopped abruptly, "What the Hell is happening out there?"

'Out there' was the front of the store, where Verna was holding a screaming Nicki aloft. The shorter and less robust Amber was desperately trying a rescue in vain. At least she had blocked the escape route and stopped a possible abduction. "Put my baby down" she cried, "please." That was not going to work and. Verna was getting angry. "Why?" she yelled, "why, is it youse all want to claim my baby? Yes, MY fecking baby, for your own? All I want is mine."

Charlie followed by Brian rushed from the shop. "Ah, Gimpy and Mr Fucking Gimpy I presume, pleased to meet you - not!" Spat Verna. A larger than the small crowd was gathering and both babies were coming distraught. Bernie did not react positively to this Irish voice as it continued. "I don't know what Mr Harvey Fucking Bright has been up to, but you fucking Gimpy', are not pairing my bairn up with your ugly brat. I've got her now and woe betide any fecker who tries to take her from me now. Right?"

Wrong!

Verna had barely finished her outburst when she felt a vice-like grip on the arm supporting Nicki on high.

Gently, ever so gently the babe was lifted from her perch and responded immediately to the soft coos as Herbert Crowe took her in his enormous left hand.

With the child out of danger, Amber delivered a mighty blow to the side of Verna's head that knocked her straight out, comatose.

Herbert Crowe bent and presented Nicki to Amber, much as if a butler delivering champagne at a Wedding Reception. "Yours I believe Ma'am," he said all polite and un-Crowe like. He then turned to the assembled crowd, crouched and bellowed "And now piss off all on yer. Gawan, Piss Off," so loud it was ear-splitting. Needless to say, the crowd bolted.

Charlie went back inside for her shopping with Brian at her side. Brian had acted the perfect gentleman throughout, they thanked Herbert Crowe and stepped around Verna, accepting Brian's invitation of a lift home.

It was his new works van, straight from the showroom, empty and spotless and took its first cargo without difficulty. This deed served a dual purpose for Brian, now he knew where Charlie was living and took the opportunity to suggest that 'friendly' drink, soon.

Only Lafferty's window dresser, Robin Lewis, witnessed Herbert Crowe's unconventional approach of administering to the sick, after the crowd had gone.

After checking her pulse, the great hands went on to ravish the unconscious Verna while the window dresser looked on. A large finger popped Verna's mouth open and it was drawn to the gaping hole now present in the maroon trousers as the fly appeared to open at will.

For once Herbert Crowe thought better of making a loud noise as the girl started to come round. Sensing the urgency of the moment he withdrew. He finished the job by hand, scattering Crowe DNA liberally over Lafferty's window and the groggy Verna. Robin Lewis sighed and nearly fainted. Herbert Crowe made his second withdrawal of the day and sloped away.

Harvey was oblivious to developments. After the girls had left he excused himself from the office, with the intent of getting a little below blotto. His staff were ok to see him go, after his dealings with that brute he was obviously quite tipsy. Only he knew how much of the empty, binned, Beefeater bottle had been consumed today. They did not blame him and after all it was officially his day off, so after greetings for the New Year he was on his way.

Flitting from pub to pub Harvey found his way home and curled up very drunk next to the pond. In his dreams, his mother rode a lilac goldfish in and out of Butchers' Shops where the carcasses of dead bicycles hung in the window. She completely ignored him until he attempted to drink from the pond then she held his head under water until he was rescued by the girls. They dragged him indoors and up to bed to sleep it off.

Charlie was concerned. "I don't like this, I'm not keen on drunks, never seen him like this, does he do it often?" "Don't worry he won't wake until morning," reassured Amber, "and if he does, he is quite harmless." She went on, "He used to do it a lot after his wedding farce, but I think you and Bernie have changed him if you haven't seen him like it. I don't think he has a problem, you know, he just gets pissed occasionally - recreational like." "What brought it on, do you say it was that Crow Man thing?" "Well, I wouldn't be surprised, imagine trying to deal with that guy. He was very apprehensive this morning and he did stink of gin when we saw him in the office."

Ambers support for Harvey was undaunted although her words were not really comforting Charlie. "My God that was this morning, mid-morning and at work! I'm not sure I can cope with this" Charlie was serious. "Please don't worry," Amber was a good emissary. "Last Friday of the year right? No matter where I am next year I will come back and give you a hand - promise" she laughed.

Charlie was less amused, "I'm sleeping with you tonight," she stated. "Good, my batteries are flat" "Oh amusing" but this time she did manage a laugh.

A girlie evening followed with the children fast asleep from their busy day, and Harvey, well, asleep of sorts. They chatted away sharing girlie secrets, aspirations and a bottle of oak-aged Chardonnay, intended for the next day.

Amber confessed a liking for Brian and was surprised to hear about his temper and tantrums "But he is such a gentleman" she said. Charlie spoke about him more than she wanted to but blamed the wine and the time apart for the mellowing of her feelings and closed that subject for the evening. They were by now a bit giggly but insisted Charlie "NOT drunk" though the bed was a good call.

From the foot of the stairs, they could hear Harvey's snoring which was threatening any kind of sleep for others. "He's on his back," said Amber, "better turn him, come on." Charlie let light drift across the bed from the landing while Amber pulled, pushed and probably punched Harvey on to his side. She then adjusted his arms and legs into a frozen running pose. Finally, she tilted his back slightly and pinched his nose, normal breathing followed and the dreadful noise stopped.

"Marvellous" Charlie congratulated, "you should be a professional" "Recovery Position" explained Amber, courtesy of my father. "You should always keep the airways clear, and if he does chuck up now, he won't choke." "Nice" replied Charlie, and they laughed. Harvey replied with a magnificent drunken fart that drove them at speed from the room.

"You know, I may just go back and choke him myself," Charlie said. "In there now" Amber indicated her bedroom, "I'd better see if there is a gas mask in the loft from the war" they laughed again and spent an undisturbed night.

Verna meets Robin Lewis

Following Herbert Crowe's departure from the side of Lafferty's, Robin Lewis recovered from his brief swoon. He went to assist Verna, who was recovering from her brief encounter with Amber's right hand. She gazed at the slightly balding man with suspicion. He had pointed features and a pale complexion and was leaning over her with a concerned look.

His breath smelt of mint, aniseed or something else, maybe Creme de Menthe, fresh anyway. She could see hints of grey amongst his sparse sandy hair and a suggestion of compassion in his grey-blue eyes. As he rose to speak, he adopted a quaint or effeminate pose.

Nothing effeminate about Verna's first conscious words. "Hey, I'm a little teapot," she addressed Lewis. " What the friggin hell happened?" she asked and continued before he could reply " And what the feck have you done to me tits. You dirty little bastard?" Which she followed with a threatening growl.

Her right breast was exposed over the top of her bra' while the left was squeezed painfully under the bottom of the framework. He was horrified, " Nothing, nothing I've done nothing, really. I work in there," pointing to the soiled window. "I came to help," he added. "Well somebody has been jiggling my jugs, and I feel like I've eaten a turd," she complained. "That is probably the shock," he said,"you were in a struggle with two young women. I could not see clearly as there was a crowd and you were at an angle to my window, but there was something with a baby. An oaf by the name of Herbert Crowe somehow got involved and you ended unconscious. Everybody scattered after this Crowe fellow shouted at them and I came to see if you needed assistance" he abridged.

"Sorry, I thought you were a perv' or something, shit my head hurts." Lewis indicated he accepted her apology. "I bet I missed my bloody coach now and it's the last one today, shit, what a fucking mess." She was not counting her blessings.

Despite the vernacular Robin Lewis felt a compassion towards this poor unfortunate, as he always did with lame ducks and innocents. He decided he would be the Good Samaritan that she needed at this time. He regretted his earlier swoon that rendered him immobile thus losing him vital seconds on the street. He would have liked the opportunity to have brushed against her bare breasts, not like an animal, not like Crowe, but just to feel them warm, firm but soft and vulnerable. He would not have abused her, he would have caressed and cared for her. He would have held her, as if she were and injured bird, with her little heart beating visibly beneath downy feathers..... He cleared his head quickly, preventing his erection from forming.

Lewis had only to make good the disturbance to the window and then he was finished for the day. He made Verna a strong cup of sweet tea. He gave her a couple of Anadin Extra as she sat in his small cupboard office while he completed his task. When he was done she felt better, her head had cleared and she had worked out a cover story. Hopefully she had found a way to stay around to sort things out with those gimpy gits, that nutty fucking nanny and Mr Harvey, fuck his guts, Bright.

Lewis listened enthralled as Verna told her tale. She had given birth unaided at Bright's house. She told how she had fought with Ronnie after he tried to sell her darling daughter, how the shock, postnatal depression and post-traumatic stress had caused her to flee leaving her beloved baby behind. Verna was on a roll as the lies flowed naturally from her brain to her mouth and she continued to captivate her audience. She explained that after months of therapy in Wales, she had returned to find that Bright Junior had gone, no surprise there, but also his father had moved on. Now a young couple lived at the cottage and were passing her daughter off as a twin to either their own daughter or the baby of some other unfortunate like her.

She told of how the couple employed a psychotic nanny to keep people from prying or asking too many questions and, how now, she was stranded. She had spent her last few pounds trying to claim her daughter and return with her to her small bedsit in Wales.

She had now missed her transport and the ticket was not transferable. The truth was less compelling.

Verna was living with a petty crook on a large unruly council estate on the fringe of Portsmouth. There she enhanced his small and dishonest income by visiting the city. Here she made many a sailor happy for a minute or two before leading them into a mugging.

The boyfriend, Greg, had heard of a childless couple who had lost a few thousand, attempting to adopt a Romanian baby. They had failed, despite the desperate need of the child. The Ceausescu government would never admit to anything untoward in their welfare programme.

He told Verna and she encouraged Greg to contact the couple. It was likely they were exhausted by 'proper channels.' They maybe willing to pay ten thousand in a simple exchange of cash, for a baby girl of less than a year old. They had most of the paperwork from Romania and Verna (mistakenly) thought how her baby, with her black hair and eyes could easily fit the description. Romanian or whatever baby, you can gurgle in any language.

No matter the truth, Lewis (Verna believed) was caught hook, line and sinker as they say on the banks of the nearby River Test.

Robin Lewis for his part was brimmed full of secrets and mainly lived a lie. His home was a small ground floor council flat close to the centre where he had once lodged with an elderly lady with failing eyesight.

The area was where people kept very much to themselves. The old lady had no friends or family and never went out.

Lewis, with her assistance, had developed an excellent imitation of her handwriting and signature. Adding a shaky hand for effect, he was able to communicate on her behalf in most things. He could order her repeat prescriptions, write and decline appointments as she willed and as time went by he did this without her being troubled.

When she died, he failed to notify the authorities and carried on much as before. Rent and most bills were paid by Standing Order and her bank account was topped up monthly by state and private pensions. The addition of a Cashpoint Card prior to her death kept the account from amassing funds and he made sure there was a small trickle out each month, to suit the needs of an elderly lady who was housebound.

Courtesy of his employment, she had opened a grocery and clothing account at Lafferty's and the modest expenditure was settled by cheque, every month without fail.

Lewis assumed that as long as the full rent was paid he would not receive unwanted official callers, and apart from annual gas and electric checks, he was right.

A caller from the Council said they needed a signature for their records and waited in the hall as Lewis obtained one. Lewis claimed she was incontinent. The Housing Officer was pleased for his help and for being spared an unpleasant encounter.

Lewis, again, rightly assumed that providing he did not let the old lady 'live' to a ridiculous age he could continue. He could bank a large part of his salary until he was ready to retire and disappear. He was not the type to draw attention to himself or kill the Golden Goose by excesses.

He registered them both every time elections were due, completed a census and did everything Maggie required. Eventually, he would milk the bank account dry, leave all accounts unpaid and disappear before HRH Queen Elizabeth II sent her telegram accompanied by the local paper. Good plan. More than enough for one person - really?

Lewis deduced his new friend would make a charming house guest for a while, although he would tell her little of his arrangements. He told her she could stay for a few days as the old lady was away for the holiday but implored her to keep a low profile or people may draw conclusions that could compromise his position.

He could smell a bit of a rat in her story, but also the possibility of adding a little to his retirement fund. So he was pleased when she politely accepted his offer.

Verna was overjoyed to have found such a friend as Robin Lewis. She was not sure if he was a fully paid up 'poof' but she had no doubt he would help out if they were short handed, so what? He seemed genuinely concerned and harmless so she accepted his offer, as gracefully as she could manage. She would get around to question him again about her tits later, but for now, just take advantage of what was on offer.

Lewis suggested Verna choose something for tea on his account. Also, if she would like to get a few bits for her stay to bolster her overnight bag, then please do so. To be paid back later of course.

He explained he had a small errand and while she was busying herself in Lafferty's he shot home on his Honda 50.

Here he rapidly tidied away a few magazines and pictures of vulnerable innocents. He then removed all keys from the internal door locks and made sure the keyholes were clear. He may just need to keep an eye on her from time to time.

Lewis told himself he would be a good friend to Verna and, he repeated, that he would not try to molest her like that beast Crowe.

His physical contact with adults was minimal and he would not dream of touching her intentionally against her will, unkindly or roughly. There would, however, be opportunities for accidental contact when they shared such small living quarters. Who knew, maybe a door left ajar could reveal plenty. He hummed as he lit the gas fire and returned on foot to collect Verna.

Lewis's idea of modesty naturally contrasted with Verna's as she waited for him with her bulging Lafferty's bags. Stuffed with clothes and accessories, her idea of tea was also off his scale. A pack of smoked salmon, two large T-Bone steaks and a large Banoffi Pie was more than he expected.

She seemed grateful and exhilarated by her purchases so he let the matter rest. He vowed to himself not to fall for that one again.

They started the short walk home sharing the bags between them. Verna unexpectedly stopped and turned to Robin Lewis for cover as she noticed Harvey across the road.

"Are you ok my dear?" he asked, a bit like a cat with the cream. "It's Harvey friggin Bright" she hissed, "I'm nor sure why but Ize think it is better he doesn't see me, for now." She need not have worried, Harvey was well into his mission. He showed no signs of his inner turmoil, as he steered a straight course to the next bar, neither looking to his left or right.

"But that's the manager of the DHSS" Lewis advised as Harvey ducked into The Lamb. "He hasn't moved, he's been at Marsden or

Langley for years Small white cottage, there before I arrived. I met him once over something for my friend and later saw him in his garden. He was there for sure over Christmas, I saw him letting the doctor in on ...Christmas Eve".

"I don't understand," Verna said quite honestly, she was confused. "Perhaps he uses his position to set people up with a ready made family or is involved in a swindle or something" enthused Lewis, sensing another opportunity to swell his personal equity plan.

He was unable to expand on his theory because he spotted Herbert Crowe. Now it was Robin Lewis who was being coy as he steered Verna down a side street. "Quick this way" he urged, cutting off the corner and the approaching menace.

Herbert Crowe's bright beady eyes missed nothing. "Well I'll be fucked" he bellowed, "The fucking fairy has got a Goblin Teasmade. Haaaa Haaaaa. Never mind her hairy legs. Whop it up her dung bucket. haaaa."

"What was that about?" asked Verna. "That was Herbert Crowe, the oaf involved in your tussle" Lewis replied nervously, relieved that he had gone.

Verna was ready for a fight,. "Well I'll fecking tussle him" she started to pull away. "No, please not now, he is err unbalanced, please ignore him" Lewis implored. "Ok, I will this time, for you, this time," she reluctantly agreed. "What did he mean about a Goblin and a fairy?" "I don't know, no idea," he lied, "like I said, he is unbalanced."

Lewis felt an involuntary shiver as he remembered the day he had the misfortune to pass Herbert Crowe a note. They were in adjoining cubicles in the butterfly roof toilets in Bristol Road. Suffice to say he was debagged and had his head flushed in the toilet more times than necessary to make a point. He also lost his toupee, that he could not face replacing.

They arrived at the flat, Verna went off to explore, while he recovered his composure and unpacked the food.

"Oh this is lovely Robin" Verna oozed. "Where will I stay, no ideas mind" she cautioned. "Good Lord no, I never asked you here for any impropriety ..." He broke off as she doubled up laughing at his pontificating.

He showed her the old lady's room which he had transformed since her death. Changing from post-war austerity to pure over the top pretentiousness and very pink. "Thank you, Robin, I adore it" again she was truthful. "You get settled in and I will make the tea, I mean dinner." He remembered the purchases - "It will take about an hour" he called from the kitchen.

"Don't rush" "If it's alright I'll take a wee bath then." "Yesss of course" he squawked, and added under his breath, "please."

The bathroom was two steps across the hall from Verna's new abode. She flitted between the two as she ran her bath and explored the contents of her carrier bags. She added some of Lewis's smelly's to the bath and then it was ready. She skipped into the room and was looking forward to relaxing in the foam.

"Fuck" she grunted as she noticed no key or bolt. She turned on the hall light and crept along the wall until she could see him in the kitchen. He was busy with the preparation and she grinned as he conducted Barbara Streisand with a bread stick through the soundtrack of Funny Girl, one of his favourites.

She returned to her bath, gently immersing her slightly bruised body into the scented water, heaven. She mused that Robin's tastes were a lot more delicate than her own, and that he was rather sweet really, as his face blocked the hall light from the keyhole.

-

Amber, Nicki and Bernie slept well, barely stirring all night. Harvey twisted and thrashed through his troubled sleep, finally waking early and exhausted.

Only Charlie had to wait until dawn before sleep came. She lay awake wondering what had happened over this past 24 hours.

Brian was the root of Charlie's concern, she had undoubtedly felt fondly towards him, and was now annoyed at her feelings. Harvey was an unfortunate bystander who just happened to drop his guard, once only, in the time she had known him. He had gotten drunk after an obviously traumatic experience with this Crowe Man chap. She loved Harvey, she liked Brian, that's settled. "Good Night, Nurse," she said affectionately to Amber's back and snuggled down to save what was left of the night for sleeping.

In the morning, they woke to the smell of bacon and eggs wafting up the stairs. In the kitchen, the two little girls were washed, changed, fed and exploring each other's ears, like a couple of primates.

Harvey squeezed some oranges and breakfast was ready. "Sorry," he said first to Charlie, who received and returned his kiss "Pig" she replied and playfully pushed him away. "Sorry and er thanks, fishpond?" he asked Amber. "Uh uh, fishpond, pig" she laughed, "let's eat."

Over breakfast, they filled him in about Verna's attempted abduction. Herbrt Crowe's intervention, skipping over Brian's presence, ending with Amber's punch. This caused Harvey to gawp in amazement.

They tried to understand what it all meant but could not make sense of the situation. It was unlikely that Verna was belatedly getting some motherhood yearning. Verna's instincts were way off course, not recognising her own daughter, or remembering her abundance of red hair, some mother!

"It has no bearing on yesterday, honestly" gulped Amber. "We'll be making tracks on Monday if that is ok. It's just that I need to sort some things out and Pops leaves around then. I better say my farewells to him and Lulu." She still had to stifle a laugh every time she spoke her name. I'll keep in touch more regular this time, honest, I'll phone you and stuff, like a real family eh?" How could they argue with that? Of course, they couldn't and didn't.

"Verna is a problem for another day. I am sure we will find out soon enough what she is after and until then we can do nothing, apart from not dropping our guard," Harvey said. "So let's not think about it until we have to, she is a very loose cannon and may just be acting on a whim."

They agreed to put Verna on a back burner and enjoy their time together. Harvey vowed that his hard drinking days were over. "Is that your New Years Resolution or a late one for this year?" Charlie asked. "Both." came the reply.

They spent a pleasant day together but could barely stay awake for the televised festivities. They did manage to raise a glass, as Big Ben woke the New Year and do the Auld Lang Syne thing. Then it was time for resolutions which they kept private and bed, with regular sleeping arrangements resumed.

-

Across the channel, in Le Havre, Claudette Golan wept alone at the side of her mother's freshly dug grave.

Chapter Thirteen

New Year Day at the cottage was a little somber as Amber made her preparations to leave the next day. "It's Nicki's first birthday tomorrow, are you sure you want o leave then?" Harvey fished. "Harvey, she won't know what day it is, and the longer I leave it, the harder it will be for all of us. I don't want to go. Gee, I love you guys, but I must go, you know that." Amber stated, of course Harvey knew what she said was true.

The Wanderlust is a terrible itch that had to be scratched until it itched no more - ah to be young.

Harvey minded the children while the girls had a girlie amble through the village. Amber, confided that she was to meet up with some old friends and hoped to cultivate and develop a particular friendship over the coming months. No more Randy Ronnie ramming it home as quick as possible - more of an Amber amble and see what happens.

Charlie confessed that she had some small doubts, following developments the previous Friday but was sure Harvey was a good sort and things would work out for the best. She would never leave him in the lurch if at all. They hugged a lot and returned arm in arm to the cottage happy with their shared confidences.

Harvey had coped admirably, the little girls were fast asleep on the sofa in his sleepy arms. A welcoming fire was licking away at some new logs atop some blazing coals. A warmth and aroma from the kitchen suggested dinner was well underway.

The walkers exchanged smiles. "Not sure I can tear myself away from this" Amber gulped. "I know I can't" replied Charlie. They grabbed a baby each and headed for the armchairs by the fire, for some serious snuggling.

Not so warming, a few miles in Chandlers Bottom, Verna and Robin Lewis were plotting their next move. They were unlikely allies but with one intention, to reclaim Verna's daughter, although their focus was on the wrong child.

After a good snoop round while Lewis was out Verna had telephoned Portsmouth. She informed Greg that complications forced her to remain in Chandlers Bottom for a bit longer. It would be worth it in the long run and may even attract a bonus. Greg was more than happy to hear the news, extra cash or a bonus were always welcome. Not so welcome was a rash he had developed, since Verna had been away, that would require a few days of a prescribed cream to make it go away. Fate had given him those few days and he was grateful he would not have to explain that one to Verna.

On his return and at his first opportunity Robin Lewis pressed the last number redial on his telephone, the joys of modern technology, and trust in one's co-conspirator. When it answered, he was not surprised to find it was a number he failed to recognised. He was intrigued, however, to find it was a pay phone in a noisy pub in Portsmouth. He was informed by the drunk, who answered the call that the stripper was on in a minute. After asking him where he was calling he was told to 'piss of now' and heard himself being described as 'some old poof on the pull'.

Verna and Robin Lewis had retired well before midnight and had not celebrated the New Year. Each distantly recorded the coming only because the nearby church bells had briefly disturbed their slumber.

As she had prepared for bed, Verna noticed the now familiar darkening behind the keyhole when she was behind a closed door.

Squeaky floorboards announced Robin Lewis was hoping for a floor show, as he positioned himself behind the door. He was completely inept at stealth never having played Grandma's Footsteps as a child. His last quarry had been easy prey due to being aged, partially deaf, and blind.

Verna was annoyed at him spying on her and her first instincts were to fling the door open to vent her anger. She stopped herself, unusually, to consider her position. In a split second, she deduced that she may be able to use this weakness of his to her advantage. She hung a coat on the door to block the view in the interim.

Later she devised little cameos of exposed flesh to string him along and then blocked the view as she was about to reveal all, and enjoyed the power this gave her.

Following a quiet morning, Robin Lewis prepared an egg and bacon brunch as they discussed their plan of campaign. As he fussed over the eggs, Robin Lewis stated in his opinion it was simple. Verna had been driven from the Bright household by Ronnie Bright because she refused to sell her child to the Franklins.

This had left her mentally scarred and in need of urgent attention, which she had received and was now fully recovered. She had obtained a home and was ready and able to look after her baby.

Verna interrupted "My problem is I have lost my doctor's notes and don't have any copies. I tried ringing yesterday," she lied. "They didn't answer and musta gone away for the holidays."

Lewis considered her for a moment, he knew she was lying and was not sure why. If the child was hers, surely she had rights and the father didn't appear to be in the picture. There again, who knew what a man in Bright's position could arrange to feather his nest.

Lewis was starting to tire of his house-guest. She totally recoiled when he attempted 'accidental' contact with her soft, fleshy bits. He was annoyed at his failure to get a glimpse of her naked. The closest he had got was the first night when she was bathing, but he had to sacrifice his vantage point to rescue the steaks before they cooked past perfection.

Lewis reasoned that similar opportunities were bound to arise, but every occasion since had ended unsatisfactorily. He was also beginning to question whether in fact he would indeed be able to reap some fiscal reward for all his efforts from this affair.

"Things are back to normal next week," he said curtly, "If you wait a couple of days you should be able to get the necessary paperwork." " I can't wait, err, they might go on the run or something. I really need to act quickly" Verna squawked, somewhat predictably.

"Well" began Lewis, "I know somebody who could probably devise a couple of official-looking forms and convincing letterheads for you but it will cost, especially if you wanted them yesterday."

"How much?" She snapped, mentally kicking herself for replying too quickly. And what good are letterheads?" "Two hundred each I would guess" he invented. "And then I can write some letters as your doctor, priest or whoever you want telling your story. They can check all they like but will only hit the same problem as you, it's the biggest holiday of the year as you say, everybody is away. If they do contact the sources, providing they are based on the ones you lost, they will concur won't they? It is not like we, or should I say you, are lying is it?" He replied smugly.

"Oh no err...." Verna was snookered, " It's just that two hundred fucking quids a lot of fucking money"

"You are quite right of course my dear" he sneered. He resembled an Eastern Narrow-mouthed Toad about to strike. "Quite right, let's call the Police." "NO! POLICE" she screamed.

"Right again, quite right" he repeated with that grin, knowing it to be checkmate. "Two hundred each it is then. I will go and get things organised and be back soon - you had better call Portsmouth again" He gloated and slipped off to produce the necessary paperwork.

Robin Lewis scuttled off elated to his little cupboard office at Lafferty's. Here he kept a small, but efficient, printing kit. Being the window dresser, it was useful for him to have access to the premises out of hours. It would appear normal, to anybody observing, to see the dapper little man mincing around the store on New Years Day.

Ultimately he had a new display for the last year of the 80's. This needed only minor adjustments for the start of the sales the very next day. Thankfully, even the money conscious management of Lafferty's would not open on a Sunday. They didn't mind breaking Bank Holidays, but the time was not yet right to offend pressure groups by tainting the Sabbath or religious holidays. In a few years, they would let Tesco and Sainsburys take the flack and open whenever suited on the back of the majors' success.

After adjusting a few drapes, pulling off a few covers and setting the timer for the illumination of his displays, all was ready for the onslaught. Bargain hunters were already starting to bed down in the main doorway. They would be the first to push, shove and swarm through, when the store opened in less than 24 hours, completely ignoring his artistic efforts.

He was pleased therefore to retire to his office and commence some really fine detail that may just need to pass some extremely close scrutiny - ah but what a challenge.

Robin Lewis's years of deception had turned an accomplished calligrapher into a mighty fine forger. He had a collection of official letters, stamps, crests, seals and jargon, that had kept his long lost companion "alive". He was sure he would be able to concoct something's that would pass muster. It helped that he could use a little poetic licence with the Welsh connection, not that he believed that one.

He worked quietly but well, after nearly three hours he had letter headings and affidavits to show Verna. His "friend" had done well and easily earned, in his opinion, his two hundred pounds a copy. Now Robin Lewis would expand on these gems by offering Verna his talents as an actor to complete the picture, another five hundred should cover it.

Verna was angry after Robin Lewis had departed to see his friend and she considered calling it all off. She would rummage around and steal what she could carry and then torch the place, serve the bastard right! First she called Portsmouth.

Greg listened then started to talk her round. "Ok so say this poof costs two gees top whack that still leaves us eight which ain't bad" he coaxed. "Just keep the old limp wrister sweet and we'll be ok. But we gotta do the deal soon or the punters will find some other kid and be gone, leaving us skint with your bastard kid to drown." "Ok but you're fucking helping me," she insisted. "I'll do my bit," he agreed, scratching his rash, "and we will get our two grand plus some back before long. This ole queer seems a bit vulnerable to me so find out what you can ok?" He rang off and missed her oath from the heart. "The bastard will regret his bit of fun and games and entreprefuckingneurial ventures at my expense," she spat and went to explore an area she had briefly glimpsed before.

After a while she had calmed a little and did not feel so hard done by. She would not be beaten and her findings had left her armed and downright dangerous.

When Lewis returned Verna was amazed at the papers he produced, the quality was excellent, the content most fitting and to her untrained eye they were perfect. She even grudgingly agreed that with the speed that they were produced made them a good investment for the money asked. "We must fill in some details, and I will rush them back to my friend to complete" he crowed. He wished he did not have to share the glory with his make believe friend, "with at least half of the money," he added as she gulped.

He then surprised her by taking one of the letterheads and writing a letter to her from a solicitor in Wales and explained, much to her confusion, that he would introduce her to him shortly.

With all the drama befitting a good thriller, he left the room in a flourish and returned moments later dressed in a black suit, dark wig with greyish temples and a dark moustache, also flecked with grey. Completing the illusion was a booming Welsh voice introducing "Evan Evans, Attorney at Law, at your service."

"Feck me, Robin, how did you do that?" She questioned him admiringly, it was so convincing.

"50% comes naturally and with my Am'Dram' background" he bragged. "And the other 50%?" she asked."Another £500" he replied. Whoops big mistake Robin!

-

Verna went to her bedroom and turned the electric fire on full. She heard Lewis change back and started to sing so he would be drawn. She noticed the shadow over the keyhole immediately. Verna hummed and danced as she removed her clothing with the expertise and tease of a professional. She could hear him puffing and slobbering on the other side of the door as she discarded her bra and pants. She lay on the bed and writhed under her own touch. First she ran her fingers under her nipples causing them to rise in the glow of the fire. Then she thrust her hands between her thighs and started to masturbate. The pattern of light dancing around the keyhole indicated that similar activity was taking place in the hall.

She reached down to the floor and retrieved a cylindrical object sheathed in a condom that she lubricated further and appeared to insert in her vagina. Several times the object was thrust and withdrawn as she arched her back using her head and feet for maximum lift as she prepared to spring.

Robin Lewis, by this time, had come in his hands, over the door and in his pants but still continued watching. Like a moth drawn to a flame he knew he was in danger, he had satisfied his immediate desires but continued spying. He had seen more than he could have possibly imagined or dreamed of but remained rooted to the spot. Gotcha!

Suddenly Verna lurched from the bed and before he could move the door was open and she was there in front of him.

"Want some PIE you pathetic little bastard?" She hissed. 'Pathetic I must look' thought Lewis, he tried to stand and cover his predicament and his semen that seemed to be everywhere. "Ok I agree pathetic but what's this about wanting pie?" he thought.

Desperately embarrassed and confused, he could not think. He did not have to wait long as she waved her impromptu dildo under his nose, removed the sheath and started to unfurl it. He felt nauseous as he recognised the Paedophile International Exchange magazine accompanied by separately rolled pictures of infantile figures orally indulging an adult penis.

She had discovered his darkest of dark secrets, she had found his cache of paedophilia literature, images and films - over exposed so to speak. How could he have been so stupid? Not only did he indulge himself with his collection but it was worth a small fortune in the right hands, or an isolated Schedule One long-term sentence in the wrong ones.

He stared at her face, even in Winter it was as speckled or freckled as a Thrushes egg, but far more threatening. It was debatable if he fainted or was KO'd by her smashing fist in his face. Either way he was unaware that Verna was devoid of the soft bits he had been lusting over.

Robin Lewis felt very warm to the point of discomfort and was very disorientated. His head throbbed, he could not see properly and his movements were restricted. At first he thought he must have experienced a stroke. As his head started to clear, he feared it was worse. He remembered the performance and that his precious collection and possibly his future were now in jeopardy.

Robin Lewis had not heard Greg's instructions to Verna to keep him sweet but, if he had known of them, he would have certainly questioned their Irish interpretation.

He lay on the floor, belly up, on top of his bound hands and was completely naked. His legs were also bound but in a fashion as to leave them wide open. Over his face was a plastic bag on which he could vaguely make out the reverse of the Lafferty's logo.

The bag was ripped open to provide a large gap around the mouth. No provision had been made for the nose and eyes but the act of inserting his head had produced a couple of tears in the plastic. He could just see, and breath, through them if necessary.

The heat was coming from the electric fire and, as he squinted through his hood, he realised this is where he now was and that fire was awfully close.

"I was fucking right about you, yous is a fecking perv' aren't you?" said Verna calmly. Noticing her captive was not fully attentive she delivered a kick to his rib-cage. This strangely, and unfortunately, began an arousal reaction in the trussed figure. She noticed the small twinge, "Ah, I thought so" she said as she strode into view, still naked as the day she was born.

Verna stood over her prisoner and lowered herself to sit astride the ragged slit in the bag hood. Her vagina covered his mouth and his nose embraced her anus.

He gulped, swallowed and fought for breath as she moved to and fro secreting down his throat. He feared he was close to death but still the arousal continued, and he cursed as his erection became complete.

Verna enjoyed being in control and climaxed freely, nearly choking her stooge, "Hmm, must remember this trick" she thought.

She then leant forward to pay more attention to his contemptuous excuse for a penis that was standing to attention for her. "Ha ha, what do we have here? It looks like a prick but smaller" she laughed, giving it an almighty slap. She was surprised to feel a draught between her legs and body as Lewis gulped lungful after lungful of 'fresh' air. She sat back hard, cutting off the supply, and grabbed his penis with renewed venom. She gripped the tight foreskin between her shortish thumbnail and forefinger then yanked it hard down the stem virtually effecting a crude circumcision. Blood oozed and Robin Lewis squirmed, but he still remained erect as she performed an ultra- violent hand job. She enjoyed the feeling of him choking beneath her. She gained momentum as she leant forward allowing him to inhale. Before he could satisfy his lungs she flooded his hood with a urine and excrement cocktail. "Special delivery for Mr Robin Lewis" she howled.

The mess filled his eyes, ears, nose and throat. She cackled cruelly as he struggled beneath her desperately trying to spit out her terrible concoction.

All the time she kept his penis erect and when she adjudged he was about to come she sat back on his face and pulled the electric bars down on his genitalia. As he shrieked in pain, she laughed uncontrollably.

She pulled the fire away more or less immediately and said, " You have been good to me Robin so I will let you go and you can have your filth back when Evan Evans does his bit tomorrow ok? I think that must be worth all of fifteen hundred don't you? Now go and pay your little friend for his valuable contribution, or maybe he would like some treatment instead eh?"

He blubbered some kind of agreement as she whispered softly "No charge for the shag Robin, hope you enjoyed it." This time, there was no acknowledgement for Mr Robin Lewis had passed out again. "That's him kept sweet then" she laughed.

Chapter Fourteen

Nicki and Bernie were the first to wake and lay content exploring each other's ears while gurgling baby talk. It was with a heavy heart that Harvey greeted them, lifting them in turn from the large cot. "Happy Birthday," he said to Nicki and, in case she noticed, "Happy Monday" to Bernie.

He took them to the kitchen and washed, changed and fed them with ease. Looking after Bernie was certainly easier while her sister was around, he construed. He then realised it was the last time they would share such moments for who knows how long?

"Morning, Amber's in the shower. She said it would be her last for a while so she is using up all my Christmas presents before she goes, the cow." laughed Charlie brightly. Then, observing Harvey, "Are you alright darling?" "Yes, of course, it's just, you know it's gone so quick. Thank goodness it's a Bank Holiday, at least I'll be able to see them off," he replied. "You're right mate, it has gone very quick, I find it hard to believe it has only been a few days. In one way it seems only hours but that's life, let's hope they come back soon." "Amen to that," said Harvey.

"What about Verna?" "Yes, what about Verna" he echoed gloomily. "I must admit I've had my head in the sand about her. It's not really Amber's problem so I didn't see the point in making too many surmises, unless the need arose so to speak. I suppose now I'll have to face up to it, she ain't going nowhere." he drawled the double negative. "Who ain't cowboy?" asked a rather rosy Amber. "Verna" they answered in unison. "Oh, understood."

Over breakfast, they chatted amicably about nothing in particular. They agreed to remain in 'regular' contact, well as regular as Amber could amble anyway. "I saw on the TV that soon, we can go to phone boxes and instead of a phone there will be a TV screen. We will be able to see who we are speaking to and them us, won't that be great?" "What were you watching?" asked a sceptical

Harvey. "Tomorrow's World, why?" "Thought so, the clue is in 'Tomorrow'. he laughed.

"I've just thought" Harvey exclaimed, "how are you travelling? Public transport is limited today being a Bank...." He was interrupted by a groaning beep from the road. Amber and Charlie shared knowing looks as Amber replied "Troy, that will be him outside" she smiled shyly. "T- Roy" teased Harvey. "Yes, Troy, Har-vee" Amber replied.

Troy was a quiet lad in his early twenties. He was shy and blushed deeply as he spoke. His accent was Southern Hemisphere tainted by travel, so he could have been South African or Australian. He appeared far more conservative than the aged, battered, sticker adorned VW camper that he drove. This had probably travelled the world, before returning to a side street in Earls Court to be sold on again.

Amber explained that he worked for a free paper that did reviews etc. on bands and concerts, new albums and releases, etc. 'If it's free how do you make money?" Harvey enquired. Troy explained that record companies, tour and concert promotors would advertise in the paper and pay for reviews and interviews. The paper could be as critical as they wanted to be providing it was fair, the only rider was if the promotors, etc. didn't like a review they could veto or edit it but still pay. On the whole, this rarely happened as there was no such thing as bad publicity.

He didn't get paid well but did get to go to all new venues, was inundated with invitations and got masses of new releases. "And he meets famous people," said Amber proudly "He interviewed Mick Jagger, they are touring America in August to promote a new album." "Oh, Amber said you knew him" Troy cut in. "Knew is probably a bit strong," he said, casting a glance at a blushing Amber "but we were acquainted back in the day. How did you find him?" Harvey asked. "Shy, and you?" " Shy," said Harvey "especially when it came to spending money. I can understand his endorsing a free paper." They laughed, Harvey liked him.

Amber loaded her meagre possessions while Troy struggled with a wriggling Nicki, wishing he had grabbed the bags first. As they made their farewells, Harvey slipped Amber an envelope explaining that it was "a little something" for Nicki's birthday and something for emergencies. Charlie also produced a Mothercare bag containing an assortment of baby grows as Amber fought back the tears.

She reached up to peck Harvey on the cheek and whispered "Thanks, now don't get so pissed too often, it frightens Charlie and watch out for the pond." She then hugged Charlie and whispered "Don't worry if he gets pissed occasionally, just leave him by the pond and don't forget the RP" Charlie looked puzzled, "Airways clear" Charlie nodded. "Are you flying somewhere?" asked Harvey and became more confused by the laughter that followed.

With more beeps than the village appreciated and amidst a cloud of exhaust, that caused Bernie to blink and cough, they were gone. They chugged down the road until the engine reached that familiar pitch, much loved by Antipodeans. This indicated that another few thousand miles across the Sahara or through Siberia would not be a problem.

"Why is it that tree huggers and planet savers always drive pollution belchers?" Harvey mused. "Dunno, but I'll miss them." "We'll miss them, but at least we have us." as he held his ladies close. Charlie joined in the threesome hug.

With Amber gone and Bernie taking a nap they curled up on the sofa. Harvey introduced marriage into the conversation. Charlie was not averse to the idea but wanted to be just that bit more certain before making the big commitment. Harvey was not disappointed by the response especially with two failed unions behind him, but he was glad he had not proposed. Then they started to theorise. If they married in say June 1990, the sisters could be cute runaround, bridesmaids.

"They would steal the show" Charlie complained. "What the fu..." She was unable to complete her sentence as an aged lath and plaster let go of the ceiling and crashed down on everything below. As the dust settled Charlie honed in on Bernie, who was scared and howling loud enough to disturb more ceilings.

"She's bleeding" she called without panic. No response indicated that Harvey may be in difficulty too. She found him on the sofa, more dazed than concussed but bleeding heavily. Being unable to find the phone under the rubble Amber put the dusty baby in a towel from the kitchen and put her in the car. She then applied a pressure pad of wet tissue, gauze and a wrap around improvised turban to Harvey's head before leading him to the panicking Bernie. "You're a bloody marvel," he said with feeling. "Are you ok? Sure? Ok, I think you had better drive if you are sure."

A trip to casualty confirmed nothing more than a gash that required three stitches in Charlie's hairline and some small scratches and bruises on her arms, she had been sheltered by the cot and was very lucky. A measly single stitch took care of Harvey's eyebrow.

"Well it felt worse" he whined. "To be honest it looked appalling, I thought you had a hole in your head," she sighed with relief. "You are all lucky you came in as you did" advised a sniffy intern. "Had you cleaned up we would have to report your child's injury to Social Services, but on this occasion you were obviously accident victims." Harvey could not be bothered to comment.

Bernie was complaining vigorously in baby terms to the unplanned outing and was clearly upset. This scuppered ideas of a meal out on the way back.

Harvey stopped to collect Fish & Chips as it started to rain. At home, they found that the room vacated by Amber was the most dust free and ate their meal from the paper. Charlie tried all she could to feed Bernie, but she would not even succumb to her favourite Heinz mush and continued her tantrum. "She's missing Nicki and she's boiling. I'll give her some Calpol and try to get her settled, fingers crossed" She half smiled and raised her eyebrows as she looked for a suitable resting place.

Harvey returned to the havoc below and started to collect the larger bits of plaster and laths which he stashed in one corner by the window. He had contemplated throwing the rubble straight into the garden but reasoned he would rather have dry rubbish inside than a soggy mess outside.

When Charlie joined him, she could see he had been working hard to clear up but with the best will in the world she could see no improvement. "Leave it for tonight, and let's go to bed eh?" She whispered, adding "You have work tomorrow, I have a splitting headache and I can't guarantee that madam will stay quiet for long, so move your dusty ass." He couldn't refuse such an offer. "It could have been worse I suppose, this time last week we were up to our eyes in sick babies and shitty nappies. At least nobody got hurt."

He looked round and caught Charlie gingerly touching her scalp where a conker sized bump had occurred. "Sorry, what I mean is that lot could have killed the kids in the right/wrong circumstances...." "Shut up, when in hole stop digging."

She bent and picked up some plaster that she crumbled in her fingers. "Cheapskate, as I thought, no hair or blood" "Sorry, you have lost me." "In the days when this place was built they would mix pig blood with horsehair, or even wool with the lime to give it a bonding agent. This is just sand, lime and water mix, blood and hair would have given it more body. Would have lasted another hundred years, do you know that the walls of Jericho had a mix of camel hair and blood?" Harvey stood back in amazement, "You are a bloody marvel, you never cease to amaze .... hang on, didn't the walls of Jericho fall down?" He ducked as she flung what may have been a cushion at him.

As Harvey prepared to shower Bernie let out a wail. "Sorry, can you get that, I'm a bit....." "Dusty" she laughed, and he knew why she was there. He showered quickly as the water appeared to be on the blink. Hopefully, Charlie will be ok.

He lifted Bernie from Charlie and walked her around and then lowered her into the cot which appeared to welcome her. He covered her and crept from the room as the phone started to ring. "If that's Amber tell her I'm in the shower." Charlie called softly, then a little louder, "You bastard, this water is freezing, you wait."

He chuckled and went off in search of the phone, instantly regretting it was not wall mounted. The ground floor lights had come out in sympathy, with the hot water, but he managed to find the phone in the darkness. The phone was reaching the end of its feeble ring, he picked it up. It bore no resemblance to its former self. He spoke into what he thought was the mouthpiece and was not at all surprised to hear a strange whine from the other part. The line cleared a bit and Harvey recognised Olivia Kitson's soft tones.

"Sorry Oli," he said in his best Stan Laurel voice. "Me too, my Bill's dead" she replied.

She had not only rung Harvey as a friend but also because she needed to talk and she knew he was a good listener so talk she did. She talked and talked about Bill. How she had met him, about his illness and bravery, about how she had loved him. About how he had died that afternoon and been taken away from her in body and soul, and on and on. Harvey listened, only interrupting when she faltered, with words of encouragement or endorsing her sentiments. On and on she went, gaining strength one minute only to lose it the next.

Charlie found him in the dark and he whispered the news to her. She kissed the top of his head and propped herself against him as he continued to absorb the outpouring of grief. When she finally ground to a halt, he advised her he was coming over but she insisted she was alright. She would be pleased if he could go with her the next day to see Bill, and when he agreed he would, she was gone.

"This is a good start to 1989" Harvey gestured to the dark. I have shed-loads at work that only my death would save me from" he said grimly. "I can't ignore poor Oli and there is all this. I know good cleaners and I have mates who are builders of sorts but not in this area." She put a finger to her lips, "Don't worry, I know a man who can." "You're a bloody marvel...."

He turned at the top of the stairs as he recognised the feeble ringing from the phone. Unfortunately, it was loud enough to wake Bernie. "Maybe Oli again, I'll take the phone," he said as she peeled away to Bernie. The earpiece was still warm, he located the mouthpiece lodged on the cradle and recoiled as a booming Welsh voice emitted from the contraption.

"Mr Bright?" The voice demanded, but continued before he could reply. "My name is Evan Evans, Attorny at Law. I represent Ms Verna McCalisky and have some important matters to discuss with you. At your convenience, of course, but not at the convenience of Royal Mail after a Bank Holiday, so it will be in person. Shall we say tomorrow? At what time?" "Fuck off," said Harvey and threw the remains of the phone across the room.

Returning to the bedroom there were two smiling faces sitting up in bed to greet him. "Who was that?" "Wrong number" he lied." Oh Grandad was rude to a Wong number" she teased but noted his grin did not hide an air of concern.

Sleep that night was a troubled affair and as usual, when the shit was flying, Harvey's mother entered the fray. Tonight she was tending a flock of Welsh lambs. They were contained in pens made from laths, but resembled futuristic phone boxes. She was attired in a lath bodice that was tightened as to heave her bosom to her chin. Every so often she would lift a lamb and carry it to her son for approval. As she approached the bed the lamb's fleece would turn a fiery red and instead of bleating it would ring like a broken trim phone. When the lamb was placed on the bed, kicking and ringing, it would start smoking and farting like a broken exhaust until his mother swatted it like a moth. She then placed it in a can of Heinz baby food. Bill Kitson collected the cans and drove them off in a VW camper. There were many lambs and it was to be a long night.

-

Robin Lewis stared at the phone in his hand. "What did he say?" Verna asked. "Fuck off" "Now don't get funny with me pervie" she snarled."That is what he said, and I quote him verbatim "Fuck Off" OK!" he shouted, not happy at the turn of events.

He had awoken, or come to, trussed and choking inside that vile carrier bag and was in extreme pain from his injuries. Verna had taken to issuing the occasional kick while he was trussed and referred to him as 'pervie' almost without exception as he lay helpless.

When she finally released him to 'go and see your little friend' he was too weak to mount an attack. Not that it would have been much of a match, even at his best. How he ever thought of her as vulnerable he could not now imagine, the bitch would have been thrown out of The Gestapo for using excessive cruelty.

In the bathroom he examined his wounds, they were many and varied and in need of attention but he would have to self-treat them to avoid awkward questions. He set about the painful task of cleaning and disinfecting himself with a vengeance.

Bathing was extremely painful but afterwards he was more mobile and a cocktail of creams soothed his ailments, sufficient for him to leave to make the final adjustments to the paperwork.

Verna had been a little annoyed that her excesses as chief torturer had rendered her 'legal advisor' incapacitated for most of the day. They had lost the advantage of a Bank Holiday visit.

As the day wore on she found that Robin Lewis had accepted his fate and was keen to help her on her way, and out of his life. She was pleased when he returned with the perfected paperwork and suggested the telephone call, but not sure what to make of the response. It must have been the right thing to do, she reasoned, that is what a real solicitor would have done surely? He sounded real enough to her so he must have come across on the phone equally as well, if not better, so why the short, sharp reply? They would undoubtedly find out tomorrow.

Lewis had left a sicky telephone message on Lafferty's answer phone, taking a couple of days off. They would not mind as all his work was done for now and he certainly sounded sick.

"Well, I'm away to my bed" Verna cooed. "Do you want a quick shag before I go?" she asked, cackling dreadfully as he bolted for the sanctuary of his bedroom and some pain killers.

Chapter Fifteen

Tuesday 3rd of January 1989 arrived in general relief of all at the cottage. "What a night" Charlie groaned, "I'm exhausted, there is nothing like a good nights sleep and, believe me, that was nothing like a good nights sleep." "Me or Bernie?" Harvey asked guiltily, he held the infant at arms length and she made happy gurgling giggles. "Both, I nearly left you two to it, but there was nowhere dust free to go. And I was scared that you may squash her on one of your trips round the bed." She was not happy. "Sorry, a bit of a nightmare, and talking of which, I've just remembered what joys await us below." "Well, firstly, perhaps you should share your worries instead of inventing wrong numbers and then they wouldn't gang up on you in the night. Secondly, I told you to leave downstairs to me - well the organising, you'll have to find the dosh, insured I hope?" He nodded. "Give me the details, and be amazed" She finished on a light note, but he could see she was being serious.

Harvey propped Bernie between two sets of pillows and sat next to Charlie, reaching for her hand. "The phone, it was Verna, well not exactly Verna but somebody representing her, a lawyer" "Representing? and you told them to eff off, you are crazy." "He was Welsh" "Oh that's ok then, you racist, do you think it it's serious?" "Yes, I'm afraid I do. I don't want to appear weak, indecisive or a defeatist, but if she has come for Bernie armed with a solicitor I'm not sure we can stop her," he said gloomily. "Please say we can try" she pleaded. "We can but try" with less conviction than he had intended.

Harvey gave up trying to get a dial tone from his mangled phone and crossed the green to use the public box, no futuristic installations yet he noted. Just the faint smell of urine and dog. It was cold in the box and grey outside, not the sort of day you would choose to start a new year, and that was without current affairs.

He was pleased to find his old boss had returned from his Christmas break and was still an early riser, despite his retirement. Harvey briefed him on the ceiling episode and asked for sanctuary for the girls while the worst of the repairs were carried out. "No problem Dear Boy" That made him feel better and he thought how refreshing it was to be in your forties and still be addressed as 'Dear Boy'. "Remember that boat I bought, we are going to check her out for a few days while she is in the yard at Hamble. Need somebody to water the plants and feed the cat so we will be helping each other. Treat the place like home from home, we were going to ask Olivia, but we heard her news last night, poor love." "Yes very sad," said Harvey, remembering something else he had to do that day. "You are my saviour yet again boss" "There is only one of them matey, and I'm afraid I don't fit the bill. Like I said, you will be doing us a favour but please don't kill the plants." "Fred, will you have time for a chat about the baby before you go?" "Problems eh? Yes, of course, we will make time when you come over" "Thank you Boss" "Splendid, see you anon." He clicked off. Harvey squeezed out of the box as one of the village church ladies arrived loaded with cleaning materials. They exchanged knowing smiles as Au du Phone Box wafted between them.

A little later it was Charlie's turn to cross the road to the telephone box. She noted with pleasure that there were fresh flowers in a small vase on the shelf above the directory. A long 20p slot bashing conversation with the insurance company confirmed all was in order. The office was inundated with Christmas claims and were pleased they did not need to shell out for, or find, temporary accommodation which they were obliged to do where a baby was concerned.

She was advised to get three quotations and if there were no major discrepancies between high and low, accept the middle one. She was told to take photographs and forward them with the quotations - not estimates which could be too open to variation. This was a simple maintenance job albeit messy.

They would send a cheque by return, providing she was prepared to oversee and sign off the work. She would produce a detailed list of damaged effects and, if that fell within a certain tolerance, a second cheque would follow. The non-existent claims history of this long standing customer allowed the insurers to proceed without inspection, providing all costs were within their projections. The call was terminated with both parties satisfied and wishing all things could be so simple.

The next call Charlie was about to make was going to be hard for her as she picked up the receiver and nervously dialed the number she had once shared.

As it rang, she could picture the two-tone grey beast, with the heavy dial, bursting forth in the office, while the ivory wall phone warbled away in the kitchen. She wondered if it had been moved away from the light switch. This had been a constant source of irritation, as the handset invariably was knocked from the cradle, when she put the light on. Her thoughts were interrupted by the beep beep, hungrily crying for a 20p to connect the call. She slurped a coin slowly into the mechanism, no need to hurry, she knew there would be the inevitable pause before he spoke. He had always done this on the grounds that most initial salutations were wasted. He deplored waste of any kind.

Eight, nine, ten.

"Good morning, Goldings - Building Solutions, Brian listening, how can I help?" "You have changed that a bit, but it still sounds smarmy," she said. "Sorry, Hello it's me 'speaking' and I hope you can help" unsure why she was being sarcastic - nerves? "Well Hello, it's a bit early for that drink but I'm game if you are." "Don't be silly, are you busy work wise at present?" "I start a big one next week but for now I have nothing on - in more than one way" he oozed. Then realising his flippancy would not be appreciated, he corrected himself, "Sorry, only joking, a bit early for my humour eh?" "A tad but better than the 75% maze mashed with Clearmont water in Jim Beam that you started the day with, she retorted." "Now shut up, how do you fancy a cash job?"

He thought he would have preferred a blow job but sensibly kept these thoughts to himself. "If it's to help you - yes. The merchants are closed still, lazy bastards, but if I can help and finish by Monday, I'm all yours." She ignored the inference and filled him in on the task. "Right, plasterboard, plaster/artex, battens, small electrics/plumbing, paint, neutral paper and all the muscle I can muster for the clear up. I have all that to hand except the muscle, but I know plenty that have overspent this week. See you there about eleven thirty, quick asses before recruiting at the pub. Cash mind - no paperwork, ok?" "Well, sort of" she explained the three quotation deal. "No problem, I have plenty of letterheads from genuine guys who have hit the skids. I'll bring all three dated over two days, all will be reasonable for the insurers, don't be late." "How can I be late you prick? I am already here. Thank you, Brian, you are my champion." She thanked him from the heart and replaced the receiver as he pranced around his office singing 'Champion The Wonder Horse' in a rendition Frankie Laine would not have recognised.

Chapter Sixteen

Charlie and Bernadette charmed Mrs Alexander in the kitchen while Harvey had an earnest conversation with Fred in the conservatory. It was still very early, but all were surprisingly alert.

"I don't like it, Harvey. If the girl has returned full of remorse and wants her child back, I don't see that we can contest it. It was not from her that you took the baby to the hospital in that shameful condition, but your son - who promptly disappeared without as much as a by-your-leave. The good Doctor and I did the best we could at the time, mainly to prevent a care order, but with her reappearance and her sorry tale we could all be scuppered."

Harvey looked resignedly dejected. "My Boy, sorry you asked for my opinion and advice, that was my opinion, this is my advice." Fred took a deep breath before continuing. "See what she wants, go lightly, check out as much of her story as you can, document anything that does not ring true. Do not offer her money on any account, that would be illegal. I don't understand the Welsh solicitor working over the holidays unless he is charity sponsored or maybe there is a church connection. Sorry Harvey, this is sounding like a lecture, but I am sure I am not telling you something you have not considered." Fred pulled a face as he gulped down a mouthful of cold tea. "You have done all you can to secure Bernie's future as we saw it and there can be no come back on that. But, and it is a big but. There is not a court in the land that would give you custody over her natural mother if she has an inkling of a case. Even if you feel she would be unfit as a mother, fair does, she has not had much time to prove one way or the other, still a kid herself really."

Harvey shivered, Verna was never a child, correction, child of the devil perhaps but that was about the nearest she got he thought. Still Fred continued unabated. "I think it would go against you if you tried to contest her right to motherhood and jeopardise any access you may want to Bernie in the future. Let her stay for a few days so she can get used to the baby and vice versa. Give you a chance to check her out, and who knows, help her out. After all, she may just be genuine. There are lots of ifs, buts and maybe's I'm afraid, but don't lose hope yet, and get rid of that solicitor soonest."

Harvey had listened without comment. He knew his wise old owl was right. As Fred concluded his opinion, advice and commentary, Harvey just stood and nodded. "Thank you, Boss, as you say, I knew as much all along, I just needed to hear it from someone whose opinion I respect. Can't let her stay, though, the place will be a building site by tonight." "My dear boy, look around, look at the space. If you want, let her stay here until the weekend with you. Mind you, if you are not at home, she may not find you directly." "Good thinking, but it's not that easy or I'd just keep moving like Amber," said Harvey glumly. "I'd better go and break the news to Charlie, but she is not stupid and probably realises the impotency of it all." "Ah yes Charlie, I understand there have been err - developments?" "Yes, but I'm not sure how she will take to just half the package." "Don't sell yourself short Dear Boy, you will be a great and supporting granddad. Charlie could be an honorary Aunt or something like that, let's no pre-suppose, come let's join the ladies."

Harvey walked with Charlie in the garden, he abridged the conversation he had with Fred and the advice he had been given. Charlie had more or less come to the same conclusion but could see no good outcome. From what she had encountered regarding Verna she doubted she had a good side, and seriously doubted her motives were honourable.

The thought of sharing the same roof as her just did not appeal at all. Still, it was for the baby and would buy time to check Verna and her story, she would give it a try. "If we fail I'll get a proper job, earn real money and we can eat out and take holidays like a real couple" she tried to sound enthusiastic.

"Oh, what are going to do about transport while we are here? Uncle is taking his car and...." "Ah, well I did have a surprise for you back at the cottage but with the sickness, then Amber, Verna, me getting drunk. Then those blasted ceilings I didn't get around to giving it to you." "Liar," she said cheekily as he blushed. "Not that, I was hoping, but that surprised me too - a nice surprise. Look if we can shoot back to the cottage it will still be a bit of a surprise. Then I must get going for work and not to mention Olivia. You ok being site foreman?" "Course, come on then, I love a surprise - nice ones."

Auntie refused to be parted from Bernie and walked her round the right angled conservatory, pointing out squirrels rummaging for their Winter stash, birds and other forms of wildlife. Bernie followed pointing fingers then wanted to be supported as she walked the same route. This was a helpful interlude as they whipped back to the cottage.

Charlie drove and he watched her intently as she negotiated the large Senator round the narrow lanes. She pulled into the drive and he asked her to park next to the large lump covered by an old blue tarpaulin. He got out and pulled back with a strained "Voila."

Where once had stood his old run down Morris Traveller there was now an immaculate version of the same model. Charlie stepped back in amazement. "Is this the....? LNH 284, Harvey it is the same, it is. How, who, what? It hasn't moved" "The very same" he crowed, pleased by her reaction. "The Potter brothers took it two months ago, when it started getting dark in the evenings, we were out. They replaced the shape with young Gordon's tube things from his family tent so you wouldn't notice.." "Mafia" she laughed. "Anyway they started work on it and this is the result, do you like it, Madam?" "Harvey it is beautiful, I love it you, wonderful man." He was rewarded by warmest hug and kiss he had ever had. "Steady on, I've got to get back up this chimney" he laughed. "What?" "Don't worry, old joke. Only one thing, a small problem before you can drive it. Sorry but the bits never came in time but I wanted you to see it for Christmas and they will fix it this week, Amber's car can wait." "What bits? It's perfect." "Get in you'll see, sorry." She climbed in the driver's seat, "Oh, I see, the pedals, my Denver Boot right?" "They are a bit close together, I desperately didn't want it to be an issue, Peter Potter said the mod' would be as new, but time ran out. A bit like giving a present on Christmas Day without the batteries."

Harvey felt like he was in that hole again and digging. "Sorry, how can you be sorry? You have just given me, me, the nicest most thoughtful present of all time and you apologise. You are mad." "It's just that it's not safe for you at present..." "Shut up. For the first time in ages I have wheels" she enthused and waved the Senator keys under his nose. "And when the bits are fitted I will have my OWN wheels, just don't mess up MY car before I drive it." He was happy to get another warm embrace, maybe all will work out .....really?

Harvey reluctantly left Charlie at the cottage while he made tracks to the office. The old car had made the journey so many times in the past, but never in such good condition. It even felt new to drive. He parked in the slot reserved for the Assistant Manager and he was halfway out of the car when he realised his error, he, of course, was the Manager and had been for some time. "Is there a bit of Herbie in you?" he asked the car before slotting into the correct space. "Can't go upsetting the order of things this early in the year," he explained to the car. "Anyway, the birds won't crap on you here - see no trees, and why am I talking to you?

He was first in the office and rang Olivia to make sure she was coping and agreed to meet just after midday. The office was filling around him then the doors were unlocked and appeared to burst open as claimants of all shapes and sizes flooded in to ensure a busy and speedy morning session.

Charlie returned to the cottage after checking Bernie was ok and dropping off a few bits. She was pleased to see Brian's pick-up parked outside. Brian was studying a copy of The Sun spread over the wheel. He hastily turned from Page Three to the sports pages as Charlie approached with a wave. "Too late, I saw you" she laughed. "Who is it today, Lucious Linda?" He didn't reply as he got out. He gave her a matey squeeze as they walked to survey the damage.

"Bit of a mess eh?" she said. "Yes, but I've got the rest of the week and once the rubble is cleared I can give it a fair go. Between us, that's me, the plaster board and my February mix we should have you sorted by Friday. It will be a bit musty for the kids, though. To be safe stay away until Monday if you can." Brian was being very nice. "Here are the estimates, the middle one is what I will charge you ok?" he advised."Thanks. These look okay" she said, "The insurers sounded reasonable when I told them we wouldn't be claiming for a hotel" "Good, bring on the cash, tell you what, it'll be easier all round if I do all the ground floor ceilings. Upstairs are already plasterboard and I have the time and materials. I can make a small adjustment to the estimates, what do you think?" "I'll try, by the way, what is February Mix?" "It's plaster that sets in the Winter" "Oh, good for it" "I'll go and organise some help..." He was interrupted by a booming Welsh voice from the open front door.

"Mister Burright is it?" enquired Evan Evans, knowing it not to be. Resplendent in a perfectly pressed black suit, impeccable white shirt and a modest tie with greased down shiny black hair he resembled Ray Reardon or a vampire. "No, my name is Golding" Brian replied politely.

"It's them, the fucking gimpys, where's Harvey fucking Bright and my poor wee child you bitch?" Verna had joined the company. "Miss McCalisky pulease," intervened Evans, "we must conduct ourselves in a civilised manner if you please." He turned to Brian and Charlie, "My client is very distraught at the lengthening separation from her dear daughter, I apologise and hope you understand." "No, I don't understand. I don't know who you are or what you are on about, and if you cannot keep your foul-mouthed client under control, you should not let her off the lead." Brian retorted.

Evan Evans squirmed as he regained his composure "My name is Evan Evans, I am the legal representative of Miss Verna McCalisky. I can't apologise enough, but we are dealing with a very delicate matter. Can I assume this is the residence of Mr Ronald Bright, aka Harvey?"

It was obvious to Charlie that the time for deception was passed. She confirmed this was Harvey's home, she passed over his office number and suggested Evans rang for an appointment. She explained that today was not good as he had to accompany somebody to the Funeral Directors.

"Fuck the fucking appointment ...." "Miss McCalisky, this simply will not do," Evans stated firmly. "But she's a friggin liar, she is stalling so they can steal away with my poor wee girl. Look, they've already started to knock the fucking house down." "I think we can take our chances with the telephone," Evans concluded, "Although our first approach was not a success"

"If you're lying I'll come back and do your other foot you.." Evans steered her to the door, but not before a well placed built up shoe forced her to trip headlong into a pile of plaster and rubble. "Oh I am sorry" Charlie lied sweetly as they departed.

"Are you ok?" Brian enquired when they were alone again. "Not really, but it's a long story. Look, Thanks again for everything, a friend in need, etc., I'm going to shoot off and try to warn Harvey. Will you be alright now?" Charlie was obviously shaken. "Yes, I have all I need, I'll just get a few troops and that will make life easier.

You take a breather before you drive off - just collect your thoughts - safer that way." Brian was enjoying being the friend in need. "Yeh, ok. I'll phone from over the road, may just catch him. I'll be ok, don't worry."

Unfortunately, she just missed Harvey, 'Ah well, they won't get him either' she thought and waved to Brian as they drove off in different directions. She hated to admit it, but she was pleased Brian had been there and he had handled the situation well. Not for the first time of late she felt drawn towards him.

Chapter Seventeen

Harvey collected Olivia, although she assured him she was bearing up, she appeared to have aged ten years overnight. They visited the Chapel of Rest and the Undertaker apologised straight away explaining there had been the usual Christmas rush of flu victims and those who found another year too much to bear.

"It's a bit crowded at present. You know we have the same number of clients all Winter, but with nearly ten days of no movement through the cemetery or the crematorium, we always get a backlog for the first week of January. Very unpleasant for the loved ones, sorry." Olivia nodded and smiled her thanks for the warning.

Harvey led the way and found three coffins in the Chapel with a discreet distance between them. They had been told that Bill was closest to the door. Harvey went left. "Oh, Oli' he looks very peaceful and if I may say, younger" "You are a knob, Harvey, Bill is here! That is the Milkman, who died at his girlfriend's."

Trust him to lighten the moment she thought. Despite his initial mistake, his comments were still relevant as Bill did look at peace. He had been made to look healthier in death than in life.

Harvey glanced at Oli, she was having her own thoughts, he squeezed her hand and let her have her last private moments alone.

The Doctor was just over the road so Harvey collected the Medical and Final Certificates. He saw Doctor Hope in the doorway having a cigaret, "I'm doing well." he advised Harvey. "I didn't break my New Year Resolution until this morning" indicating the glowing cigaret. Harvey raised his eyebrows and gave a tut with a smile. "Not the right time I know, but don't forget your test sheet." Harvey nodded again, wished the doctor a Happy New Year and went to rejoin Oli'.

The Funeral Director and his staff were professional and very accommodating. They knew exactly how to deal with Oli' and the arrangements were made. They were advised that they should visit the Registrar and to hurry as they had just opened.

They were the first there and again were treated with care and consideration, as they registered the death. They got the Death Certificate and a couple of copies for the bank and insurers.

Next the bank, no real surprises there, Bill had not worked for years and Oli' was not at all provided for. She would be forced to eke out a living as best she could.

Thank goodness there was better news at the Prudential, they had taken a penny policy when they first got married so the funeral would be paid for at least. There was also a small endowment policy she knew nothing of that Bill had frozen when no longer able to keep up the payments. They were told that their agent had researched the best option and there would not be a bad return, albeit, not a fortune. "Thank you Mr Tarrant" Oli blessed the long departed agent.

Armed with the figures, Harvey was able to give advice on her entitlements. Proud Oli' insisted that she would not be a burden on the state for as long as she was able. Harvey settled her down with a cup of tea and made his apologies, he really had to return to work. He vowed silently to keep an eye on Oli' from this moment on, he owed her that.

As he was leaving, Oli' grabbed his hand. "You are a good friend, Harvey, even if you couldn't recognise my Bill from that Randy Milkman." She smiled, "Will you do one more thing for me, please?" "Yes of course" he replied, it did not matter what, he would do it or die in the attempt. "Find Ronnie and makeup, please."

Chapter Eighteen

After lunch things were much quieter at the office as claimants regrouped in the local pubs. Thankfully normal services and a more sedate pace were resumed. Through the new computer system, Harvey was able to find out that Ronnie had been living in Hounslow. He was, or had, been claiming benefits. He had no fixed abode and was under investigation. Probably working while claiming, which had been put on hold as all resources were concentrated on a major case. A newspaper exposure over the holiday reported a massive fraud in and around Heathrow.

An undercover reporter had found contractors using benefits claimants as 'casual/slave labour'. They had been employed with false references, and gained access to very secure areas. There was no suggestion that the airport was in collusion, but some processes were highly questionable. Ah well the heat was off for the present from Ronnie's back.

Harvey wrote a short letter explaining about Bill and asking him to get in touch. He made copies and addressed them to the last known whereabouts of Cass and her associates. Hopefully one would reach Ronnie. He had not mentioned the present predicament they were in with his children. His thoughts were drifting in that direction as the phone rang.

It was Charlie. She was more than a little upset as she related the encounter with Verna and her legal representative. Now she was adamant, that no matter what the outcome, there was no way on God's earth that she would stay under the same roof as that 'foul-mouthed Monster from Hell'.

She then recounted the contact with the insurers and her update on estimates - including the 'extras'. As per their current slogan, Commercial Union had not turned a drama into a crisis. The repairs were acceptable and she now needed to make an inventory of damaged contents. He was pleased she had this distraction. He had the impression that John Lewis and January Sales would be the topic of the evening as she rang off with a kiss.

Herbert Crowe could not claim to be in the same league of crisis management as he flew into Harvey's office. "Help me please, Mr Bright you have got to help please" he pleaded. Harvey jumped out of his chair, and nearly his skin. At first he thought the fateful day had arrived when the maniac had lost control and gone over the edge.

"What the..." Harvey began. "It's Maude, theyme got her, aagh, help me. It's my fault, not hers, now they got yrr and won't let yrr go, or me near like, help." Harvey considered slapping his face to calm him down but decided that may not be the right thing, deep breath.

"Sit down," he said, with remarkable calmness, deep breath. "Come on now Herbert, I can't help if you don't tell me...DON'T start again! Now from the beginning please." Harvey was strangely in control of the beast.

"It's Maude, yoom know, my sister - you knows, she's on my claim..." he began. "Yes, go on." "Well with New Year an' all, I been, well, err - missing." "I understand, don't get up, you are doing fine." "Well, she cum into town, fuck knows how like, but she goes to Lafferty's and err went shopping like" "I'm with you so far, then what?" Well she never been to town before, let alone shopping on her own and she don't know, you know, she ain't got no money..."

"Ah, I think I know where this is leading." Harvey felt like he was drawing teeth. "Well, she gets the bits she knows like, not many, just bits. When she goes to walk out that bumped up stroppy bitch from out your way, you knows her, all tits and lacquer, well she grabs her. Maude gets all fucked 'n' flustered like and ends up with the fucking rozzers taking her. Now they got her and won't let me in, threatened to shoot me them did. You got to help me please, you the only cunt I knows who works in a suit, you gotta help me"

"With such an endorsement how can I refuse?" Harvey muttered. He was whisked from his chair, by the strongest of strong grips, and soon found himself outside the Police Station, which appeared on full alert.

They started to climb the flagstone steps, but two officers in full riot gear emerged and blocked the door. Crouching behind them

Sgt Snape called to Harvey "You can come in Mr Bright, but that lunatic stays where he is, OK?" "Ok. Ok, stay here." Harvey instructed Herbert Crowe and surprised himself by giving him a reassuring squeeze of the arm. Not that it would penetrate the elephantine thickness of his skin.

Herbert Crowe accepted the encouragement, he lifted himself to his full height and bellowed at Snape "Yuum for it now. This is Mr Bright of the Government, he'll sort you out you, you fucking bastard sister snatchers."

Snape crouched even lower as he reached between his men to permit Harvey entry. Harvey just managed to cram between the small opening in the double doors. Before closing the doors tight, Sgt Snape raised his voice and said, unnecessarily, to his officers "Watch him" adding "and if he moves, shoot him!" "Blimey, that's a bit extreme isn't it?" Harvey exclaimed, "I thought he was exaggerating." "Can't be too careful with that one" snarled Scape. "The last time he ran a muck in here it took fourteen of us to hold the bastard down and he still managed to push his thumb up the fanny of one of our most promising WPC's, big girl too she was, the bastard." "Was?" Harvey asked. 'Was, is, she transferred after that and is one of the new Traffic Wardens now! Anyway, every time that lunatic sees her he sucks his thumb and she books somebody on the spot, the bastard. And the Super let him off with a slapped wrist. The bastard, anyway, as much as I would like I'm not allowed to shoot him, he's a protected species."

Harvey blamed the rambling on the pressure of work. "Ahem, the matter in hand Sgt Snape." Harvey brought him back to the present. "There is no matter in hand." Snape snapped. "Miss Maude Crowe...?" "Free to go." "Then why....?"

Sgt Snape took a deep breath, he was willing to explain, but only once. "I told you before, he's fucking mad. It was obvious to all that she is as dippy as a rabbit that has strayed down a foxhole. When we saw her in Lafferty's, we told them to retrieve their stuff. If they wanted to prosecute they would find us less than sympathetic in future we then brought her here. We didn't know who she was, thought it was another of Maggie's Care in the Community fuck ups."

Snape drew breath. "We were in the throws of finding which unit she had wandered from when Rambo out there comes charging in the doors. Fortunately, the reception was crowded with people complaining about the new Traffic Wardens, yes the same, now nicknamed Adolph and Eva. We managed, in the crowd, to push them all towards the door and he sort of fell back on the street before he could start swinging them fucking great arms of his about. We locked the door and the siege began."

He sighed. "She could have been home hours ago, are you ready to take her?" he pleaded. "Yes, I suppose I am. Can I have a few seconds to get my breath back?" Harvey asked. "Yes, you finish my tea and I'll bring the lovely Miss Crowe along. That brute can fume a bit longer. He can only damage those professional moaners out there, with luck maybe they'll kill him. After all he is indirectly responsible, or maybe they will fuck off and go to the sales - if we haven't towed their cars."

"What's she like?" Harvey was curious. "Him, unfortunately, except she is smaller and got more facial hair, she is much milder mannered thank God. The thick cow must have got confused when they were doling out the ugly pills and gone back for seconds." Harvey hoped he was exaggerating.

On the steps of the Police, Station Herbert Crowe was indeed fuming. He was also raging and steaming, much to the chagrin of the mini riot squad assembled inches away. Behind what was appearing to them now to be an extremely fragile door. The traffic complainers had understandably dispersed.

Herbert Crowe glanced round for somebody to berate and glimpsed Verna and a strange looking gent emerging from Harvey's workplace. Although they turned sharply, they were not sharp enough to evade the eagle eyes of Crowe. Verna, he recognised immediately, then the identity of her companion dawned on him. "Ha argh, it's the fucking fairy all got up, how's your teas maid? Haaagh, never mind her hairy legs, whoop it up her dung bucket." He laughed, relieved to be back on familiar territory, he screwed his mighty fist into the side of his nose as tears of mirth ran down his cheek.

The officers guarding the front door became suspicious with the sudden calm and craned to see what tactics the giant loon was adopting. It appeared that he had become engrossed in the movements of a couple across the road. From their disadvantaged point behind riot shields, doors and Crowe's enormous back, their view was somewhat obscured What little they did see did not warrant the uncontrolled hilarity that emanated from the beast.

"Mad," said Officer One. "As the proverbial Mad Hatter' agreed Officer Two. "Should we, could we lock him up?" asked One, looking to Two for guidance. "Over my dead body." "Me too" concurred One, "in fact if you had said 'yes' I would have killed you and locked myself up!"

Harvey instinctively stood as Sgt Snape returned accompanied by a miniature, female, version of the beast outside. "Mîss Crowe this is Mr Bright, Mr Bright - Miss Crowe." "Pleased to meet you." Harvey lied. "Very delighted I'm sure Sir" reciprocated Maude, in much softer tones than her appearance gave credit. "Well we can't stand gossiping all day, let's reunite you with your brother shall we?" Snape was in a hurry for the riddance.

"Please, sir if you may. I only been out once before on my own - when Herbert was really bad. I went to the Priest because I used a bad language word. "Snape's ears pricked up, maybe there was a collar after all. "Really bad eh? You should come to us if he is really bad, what had the bas.. Herbert done?" "He was misplacing himself in a chicken on the table.." "Grief, was it dead?" gulped Snaped. "Oh yes sir it was one of them bald iced ones, they comes in a bag" "What did you do," asked an astonished Harvey. "Well, I said (excuse me sirs) I say 'That's my fucking dinner you dirty bastard' then I snatched it off him and put it in the oven. Then I went to the Priest. He said not to worry it was ok and I was forgiven. He said he would have done the same, I think he meant the bad language words not the thing with the chicken, he was a nice man. He did it with Trigger the goat once, Herbert not the Priest, and he ran off for a week, Trigger, not Herbert, he's always running off, that's why I'm here...."

"Time to go," said Harvey, it was distressing to see a hardened Policeman crumble before him.

On the steps of the Police Station, Herbert Crowe had returned his attention to his plight and was hammering on the doors with his mighty fists and yelling for all his worth. "Free the Chuffers One, Free Maude Crowe, Fucking Sister Snatchers".

Onlookers swore the building was shaking, the officers inside certainly were. Snape bravely pushed them aside to reveal Maude and Harvey. Crowe stopped his pounding and gently the door opened. Taking Maude's hand Herbert Crowe led her gallantly down the steps to the street as the small crowd scattered. Harvey followed a pace behind as the doors, not so gently, closed firmly behind him.

"Free, free, you dun it Mr Harvey Fucking Bright, you dun it, I knows you would." Crow's joy was unconfined. "Kiss him Maudy" he instructed. "Err, that's not necessary, really." Harvey insisted.

"Kiss him" repeated Crowe, "and then you kiss the pavement." "Why," she asked. "Cause that's what all them Irish and murderers do when thems gets let out, they all does it. Must be ok - even the Pope does it. Mind that dog shit mind." "Airports," said Maude. "What's fucking airports got to with the price of fish?" demanded Crowe, for once baffled. "The Pope does it at Airports, not when he's just murdered somebody. Probably because there is no excrement from dogs at airports" replied Maude." "The Pope ain't murdered nobody you dopey cow, well not this one anyway, and how you know 'bout him and airports?" "I seen him on the radio" "You reads to much."

Harvey saw an avenue of escape during this Papal discussion and started to slip away. A large hand grabbed him for the second time that day, and dragged him back "Don't be shy Mr Bright, Kiss him" commanded Crowe, "no tongues mind or it's Romsey Abbey next stop" he guffawed.

Like her voice, Maude Crowe's kiss was a lot softer than one would expect. Harvey put this down to the facial hair and silently cursed his little pill for generating a slight stirring below. He managed to withdraw quickly before there any question of tongues or Romsey Abbey, and this time made good his retreat.

He looked frantically over his shoulder in time to see Maude embracing the pavement. "No Comment!" Shouted Herbert Crowe at nobody in particular, and then contradicted himself by bellowing "I'll not forget this". This had a different meaning to Harvey than it did the incumbents of the Police Station, who produced damp patches in their undies.

What a day thought Harvey, thank God it's nearly over - oh so wrong.l

Chapter Nineteen

Verna and Lewis, in the guise of Evan Evans, were having a bad day. First the encounter with the strange couple in the remains of Bright's cottage, what was that all about, all that damage? The phone call the previous day had been extremely brief but contained a home style "fuck off'. That was said with feeling, not the throw-away type of language common to builders and the like. Next, phone call after phone call to Bright's office only revealed that he was "with a client". "Engaged" or "at lunch" and were possibly evasive tactics while he got his act together. Then, most worrying, their unannounced visit to his office where they were told he was he was at the Police Station. To add to their predicament, they were then maligned by that oaf Crowe as they scurried back to Lewis's to reconsider their position.

Harvey returned to his office and explained the odd goings-on at the Police Station. He was duly advised that he had missed a pair of strange visitors calling on a personal matter. Maureen, who had been at the front desk, thought they had made a hasty retreat at the mention of the Police, but she couldn't be sure.

She went on to describe the female, who could only have been Verna and the male matched Charlie's description of her solicitor. This was a very odd day, but there was no time to contemplate as the pubs closing had filled the office again with claimants, refueled and demanding. Everybody was needed at the front and Harvey undertook many interviews himself.

Verna would have settled for an interview with Harvey. After all the chasing around of the last few days, she was convinced if she could get to him and put her case he would see reason. Then she could be on her way. She was convinced her documents would stand scrutiny and he would have to release his charge, especially if Evan Evans did his stuff. She knew that Harvey was basically a nice man, and all that Ronnie had told her about him made her feel she had adopted the wrong approach. She should appeal to his better nature. Hopefully, it was not too late to change tack.

Lewis was taking a break from Evans as they tried to decide their next course of action. "We must get to him and soon" she declared. He was not sure, "I'm not happy about the Police involvement. Ok there is money at stake but is it worth risking our hides for?" "Listen, you pervy bastard and think. His house is wrecked and he works with dodgy people, there could be many reasons he went to the Police and one of them may not be us. Now you can either get caught and go down for helping me, or I can make a call on my way out of town and you will go down for not helping me. If you get my drift."

Lewis sat upright and started to pay more attention to the campaign. Verna was amazed how she could bully Lewis but not Evans, who was so dominant. "Go and get Evans, pervie, we need a man on the case.

He slunk off and returned in full garb. He resumed his seat but was so different and decisive. "Right," he said, "the time is now three forty, Bright's office closes at four, I suggest we go straight there now and confront him. If he is planning a surprise for us, it will be we who have the initiative. I don't think he will be expecting a recall today at this hour in his office. His defences will be down and any plan he has is either for this evening or tomorrow. However, if he is fully prepared or there is a hint of a trap we are out of there. I will get you back to Portsmouth and that will be that. Believe me. I will not go back on my word, and what was agreed in, shall we say, unfortunate circumstances. But, I will not be blackmailed when I have done my best." he said forcefully, he paused for the climax. "If you turn on me later I'll turn Queens Evidence against you OK?"

His piece said, he looked her straight in the eyes and repeated "OK?" She held his gaze, not sure what Queen's Evidence was, but it didn't sound good, she dropped her eyes and said "OK."

Harvey stared at the clock high on his office wall and was sure it had stopped, one minute before the doors close, another hour and home, well Fred's anyway.

Harvey was reading a letter from a former director bemoaning the 'ludicrous cost of legal advice. He was attempting to sue his former employer and asking if he qualified for any kind of benefit. Harvey was about to look up Legal Aid in civil matters to rid himself of this problem when the intercom buzzed.

He checked the clock before flicking the switch. "Yes, Maureen" "A Miss McCalisky and Mr Evans to see you Mr Bright. They do not have an app.." "Ok Maureen" he sighed,"send them along, please."

Harvey rose and opened the door as they arrived. "Verna" he greeted them amicably, nice to see you again, and you must be Mr Evans. Do come in please and take a seat. As they sat, he looked at Evans, 'makeup?' he thought, 'why?'

"Firstly I would like to apologise for the call you made to my home last evening but, as I answered the phone, the blasted ceiling decided to crash down on my head. I'm afraid it caused me great alarm and cut you off, I hope, before you heard my response to the incident."

"Ah, that explains a lot" responded Evans, with a sideways glance at Verna, who made a silent 'ouch' as she studied his small wound. "Now, how can I help you, Verna?"

Evans rose, cleared his throat, and spoke as if addressing somebody in the next street. In a heavy Welsh accent he broke into a lengthy eulogy. He told of the misfortune and heartbreak suffered by his client brought about by the general misbehaviour of Mr Bright Jnr. He continued to describe how the enforced separation from her daughter had brought on a mental breakdown, a general deteriation in her health and well-being.

As he spoke, Evan Evans strode the length and breadth of the small office. As he spoke and strode, he produced document after document, in a flourish from his large black briefcase, in support of his testimony. As he spoke, strode and flourished, he was magnificent. He was omnipotent. He was Evan Evans the all powerful, Evan Evans the all empowering, Evan Evans the almighty and he was proud to represent such a deserving case.

Harvey sat like a rabbit trapped in the headlights of an evil poacher. Vena sat silently and just gaped. When Evans had completed his oration silence fell like snow at Christmas, while thoughts were gathered.

Harvey could not entirely agree with his version of events, but it was close enough and with that delivery it was compelling. He trawled over what his friend and mentor had advised earlier. He could see no way out of or around the predicament, Verna was Bernie's Mother.

As an exhausted but fulfilled Evan Evans sat Harvey rose to begin his damage limitation exercise. His thoughts went back to school where he won debates on topics he didn't care about, or even agree with, this time he cared with a fervent passion.

"I hear what you say. Obviously I accept that certain matters have not been dealt with or handled satisfactorily. That said, I was left in an awful position with my granddaughter needing thorough and total support. I am not prepared to go into certain matters, but I am aware that Verna was not contemplating motherhood with any great conviction. They are both young people who both behaved irresponsibly and I need a little more convincing before discharging my duties as Guardian. However", he raised his voice to stifle Verna's protestations, "I am prepared to visit Wales with you Verna, and if I am satisfied that a loving home awaits my granddaughter, your daughter, then I can not and will not stand in your way. There are legalities to come and I will insist on visiting rights." He glanced at Evans, who nodded readily as he folded and unfolded some half moon glasses.

The intercom buzzed to say the office was secured and Harvey bid Maureen goodbye. He continued, "I will help you all I can both financially and any other way I can or require. I am professionally placed in a position to give you the best possible advice on state benefits that are the same in Wales as here." He again looked at Evans, who nodded enthusiastically.

He gulped as he fought the lump in his throat, "We called her Bernadette by the way, she is a lovely child and we love her dearly....I, we want the best for her..."

He tailed off as the lump in his throat choked him and he could not carry on. Evan Evans rose in partial victory and fought a genuine urge to throw his arms around Harvey.

It was agreed that Verna and Evans would meet Bernie the next day at noon, when arrangements would be made for Harvey to visit Wales. If all went well, over the next few weeks, it was mutually agreed that the child would be drip fed towards full repatriation with Verna. Not discussed was that the breathing time would give

Harvey time to check out everything, and ensure Social Sevices were alerted.

When they departed, Harvey showed them out and returned to his desk with a heavy heart and slumped in his chair. He glanced instinctively at the clock and found this time that an hour and a half had passed.

"My how time flies when you are having fun." He said to himself aloud and launched his paperweight at the offending timepiece. A direct hit ensured that it's last tick never made it to toc. He grabbed his emergency bottle of Plymouth from the bottom drawer and took an almighty swig.

Returning the gin to the drawer, his eyes fell on the letter he had been reading. The phrase 'ludicrous cost' jumped at him in six inch print. He sat back in his chair and asked out loud "How on earth can she afford HIM.? He should be representing The Guiness Four, now where is that book on Legal Aid?"

Chapter Twenty

On the street the dubious pair were again under the scrutiny of a larger than life character. For one of the few times in his life, Herbert Crowe, showed a little decorum and restrained the urge to holler insults in favour of a little covert surveillance.

He was curious and determined to discover the reason for their alliance and the purpose behind Robin Lewis's disguise. As they approached they were deep in discussion and failed to see him squeeze into the shadows. When they passed he emerged and stayed within earshot on the short trek back to Lewis's flat. Herbert Crowe was adept at stalking and throttling prey, he was also equipped with the most precise hearing that nature could provide. He found this short pursuit amusing as he got within touching distance of them.

They did not walk fast but spoke aplenty and gave Herbert Crowe a fair appraisal of the situation thus far. As they reached the flat Lewis shot off like a scolded cat to avoid being seen and Verna went to use the public telephone shadowed by Crowe.

My how they had jabbered, the evening was dark and miserable, which matched the mood of the Irish girl whilst Lewis/Evans was elated with his performance. He had carried out a master performance and had even fooled himself to the extent that he smelled victory.

It was only as Verna began to question the logic of visiting a mythical Welsh home with Harvey in tow that it dawned on Evans that he was in fact Lewis and he was not a knight on a white charger.

They paused in their stride and Crowe nearly bumped into them. "Well you were very quiet in there, why didn't you say something?" Lewis muttered. "Don't fucking give me that" she snapped. "You were the man of the moment, you were good, very good but when you think about it, he was better. What could I do? I could hardly contradict you could I? More to the point, what do we do now? He has all the aces, our story does not stand up does it?" "Shut up you daft cow, I'm thinking." Lewis was tiring of Evans now he appeared fallible and started to think with his own sly mind for a while. "Come on" he said as they started to walk a bit faster, to Crowe's relief, he was starting to feel exposed. "Ring Portsmouth, not from my phone. He has transport?" She nodded "A van" Good. Get him here by noon, we'll keep our appointment. I don't think our Mr Bright suspects anything is amiss, you saw him, he was nearly in tears. While we talk about some details, you make a big fuss of the girl. Ask if you can take her to Lafferty's to buy her something in the sales. He won't refuse, I will be there with all the papers, I will explain them all to him, that should take a while. Meantime you are out of the door in the van and away." "Brilliant, Robin, fucking brilliant."

He noticed that she did not ask how he would make his escape so he volunteered that he would complain of a bad stomach and go to the toilet and he too would leg it. Once home, he would put Evan Evans to rest and resume regular duties at Lafferty's.

"There is just the small matter of, shall we say, personal belongings?" Herbert Crowe stopped breathing. "Oh, you mean them pervie mags, photos and videos you dirty bastard. How did you get them kids to do something like that? Fucking near made me puke, and you got yourself in the frame too. You, you're dis-fuckin-gusting, that's what you are." she spat with genuine revulsion. "You don't understand, I love.." "Fucking right I don't know and I don't want to either, God save us, love huh." Crowe did not understand either but soon would. "Don't worry, you'll get your filth back in the morning. As you saw, I made a couple of your filthy mags soggy. But, I don't expect that is the first nor last time they will get soggy from body fluids you fucking perv, now piss off whilst I phone Greg." "Who?" "Portsmouth." "Ok, see you later."

He scampered off to make sure he was well and truly safe in his room when she got back, less she decided on some form of retribution for his 'weakness'.

True, Robin Lewis did disgust Verna but she needed Evan Evans for one more day. She would make him pay, that was for tomorrow, or Greg to decide, for tonight Lewis was off the hook.

The telephone was in similar mode, courtesy of some ne'er-do-well. Not wanting Lewis to hear her conversation she sought out another box. Herbert Crowe had to use all his skills to leap silently into the shadows to avoid contact as Verna doubled back. He followed her to another box a few streets away and was able to hear clearly Verna's side of the conversation. As she was concluding, he took the overgrown path that would eventually take him close to Lewis's flat. Here he could observe her going in, he had gathered there would not be much more to gain tonight.

At the end of his sortie, Herbert Crowe was armed with enough to repay a debt, earn a few bob and best of all, have some fun at somebody else's expense. "Haaaargh, fucking Haa aargh, never mind her hairy legs, shove it up his shitter, and make sure it hurts," he bellowed into the night. He laughed and gulped so much he gave himself a stitch. This made him wheeze so much that he bent double in pain. The Asthma then took hold, but he still could not contain the mirth as he wheezed, gulped and bellowed. The noise was a mix of industrial processes and animal husbandry, as he fought for breath.

After her animated conversation with Greg, Verna tracked her way back through the darkened streets. Close to Lewis's flat she heard what appeared to be an animal in pain, indeed as she got closer she imagined it was a large creature in considerable pain, this made her wary. As a child, she had spent a little time with relatives in a run down part of Dublin. One of the pass times, and in some cases passions, of the local children, was to tease and torture the many horses that wandered the sprawling housing estates.

She had witnessed these large mangy beasts being stabbed, pelted and even beaten as they were backed into large open drains. The noises they made were almost the same as greeted her now. She was approaching cautiously now, sometimes these beasts had a way of kicking free causing dreadful injuries to anybody in the vicinity. In those days, she was too scared to intervene and sometimes threw the odd stone but did not subscribe to harming the ragged animals. Her recent dealings with the distasteful Lewis and trying to get Greg off his ass and away from the bar made her feel like helping this stricken beast.

Rounding the corner the noise suddenly changed from a wheezy whinny to a wheezy chuckle, as the bent over the figure of Herbert Crowe was slowly backing out of the pathway. Verna stopped, she recognised this large form and all thoughts of aid slipped from her mind. For once Herbert Crowe was the prey. Pumped with adrenaline Verna took careful aim and delivered a murderous kick between the open legs of her quarry before fleeing, vengeance complete. Herbert Crowe let out an enormous belch, sank to his knees, then all fours and uttered "Thank you ma'am" as his breathing returned to normal.

Harvey had returned to Charlie and Bernadette, snuggled together in their large temporary home by a warming fire. It was not easy to relate the happenings of the day, but he tried to struggle through. When Bernie was safely down for the night, they sat in loud silences of depression. Each thinking their own lives through post-Bernie, and thinking what lay in store for the little one gurgling herself to sleep upstairs.

Crowe's exploits were forgotten eventually and even poor Oli was barely mentioned as Harvey mulled things over, he had not even inquired about the cottage. Charlie did not volunteer that she had made three site visits (five in all) and things were progressing well. Brian was a diamond and in truth she felt rather guilty about certain thoughts that had crossed her mind during the day.

"Don't breath in the fire" she sniffed, and they retired for the night. Charlie dreaded the moment the bedroom light was turned off as she contemplated another fitful sleep from Harvey and a sleepless soul searching night of her own. She made an excuse and went to sleep in the single bed in the next room, he said that he understood, as she kissed his forehead she hoped he didn't.

Charlie surprised herself by sleeping through until morning. After weighing the pros and cons of the older Harvey against, the younger Brian she had come down on the side of the demented soul circumnavigating the bed in the next room. The demented soul for his part was having trouble focusing on any topic in particular. He ended up with a kaleidoscope of events from riot squads, through bearded ladies to Evan Evans. His mother sat quietly on the bonnet of the old Morris in the pose off Rodin's Thinker. When the characters slipped from view and the car melted away, his mother rose and whispered "How can she afford HIM?"

Harvey reached under the bed for a comforting snort of Beefeater, this resulted in him finishing the contents of a neglected hot water bottle. Harvey didn't notice as sleep finally took over.

Sleep was far from Sgt Snape's thoughts as he prepared to sign off an eventful day. He was contemplating a single malt on the way home and was a little annoyed to be summoned to the front desk. But the young Constable had sounded most insistent and a little edgy.

Snape recognised the sounds of Herbert Crowe before he saw him and took the precaution of drawing his truncheon. He opened the door and was amazed at the scene that greeted him, although by now nothing should surprise him where Crowe was concerned.

Ahead of him Crowe was in a genial mood and the young Constable was carefully examining what, at first sight, was a couple of cricket balls proffered by the former. On second glance, and Crowe's stance, Sgt Snape realised he was staring at a pair of testicles. In fact, Crowe's much-battered testicles as the giant perched on tip toes to get them on the high desk. Snape was furious to note that they were barely an inch from his favourite Horlicks mug. He brought his truncheon down with such force that what was left of the contents of the mug splattered the testicles.

"What the blazes is going on?" he demanded from the greenhorn. "Steady on," said Crowe, "thems 'ad enough for one night." Without further explanation Crowe tenderly pushed his bits back where they belonged. "Super in?" he enquired, having seen his car outside. "What's it to you?" Snape snapped. "Good, tell him I want him," Crowe commanded and let himself into an interview room and gingerly sat down.

Sgt Snape dispatched the Constable to summon the Superintendent while he finished the serious business for the night. He made a note to change the codes that opened the interview room doors, that bloody oaf knew everything. As he was leaving the Superintendent bade him good night and knocked on the interview room door. "Come in," said Crowe and farted loudly. "Amazing," Snape muttered to the Constable. "Let's hope they fucking choke," he said with feeling. "By the way, what was that performance about earlier?" "Said he'd had an Asthma attack" replied the Constable. Snape decided that one single malt would not be enough.

Chapter Twenty-One

Bernie had been fed and Charlie was breakfasting as Harvey got to the kitchen. Despite a heavy day ahead the mood in the cottage was much lighter. He made himself a messy sandwich from the bacon and eggs that were awaiting him and dropped bits over Bernie as he reached to kiss them.

"Careful clumsy, why don't you sit and eat?" "I'm popping in on Oli on the way through and then I thought ...err". "Go on" she urged,"...well, I thought I, well if there's time, maybe I will try to catch Snape. He sort of owes me one, what do you say?" "The Police Sergeant? About time, that's what I believe. She has to be up to no good. Have you any idea what even a bad solicitor costs? You say this one is dynamic and ... he's been with her for days - legal aid that ain't, even if he has some fancy computer link, it does not ring true. There that's what I think." He smiled in thanks.

He reached for the car keys, "You ok with the Vauxhall?" "It will be over soon, and your car will be ready too, promise." "See you at noon, High Noon, James Stewart." "You're too young to remember that.." "Tick toc, Tick toc, Oh don't forsake me oh my Darling" she sang. "Too many repeats on the telly nowadays," he laughed, hoping for a happy ending as the film. She laughed back, she didn't say that Brian had been singing it yesterday - he was a big Frankie Laine fan, and she felt like Jezebel.

"Come on, come on will you? I've got all you're filthy shite ready, now come on." It was 11.20 and Verna were getting impatient. "Alright, we have plenty of time, it's only down the road. A bit too close really, we have to be careful leaving." He glanced at his sordid array of literature, videos and incriminating photographs that she had placed on the table. "It's all there" she snapped. "Even the ones that got a little damaged, but it was for your enjoyment."

He shuddered as she cackled. "I don't want any of the filthy muck so don't bother checking. It's all there, under different circumstances....., well let's say you are lucky, you helped me so that's that. Oh and here is your spare key, oi, manners, no need to snatch."

Evans pocketed the key. He went to the airing cupboard and brought a sheet to cover his belongings. She grabbed it from him and covered the lot in one movement. "Now get your pervie ass in gear" she snarled and this time Evan Evans was ready to perform.

She glanced around at his elegant possessions on their way out, she pushed Evans ahead and coughed loudly as she slipped the catch on the Yale Lock to the front door. She coughed again, loudly, as she slammed the front door. "Nervous?" he enquired. She nodded in response and shepherded him down the road, past a parked Luton van.

Greg and Stringer watched them pass and then reversed the large van a smidgin closer to the front door. Thankful that it was a ground floor flat, and facing the road. A nudge was all that was required to gain access, thanks to Verna's nervous cough.

Inside they found everything more or less as she had described it. Working hard as a team they had soon cleared the place of it's nice things. Most of it's not so nice things and several of it's nasty things - they wouldn't tell Verna about this. Or the fair amount of cash they found squirrelled away in nooks and crannies. Greg and, his drinking buddy, Stringer were a light-fingered pair and used to working quickly together when the opportunity came along. Usually in similar circumstances to this.

Within twenty-five minutes, they were back in the van and on their way to rendezvous with Verna. They had left the door open and Herbert Crowe glided into the plundered dwelling.

Herbert Crowe was again enjoying himself, he loved prying about where he should not be and confident in his animal cunning to keep him safe as he snooped. His enjoyment was short lived as there was little left to snoop at, some chairs, some over the top pink furnishings and some glossy photos. He picked one up, hoping it would prove to be Lewis in school uniform or, heaven forbid, as a naked baby on a rug. He chuckled at the thought. The chuckle died in his throat. The laugh was unforthcoming, it remained in his belly, stifled, where it became transformed into a rage. Not the rage of a man catching his unfaithful wife with her lover, no. This was a fiery rage of dying bull as it launched itself towards the hapless Matador.

This was the full blown rage of an injured rampaging beast with nothing to fear. This was hell on fire.

That a grown man could ever want to encourage an infant to perform sexual acts was beyond his comprehension. That this same man should capture the act on film, and ensure that his slimy face somehow got in the picture, was as far from reality that Herbert Crowe could ever believe.

Like a wounded Sampson, but blinded only by tears, Herbert Crowe picked up a large, heavy chair and wrenched a leg from it before smashing it to matchwood. This leg was his ass's jawbone. What Greg and Stringer had left was reduced to nothing in the ensuing tempest. What Lewis and Verna had left a short half hour before was completely destroyed or just gone.

Harvey was having a morning of differing moods. First came initial optimism at the cottage, then sadness while he shared a cup of tea with Oli, as she cleaned egg off his tie. Confusion followed at the Police Station, there was no sign of Snape, but he had left a message advising him that was all under control and to play along?? The final mood of the morning was a mixture of sadness and despair. His new digital clock announced 11:59 in red flashing dots as the intercom buzzed.

Verna looked at a well cared for, happy baby and gasped. "That's not my wee child, where's my fucking baby you gimpy bitch?" Charlie looked Harvey cold in the eyes, ignoring Verna, "I told you she was evil, she does not have Bernie, she does not even recognise her." "Where's your bleeding Nanny with my bairn?" Verna continued. Harvey looked at Evans, he was equally confused, and then to Charlie, who was not confused but furious. "Nanny, what's happening here?" demanded. Evans.

Harvey explained about Verna's first visit to the cottage and the encounter with Amber and their initial reaction of passing the girls off as twins They didn't really know who Verna was or what she wanted. It was a precaution he explained, Verna had seen through that, and had assumed that the elder child was hers, because of her taking after Ronnie. Bernie as they could see had the Verna look. The penny began to drop.

Verna listened and realised she had made a big mistake. "Never assume" she had once been told. She looked over Charlie's head to

Evan Evans for assistance, he was now composed and ready. Leaping to his feet he began his now familiar delivery. "Mr Burright, it is obvious that my client has suffered greatly. Even now it has been confirmed that persons in this very room have conspired to hide the truth from her. I ask, is there any wonder she is confused? Miss McCalisky has barely seen her child since birth and had no chance to succour her before being cruelly dismissed. Despite all you may read about a mother's instincts and the wonders of nature, if a young person is deceived, and she is young, and is deliberately mislead, well I ask you? She cannot be condemned for being a victim or believing such a cunning deception." He glanced at Verna, who suddenly became young and vulnerable.

"Do you think I can hold her, please?" Verna asked meekly. Harvey looked rather guiltily at Charlie after Evans's rebuke and they both nodded sheepishly in consent. The baby looked up at Verna wide-eyed, Evans could be wrong about instincts albeit if they were one-sided. Verna looked down at the babe wondering how the fuck she could pass this carrot headed, freckled faced, thing off as a Romanian. Ah well, one thing at a time, back to the script.

After a few minutes, she looked up and asked if she could take the baby to Lafferty's to buy her a belated Christmas gift. Too soon thought Evans and interjected as he sensed apprehension in the room. "Naturally in the company of Miss err, Charlie," he offered, "or indeed the whole company if preferred."

In the event, Charlie led the way with Verna following, doing a fair job as a novice, of negotiating the passages to outside, with the baby carriage. They crossed to Lafferty's. When Charlie bent to assist with the steep kerb Verna anticipated correctly and discreetly floored her with an accurate uppercut. The blow was similar in force and delivery to that of Amber on her in the same spot a few days earlier.

With Charlie out cold, and in the arms of a helpful stranger who thought she had tripped, Verna pulled Bernie from the carriage and high tailed it to the van waiting on the corner. Stringer was in the back, taking stock of their acquisitions, so she scrambled in the front as Greg hit the gas.

The sudden movement had frightened Bernie, who began to scream. "Shut that thing up for a start", he snarled unkindly as he pulled out in the flow of traffic. They cut up a car containing four serious looking gentlemen, they did not hoot or complain as he picked up speed. "I'm doing my fecking best" replied the less than perfect vision of motherhood. She didn't need to waste too much time comforting Bernie, who settled with the throb of the engine as sleep took over.

As they reached the top of the hill, that would descend to the by-pass and the Portsmouth road, they were directed to pull over by a uniformed Police Officer in a day-glow jacket. The car with the grave gentlemen pulled in behind and the miscreants were all promptly arrested. The baby was put in the care of a WPC and the four gentlemen sped back from whence they came, this time with a blue light flashing on the dash, and twin tone sirens blasting.

Harvey was half-heartedly studying the documents Evan Evans had flourished the day before, but could not get a niggle from his brain. He contemplated offering a drink but decided he would wait until the others returned. Suddenly a light came on in the back of Harvey's head as he remembered his dream and Charlie's remarks at breakfast "How can she afford him?" he muttered allowed.

The new office clock showed that the five minutes had elapsed and Evans rose, fidgeting his way to full height, he realised or thought he had been addressed. ""Sorry Mr Bright, I was absorbed briefly in my next appointment, you were saying?" Harvey felt his heart sink again. "Oh, you have more cases in the area? I was just saying it was unusual for a person such as Verna to acquire your services, more or less exclusively, for what? Four days or more?" "More" replied Evans, twitching slightly, "but if you are really interested, and as we are able to deal so amicably I am prepared to show you this." He flourished yet another sheet of A4 that he lowered to the desk. "As you can see..." he was saying, but Harvey could not see. The page was blurred or gibberish, the script was badly typed, purposely obscure, Harvey lowered his head and squinted, it made no sense. "I'm sorry Mr Evans I ...." The paperweight of clock killing fame came down on his head, Harvey slumped over his desk, the sentence remained incomplete. Evans bolted.

In the passageway Evans encountered a dazed Charlie, the poor girl was floored a second time as he caught her a blow with his elbow, strangely raised in defence as he charged. He flew down the street and heard a distant siren blaring. He glanced around, he was not being followed but was attracting curious glances as he ran at full pelt. He decided he was not being chased and that a fast walk would be more acceptable. It was lunchtime and appropriate that one dressed as he should be in a hurry. Now he was not attracting any attention and felt safe to proceed home. There he could get rid of Evan Evans quickly, stash his cache back where it belonged, and backtrack as Lewis to Lafferty's.

He opened the front door without the key. "Bloody girl" he complained. Then, as he regained his composure he put the door to his back and, with relief said "Safe at last" before noticing something was definitely amiss and a car screeching to a halt outside.

"Wrong" yelled Herbert Crowe, who emerged from the shadows. He catapulted Lewis the full length of the small hall and crashing into the remains of his lounge. Lewis struggled to his feet, he barely recognised his surroundings, had he stumbled into Brights cottage? Confused he did not move and Herbert Crowe grabbed him by the scruff of his neck and hurled him at the wall with all his might. The intention was to break every bone in the degenerates body, but Crowe was so angered that he missed by a yard and Lewis sailed through the window, taking the frame with him. He was badly lacerated and landed heavily amongst two pairs of shiny boots. He looked up through bloodied eyes, "Arrest me please." he pleaded and characteristically passed out. Officers One and Two bundled him in the car as Snape and the young Constable came from the rear. "Go" shouted Snape. "Hospital, go. Not you lad, you stay with me - he's your mate."

The car sped away, Officer One related the scene behind to Two. "The fucking maniac is out, he's got Snapey, they deserve each other. No wait, not you wait you, idiot, I was talking figuratively. He's waving something at Snapey and pretty excited he is too, the maniac, not Snapey, shut up or I won't tell you anymore. Snapey's got his radio - one, two three." Snape's voice crackled through their radio. They were advised that their charge was suspected of offences of the most serious nature. He should not be unguarded for a single moment and it was relayed that Herbert Crowe may not have finished with him yet. Reinforcements would be sent to the hospital.

As Lewis came to in the hospital A&E area, Evans had all but disappeared. Only tatters of the disguise remained and nothing of the bombastic Welshman was evident. Officer Two advise him he was under arrest and read him his rights. He helpfully advised him that there were not enough officers in Hampshire to keep Crowe at bay if he decided to come after him and said he hoped whatever he had been up to was worth it.

At his request, Lewis was escorted by both officers to the toilet, he was starting to vomit and appeared to be filling his trousers at the same time. The disabled toilet had no window so they did not fully follow Snape's instructions as they pushed him in to sort himself out.

He was certainly disabled and there was no escape - but there was one way out! They were on their second cup of tea when they decided he'd had long enough and indeed he had. "Fuck," said Two. "What?" "Belt, laces and bracers, he's under arrest." "You stupid twat - you arrested him," Officer One mimed washing his hands in the best Pontious Pilate tradition.

In his last few moments, Evans was gone and Lewis was alone and vulnerable. As a Schedule One Sex Offender he would probably be fed glass in his food in prison. He decided to start early before Crowe got to him. He kneed the low mirror and with a large shard of glass he cut his wrists vertically, his throat horizontally, swallowed some smaller shards and for good measure chopped off his penis. With his remaining strength, he removed his belt and, using the hoist, hung himself until he was quite dead.

Beltless, his trousers fell to his ankles. Due to his earlier injuries at the hands of Verna, he was without underwear. Officers One and Two decided two things there and then. Firstly Lewis was a selfish bastard to take advantage of their good nature and secondly, that this job was not for them. They wondered if any more Traffic Wardens were wanted.

Snape and the young Constable arrived. Snape was speechless as the young Constable observed Verna's handiwork. Lewis's testicles were now bloodied and exposed. "Asthma" he said with authority, a job at CSI awaited him - no doubt. "At least he never used his laces" observed Two.

A little away from the excitement, Harvey and Charlie were reunited with Bernie as they had their bruises attended for the second time in a matter of days. They were told little of events as the Police closed ranks, so they retired back to Fred's. They slept undisturbed and even missed the excitement of the nearby school burning down, an unrelated oddity to an odd day.

The Aftermath

The fire at the school gave a breathing space for the Police to implement a good old fashioned cover up. This was aided by a local newspaper reporter stumbling over a couple of youths hiding at the scene of the fire. He was able to interview them and get a confession before he pointed them out to the Police and got his recognition for a fine piece of investigative reporting. This was the breather the Superintendent and Snape needed.

Lewis was duly un-arrested as he hung dead and bleeding like a kosher goat, before the medics were called.

The story presented to the press was that a routine traffic stop had discovered items of a serious nature and were linked to a burglary at the home of a local window dresser. The window dresser, having discovered his incriminating cache of child pornography stolen, had panicked and fled the scene.

His fear had brought on an asthma attack and he had been helped to the hospital by one Herbert Crowe. Crowe had alerted the Police after hearing that they were looking for the dresser. Lewis was about to flee the hospital as the Police approached and had committed suicide before he could be apprehended.

A further press release would ensue relating to the burglary, and other matters currently under investigation. The local paper was filled with the exclusive scoop from the school fire, Robin Lewis made page five, and a small editorial.

Greg and Skinner were remanded in custody and were sent to Winchester Prison. Verna was released on Police bail after turning Queens Evidence, on the condition she would make no attempt to contact Bernie or any member of the Bright household.

Herbert Crowe received a payment from the Superintendent's Informers Fund and was told in no uncertain terms to discuss the matter with nobody. He promptly went to the local paper to advise how he had helped capture a major criminal and was told to piss off by the School Scoop reporter, who did not want his limelight to be diminished.

Chapter Twenty-Two

Following the hectic days since New Years Eve, things calmed to a more natural pace. The usual backlog of funerals started to clear and Bill's took place the following week. The delay prolonged Oli's agony but did give Ronnie time to appear, for which she was grateful.

Ronnie looked well and stayed on with Olivia for a few days while she came to terms of being alone. Harvey was pleased he had made the effort and more satisfied (he hoped) that the computer report of him being in Hounslow was wrong. In Ronnie's world, it was easy to use somebody's name, date of birth, etc., to get benefit. Ironically, Data Protection in some cases aided this process, data sharing was virtually unknown, and fraudsters had a 'Purple Patch'.

Ronnie had in fact been working with Cass in her developing business and was there when Harvey's letter arrived. Oli had been a major part of his life and even Ronnie had some heart. He, however, showed little interest in his daughter, but his appearance did help with the formal arrangements concerning the Guardianship. Typically, after a few days he was gone.

Brian did a good job of the repairs to the ceilings (all) and in good time. Charlie had dealt with all aspects of the works, insurance and refurnishing to a high standard but within budget. She had also enjoyed herself, and Brian's company.

Brian had commented, and flattered, Charlie several times. He advised that she had a natural bent for interior design and project management. He asked her to consider working with him again. On a professional basis, of course, combining her office skills with her new found talents. He explained that in difficult times people were using their resources to improve their home rather than move. Working together they could offer a complete service. She was more than flattered but declined, for now, claiming she was happy with the status quo.

In due course, Verna's 'gang' got their just deserts, having lots of previous convictions, they were sent down for five years. Verna herself faced no charges. She received a Police Caution, Lewis was gone and the couple who wanted to 'adopt' Bernie had disappeared. The caution was strong enough to make her swear never to set foot in Hampshire again. She relocated to Brighton and provided 'services' to gays and businessmen who liked to be punished.

Lewis's funeral was very low-key and he was cremated, it was delayed somewhat by a certain missing body part that was eventually discovered in the locker of the young Constable. He was not charged, after threatening to 'tell all', but did take a career change by becoming an assistant in the mortuary. Strangely, the only person in attendance at the funeral was Maude Crowe, who on the advice of the Priest, was 'getting out more'. She found funerals a comfortable pass time and sometimes the teas were very nice afterwards.

Harvey decided to rest the pills, he would not tell Dr Hope. He had enough experience to complete the forms and his body readings were good, with or without assistance. Harvey loved Charlie and thought that would cover for some inadequacies. He visited Oli regularly and became increasingly worried about her welfare. She was finding work ever harder to get and consequently compromised on heating, food and other luxuries.

Brian contacted Charlie almost as regularly as Harvey saw Oli, trying to get her to join him in business. Although rebutted on every occasion, he was encouraged by her weakening resolve - he sensed it, he knew her so well.

In the Spring of 1989 Amber, Troy and Nicki paid a visit to the cottage and a mini reshuffle ensured they could be accommodated. Troy, it transpired, was a New Zealander where vowels were random and had American Grandparents on his mother's side, that explained the accent. His name came from his mother's birthplace, Troy - Michigan, and she claims to have got one of the best educations the USA could offer.

He had been commissioned by an unknown source (to him) to cover the Stones US tour for his paper, in preparation for the European version in 1990. It would coincide with his Grandparents' Golden or Diamond Wedding Aniversary and he would return around Christmas, as the tour moved to Japan. He wanted to take

Amber, but she would not be separated from Nicki for so long and temporary lodgings (hint hint) were being sought.

All were pleased to see the sisters reunited and they in turn performed for their audience. Both were walking and communicating well as they went off hand in hand to explore. Bernie was still the bigger of the two despite Nicki being older. Amber referred to the difference as one being 'cottage size' and the other 'camper size', it was a tempting as nicknames but only in-house.

They filled Amber in on all the excitement she had missed during a trip round the village in the restored and now adapted Morris. As they passed the Potter brothers garage, Amber spotted her Fiesta looking forlorn in a shaded corner.

Harvey noted the look, "They have been around asking what to do, the engine is shot. When did you last check the oil?" he asked. "What oils?" "Say no more, it can stay there a while but with the current climate .... well fair to say they can not spend money until you come to some arrangement." "Ok, I will see them tomorrow and call Pops, and smile nicely at the younger one when Troy has gone", she laughed as Troy gave her a sideways glance. "Well it could be a long trip," she joked as he mimed a strangle on Nicki balanced on his lap. They pulled over at the Off Licence and bought some wines of Antipodean origin recommended by Troy.

A pleasant evening ensued with Troy showing off his skills as a chef and wine waiter. His choice of food and wine exposed a hidden talent. "Why is New Zealand wine, good as it is, so much more expensive than the Australian ones?" Harvey enquired. "Because the Aussie stuff is mass produced shite, this one is developed, not forced," came the indignant reply. Troy left after a few happy days, an unspoken invitation for Amber to stay was unspokenly accepted. Troy hoped to send her a ticket for a flight and concert once he was established if that was ok. She said she would Potter about until she heard from him, this raised an eyebrow and a cautionary grin. As usual Amber took everything in her stride, though it was obvious he would be missed.

One day Harvey returned home to find Brian driving away. He was not at all concerned by Charlie's ex-boyfriend's occasional visit or phone call and did not consider him a rival for her affections.

She appeared happy, had Amber for the company and their domestic life was running smoothly in most directions.

"Do you think he could do a small extension for us here in the near future?" Harvey asked Charlie, indicating the departing builder. "Why, are we planning a baby or has Amber requested a potting shed?" she teased. He coughed a little and may have blushed a bit. "Seriously, I have been thinking about Oli, I'm not sure she is coping on her own, she has no work of sorts. It's only a thought, what do you think? I've not said anything."

Charlie mulled it over before speaking, her response was positive with reason. She agreed it could be a good move all round if Oli were agreeable. She explained that Brian had just made her a serious and sensible offer of employment. Oli being on tap would help her decide. She explained Brian's thoughts on people wishing to improve what they had rather than search for a larger property plus, the expense of moving and all could finance a reasonable upgrade.

She could deal with all the nitty gritty while he did the business and then they could offer her as an interior designer as a complete package. New TV programmes were already selling this concept, he was not a fly by night cowboy and had good local connections.

Brian had researched well and his argument held water. It was not by coincidence that he would target those such as Harvey, those on a regular salary, mainstays who did not want to move but needed more space. These were the types who would not gamble on a large mortgage increase for a mansion but would be interested in cashing in on the price incentives a recession delivered. The building industry was in the doldrums, builders merchants were 'giving away' materials for cash flow and skilled labour was in abundance. Add to this a good looking conscientious internal designer and the job's a good 'un.

If Oli were willing to look after Bernie in exchange for full board, Charlie could seriously consider Brian's offer. She would ring Brian for extension ideas, he had a flare for those things, once Oli was on board.

She was getting excited now, but first 'What about Amber and Nicki?" she needed to know. This would not be a problem, he explained that Oli was mortgaged up to the hilt and struggling.

Harvey would employ some delaying tactics with the building society on her behalf. This could freeze the interest or capital repayment for a while. Hopefully she would find a buyer that would not leave her in negative equity.

"All that will take at least six months, by which time our master builder (and new assistant) could have this place up and running. We had better allow space for Amber's visits, though, hey, she is here for a while yet - you could start working next week if you want." "Slave driver" "No rush, but you know what I mean. Do you think it will be ok to do the work in the Winter?" "February Mix and he won't break through until the last moment so we can take a break away until the dust settles." "What?" "February Mix holds stuff together so you can build in the Winter and he can build the new bit without disturbing the main part until it's ready. Or something like that." "Bloody hell, you're talking like a builder already" he laughed. "No, I'm fucking not." "Ha ha, you lose me with all that technical stuff."

"One-Parent Family Allowance, you fraud" she countered. "What?" "Well with you, me, Amber and now Oli, how come you can claim that allowance, don't lie, I've seen the book." "Perks" he laughed. "Anyway, I've been giving that to Oli, Maggie can afford it, so up yours." "That would be nice for a change."

Oli, of course, was delighted by the prospect of moving into the cottage and becoming a part of the family unit. She was more than happy for Harvey to deal with her financial and other worries. She was hiding her despair and in all honesty had contemplated an early reunion with Bill as a way out.

Brian had come up trumps with a buyer, who was in a predicament and needed to downsize urgently, and everything was bumping along nicely. Oli insisted a condition of her impending move would be that she assumes certain household duties and responsibilities as she had done for Harvey before - music to his ears. "After all" she had declared. "I don't want to be made redundant when Bernie outgrows me do I?" "Don't worry, we'll have you put down or stuffed when the time comes" Harvey assured her.

The year drew to an amicable close with no bumps in the road. Christmas and New Year festivities passed without illness, incident or a mention of the turbulent times faced the previous year. Even his Mother had been missing apart from the odd visit, and Harvey was starting to think she had finally found peace or at least a resting place.

Since resting the pills Harvey's lovemaking had taken a slump and he concluded that he had to introduce the odd one if it were obvious things were going that way.

Herbert Crowe's annual settlement was agreed on friendlier terms than had been previously known and he divulged that Maude was getting out more. She was a regular visitor at the new hospice where she was popular as a good listener. Her grasp, or her interpretation, of current affairs, were an endless source of entertainment. In return she was provided with an endless source of funerals to attend. She was also an honorary cleaner at both the Catholic and C of E Churches were the fresh woodland flowers were a welcome addition. The only fly in the ointment was Planning Permission for the small extension, but Fred Alexander pulled a few invisible strings somewhere and finally it was granted.

Troy returned in time for Nicki's birthday which was an unexpected bonus for Amber. He was full of apologies for failing to get Amber tickets to join him but this was never an issue, she had just missed him terribly. His coup de grace (in the nicest term) was the production of tickets to Japan for Amber and Nicki so they could join him on the tour. He explained that his articles were a success and he had been privy to much inside information which he only passed on when he got the nod.

After Japan, they would follow the tour on its European leg which, he divulged conspiratorially, would be Bill Wyman's last tour with the band. This would be his scoop when they were ready for the public to know. He had already reported on the squabbles and tantrums he had been allowed to drip feed to the paper. He said, he had Harvey to thank for some of his inside dealings. He had name-dropped him as a feeler, and was pleased that he was remembered as 'part of the scene way back' - it's not what you know ..... A week later they were gone with the assurance that they were welcome back whenever, in return, concert tickets were promised, with backstage and after party passes of course.

Oli moved into the spare room and resumed duties. Brian commenced the conversion towards the end of January, promising all would be ready by the end of March. Digger Daley manoeuvred his JCB expertly around the back of the cottage where the footings were duly dug and he departed before Harvey spotted him and could question his unemployment claim.

Complete with his February Mix, Brian toiled as Norman Fowler left the cabinet 'to spend more time with his family'. He sweated as about 600 new cases of BSE were being identified each month, and his army of Dole Claimants topped out as Nelson Mandella left Victor Verster Prison, a free man for the first time in 27 years.

Brian laboured on alone as Buster Douglas floored Mike Tyson, he broke through as Farzad Bazoft was hanged by Saddam Hussien and completed as Poll Tax Riots were taking place in London.

A delighted Oli moved in and a happy Charlie began full-time employment on April 2nd, the Eve of Bernie's birthday. Amber, Nicki and Troy paid a surprise visit, albeit fleeting, and although it was a bit hectic for a few days, the little cottage and it's new extension coped well.

Brian had been pleased with the cottage conversion and had stretched himself to the limit to ensure all went well and to programme. This was not for Harvey's benefit, or even Charlie's, but for his ego.

Now he had a new project to channel his efforts into - a partly converted Charlie. He was very subtle at first, charming here, flattering there, offering encouragement when needed and mildly chastising when he felt like being superior. Charlie was enjoying the work, this enabled her to ignore his double meaning invitations to 'stay on for a bit' and the like. She also overlooked his other irritating ways of showing off and acting the 'Big Boss' in front of clients. She knew deep down that she could handle the situation as long as there was no sign of his old ways returning.

The experience she was gaining was invaluable, this was a line of work she had more than a flair for, and if he became difficult again, she would take her talents elsewhere.

Brian for his part, was a man with a mission. He was an achiever, in his mind, whatever he wanted to accomplish he did. Anybody who got In his way or tried to get one over on him would regret it. He had been through the mill and came out a survivor. Charlie would learn this if she did not know already. She had taken it upon herself to end their relationship before he was ready. He told himself that he had wanted to stop it, but she had beaten him to it. This he could not accept, this was unfinished business. All loose ends had to be tidied up, no matter how long it took. Thanks to two spotty kids, he had half frightened to death, the school that had humiliated him as a youth now lay in ruins.

Chapter Twenty-Three

Life at the cottage was enjoyable and the new arrangements worked well. Oli was a dear and had a knack of when and where to be, or not to be, at all times. She enjoyed her privacy and respected theirs.

Bernie loved Oli and kept her going all day. She in turn adored the child but was quite pleased to retire to her room after dinner, and watch her favourite soaps with her feet up, and dry sherry to hand.

Amber and Troy were regular visitors with Nicki throughout the year. Tour dates and cheap European flights were very friendly in their favour. Late July, they skipped a couple of dates and turned up with the much-coveted tickets for the last concert in Wembley at the end of August. As earlier predicted this was to be Bill Wyman's final performance with the band and was a memorable occasion.

Towards the end of November, as storm clouds were closing over The Iron Lady in Westminster, Amber called requesting a special favour. Pops had invited them on an all expenses trip to America for Christmas. It was pretty evident from the itinerary described that this was not a child orientated happening and Amber was torn.

Oli was consulted and it was agreed that Nicki would spend another Christmas with her larger, little sister. The period passed very quickly which is always a good sign that things were going well. There were just two festive 'flies in the ointment'. One was Brian's exploitation of the mistletoe which made Charlie uncomfortable and the second was Harvey's unscheduled stop at the fish pond following a difficult time with Herbert Crowe.

Harvey was fortunate that Charlie was madder with Brian than she was with him, Brian very stupidly missed an opportunity of gaining 'Brownie Points'.

Both were eventually forgiven but Charlie was slightly disconcerted by the episodes and she confided in Amber on her return. Amber was not too surprised by Harvey's performance and by then Charlie had accepted it as being an irregular occurrence. Amber, as expected, played up Harvey's good points and talked down the misdemeanours.

Brian's attempts or approaches had been carried out without the benefit of alcohol and Amber advised that they should be viewed with a degree of caution. She told Charlie it was obvious he still had 'a thing' for her and perhaps following their good year in business he had got a bit carried away. "Think how you would have felt if he had ignored you," she said. "Men, they never get it right, just be on your guard, you know."

She then hurled a cushion at Troy as came down the stairs with a squeaking girl under each arm. Charlie decided to put both on probation lest they transgress again, but as the year moved forward the events were shoved to the back of her mind.

As if from nowhere 'the customer' "Customer Care' and 'Charter Marks' became buzzwords, and the infatuation of the early nineties. As Mr Major found his feet - probably after somebody had told him they were on the end of his legs!

It was not long before Harvey was lined up to attend various courses to make his staff more 'user-friendly' to the nation's citizens. One course on Customer Satisfaction, at the Queen Elizabeth II Conference Centre, in London meant he would have to overnight in the city. He would be afforded an excellent hotel and asked Charlie if she wanted to go along to catch a show or something. He was not surprised that Brian had been reluctant to lose her for a couple of days mid-week, and she in turn said she was in the middle of something, so he went on his own.

He telephoned from the hotel and received a lengthy story about her dinner from Bernie and how she had made her name from Alfrebetty Spaghetti. He filled Charlie in on his day and the fantastic view of Big Ben from both the conference and his hotel. She told him to stop trying to make her jealous or guilty, or both as he explained they had another seminar shortly that would've followed by a slap up silver service meal.

She laughed that she and Oli would probably have a takeaway, on him. He promised to ring later if not too late, she took his details and said she would ring before going to bed, and warned him not to ring her after.

Charlie tucked Bernie into bed while thinking of slap up meals and got to the phone on the second ring. "Forget which fork to use for the soup? she joked. "I'm sorry!" It was Brian. "Oh sorry Brian, I thought..." "Don't worry, actually it's me that should apologise, I've got something I'd like you to see and I think you would hate me if I made you wait until the morning." "Err..." "Shall I have a word with Harvey?" "No it's ok, he's away tonight, it's not a joke though is it?" "Of course, I forgot," he lied. "No definitely not a joke," he replied seriously, "will you come?" "Ok, but I can't be long, I'll just tell Oli and come now." Brian hung up the phone knowing she was at this minute on her way at his bidding. He considered it a nice touch of deception asking to explain it with Harvey when he knew him to be miles away.

The phone call and deception had aroused him, but he controlled the urge to masturbate and set about preparing the dining table. He barely noticed the change in the weather, thanks to his double glazing, and Frankie Laine.

Charlie checked with Oli, who was only concerned because Charlie had not eaten and the July sky had taken a turn for the worse. The weather forecast was promising heavy downpours and duly delivered.

Charlie drove off wondering what Brian had in store and cursing the weather. Maybe she should go back to the Senator and then remembered it was at the station. The old Morris was not very good in heavy rain and she struggled to see through the single speed windscreen wipers. The Summer had been relatively dry and surface water abounded in the small lanes. BSE worried farmers had been less than diligent in clearing blocked culverts.

The Peking & Cantonese Takeaway driver was the first to brave the storm and flooded roads to Brian's that evening. The proprietor was so pleased to have such an excellent order this early in the night that he threw in several complimentary cans of Chinese lager, that were only a little out of date. The meal had apparently been chosen by a connoisseur for its gastronomic appeal rather than the price, and differed from the curry and chips ordered by the yobs at closing time. Brian accepted the order paid and tipped generously. He eyed the larger curiously and started laying out the feast - not long now!

Charlie passed the delivery van just outside Marston on its way back to Chuffers. Her hunger hit home as her thoughts drifted, to long gone Aromatic Crispy Duck, fine wine and nights of romance. She pulled up safely at her destination, breathed a sigh of relief and ran the short distance to the door, maybe Brian would drive her home. The door opened before she could knock.

Herbert Crowe was having a miserable day, his friend the Super had failed to pay up for some less than plausible information he had given him about the local antique dealer. The Superintendent knew that Crowe was embroiled with the dealer concerning some doctored furniture he was trying to offload and did not want to get involved. For once he sent the big man packing with no reward.

Next Crowe had lost several pounds on some dead certs who, unfortunately, preferred heavy going. That would have been great tomorrow after this rain, but today the ground was rock hard. Then to top it all, he had been asked to pay his tab at the pub and had been refused any ale because he was fund-less. By this time he was depressed and left without argument, after blowing his nose on the bar towel. But it was only a parting gesture and his heart was not in it.

Half way home he was half soaked and raining harder. He heard the takeaway van approaching, stuck out his thumb, and thought he might scrounge a ride. The little Chinese driver thought otherwise. Recognising his tormentor of many late nights, and a long since flying bicycle incident, standing by a large muddy pool was too much to hope for. He took the action that his most inscrutable upbringing had taught him and drenched Crowe from head to toe.

The large man leapt into the air as if scolded and many an oath ensued as he wiped what he hoped was mud from his eyes. Neither man could believe their luck when offloaded at Brian's he was able to repeat the exercise on the return trip. He went on his way happy in mind and richer in pocket.

Vowing to do unmentionable things to the 'little slant-eyed, slant arsed' bastard next time they met Herbert Crowe took to the woods as it began to thunder. He was not concerned with the trees surrounding him. He reasoned that with so many trees in the wood, and him on the move, he was less likely to attract a lightning strike than being drowned by a 'fucking Kamikaze slant-eyed van driver.'

Herbert Crowe had only been wood side a couple of minutes when he found he was level with the front of Brian's house. There were more headlights and the old Morris pulled up to the front of the house. He recognised Charlie immediately and was aware of her previous relationship with Brian though his terminology was less delicate.

"Hmm," he said to himself, forgetting the rain, "bet she's come for a shagging, old Brighty can't be up to much, no wonder he was so grumpy at Christmas." He waited for her to enter and crossed the road to investigate, he was starting to feel happy again.

"What a night, I hope this is worth it Brian." Charlie hesitated as she recognised the familiar aroma of oriental food, she was incredibly hungry and began to tremble.

"Da la," Brian sang out, he took her hand and led her to the feast laid out in the tastefully appointed Dining Room. This was now candle lit and had soft music playing.

"You shit," she cried, "is this what you got me out here for?"

"Yes, don't you like it?"

"Well no, actually I'm afraid I don't, Harvey's ....."

"Fuck Harvey," he said nastily.

"What?"

"Oh sorry, you do that already, DON'T you?"

"What's going on Brian?" She was scared but tried to be calm and casually tried to back away.

"Eat" he snapped, pulling her back to the table.

"Oh sorry Brian, you should have checked, we've already eaten..."

"LIAR. You have not had time to eat and I know there is no 'we' this evening, do you think I'm stupid?"

"No of course not, I meant Olivia and me. It's just that we are colleagues now and not you know.," she was careful with her words.

"I know that you walked out and left me when I needed you when I had nobody and for - HIM! Now I have gone to a lot of troubles to reward you for your hard work - as a bonus, we can both enjoy. So now I would appreciate it if you would join me for some supper before it spoils."

She knew the signs, the build up, the ranting, the calm and then the violence. "Yes, of course, thank you. I'll just pop to the loo, won't be a mo', don't eat it all before I get back, Ouch!" A can of cold Chinese lager glanced her forehead and exploded against the architrave. "Eat" he screamed and grabbed her hair.

He pushed her face into one of the sauces and she recoiled from the heat. She kicked and struggled as he forced the crumbling duck between her teeth. She began to choke but managed to bite him, hard. He was extremely agitated and became aroused at the pain. "You ungrateful whore, all this was for you, now you've spoilt it" he ranted. Now his hands were all over her at once, feeling her, groping her and pulling at her clothes. She hung on to her panties desperately, they were being removed, he was too strong, she must keep her head.

Brian embarrassed himself before he could effect penetration and during his momentary lapse she was able to produce a debilitating kick to his groin and make her escape. She rushed to the car and slipped in, thankfully she had not locked it. She said a quick prayer and the engine turned over straight away. She was nearly free when his large fist shattered the side window and made a grab for her. Charlie pushed hard to the floor but her wet shoe slipped from the accelerator and he punched the side of her face.

Partially sited, she managed to pull way. She could hear him screaming. "You're sacked, you fucking prostitute, try and get one over on me would you? I saw you coming you bitch, you'll never work in this industry again, you hear me bitch?" She heard no more as she gunned the old car on its way.

Peering through the window Herbert Crowe was enjoying the show. He enjoyed the sexual activities of others and never ceased to be amazed at the antics. This, however, was a new slant on anything he had seen before. He appeared to be waltzing her to a heavily laden table - foreign muck by the look of it. She wasn't dancing that good but, of course, she had that fucking great boot on one foot so would never win a competition.

Then they were shouting, now smiles, then he bounces a fucking can of larger off her napper, bloody Chinese crap it was too. He recognised it from his late nights at the takeaway. He chuckled a wheezy chuckle, this was good fun. Now he was pushing her head in something and was trying to force feed her, it reminded him of the Tom Jones film he had once seen, but was a bit more violent.

It was hard to tell if she was enjoying it or just acting as her moods seemed to be very changeable. "Now, she's gonna have him whether she be ready or not" he spluttered. Convinced he was privy to some posh foreplay, "best lay back and enjoy it before the food gets cold" he silently advised. Brian forced her onto the table and grappled with her undergarments, Crowe pushed his massive fist to the side of his nose and stifled his inevitable catchphrase. "Here comes the helmet, well I never, he shot wide, randy bastard couldn't wait."

Oomph he groaned as a foot or knee made contact with Brian's naked groin, and she bolted. Herbert Crowe laughed to himself, "Bet old Brighty don't do that, still a bit of rough never hurt nobody" he wheezed.

He continued to watch as Brian delicately got to his feet and rushed after her. The ensuing noise and insults at the front of the house made Crowe wonder if what he had witnessed was a game. After the car window was smashed and he punched her in the face, he realised that she had not been a willing participant. Well at least she hadn't been hurt, much, at any road. As Brian was spun round by the old Morris Herbert Crowe gave him a mighty kick in the balls and as he lay groaning in the rain, he pissed in his front door for good measure.

Eyes filled with tears of fear, hate and dismay Charlie struggled to watch the road. The wipers were again useless and she did not see the mass of water where the culvert was inundated. She hit the water at speed and aquaplaned into a one hundred-year-old oak tree, she died on impact.

Chapter Twenty-Four

Harvey lay on his back with his eyes firmly closed against the early morning August sun, his left arm was cold and wet, his head was throbbing. That was a hell of a dream, the hotel, the Police, several visits from his mother, grief, sorrow and great sadness. He heard distant voices and the rumble of a lorry, back to the dream. Amber, Oli and the little girls, no Charlie, the funeral, whose funeral? CHARLIE'S FUNERAL!

He tried to sit up but the gin induced hangover made it impossible for his shoulders to bear the weight of his head and he slumped back down. Head splitting with pain, he lay with his gut churning with bile, heart pounding and breaking from realisation.

It had not been a dream as it had not been a dream for the last nineteen days and TWENTY nights.

His dry arm made contact with a firm object and his subconscious made the connection that it was a Gilby's Gin bottle. Harvey lifted his wet hand from the pond and the bottle to his lips, he poured the remains down his throat chasing the bile back to his stomach before it saw the light of day.

The draught went coursing through his system, his veins took over and distributed the gin equally to caress his aching head and sooth his turbulent stomach. The gin was a good measure and chased the demon thoughts from his mind, he rested back and let himself be taken to a distant plain.

The voices were closer now, he recognised Amber and Oli but made himself invisible so he would not have to explain his condition. They were very close now. "Told you," said Amber, "he will drown out here one night, I've read that it is possible in two inches." "Poor man" Oli was deeply concerned, "let's get him in before the girls see him, he wouldn't like that." "You're right but who lets him get in this condition?" Amber asked angrily. "Look he has a bottle, would you sell him a bottle in his condition?" "I think everybody feels so desperately sorry that they think it will help him forget. They don't exactly encourage him, just humour him I suppose." "I guess you are right, it's just so worrying trying to figure out how long it will go on. He loved her so much .. so did I, still do and him" she couldn't help giving him a kick. "I know dear, me too, let's get on shall we?"

They half marched, half carried Harvey to bed. Lack of food made him quite a lightweight even in his condition. Amber undressed him, mopped at dried sick and generally gave him a bed bath. She put him in the Recovery Position and kissed his forehead "You prick, stop this," she said as her tears made rivulets down his face.

In the late afternoon Harvey woke, this had been a better sleep. He was parched and reached for the jug of water he somehow knew would be there. Amber, the Goddess of the tap, had delivered.

He gulped greedily from the jug and realised he was not alone. Ronnie was standing at the foot of the bed, he felt the presence of another, closer. A significant character in loud striped cheesecloth trousers, baggy jumper and hiking boots was smoking a prison style roll-up. She was making wispy smoke rings and a deep impression in his mattress.

Harvey blinked to clear his head and his blurred eyes. He toyed with the idea that his mother had had a sex change and become some kind of circus act when Cass spoke.

"Hello Harvey, how are you?"

"Dreadful"

"It's not surprising is it?"

"No"

"Well, what are you going to do about it?"

"About what?"

"Feeling dreadful, what are you going to do about feeling terrible Harvey?" she asked patiently.

"I'm going to have a drink and not listen to so many questions."

Something snapped, Cass reached across the bed and grabbed Harvey by his hair and pulled him within inches of her face and snarled "Well let's try some fucking answers shall we? You have lost somebody very dear to you and you are in danger of losing all the others that love you. You may wish to drink yourself to death, and probably will. But, unless you mix some arsenic with it or ingest twice as much as you do now it's going to take an awfully long time. When that time comes, those who have loved you, cared for you, will have despaired and will hate you. And, you them. Those lovely little girls who adore you, Mrs Kitson who depends on you and Amber, who has adopted you as her surrogate father will hate you. One last question. Do you fucking understand?" She let him go, he hung on and sobbed, she held him tight, really tight.

Nineteen days/Twenty nights of anguish and despair welled up and poured out. His cries could be heard from the road and surrounding area. Those who heard it, and meant him well, were glad, it was over. Cass and Ronnie held him until he could cry no more. Cass managed to feed him a sleeping powder Dr Hope had left. They watched over him as one by one the demons left him and he slept peacefully.

By the following week, he was ready to return to work and he got stuck into the backlog with a vengeance. The energy he had expended on self-pity were now obsessively channeled into his work. He would never let the pain go away but would deal with it. He was comforted to know her head had been filled with good thoughts at her death. She was a treasure and he owed it to her to carry on.

The inquest was finally held in late November. The Coroner recorded a verdict of Accidental Death, blaming the atrocious unseasonable weather as the contributory factor. Brian had born witness that she had left him in good spirits during a lull in the storm.

The project she had been working on was going well and he read out a fax from a client that he had shown her that was very complimentary. He blamed himself for calling her out but wanted to share the news with her, if only he had waited until the morning. He blamed himself for not offering to drive her home but was suffering from a migraine and she would not hear of it. She left looking forward to a cozy meal with Mrs Kitson and, he repeated, in good spirits.

Sgt Snape thought it prudent to withhold information that she had not been wearing underwear and the presence of what appeared to be semen on her clothing. He had suspected a liaison and should have investigated further but what good would digging around like that do? The poor girl had hit a flooded culvert, the car had hit a large immovable tree and nobody else was involved. There was no need to put her family or Mr Bright through any more pain, let the poor girl rest in peace. He agreed with the verdict.

The takeaway driver knew nothing about the accident, after laughingly telling the proprietor, about soaking that oaf Crowe twice he was transferred to an outlet in Glasgow. Herbert Crowe knew as much or more than anybody about the events that night but decided to keep his own council. He unknowingly shared Snape's opinion and anyway he had his own methods of dealing with things.

After the inquest, Harvey took Brian for a drink and implored him not to blame himself in any way for the accident. They got drunk as they discussed Charlie's attributes. Brian confessed she was a great loss to his business and things were not going so well. Herbert Crowe gate crashed the discussion and lifted the mood.

He made sure the glasses were topped up until Harvey and Brian confessed they could not drink another drop. He escorted Harvey home and helped him to his rear porch, as he had done many times after Charlie's death. Herbert Crowe made a strange Guardian Angel but was nonetheless effective and took his role seriously. He watched to make sure Harvey was not creeping back to the pond and was pleased as he fell through the back door.

When Harvey landed on the kitchen floor, Amber was happy to see it was the Dudley Moore character that had rolled in and not the dark spectre of before. She happily helped him to his bed and tucked him in, water jug at the ready. It had taken a while but he was stronger for it and she knew Mrs K would be able to cope from now. She rang Troy and would leave with Nicki the following day, after Harvey had surfaced.

Herbert Crowe helped Brian most of the way home, taking him through the woods and showing him places that Brian never knew existed. Less than a mile from Brian's home they rested on the edge of a long disused lime quarry. In the distance a one hundred-year-old oak prepared for Winter.

"I goes that way," said Crowe, indicating a trampled path. "You're a good chap" Brian hiccoughed, "I can see mine from here, amazing it is so close and I've never been this way before." "I know, and I saw you that night, you know that"? "What night, what are you on about?" Brian sensed a change in the atmosphere and shivered. "Less than a mile from home she was, like you now. 'Cept that their tree was a bit closer." "What are you getting at?" demanded Brian. "Nuffing, I just wanted you to know that I seen you and her that night, that's all."

Less than a mile from home, on the edge of a long disused lime quarry and in view of a hundred-year-old oak tree, Brian Golding was thrown to his death.

At his inquest, Herbert Crowe said he left him in good spirits. As they parted to wend their ways home, he added that Brian ensured him he was familiar with the route, after walking it hundreds of times in the past.

Chapter Twenty-Five

The Hampshire countryside that Charlie loved so much remained the same. The cottage that had been a real home for her and Harvey was still an idyllic picture, but the plans, dreams and aspirations they shared were gone.

Life without her was difficult to come to terms with, for nearly three years she had been the central part of his being. When he was down, she was always there to pick him up when a problem arose there was no problem and so on. With a simple common sense approach, invariably smattered with her innocent but effectual sense of humour, she kept his life vibrant and fulfilled. With Charlie he was complete, without her he felt many years older and without purpose.

Bernie was the exception to his life without purpose. She needed Harvey more now than ever. Thankfully he was able to steel himself and be there for her. She in return developed into a lively boisterous child, extremely intelligent with only the remotest touch of what he perceived was Verna's temper. With Bernie, there were not many dull moments and she kept both Harvey and her beloved Oli on their toes from morning to night.

Oli for her part was the mainstay of the trio and carried on with whatever was needed without complaint. All she asked was a couple of hours to herself every evening. Amber was also a stalwart and a regular visitor who was always Amber and ready to help out. Troy was away a lot but doing well and she finally managed to get her car moving again.

Soon it was the first anniversary of the accident which was marked by Mrs Alexander falling and breaking her hip. The ensuing pandemonium resulted in the tragedy being forced to the back of their minds while her predicament was dealt with.

Still a fan of Maggie, 'the truly elected Queen of the people", Fred had followed her advice and taken out private medical insurance. The excellent service his good lady received made every penny worth the outlay. After the best treatment going, Mrs Alexander was up and about within three weeks. Albeit physio would go on for longer and she would need plenty of rest, but the recovery was well in hand.

This period served as an appropriate diversion and so was Fred. His attempts at the most simple of domestic chores were beyond him and the smoke detector announced his arrival in the kitchen. He was the one in need of constant attention. Fortunately, Amber had returned to be with them 'just in case' and found herself taking over at the cottage while Oli moved in with the Alexander's until the end of August.

Harvey and Troy bonded well during this time. Troy confided that the work with the paper had cured him of his wanderlust and Amber, as always, was ready to settle down. Troy's excellent work on the tour and subsequent gigs had earned him respect in the industry and he was rewarded with two job offers.

One was his own tittle tattle gossip column for New Musical Express and the other was as an entertainment boffin for Capitol Radio. Both jobs were London based, although the column could be compiled anywhere, he would need to attend clubs, concerts and venues in the city. As far as he could tell, the radio job was partly live and partially recorded and he was advised that the kudos he gained working for NME would aid his radio work and vice versa. In the event he accepted both offers, Amber was delighted.

When Oli returned to the fold they held a straight talking conference, where all views were aired, was the order of the day. The outcome was, for the time being, Amber and Nicki would move into the cottage. Amber would help with the children and maybe attend the local college as a mature student. They could share Amber's old room and Troy would live with or look after the apartment of an NZ pal in London, he would come to the cottage midweek most weeks.

Oli pointed out that all this would be fine, but even with her extension, the cottage would be very crowded at times and must be viewed as a temporary measure. The little ones were growing up fast and could spend a lot of time together, which very soon would include starting school. They too would need their own space.

So it was agreed that all would keep ears and eyes open for a more substantial arrangement close by for Amber, Nicki and Troy. If Charlie were watching, she would be pleased.

The presence of Amber's level head would allow Harvey the occasional fall from grace and night out by the pond. He had been resting his little pills and the odd influx of alcohol would ensure that any urges remained dormant. It occurred to Harvey that Charlie had been the only person he had been happy making love with and now she had gone so were his desires.

Dr Hope accepted the respite and falsified Harvey's reports, after all the trials were nearly over, as long as Harvey was available for the tests all would be ok. He would still be entitled to his withdrawal pills if he ever needed them, and Dr Hope was a firm believer of kicking sleeping dogs.

Harvey's 45th came and went without mention. He may not have been openly mourning but he was not yet ready to celebrate a nondescript event, and those around him knew. One day maybe but not yet. His mother did appear briefly but, after having difficulty blowing out 45 candles, she left without comment.

With the domestic situation on a hectic but even keel Harvey threw himself into his work. He emerged himself in case review after case review as his staff became increasingly despondent. Clouds of Doom and gloom were gathering over the future of his staff, the office, and him in particular. Transfers to more secure offices, early retirements and voluntary redundancies were in an abundance. Despite being a small team he seemed to be hosting a leaving do every other week.

Compulsory attendance at pathetic courses on 'back to basics', 'customer choice' and other nonsensical subjects took no account of his workload. He realised that by now his age was also against him. Other course attendees were from larger branches and years his junior. They were ambitious and full of cost cutting ideas that would see it inevitable his office would soon be swallowed pips and all.

Still he continued to fight for his team and secure the best for them. He was not rewarded for his efforts and found loyalty a forgotten word.

One Friday he received a visit from a small man who explained he was the football pools collector. He had not been paid for weeks and was now considerably out of pocket. He was advised, it was not an official syndicate, but Harvey was a contributor. He did remember sharing in an occasional small payout. But, had not been asked for any money for a while and thought it had been disbanded. He checked the unofficial list the man presented, nobody was left and it transpired nobody had left any monies to cover their dues. Harvey was the sole survivor.

"How much?" he enquired. "Fifty-Four, Ninety, I put this week in already, it would help if you could keep it up for a bit. I have been wedging it for a while." They agreed that £60 would take the existing arrangement to closure. Harvey paid another Sixty on top to continue a smaller plan on his own, until that amount was exhausted. The man went away happy having received his back pay and an advance payment for the foreseeable future. He was a decent chap and Harvey had dealt with him as such.

In the Spring of 1993, Harvey received a visitor from Head office who presented him with a business card bearing the name of John F Kenedy, Personnel and Management Services. "Soon to become Human Resources, HR" he advised. "Hardly Relevant" Harvey muttered. The visitor missed the point. He was a tall chap who looked fresh from school and had yet to develop a sense of humour.

He handed Harvey two envelopes, one he explained contained the (unattractive) conditions of his future employment, in the central office, and the other held the terms of his voluntary redundancy.

From his nervous and sweaty appearance, Kennedy was obviously happier writing such letters than facing the recipients. Mr Major probably had an NVQ for this function, so hand them over he did. Harvey noted the 'Personal by Hand, for Addressee Only' on each envelope and put them on his desk with barely a glance. An extra set of sweat beads appeared on Kennedy's top lip as Harvey ignored the envelopes.

"Cup of tea Mr Kennedy? I'm afraid we have to send out for coffee." "Jack, please call me Jack, everybody does, Ronald" "Mr Bright, please call me Mr Bright, everybody does Mr Kennedy. Now was it tea or something else?" "No, I'm okay Ron. Mr Bright, are you not going to open your letters?" "No, Mr Kennedy, not yet. I had no control or anticipation of their arrival, but I shall open them when I'm good and ready, is that ok?" He rose, tucking the envelopes in his pocket, and Kennedy's course on Body Language told him the meeting was over. Kennedy had to get a decision to enable him to tick the box on his Performance Indicator Chart. He had been given this task at his last Assessment but advised Harvey he could take his time. Would he ring him the next day, please? How generous.

The envelopes remained in Harvey's pocket where he willed himself and refused to look at them until he got home. Then he shut himself away. There, he concentrated his mind on his future in a large impersonal office. Or an unsure one, unemployed, albeit with an acceptable short-term amount of redundancy, and an index linked pension in twenty years. He decided to opt for the latter. After all, it may be fun on the other side again, especially if he could pit his wits against prats like 'Jack' Kennedy. The pretentious prick, at least that would be better than working with him.

Once decided he descended to the kitchen. "I know your not a fan of liver" said Oli "but to hide away is a bit extreme, even for you." He smiled and called for Amber to join them. "Bernie wants to put a condom on a carrot" she laughed. "What?" "She has a little friend with an older sister who has started sex education. Don't worry, she wanted to dissect a fish's eye yesterday." "Better than liver," said Harvey.

He told them about his letter and his thinking. They agreed with his reckoning, together they would be ok. They were a unit, they had dependents and rights, they would never starve.

It was with a much lighter heart that Harvey returned to work the following day to relay his decision. Behind his back, his team had been given an envelope offering employment in the head office. Most would take the offer and a couple were consulting the union.

He did not give Kennedy the benefit of an early call and when he eventually rang a young voice answered. "Mr Kennedy, you mean JFK?" "What?" "Really that's what he likes to be called, what a prick eh? Err, you are staff aren't you?" "Yes, don't worry, I only met him yesterday when he was Jack. I would say he was certifiable." They both laughed as she connected him.

Harvey informed him in a matter of fact way that he would take the redundancy, after checking it out with the union. Kennedy was quite relieved, he would probably have been in close contact on a daily basis and thought this may have been a career disaster in the waiting. "Please check with the union Mr Bright, they have been on train since we left the station, better terms for voluntary redundancy and we, err they, look good at the end. Leave all the paperwork to me and I'll get back to you."

He changed to what sounded like genuine sincerity in passing. "I've checked your leave and circumstances, if you don't take any time off, sickness, etc. excluded, you can probably go in about six weeks. Your increment is due in two months, so take your holiday after six weeks and you will be on the books for another three months from now. You'll get the annual pay rise and the increment. It may not seem important now, but inflation-linked in twenty years - well you get my drift, fair does, you have a good record and it should be rewarded."

Despite himself, Harvey ended up thanking the twit, he was obviously better at that end of the phone than in person. Maybe he needed a course on interpersonal skills.

Six weeks is not long when you have a lot to do and Harvey was committed to leaving as little undone as possible. In true Alexander style, he set about reviewing all his cases and, when he was satisfied, he turned to the one that needed his most urgent attention and ingenuity.

Herbert Crowe's case took him nearly a week of late, lonely evenings but when he was finished, he hoped it would pass the very closest scrutiny. All that Crowe had to do was follow the simple instructions that Harvey would supply and he and Maude should be covered for as long as the present circumstances allowed.

John Major was on a sticky wicket, ok he had to cut civil service jobs, but he was up against it with his own party. Divided on Europe and many other matters. The farmers were in crisis and with so many people on the dole he would not look at benefits until he was re-elected. If he lost, Labour would not start off by lopping benefits so the Crowe's were as safe as he could make them, for now. Over the years, Harvey's feelings for Herbert Crowe had softened and he would not have felt easy leaving him at the mercy of the likes of Kennedy. He decided he had better visit to explain things.

He found the place eventually, or what was left of it. Herbert Crowe had been using bits of the carriage for the fire and metal for scrap. What was left was not fit for an animal shelter. It was worse than he could ever have imagined. A series of old car batteries gave a single light some glimmer, and Maude's ancient TV a snowy fizzing representation of the outside world.

Cooking and toilet facilities were outdoors, namely a fire with a metal tripod supporting a pot, and a shovel for digging holes for latrines.

"Maude's out" declared Herbert Crowe as he removed the skin from a rabbit with a practised shake. He then disemboweled the creature and tossed it in the pot. "Staying for dinner? She'll finish off when she gets back from the hospice with some cake and sandwiches, good they is."

Harvey explained the reason for his visit. "I've produced an idiots list for you to follow" he regretted using this - bloody courses. "I'd better find a fucking idiot then ain't I" laughed Crowe. He surprised Harvey by producing a pair of half-moon specs and checked the list. "But before you do any of that Herbert, get yourself today or no later than tomorrow to the Housing Department at the Council Offices in Chandlers Bottom. If you have to, drag somebody out here, from my limited experience you are a priority housing need and you cannot continue to live like this." Crowe nodded. "You will see, I have suggested you get some kind of medical certificate for you and Maude. stating you are unfit for work - play on your Asthma. To be honest, I'm surprised you don't have pneumonia living here."

"Doctors no problem, I knows old Hopey is shagging that bit in the tobacconist, don't know where he gets the energy though at his age." Harvey had an idea he knew the answer to that one. "Anyway, he knows I knows, so he won't be a problem. I reckons its fair does anyway with all this fags he smokes."

"Next" Harvey continued, "be bloody careful with your cash jobs, scrap and the like. There are plenty of snoopers and investigators looking for those claiming benefit while working, so be careful or you can just put that bit of paper on the fire now." "These snoopers get paid? I know hundreds on the fiddle...." Harvey left, Herbert Crowe would survive.

Chapter Twenty-Six

Through Fred's contacts (again), Harvey was offered a two-year contract with a local Housing Association that had inherited many local authority properties in need of repair. The job would entail decanting tenants from the dilapidated properties to either temporary accommodation, so they could move back when their homes were renovated, or newly built ones that were springing up.

The Housing Association was more eligible to attract funds than the local authority. Harvey's part in the grand scheme was to arrange storage for those wishing to return or arrange the relocation to the new properties. His office was a Port-a-Cabin that was moved from site to site. He arranged everything from removals to new carpets, curtains compensation et-all. It was not particularly hard work, nor was it very rewarding. Given so many options and choices mankind, in general, was a selfish bastard. He did not want necessarily what was best for him, but he certainly did not want less than his neighbour.

Harvey's debating and mediating skills were invaluable tools in getting the right pea in the right pod. The Local Authority had nomination rights to the new build properties, but he was able to mix and match with the renovated ones. His sense of mischief came into play as he put snobby types in their preferred location only to move a large family of uncontrollables next door after a few days. This is where he got his job satisfaction. It was rewarding to house nice people next to nice people, but it was good to play around with the others.

He had been instructed to spread the mix of tenants so as not to create good and bad areas, His manager seemed to change on a regular basis, which left him influencing the course of events.

He had heard that Herbert Crowe had been placed in Local Authority temporary accommodation and was relieved.

These were a good two years, his redundancy and salary served them well and the 30 hours a week sped by as his peas were nestled in their new pods.

He was remote enough to be removed from neighbourhood quarrels and Mr Major's Tenant Groups could sort them out, or not. Once housed these people were not his responsibility.

The set hours and regular breaks meant that Harvey was able to spend time with his granddaughters, and take them to theme parks, kite flying, the New Forest, the seaside, and even cricket where Robin Smith was a firm favourite.

Smith had a young son and was happy for him to mix with other kids as he scored run after run for Hampshire.

Harvey also took the girls for a week to Butlins at Bognor Regis, which they enjoyed so much. He was a bit of a magnet to a group of single mums but kept things at a respectful distance. He was not yet recovered enough for anything more.

The more they spent together, the more the sisters grew alike in looks and ways and he couldn't imagine life without them. Amber could no longer say they were Cottage and Camper size as they were soon both Cottage size.

Troy's work was going well. His gossip column was successful and he developed a rapport with all the presenters whose shows he gate crashed on the radio. After the hourly news, weather and traffic reports he popped up with snippets of gossip that often scooped.

Despite a fall in property prices both London and Hampshire remained out of their reach and rentals were hard to find. Harvey had no strings to pull at the Housing Association, but with Oli ageing it would be desirable for them to find something.

Things improved the day after Bernie's birthday when Harvey was advised he had won Two Hundred and Sixty Three Thousand Pounds and Nineteen Pence on Littlewoods Football Pools. This he discussed with, or divulged to anybody. Dispute wanting some good publicity, Littlewoods respected his desire for anonymity. He was accredited in the press as being a retired Civil Servant from the South East who was going to move to Spain - close, but not close enough!

Shortly after his win, the cottage vacated many years earlier by Gwen Orchard was up for sale. Claiming a draw on his redundancy money to the family, Harvey was able to buy the cottage and furnish it for Amber.

Having started a spending spree, Harvey took his granddaughters to Butlins again and dispatched Oli and her best friend Babs, from her Nursing days, on a mini-cruise roundtrip from Harwich to Malaga. This gave Amber and Troy all the space they needed to achieve the move.

For his part, Harvey would take a break in Spain. The press release from Littlewoods had whetted his appetite to visit his friends on the Costa-del-Sol, but he would await the end of his contract in a few weeks.

To keep his recent good fortune a secret, he invented an end of contract payment that would finance his trip. He would also charge Amber and Troy a fair rent which would be put in trust for his granddaughters. They could afford the rent and he would sign the house over to them eventually.

Despite the win, he was not wealthy by modern standards. He was comfortable though and soon would be benefiting from a couple of endowment policies that were paying good returns.

He felt a twinge of guilt, not sharing any of his winnings with Ronnie, but the lad was at last gainfully employed with his mother and doing quite well. Harvey did not want a sudden windfall to disrupt this, Ronnie would benefit a bit later.

The last two months at the Housing Association were very hectic due to the delay in a new development becoming available. Goldings, built on Brian's old house/yard site was hopelessly behind schedule, rather ironic after Brian's obsession with finishing on time, and may require an extension to Harvey's contract. Not what he wanted, he wanted Spain.

In the end, he agreed to another month. He did this after viewing the lettings list, he could have some fun. Tthe Association approved an exgratia payment that would indeed finance the Spanish trip.

The development finally came on stream (as a certain JFK may say) and the fun began. Goldings was a prestigious development of which the Association was duly proud, it had views, energy efficient design and were surprisingly spacious and light.

The Housing Minister cut the ribbon with particular pride, this was his constituency and his broad smile gleamed down on the assembled press and local dignitaries. Although the dwellings had the same facilities all had differing attractions whether it be South facing, closer to the road, further from the road, a corner plot, etc., etc. A deal struck with the utility companies ensured a mix of electric and gas heating. Only one had solid fuel as the heating source, and although a Multi-fuel appliance that could burn both wood or anthracite was installed, it was the least sought after, albeit being in the best location.

Ugliness and selfishness abounded until all but the last property were occupied. The prime plot was the last to be allocated and occupancy was delayed to Harvey's last day for some unknown reason.

Speculation about the lucky residents of No.1 Quarry View were rife, was it a relative of the Housing Minister - surely not. Harvey watched with amusement from his elevated Port-a-Cabin as a belch of smoke from an old Massey Furgeson tractor announced the arrival of Mr Herbert & Miss Maude Crowe. Maude sat up front and acknowledged the despairing ensemble as if she was Queen for a day.

The old tractor and flatbed trailer managed to demolish several new fences and churn up newly seeded lawns as Herbert delivered their worldly goods. The same performance followed as a hundred wooden pallets and the remains of the rotted railway carriage were piled in the front garden in readiness for a Winter six months away. As the goats began eating newly planted flower beds, vegetable patches and the contents of rotary dryers, Harvey padlocked his portable office for the last time.

Part Two

Harvey removed his James Brown cassette as he left the M25, half an hour to go, perfect. He inserted a prerecorded tape of From Our Own Correspondent for the last leg of the journey. Apart from the obligatory hold ups on the M25 it had been a good trip. The weather started to deteriorate behind him and it did not bode well for early June. But you selfishly don't mind when heading for sunnier climes. He took the slip road that announces 'For Gatwick use Both Lanes' and was soon entering the long stay car park at the South Terminal.

After finding a slot, Harvey reversed in and sat back to listen to the end of his tape. He was about to note the aisle and row on the back of his ticket when he noticed with amusement it was 1F, he would remember that one for sure.

The driver of the courtesy bus waited politely for him to cross from his car and load his case before setting off. 10.55 read the clock above the drivers head.

Harvey checked in with the minimum of fuss and went for a pint in the 'pub' in the airside Gatwick Village. It was his first experience of Guinness Extra Cold and it slipped down so well he had another, making him pay a visit to the toilet prior to boarding.

In the toilets, he looked at his reflection in the sparkling mirror and stared deeply into his own eyes while washing his hands - not bad. After drying his hands, he did a twirl to examine his new lightweight linen suit - very nice. He patted the coin pocket in his jacket and felt the little pack of purple pills and the note from Dr Hope that testified their legality. He then inserted two one pound coins into the vending machine and retrieved the slim pack of condoms. He was on holiday H'ray. For some reason he thought of Roy Plummer and felt suddenly mischievous.

On his way to the door, a small Oriental man was standing on the scales struggling with a larger than large hand luggage case. For some reason best known to himself, he wanted the combined weight of himself and the case.

"Please, how much?" Harvey guessed he could not read the scales but he was feeling mischievous"A Fiver?" The little man looked puzzled. "Tenner," said a passerby and winked at Harvey, "Score," said another, "Pony" another joined the gang.

The little man started to understand he was the subject of some kind of auction for what purpose he shuddered to think. When a large man shouted "A Monkey, in yer hand now, good as it gets" the little guy screamed. A passing American said to Harvey "Pearl Harbour was a shithouse trick, you look like a nice guy, go piss on that Jap." With a scream he yelled indignantly "Me Korean, no Jap,

Fluck you all" and the little man tried to flee. "Even worse," said the American, a Veteran of that conflict, and punched him in the eye.

In the disabled toilet, a businessman in a pin-striped suit and pink tie withdrew from the Pakistani cleaner, distracted by the noise outside. "Better go quick, Police come," said the cleaner urgently and relieved. The man adjusted his dress, slightly aggrieved. He had been enjoying himself, admiring his thrust and retreat in the knee high mirror. First bareback since Rock Hudson died too, damn the racket. He bent to comb his hair with the aid of the low mirror and snuck out of the door. "Pain in the ass," he said and aimed a kick at the floored Korean.

Back in the toilet, the Pakistani was thinking the same as he examined his anus in the knee high, not bad, good stuff Vaseline. He spotted something shiny on the floor, a gold money clip, stuffed with notes, which he pocketed - not bad. He pulled up his pants and signed the sheet to say he had cleaned the toilet.

He did up his work smock and retrieved his cap from the CCTV camera. This was positioned over the door to deter double occupation by able-bodied passengers.

He eased himself into the mob. "Make way, official cleaner" he demanded. He helped the Korean to his feet and gave him the Vaseline for his bruise. This was too much for the Korean, he had heard many tales about brown devils and Vaseline, "Fluck you" he screamed and grabbed the Pakistani by the throat as the Police arrived. Both were arrested for affray.

'Getting out of hand' Harvey chuckled and slunk away, Roy would have been proud. He had no idea what this holiday had in store but whatever it was he was going to enjoy himself.

Away in time and space his elderly deceased mother was trying on her sombrero.

Chapter Twenty-Seven

Claudette Golan

Claudette Golan ignored the laughter aimed at her as she took her seat at the front of the coach next to Henri, the driver. "Merde" she exclaimed realising she had squashed her new sunglasses that had been purposely placed where she would sit on them.

For the last half an hour or so she had been searching the hotel, and surrounding area, looking for one of her charges. Only to find him hiding between the seats at the rear of the coach.

Since shunning the advances of the party, Claudette had endured an endless stream of practical jokes at her expense. Coupled with anonymous explicit notes, and drawings, even a semen filled condom had been dropped in her bag. The donor was either related to a whale or had several accomplices.

Determined not to show weakness she glanced fiercely over her shoulder and the noise subsided at her icy stare. She remained calm though fuming inside.

Henri raised an eyebrow in a question to which she nodded. The idling coach inched forward through the crowded streets of Madrid. She squinted against the brightness as she caressed her bent frames back to shape. Ahead lay a long, uncomfortable drive to Seville, for a few nights stay. A visit to the tomb of Christopher Columbus among other activities were arranged. If things carried on like this, she would be tempted to give the late departed explorer some young company.

As Henri stepped on the gas, they put behind them a distraught and broken professor, a hotel in disarray and a hotel manager who would have to face on the return trip, Cie la vie!

Henri eyed his companion and wondered for the hundredth time if she was up to the task in hand. She was very young and the job was arduous with little reward. The wealthy parents of some thirty fifteen - seventeen-year-old youths from various French boarding schools had signed them up for a three-week cultural and recreational tour of Spain. Wishing to extend the school calendar and subsequent absence of their siblings, the parents had had happily loaded them up with designer wear and oodles of filthy lucre before shedding their responsibilities and heading South.

Professor Jean-Pierre Megret, his young assistant Claudette, and driver Henri viewed the youths warily as the clink of bottles sang noisily from their hand luggage as they boarded.

The first hour had gone quite well as Professor Megret explained the tour and expectations over the coach PA system. They drove through the suburbs of Paris and beyond. The youths interacted well with the professor and encouraged him to waffle on as they rolled joints in preparation for the first coach stop.

After besieging the first service area and getting into a fracas with a coach load of Italians, they became a rabble. By the time they reached Bordeaux, for their first stop-over, the lunatics were running the asylum. They were already beyond the control of mild mannered Megret.

Henri was able to instil a little bit of power on the coach, and the girl could stand her ground, but as for Megret! By the fifth night he was a shambling wreck. All his plans of cultural exchange lay in tatters, as the group self-indulged themselves in drink and other substances.

In Madrid, Megret rang the tour office and said he was quitting. The English named, but very French, Peter Ponting asked the other two in turn if they would continue while he found a replacement. After an offer of a bonus they both agreed. A later call to Ponting revealed that he would have a replacement meet them in Seville. He advised that he was working on the bonus with the parents.

Ponting had indeed dispatched several telegrams and made telephone calls to contact numbers demanding an additional 15%, or the immediate return of their loved ones, he was not surprised to find the money rolling in by return.

Money was the main reason Claudette had signed up for the tour so the mention of a bonus made the journey a little more bearable.

They were nearly through week one. In three weeks this would be just be a bad memory, and she would be leaving France to take up a job in a Summer Camp in the USA. If all went well in America, it might lead to something more permanent, but first she had to make the best of this debacle.

The coach grew quiet as the sweet smell of marijuana wafted through the air conditioning, she gave Henri a 'What can I do?' shrug. He responded by lifting his nose and lowering his top lip, in one of those French gestures impossible to translate. Men, or, in this case, young men, she thought, 'Who needs them?"

Claudette was a slim, dark-haired, dark-eyed French beauty with that olive sheen one gains from being Mediterranean. She was part French from her Father and Italian from her Mother. She spoke both languages fluently as she did German and English.

When she spoke English, it was with an accent that would make any man's neck hair rise and his toes curl. On first sight, Henri had described her to himself as joli, but soon corrected this to tres, tres joli, after he witnessed her smile. She had a strongly determined character that belied her meagre twenty years and it was this that would hopefully see her through to her bonus. As the Spanish countryside sped by she reflected on how she had reached this place in her life.

Her father, Pierre Golan, was the first man Claudette disliked because of his appalling treatment of her mother, Maria. All the reasons he had been attracted to her he tried to beat out of her once they were married. He despised her Italian ways, her commitment to God and even her delicate looks with her trim figure.

In truth, Pierre was scared that others would be drawn by Maria's beautiful qualities and he was jealous of these imaginary rivals, to the point of obsession. This obsession had caused her to flee with Claudette, but he always managed to track them down and return them to 'his' home.

Once they had fled to Naples, on to Sorrento, down to Sicily and finally Malta where Pierre caught up with them and administered a cruel public beating. They had been staying with family all through their trip. Unfortunately, the male members were all firm believers that marriage was for life. Whether good or bad and kept Pierre informed of their whereabouts - men!

After the Malta episode, Maria's spirit broke and she never recovered. She died fourteen months later and was buried on New Years Day 1989. It was in Claudette's fourteenth year when a girl really needs her mother.

With Maria gone, Pierre lost all interest in his daughter. He initially tried to enforce a strict regime but when this failed he could not be bothered with her. He withdrew into his own space where he mourned his beloved wife, and prayed for his daughter.

Claudette had developed rapidly, drifted in and out of school and absconded regularly. She had experienced sexual relations freely and at will. She used the term 'experienced', rather than 'enjoyed', as she found all but one un-fulfilling. This one was with an Englishman over twice her age.

He turned out of course to be a shit, who was cheating on his wife. But, he had treated her well, with the respect, she had not known before. When the time came, he let her down gently. The young ones were just arrogant who lost interest once she had given herself. If only she could find another gentle Englishman.

Her last experience with a young Parisienne, had ended badly. As she was packing her meagre possessions, she had spotted the advertisement for both the American camp and this tour. Ironically on the same page - destiny or coincidence? Either way she had applied for and was accepted for both.

Until she had met the others, in Peter Ponting's office, she had been unaware that she was the only female on the trip, pah - Men, who needs them? Surely Mr Right was out there somewhere.

Seville was a nightmare. The promised reinforcements were not forthcoming. All attempts to contact Ponting failed. The hotel had mistaken the booking for the party and had reserved family rooms, believing it to be an all male group.

Despite Claudette's protests, they could only promise her a single room in a day or two. For the first night, she shared with Henri and two of the younger boys. The boys seemed sweet, but they were open to a bit of coercion. When she thought she was alone, they returned and let some older boys in while she was taking a shower. Fortunately, it was nothing more serious than teenage voyeurism but it was not nice.

She then experienced an uncomfortable night listening to Henri snoring and the two boys farting and giggling. Claudette willed herself to stay awake in case they had been talked into more skulduggery. She was sure at one stage they were engaged in communal masturbation, or even a bit of something else she would rather not know about.

On the second day, Henri took a peculiar turn when he could not find his medication, needed to control his blood pressure. One of the boys had recognised them as a relaxant and pocketed them to share out later. By the time Henri had found a friendly Pharmacist, he had declared himself unfit to drive the coach on the planned excursions for the day. In fairness, he looked very pale and was sweating more than the climate warranted, so retired to his room.

This left the boys rampaging through the hotel and local bars, with plenty of money in their pockets. They were soon in possession of some E's and other designer drugs. Claudette tried to take control but was outmanoeuvred as they split into four directions and ran for it.

When her single room had been sorted out she collapsed on the bed and took a well-earned nap. To Hell with them, she hoped they would all be locked up. She was woken after an hour and asked to go to the managers office. He advised that the boys were upsetting the other guests and unless the were reigned in they would all be thrown out.

She urged the manager to ring Ponting and was pleased when he answered. He was all charm and apologised for the missing reinforcement and blamed illness. He had spent the previous day trying to get somebody and asked her 'to hang in there' as there would be help soon, a bit further down the line.

Ponting told her to check her bank account, he had secured funds, and as a goodwill gesture, the agreed bonus had been paid, with more to come. He then smoothed things over with the manager by promising further trips which would be catering for a more sedate client.

She asked Ponting to check Henri's medical declaration, as she was unhappy at how easy he had been incapacitated. She felt a bit disloyal but what if it happened again, or worse still - he could be driving.

Ponting had listened to her concerns and reassured her on every issue. She returned to her room a little more confident than when she had left it earlier.

Claudette moved furniture in front of her door and, when she was happy with the barricade, she took a relaxing shower. She then lay on her bed hoping to resume her nap of earlier. She was dozing to P. P. Arnold on her Sony Walkman when a loud hammering on the door again interrupted her rest, before it began. For a moment, she lost her bearings then realised she was being summoned. She dismantled the obstacle course and man traps to get to the door.

It was Georges, one of her companions from the night before, he was supporting the other youngster, Paul. The latter stank of drink and vomit. A look in his eyes betrayed the presence of something else. "What is the meaning of this?" Claudette demanded. "Am I supposed to babysit you, stupid delinquents, every moment?" "Sorry Claudette, but I did not know what to do, he is very ill" Georges sobbed. "Bring him in and you had better explain yourselves. But beware, if this another infantile attempt at humour I will stroke your testicles with a steak mallet," she growled and meant it.

They lay Paul on her bed, but it might well have been an ants nest as he writhed about snatching at non-existent flying objects. Georges explained they had been in a bar with some of the elder boys. Paul had been holding his own in a drinking contest with Guy, the eldest member of the party and self-elected leader. Fearing that he may be losing out to the younger, Guy had produced two pills, and Paul had grabbed both and gulped them down before anybody could stop him. He followed this with another beer and then began the reaction she was now witnessing. His eyes were bulging and he complained that his jaw was locked.

Claudette took control. "Go to the bar or restaurant, anywhere that you can find sugar, water and lots of ice, go as quick as you can. Go, stop whining go!"

Georges stumbled over Claudette's defences and flew out of the door. She tore at Paul's clothes to loosen them, he was sweltering. She soaked her large bath towel and wrapped it loosely around him, but he was still shaking. She fed him water from the shower, it would probably give him the runs later, if he was lucky. Georges returned with a large ice bucket, mineral water, an ashtray full of sugar sachets and the. Bar Manager in pursuit.

She grabbed the ice and packed it inside the towel, then she forced a bottle of water down the boy. She then mixed sugar with another bottle of water and forced him to drink this also.

She filled a hand towel with the remaining ice, rolled it and placed the sausage in the nape of his neck, she covered his eyes with a wet flannel. Within a few minutes the haunted look of despair left the youth. His breathing and temperature became more normal so she put the earphones from her Walkman in his ears and he rested peacefully. "Bravo" cried the manager, clapping her on the back, as Georges wept with relief.

Claudette had acted on instinct, common sense and a little experience but was happy with the result. Only a tear of relief spoiled the picture of total composure.

The wild racing around by Georges had attracted a small crowd. They were about to applaud when the Bar Manager beckoned silence. The hotel Doctor was admitted as Guy melted into the background. After a couple of hours, Paul was escorted back to his room and Claudette again resumed her siesta.

The next person to wake her was Henri, on the instruction of the hotel management. She reported again to the office of the manager. He advised her that the party was no longer welcome in the establishment. Their unruly behaviour and the episode with Paul were the final straw. His staff were already clearing the rooms, and assembling all their belongings in the reception area, ready for their immediate departure.

Claudette was permitted to telephone ahead to the next hotel in Cadiz. She was advised that there was no problem arriving ahead of schedule and she was pleased she did not have to make up a story in front of the manager. She then had to listen to the manager while he rang Peter Ponting berating her efforts at controlling the group. She knew the group had behaved appallingly, but she has done her best and to hear this supercilious little man ranting on was too much.

She was about to interrupt when he passed her the receiver. Ponting assured her that she still had his confidence and Henri had already spoken well about her efforts. The manager had developed a sickly grin when he believed she was receiving a dressing down. He was very surprised when she emptied his inkwell over his head and left.

She returned to her room to pack. Her anger increased as she noticed the door open and her belongings strewn over her bed. This was not the work of the hotel staff. In her hurry to report to the manager she had again left herself open to these juveniles. She never checked but had the feeling some of her underwear was missing, she shuddered slightly at the thought.

The youths could tell her mood and for once there were no stragglers or practical jokes. Claudette sternly herded them on to the coach for the head count. A quick conversation with Henri convinced her he was rested and able to continue driving. He was more than a little embarrassed by his earlier incapacity, but the journey was for once a pleasant one.

As they entered the sea port of Cadiz Henri advised her that Sir. Francis Drake had torched the harbour in 1587 resulting in many deaths. She couldn't help wishing a certain hotel manager had been present in an earlier life.

Providing they could now stick to the itinerary, a day in Gibraltar would follow Cadiz. Then a whole week in the Costa-del-Sol soaking up the sun, sea and whatever came along. Hopefully, her reinforcement would be waiting at the hotel so she could take a breather. After the week on the coast would be a trip through the Sierra Nevada returning to the Madrid hotel, another bumptious manager, then the last leg home. In two weeks Claudette would be America bound, and not a moment too soon.

Chapter Twenty-Eight

Ruben Del Taurino

Ruben Del Taurino moved his ungainly form on the high stool behind the reception desk of Hotel El Torro.

He viewed the guest list for the coming week. This was almost high season on the Costa del Sol. The El Torro was was as finely placed as any hotel in Fuengirola, but the empty rooms and lack of bookings were a grave concern.

True there were stories of half empty planes landing in Malaga, but this was Espania's finest Costa. Fuengirola was an excellent resort. Ok, long hauls and all inclusive were becoming popular. But, they were more for Winter time. The peseta was good value against the UK and Northern Europe currencies.

Hotel El Torro was a good hotel, the area was a bit dated, but was not subject to major roadworks, or over developed like so many he could mention. There were plenty of people passing, he could see them, but they were not coming in.

Ruben blamed the Delgado brothers, the owners, for refusing to talk to the major tour operators. They stubbornly refused to cater for the masses and wanted to indulge the independent traveler. They could take the full levy without passing on a huge percentage to a faceless foreigner. They would, of course, consider the odd case of overbooking. They prefered overnight stranded tourists, when there were problems with flights. This was at their rates and not those of the operators.

They did not want to kowtow to some slip of a girl in a multi-coloured uniform who would skim profits from trips and excursions, that was their job. This approach may have worked in their Mother's time. You had to follow the trend or end up boarding up, and giving the keys to the bank.

Due to the lack of bookings Ruben, as Assistant Manager, and most of the small number of staff were on double shifts. For little more than the single shift rate. With the few guests they had, the work was demanding. The clients usually wanted more than was on offer. This and the long hours made tempers short and his position the least enviable in the establishment.

His job title, as Assistant Manager, did not actually reflect Ruben's stance for there was no manager for him to assist. The Delgado brothers both assumed the position of General Manager without setting foot inside the place. There was also no Receptionist or Night Porter. Ruben started work at 2:30 in the afternoon. He took his evening meal in the restaurant, when he was able, and remained in post until midnight.

Then he was management and staff of the 116 room hotel until the restaurant manager arrived in the morning. With few breakfasts to manage, he was invariably late and not one of Ruben's favourite people. He had however taken over to allow Ruben back to back days off. There were only messages left and little else to prove he had done anything of worth.

Ruben yawned as he again consulted the list, the residents ledger had not been filled in and he had bits of paper to scrutinise to find out the current position. Mrs Fairbanks and her companion, Miss Riley, were still there, but that was no surprise. The elderly ladies had spent July at the hotel for the last fifteen years.

The formidable Mrs Fairbanks commanded the same recliner every year, every day in the same shaded area, away from the pool. Here she boomed out her thoughts on the downhill progress of the hotel, the weather - that never suited her, fellow guests and the world in general, to her slightly built companion. Miss Riley was never more than a few metres away. She was incredibly resilient, stupid or possibly as deaf as a post.

There were an odd smattering of nationalities, apart from the English ladies. There were a honeymoon couple from Yorkshire. French numbers were up, but they were few. The Italians were down in large numbers from previous years. There a party from Canada with two days left (no,one day - damn that man and his slips of paper), and not much else.

Ruben flipped the page to see what if anything was happening tomorrow. Two sheets of paper freed themselves from the book, one fell to the floor.

Tomorrow, in a few hours, a lone Englishman by the name of Bright was to take the place of the Canadians, and that was it.

Ruben rose and smiled. Behind the high reception desk he marched an exaggerated slow motion goose step. As performed by the English actor and comedian, John Cleese.

Ruben was unusually tall for a Spaniard and, from watching Monty Python's Flying Circus over and over, had practised this walk to perfection. His command of English was excellent, but despite the walk and odd sketch, he understood little of the humour contained in the programme.

When the hotel was patronised by many English in the good days, Ruben would raise regular laughs as he 'Cleese walked' through reception for their benefit. He enjoyed this, which is why he had developed the walk. But for a few years it had been a mystery to him why the English referred to him as 'Basil' or 'Mr Faulty'. In the street, they would shout after him and roar with laughter, like the TV programme, this was beyond his comprehension.

The previous year he had passed a new bar on the strip called Fawlty Towers, in the window, was displayed a small group leaning on a reception desk. Ruben stared at the picture in disbelief, there staring back at him from the photo was his funny walk mentor, John Cleese.

He was fascinated and could not resist going in for a coffee. The English owner took a double take as he entered. In conversation, it transpired that that the owner was a big fan of British comedy called Fawlty Towers, that featured Cleese. He explained, although it was a short-lived series, it was hugely successful and had developed a cult following. Being a big fan, and wishing to attract the English, the owner had named and themed the bar around the programme. He also disclosed that on first sight he had thought, Ruben to be Cleese. He also exagerateded, that Ruben and Cleese were so alike in appearance, that their respective wives would have difficulty telling them apart.

For a time, Ruben took the occasional coffee in the bar (on the house) but the owners finances did not match his dreams and it was now closed, even with Ruben's cameo appearances. Ruben also tired of, and became to resent, the 'Basil' taunts.

Ruben stopped daydreaming. He noted glumly that Mr Bright was a referral from a tour company, as a late booking, and not an independent. He rang the company to confirm the booking and 'yes, we are not charging a single room supplement'.

Ruben decided he would show Mr Bright some Spanish humour and have the first laugh by putting him Room 217. He would, of course move him later. But, if Ruben were to endure the 'Baazeel and Ah Fawlty' routine for two weeks, he would strike first.

Room 217 was on the quarter landing a few steps from Reception. It had previously been a storage cupboard for the cleaner. With a little imagination and even less effort, 217 had been converted to a windowless, cramped cell that a Trappist Monk would find oppressive. The introduction of a bathroom made it possible to touch all the internal walls without moving from the bed. Ruben chuckled aloud "Welcome to Hotel El Torro, Señor Bright".

The telephone rang sharply cutting short Ruben's mirth. He spotted the slip of paper on the floor 'Peter Ponting' it read, followed by a French phone number, damn that man.

He lifted the receiver and stared at the phone and the paper as a voice said "Peter Ponting". "Ah, Señor Ponting, I am in the presence of calling you" Ruben recovered. After a brief conversation, Ruben found another reason to smile. Ponting had explained about his cultural tour being let down by an overbooking and Hotel El Torro had been highly recommended as an alternative.

Ponting explained that he had taken it upon himself to deal with the matter rather than let the other hotel take the credit and no doubt a fee. If Ruben could assist with this current dilemma, Ponting would ensure that El Torro would get first refusal on all future tours.

Ruben took all the details and promised to call as soon as he could match the requirements to the availability of rooms (at such a busy period) with the General Manager. What he really wanted was to check that the promised method of payment was good and would be honoured, that was not possible at this hour.

Ruben permitted his smile to broaden to a broad grin. Of course the rooms were available, he went over the guest list again in his mind. With the small group of Canadiens leaving and the lone Englishman arriving there would be little else for the staff to do over the next three days until the party 'of well-connected students' arrived.

Once he had confirmed the credit arrangements, he would call Ponting and insist on a 50% through a Western Union transfer as deposit for the rooms. He would also request a fax list of the party. He would scan this list personally for any familiar names that he could impress.

He closed the main doors and fitted a broken pool cue behind the large glass-pad handles securing them shut. The Delgado brothers would not be happy with this practice because they insisted that the doors should always remain open and the staff ready to serve. Whatever the time of day or night. Closed doors never sold anything. Delayed flights, etc. could produce customers at any time - fuck them, let them phone, thought Ruben. He settled in a large chair by the door.

30 well-connected French tourists, two cultural guides and a driver. 33 persons for one week on premium rates. Plus a little extra for a secure berth for the coach, not too bad for one telephone call in the middle of the night. This could be fortuitous for the Hotel El Torro and Ruben Del Taurino personally. With this happy thought whirling around his head he fell peacefully asleep.

Life had not always been so peaceful for Ruben. He was born in July 1937, in the centre of General Franco's Nationalist-held Madrid. He had the great misfortune to be the son of Niño, a staunch and active supporter of the Republican Government of Manual Anzana. Niño led many an attack on the forces of Franco during the Civil War and was a principal stay of the Republican movement. Niño organised bands of the International Brigade into some semblance of a fighting unit, that gnawed and niggled away at the fascists.

Each action was followed by reprisals of horrific proportions. This made Niño indirectly responsible for more deaths of his own side than the enemy, but who counts such things - only Historians. After one such bloody reprisal, Ruben was born and Niño thought it best to get his wife and son out of the city. They could prove a weakness to him.

Bloody reprisals meant lots of bodies and this one was no exception. Niño had his men collect a few corpses and made a comfortable framework of his ex-comrades on a handcart, in which he nestled his family. A net was placed over the bodies and rotting limbs, from an earlier fracas, were threaded into the netting. It was assumed, correctly, the cart would attract only the most cursory of examinations by the Nationalists. This was a tried and tested method Niño used to move weapons and significant personnel around the city, and never failed.

After the city cart ride, the family were escorted via a network of sympathisers to the village of Mijas, in the hills above the small fishing village of Fuengirola. Safely away from the action. Escorts had changed frequently and now Mother and Son where all but anonymous as they settled and integrated into the community.

Politics was rarely raised and what harm could a refugee and her young son be? They survived the aftermath of the war when many did not. Some suffered just for being remotely connected to sympathisers, Heaven knows what would have been their fate if their real identity had been known. They starved along with their neighbours but, as time slipped by, the fishing began again and from then things slowly improved.

Alas not for Niño. Once his family were settled, he led an attack on Ronda. His contingent of International Brigade volunteers and a company of Russians were greatly outnumbered and overwhelmed.

The makeshift army of actors and idealists were all foreign. They were offered amnesty and repatriation if they could identify Niño, who was skulking in their midst. Realising he would be taken even if they did not give him away Niño took action. He jumped onto the parapet of the town bridge and dived to the rocks below, which is what the Nationalists were going to do anyway - ah well.

The Russians slunk back to their submarine, the ragtag band of foreigners drifted home to glory, and prestigious careers as authors or in the Luvvy Industry, where they played heroes. The bridge that took so many lives now is a familiar backdrop to holiday snaps - Niño who?

Towards the end of Franco's life, Spain was poor and sought the foreign currency tourism would bring. Slowly things began to pick up on the Costas. Although British tourists were only permitted, by the Wilson government, to take £50 on holiday it still bought a lot in Spain. Ruben tired of tilling the dusty land and his hoe joined the pile, as he embarked on a career of catering for the interlopers. At first established hotels benefited, but younger tourists wanted sun, sea, sex and sangria in no particular order.

Newer plusher hotels sprang up along the Costas, the tourist flocked to them and Ruben was waiting. He was first a Bell Boy/Lift Hop. He became very adept at scrounging or stealing unopened packs of Benson & Hedges, Dunhill and other brands of cigarettes from the punters on their arrival. After a few days, when their duty frees had gone and the tourists had choked on local fags, Ruben would sell them back their cigarettes.

He advanced through the ranks and became an excellent all-rounder whether it be a bar, restaurant, reception or whatever. He never stopped learning and gaining experience.

Eventually, Señora Delgado beckoned and he accepted. There was no job description but Hotel El Torro wanted him and he obliged.

Eventually by the late 1980's the area bristled with hotels, apartments and villas. Timeshare became a buzz word. As the area reached a point, between acceptability and saturation, most of the developers moved on. Many British settled, some less desirables, and there were odd shootings to settle old scores.

Famously, Ronnie Knight attracted the occasional tired journalist, friends and curious tourists to his RK Club before he was lulled back to warm beer and warmer porridge.

Small brothels had existed for many years but were low profile, they attracted odd tourists but not sex tourists. They were generally frequented by locals and 'in the know' ex-pats. These were service providers, offering wholesome satisfaction, to those seeking a little excitement.

Manolito Soler's establishment was one and was situated close to Hotel El Torro. Enquiring guests were duly advised, some staff were also clients.

Ruben slept well through his second shift, dreaming of a business relationship with his prestigious French tour operator.

He had barely removed the cue from the front door when the 6 am - 10 pm crew arrived. Juan, the Bell Boy cum dogsbody, eyed Ruben's red eyes and unkept hair with suspicion. If he were able to sleep while on duty, then it would only be fair for the boy to take a siesta later.

Juan felt the need to make up for an unscheduled stop at Mani Soler's on the way home and thought that 217 would do nicely.

Ruben briefed them on his overnight dealings and received a round of applause for his efforts, Juan yawned, that may explain the unkept look, but he had his doubts.

Chapter Twenty-Nine

The plane dipped to the left and Harvey caught his first glimpse of the fabulous blue Mediterranean below, he had arrived. The chatter that had subsided over the last hour picked up again. The passengers eagerly anticipated their next seven, ten or fourteen days.

All but one craned their necks to take in the views over the heads of those in window seats. Ellen screwed up her face and moaned as she sank her right-hand fingernails into the armrest and gripped Harvey's arm in a vice like a grip with her left.

Not for the first time Harvey recoiled with pain, he watched Ellen's knuckles turn white. Increased pinging off the aircraft pinging system, and a rumbling beneath, signified that the landing was imminent and the ground came closer.

Harvey missed an announcement because his ears had reached a stage of nearly popping but not quite, but he could hear the increase in engine noise. It took several hard sucks on his boiled sweet before a loud crack in his left then right ear restored his hearing to semi-normal. At the slight bump as the plane touched down, Ellen exhaled in relief then let out a scream causing her sweet to fall from her open mouth.

Harvey had taken his window seat at Gatwick and was joined almost immediately by Ellen and her granddaughter, Janine, who was about eight or nine.

He would not have taken Ellen for anything more than the child's mother but the lineage was volunteered in initial salutations, as Ellen was babbling on about everything and nothing in particular.

The youngster was fidgeting and trying to look through the window, Harvey being Harvey suggested she take his seat, and he would swap with Ellen in the aisle position. Janine jumped at the offer and nearly ended up on Harvey's lap as she scrambled eagerly to take her place. Ellen flatly refused to vacate her seat stating that she was petrified of flying and only agreed to board if guaranteed an aisle seat. Harvey took the inferior, middle position between the two.

His mischievousness was still lingering as Harvey said he didn't mind flying, but disliked crashing. One look at her face and the tears that ensued made him realise Ellen was deadly serious, Janine giggled.

Ellen began whimpering and gripping his arm as the doors closed. As the began to taxi, and were being shown the safety drill, she began to hyperventilate, surely you wouldn't fly if you were this scared.

Here was an attractive, worldly woman in tight jeans, denim waistcoat and very little else, displaying all the tendencies of a child being left at the school gate for the first time. She must love Janine to put herself through the trauma.

The youngster was a delight as she chattered away. Their destination was an 'Uncle's' Timeshare in "Belly Mandarin". The Hostess presented her with a complimentary fun bag. She and Harvey were then engaged in puzzles, colouring, joining dot to dots and discovering beach items in a large picture. They were told there were twenty, but they could only find seventeen until Harvey cheated. He peered through the gap in the seats at the efforts of a boy in front.

The bit of naughtiness made Janine giggle again, happy with the full tally, she let Harvey colour on his own for a while. Being right handed put Harvey at a slight disadvantage with the colouring as Ellen kept a tight grip on his arm.

"Ladies, Gentlemen and children. Welcome to Malaga, where your local time is five minutes to five. Due to a favourable tail wind we have arrived ahead of schedule" a small cheer/ "On behalf of Captain Underhill and the crew I would like to thank you for flying........"

With a numb arm and the plane on terra firma, Janine and Ellen were reunited as everybody shuffled to the front and rear doors. Ellen was back in control and waved fair well as they climbed aboard different doors to the waiting bus. They were reunited briefly while waiting for the luggage console to chug into action. Their bags were first off. Harvey's was last, he had missed it first time round, as Janine gave him a hug goodbye. He passed through customs and passport control and looked for his tour operator.

"Harvey, Harvey, I don't believe it," a young man exclaimed. "Nobody said you were coming, it's me Enzo" "Enzo, well blow me, and all grown up too"

Harvey recognised the son and heir of Hillstreet Blues. "Oh sorry Saz, this is Harvey, Harvey this is Saz, my girlfriend - she's English too." "Hello Saz, I guess you are Sarah, yes? Pleased to meet you." "Harvey's the person who.." "Saved your Grandfather's life. Sorry Harvey, I've heard that story a hundred times. Yes it is Sarah but you know how it is with us young ones" she laughed. "Harvey really pleased to meet you, but I have to check in, I'm probably jumping on the big bird you just departed." "Blighmy, you pushing it," said Harvey. "No worries mate, she's one of them, in the trade, won't take her long to get through, wait here mate I've got the van outside." "I'd like to but..."

"Mr Bright?" interrupted a slip of a girl in a multicoloured polyester uniform, checking his luggage label as she addressed him. "Follow me we are waiting, you are the last, expect some boos as you board." Harvey shrugged and picked up his case.

Enzo looked at the label, "El Torro, don't know that one, but it can't be far from us if it's Fuengirola. Come and see us, please. But make it today if you want to catch Dad, he is going to Italy tomorrow I think, Granpa's not so good, cheers mate, happy to see you."

"MR BRIGHT, Come!" Miss Polyester was creating static in her knickers. "Yes of course I'll come, sorry about Enzo, Enzo". Harvey gave the boy a hug and followed Miss P. "Bye Saz, have a good one" Bye she called, catch you next week maybe"

"Harvey, don't forget, keep Fuengirola to your back and the sea to your right and you'll find us" the boy shouted as Harvey prepared to be booed. He need not have worried, the passengers dotted around the coach accepted his raised eyebrows as an apology.

A group of Welsh lads at the back broke off singing a dirty ditty to wave their cans of beer at him and cheer. "Hey, Hugh Grant, do you want a beer boyo?" Harvey smiled at the compliment, he could probably give the actor twenty years - must be the suit. He declined with a wave and took his seat. The lads returned to their dirty ditty, which they completed in perfect harmony.

The coach PA system crackled, followed by an annoying thump, thump, woosh, woosh, as Miss P prepared to address the nation, or the captured audience on the coach.

"Well, Hello" she bellowed, "Hullo" came a muted response. "I can't hear you, Hello..." The response was a bit louder. "Well, that will have to do I suppose. Welcome everybody, my name is Lyndsey, I am your transfer rep and your driver is Abel, wave, Abel." Abel waved like a trained seal and moved the coach out of the bay.

"Now Mr Bright has joined us" "Don't be nasty" shouted one of the lads. She continued "..Abel will be dropping you off at your hotels in the following order ....."

The lads got bored and started to sing. Harvey managed to glean that his hotel was after the Fuengirola Park, and before the El Puerto. But, he missed the name of his rep, who he 'MUST' meet at the welcome meeting in the morning. A good excuse for being absent.

Judging by the cheer from the rear, the lads were staying at Fuengirola Park, no cheer greeted the calling of El Torro.

As the coach cut through the hills, Lyndsey droned on about the joys of being in Spain. All the tours that should be enjoyed, booked through your rep, of course, but most of her eulogy was lost on nearly everybody.

She upped her tempo a little and spoke "on a personal note" that she ran a dog refuge for sick and unwanted doggy woggies with her boyfriend, which received a spontaneous round of applause. One of the Welsh lads whipped off his cap and went round the coach collecting."Oh, you shouldn't" Lyndsey fawned, happy that her "on a personal note" had worked again.

After a few stops to disgorge passengers, they pulled up at a place Harvey recognised. The Welsh lads collected their belongings and disembarked, singing, belching, shaking hands and crushing beer cans in their wake. Harvey was half tempted to see if he could change to the Fuengirola Park but reasoned that even if the lads wanted him to tag along he would have difficulty maintaining their pace for fourteen days.

"Fancy a shag later" the lad who had organised the collection enquired of Lyndsey, she bristled but replied "I may come for a drink later, have your passports ready, please."

Abel was busy unloading suitcases, the coach throbbed idly as the lads assembled in the dust alongside the manically busy road. Lyndsey grabbed the arm of one lad who nearly stepped in front of a speeding car. "Careful, this is not Wales," she cautioned. She then led the small procession to the hotel. After a few minutes, she emerged. Collection Boy followed her and gave her a lingering kiss. Harvey began to doubt the boyfriend and thought the nearest she got to a sick or unwanted doggy woggy was probably as Abel sped past them on the coach.

Harvey got his bearings, ahead on the hill was a large black replica of a fighting bull. He had no features and was, therefore, watching the road from whatever angle he was approached. Harvey knew it was no distance to the seafront and Hillstreet. He felt a tinge of excitement as he spotted the underpass that led to the beach, and his hotel was next. He spotted Whispers nightclub, but it appeared to shut down, and he wondered if the drains had finally won their battle of domination.

Lyndsey returned and Abel left the hotel in a cloud of dust and joined the main highway, that claims many lives and doggy woggy's each year. They passed apartments Harvey recognised, the raised station, the market, the statue and the area he knew. All disappeared in the distance. He was a bit disappointed, he had hoped to be closer to The Hill.

Maybe he would attend the Welcome Meeting after all, if only to get his bearing. Lost in thought he failed to notice Abel had pulled into a side road. Ahead was the El Puerto all brightly lit and magnificent.

Harvey watched the traffic lights go through their sequence twice before he realised he was being addressed, "Mr Bright, do come on" Lyndsey squalled into the microphone. He spotted Abel in the road impatiently waving his suitcase at him. Harvey rose and bade the remaining passengers farewell and a good holiday. He received no response, miserable shits.

Abel thrust his case at him with gusto as he disembarked. Harvey pocketed the folded note he had intended as a tip and followed Lyndsey - fuck him. He wondered where the El Torro could be hiding but was pleasantly surprised as she turned sharp left and led him into the hotel foyer.

The foyer was spotless, airy and furnished with deep armchairs. The chap behind the desk had a familiar ring to him too, but he could not quite place it. Harvey heard Lyndsey whisper to Ruben, "Bit of a problem this one" unnecessarily indicating Harvey with a flick of her head.

She took his passport and went through the formality of handing it to Ruben, he gave it a cursory glance, placed it on a ledger and handed him a registration card. "Well that's me done Mr Bright, have a really nice holiday," she said falsely. "Thank you for all your help" Harvey replied sarcastically. "Good luck with the doggy woggys' and the sheep shaggers", she left without further comment. "I had better watch him," thought Ruben, "bloody tour operators".

Harvey completed the registration card, it was a simple name and address job, and handed it to Ruben who placed it with his passport and gave him the key.

"Muchas Gracias, I am er sorry, los soleto, I don't speak your language, well only badly" Harvey stumbled. "Señor you do not even speak my language badly, but thank you for trying" Ruben replied with a smile. "Now that you have got that out of the way you may return to your native tongue for the duration of your stay. English is widely spoken in the area and all my staff speak it well, but if you find someone who does not, we will have them a shot."

Harvey looked up, from his key sharply, and saw a stiff upper lip smile that showed off Ruben's front teeth. This, following the snap delivery and facial contortions were remarkably familiar, why? Harvey returned the smile. "A tip Señor, if somebody does not understand you, try speaking a little slower, don't talk in a voice unnatural to you, don't wave your arms about or shout. Pointing helps, if you point with a bank note you will find that you are speaking perfect Spanish" he laughed at his own joke.

"Thank you, do you provide a security box?" "Regrettably nowadays it is advisable, equally unfortunately there is a 2000 peseta deposit. All but 400 will be returned on the safe return of the key."

Harvey coughed up and Ruben gave him a solid brass key, "You will find the box in your wardrobe Mr Bright, enjoy your stay." Ruben handed over a receipt for the deposit.

Juan stepped forward, took the key from Harvey's hand and picked up his luggage. He eyed the key incredulously, "Moment Señor." He put the bags at Harvey's feet and spoke rapidly in Spanish to Ruben.

Ruben walked stork like towards them, began his response and reached for the key. Juan interrupted Ruben's flow with the single word "Que?" Ruben was about to continue when Harvey erupted, "That's it, of course, Basil Fawlty, Mr Fawlty" he roared, his eyes brimming with mirth. Ruben retracted his arm and spoke sharply to Juan, who picked up the bags again and said "Please Señor, this way."

The conversation in Spanish had gone along the lines of.....

Juan, "What is this? We are nowhere near full, 217 is a shithole, even with your new deal, we do not need to resort to 217." Ruben had replied, "OK, you're right, the rep said to watch him, and you can't get closer than 217. But he seems ok, and quite smart, give me the key and I'll change it." "Que?" "The key, give it to me..." Harvey had then erupted. Ruben stopped reaching for the key, "See, trouble, I want to watch him. If he learns some manners we can move him, now go!" 'Let's see how he likes the joke' thought, Ruben.

Juan moved off with Harvey in close pursuit, wondering what the quickfire exchange had been about. Four steps up from the foyer he collided with Juan's stationary back and bounced two steps back.

'Drunk' thought Ruben. Harvey looked up to see Juan step inside a hole in the wall and followed curiously. He blinked in the gloom, this must have been the reason for the conversation. His room was not ready and they were storing his luggage in the interim. No matter, it was early evening, not sure why they bothered.

Juan had put the baggage on the floor and with difficulty shuffled to the end of the bed. The room was stifling after being shut up. He opened the full sized drapes and revealed a small opening light window just below the ceiling. The gloom decreased by an ion.

Juan stood on the bed and pulled the ring catch on the window and lowered it a few degrees towards him. The smallest of breezes puffed at his wispy hair.

Harvey watched with growing concern. Juan returned to the floor and sidled back to Harvey. He reached behind him and flicked on the light switch. As Harvey looked around astonished, Juan pocketed his tobacco tin ashtray he had used during his siesta. He then pushed the bed noisily towards the end wall with the window and pulled the headboard towards himself and Harvey at an angle. Squeezing behind the headboard Juan pushed a sliding door to reveal a chest of drawers with a small safe on top and a hanging rail above. Sliding the door, and the one it was covering, back the other way revealed another hanging rail and a free standing shoe rack. With difficulty, he reached inside and retrieved a remote control handset.

Reinstating the bed, he backed a stunned Harvey into another hole in the wall behind him and flicked a switch to illuminate space. A bath was crammed along most of the wall in front with very little of its enamel surface intact. A wash basin fitted on the bedroom side wall overhung the bath. To reach the toilet and bidet, the cistern of which also overhung the tub, you had to step into the bath and out the other end. It looked as if it all had been dumped in readiness for collection but a clanking, vibrating extractor fan announced it all as a functional bathroom.

Juan stood with one foot strategically placed between Harvey's stance and the other one nearly on the landing. He began demonstrating the TV set, that was precariously perched above the door. The screen was probably only visible from the bidet.

For the second time in half an hour, a crisp banknote slipped back into Harvey's pocket. "This, err, this place, this is my room is it? The bed is not even ready. It looks like somebody just crawled out of it" "Si Señor, your room" Juan replied, silently cursing Ruben, then added cheerily "you like it yes?" "No, do you?" "Si Señor, very much" "Then you are fucking welcome to it." Harvey fumed, grabbing his wallet he stormed from the room and fell onto the small quarter landing.

Ruben was waiting with another room key in the enclosed palm of his hand, he had rethought his joke. As Harvey approached, a large grin spread across Ruben's face. "Is everything alright Señor?" he asked politely. "No it fucking is not alright" Harvey replied, rudely, and continued with more venom than was really necessary, "and take that grin off your face, you great lolloping freak. That room was probably last used in the Inquisition you bastard and now you give it to me, this is war - remember the Armada!"

Ruben let the key and his smile drop at the same time as he fumed inside.'Great lolloping freak, bastard, war, Armada' he thought as he took great lolloping exaggerated steps behind his counter. "We'll see about that Señor," he said to Harvey's retreating back. "I don't think an Armada will be necessary" but his retorts were unneeded - Señor Bright had left the building.

Harvey stepped into the street and considered his position. The hotel was pleasant enough and the manager, or whoever Fawlty was, had seemed amicable at first but why that appalling room? It was not in keeping with the facade of the hotel and surely the tour operator viewed such basics as the rooms before signing up these places. He would have to attend that blasted Welcome Party tomorrow and either sort it out or request a change, maybe the Fuengirola Park after all.

He decided to put it behind him for now, he was on a well-deserved break, he was not going to have it spoiled my some mix up over accommodation.

'Maybe it was retribution for the Korean at the airport' he thought, and his mood lightened as he thought back to the toilet incident, 'poor bloke - ha ha.' His outburst at the hotel had been uncharacteristic and he considered going back and apologising to 'Fawlty' but thinking of the room again he decided to let him stew, fuck him with knobs on.

Harvey returned to the traffic lights, where miserable Abel had dropped him off, and probably started his bad mood. He headed towards the sea and was pleased to find the London Underground club. He could not rightly remember the distance to Hill Street but remembered to keep the sea to his right and proceeded down the Paseo, dodging the ongoing repairs to the pavement.

The El Puerto loomed large and new. He wondered if it was listed with his operator, whatever it lacked in history and big comfy chairs, the rooms had to be better than his cell.

He walked at a leisurely pace enjoying the sea breeze and started to unwind from his travails of the day. The sun had set quickly and he passed a procession of late bathers as they made their way home to change.

The jet black 'Lookey Lookey' men in their African robes were still trying to tempt the retreating holidaymakers with their 'excellent' 'genuine' and 'designer' products. All guaranteed of course. Not for them a quick shower and a night on the town. They merely swapped tramping the beaches for the streets and bars, until the last holidaymakers had retired. They had the same routine all day, every day, despite being hassled by the Police, chased by Bar Tenders and traumatised by the children of the tourists. At the end of their long day, they would huddle together and share a joint or two before sleeping under the stars.

Harvey marvelled at their good humour as his returned. "Lookey, very good, Cartier - genuine, look". The large smiling man accosted Harvey. "Sorry, no dosh" he replied. Encouraged by the exchange the African approached, he examined Harvey's paler than pale complexion. "Ha ha, so white, not even pink yet, must be first night right?" Harvey nodded. "Don't worry Brother, I got plenty of time to wear you down."

They both laughed as he waved Harvey on and he promptly fell over a crouching Moroccan, who tried to sell him a carpet before he could get up. He could hear the large African laughing as he extricated himself from this latest encounter and crossed the road. He was not so vulnerable here as he mixed with promenaders looking for the best deal for their evening meal.

Harvey realised he was somewhat hungry, the plane meal was long forgotten, but he wanted to get to Hill Street, it must be close now. He also had no loose change yet and wanted to ring home to check in before it got much later. He had hoped to do this from the hotel - some chance!

Harvey had no idea of the time. He had only brought a small travel alarm clock with him and this was resting in his luggage. The jovial African would have spotted the lack of a timepiece and marked him down as a customer.

To his right Harvey heard a train breaking overhead, he quickened his pace, not far now. He crossed the wide road that incorporated the taxi rank, familiar but different. He kept walking.

"Harvey, where have you been you old bastard?" He looked up and saw Marco - a slightly portlier Marco, hanging out of a window of what must be an upward extension of his emporium. "Marco, I'm so glad to see you, thought I was lost" he called back. "Now get down here and get me a San Miguel." "Watch this." With no more ado, Marco squeezed through the opening and scrambled down a large pipe to the ground. "At your service," he said as they embraced.

Hill Street Blues had undergone quite a few changes since Harvey's previous visit. Some were planned, like, staff living quarters cum hostel above, and moving the bar back into Enzo's old living quarters. This increased the dining area and provided room for a pool table. If you didn't, mind taking some shots from the pavement.

The demolition of the glass panels under the awning, that had served as extra space and dividers between establishments, had been at the hands of the Police. For some reason, after many years of existence, the local law enforcers suddenly took exception to these temporary structures encroaching on the Paseo. They had warned all the owners they should be removed.

This being Spain, all the bar owners adopted the Manyana approach. To their cost.

One night a Police Land Rover mounted the paved area and drove along the front of the bars, demolishing all in its wake. The owners got the message.

Although they still continued to use the area. Nobody was foolish enough to put anything but plastic furniture, or the odd metre of pool table, in front of their legally owned bit of Spain. This was probably what had thrown Harvey into thinking he had been off course, prior to hearing the train.

Harvey drained his beer quickly and phoned home. All was ok their end and he assured them his hotel was beautiful and he had met up with friends already. He gave the number of Hill Street, just in case.

Amber had promised not to ring and he did the same, but it was good to have a contact number, he went back to a new beer, happy.

Over their beer, Marco cited the removal of the panels as yet another cross to bear in the struggle bar owners had to contend with."Diversification is the name of the game now my friend." "I thought you had that one summed up by cornering the market in leather jackets and ketchup" they laughed and reminisced over roast lamb, served by the boys.

Mario and Marco Jnr barely knew Harvey but were well versed in his 'saving Enzo Snr from a rampaging hoard'. He was treated with much respect.

Marco said Roy had told them of his loss, they had tried to contact him but had been told that he needed time. Moving quickly on Marco said "And talking of Roy, have you heard from him lately?" Harvey shook his head. Marco explained that he was living with a semi-retired Page Three Girl, who was half his age and twice as fiery.

Their relationship was one of turbulence, they were often bruised through spite or passion. or both at the same time. When they were out it would inevitably end with one or the other getting jealous and many a good evening ended badly. Harvey was disappointed as he would have loved to meet up with Roy, but it didn't sound like a good idea at present. Maybe when he had chilled a bit.

Harvey explained his arrival at the Hotel El Torro. "Funny indeed, what you learn in school doesn't prepare you for real life," he bemoaned. "Not when ye mention the Armada and the Inquisition you daft bastard" Marco laughed.

"Don't worry, with things as they are he would be stupid to upset a guest, especially an esteemed one like you. I can send Enzo over to have a word if you like, smooth things over..." "Enzo will do what?" the lad enquired, as he approached. They filled him in, "I don't mind, may get a sale out of it?" "Don't ask, I'll tell you later" Marco advised Harvey, but it was agreed that he would fight his own fight.

Marco' wife, Mollie, had returned home some time ago to nurse her aged mother. Although the old lady had since died, and Marco had gone to the funeral, she had not returned with him. When they spoke on the phone it was amicable, but neither mentioned the time that had elapsed, or when she would return.

They had never had a cross word and he hoped she would come back when she was good and ready, meanwhile he was here and she was there. "Let's face it, Harvey. Once she saw them rolling hills again that was it. There's not a lot of greenery around her my friend."

"She was getting a wee bit homesick Harvey." Enzo explained. "Now the boys are older why not take a break? You don't mind do ye, Dad?" He enquired, as he cleared the table. "Ha ha, no son, the life of Reilly me aye?"

They had done the meal justice and followed on with the beer as they relaxed on the forbidden territory at the front of the bar. Enzo explained that Saz was his girlfriend of some standing. She would be back in a few days to help out while Marco was in Italy.

He told Harvey that she was a full-time rep and worked for the company all year round, even Christmas Day. This gave her a few privileges and this two-week break early season was one of them. He also let on that she knew Lyndsey, who was known for 'being a bit above herself, "Not just me then?" Harvey was relieved to know.

"Yes, sorry I have to go my friend but the old warhorse is a wee bit poorly, but we have two - three days to catch ...."

"I thought you were going tomorrow," Enzo said accusingly.

"No, you must be mistaken..."

"Mistaken be fucked, why am I working tonight then?"

"Harvey's here ..."

"But you did nay know 'till today did ya? Not until I came back from the airport, and you lined me up for this last week. You couldn't have known could ya? Unless Harvey had told you and he did nay, did he?"

They both looked at Harvey, who was diplomatically draining his glass. He was, therefore, unable to speak and avoided eye contact. "No, but you're here now so Harvey and I can go fishing tonight. Your brothers are lolling about in the kitchen. Lenny has gone for Neta and they are due anytime. The same routine tomorrow so you won't miss me, I have to entertain our guest, it's expected" Marco stifled all future complaint with his incorrigible grin. "It would have been nice..." Enzo broke off.

The arrival of a battered motorbike of unknown origin drowned out any further conversation as it pulled up level with their table. It stopped speedway style amidst a cloud of dust and exhaust gases.

Not only was the bike unusual, but it carried an unlikely duo. The rider was a pretty blonde girl who Harvey guessed was around five feet nothing tall. She was beautifully packaged and could barely see over the raised handlebars. She was dressed in a baggy safari suit that she had tied up to expose her brown tummy. If the shorts had been cut any shorter - well enough said. Her passenger was much taller, maybe a foot. She was slim, fair - rather than blonde and equally beautiful. She sat high on the raised pillion literally dwarfing her rider. She was dressed in a classic boob tube and mini skirt combo, in electric blue, and had legs to leave home for.

They were Lenny and Neta, Marco's bar staff. As Neta dismounted, Lenny battled with the bike. She finally killed the engine and got it on its' stand.

Some teenage lads who had been playing pool, quietly at the side of Harvey, were now hovering behind him and drooling. They had only been staying in the hostel a couple of days but knew that the sound of that bike heralded the entrance of the girls. Only a fool would want to miss Neta dismounting.

As Neta stood waiting for Lenny she absentmindedly played with her chewing gum. She pushed it slowly to the back of her mouth with her middle finger, down to the knuckle. As if she had just realised she was being watched she removed her finger slowly and said "Sorry, only dreaming." The lads flushed and flew back to the pool table, not that they would be able to take a pool stance until their shorts returned to normal.

"Neta, if them lads starch my sheets tonight you are on laundry tomorrow" Marco chuckled. "Watch these two mate, if they had a band 'The Fornication Sisters' would be a good name for them." "Dad, they're not that bad" Enzo complained.

The girls stepped over and Harvey stood, the others remained seated, but he felt no embarrassment, it was something he did naturally.

"My, a gentleman Len, pleased to meet you," purred Neta. She was more stunning close-up and could have been a supermodel with little effort, she even had the walk. "Put your talons away Net, it's my turn, this one is mine." "That boy didn't count" Neta snarled indignantly. "As I was saying, Hello my name is Lenny, well Lenita actually or even Len. The tall, gorgeous one is Neta or Net..." "Well, it is Anetta actually but my mother couldn't spell"

Harvey wondered if the introductions would ever end. "Anyway, as I was saying, shut it Net. She is the tall one but why go for long when you can have a quick short eh?" This one was no super model, more Barbara Windsor or even Marilyn Monroe. The voice was Manchester/Lancashire thrown, and she was certainly no less attractive.

"Now girls behave," said Marco rising, he turned to Harvey, "You'll have to forgive them mate. I'd like to say they are not always like this but they are. I also regret that what I'm going to say next will make them worse. Girls, I'd like you to meet our old family friend and true mate Harvey, Harvey this Lenny and Neta ..."

"No, not Hero Harvey" Lenny squealed. "We hoped you existed but started to think Enzo had made you up. Leave him Net or I will kill you." She gave the bottom 75% of Harvey a big hug.

"Well, worth dying for" Neta replied in a slight accent. Taking over the top half of Harvey she planted a big kiss on his cheek. "We've loved you since we first heard of you. Lenny has a boyfriend, but I don't, I don't like little boys." One of the pool players miscued. "Bitch," said Lenny.

"You're very Hugh Grant, as I imagined, I love Hugh Grant" Lenny continued, Harvey felt a twinge, "Well you'd be better off with Danny Devito" snarled Neta. "Dutch Dragon" retorted Lenny, "Manchester Midget" put in Neta. "Bitch," they said in unison.

"Bloody Hell, behave. Harvey is here for two weeks so you don't have to fight over him tonight. I'm sure you will both have the chance to cross him off your list. Now go and get us some drinks and bring one for yourselves. BUT, keep an eye on the bar, Enzo has a strop on." Marco teased. He got a sharp look from Enzo. "I'd like to get you out of this bear pit soon Harvey my friend, while you are still in one piece."

Harvey looked a combination of flattered, quizzical, flustered and embarrassed all at once. He also thought he was getting telepathic messages from the little pills in his coin pocket. Marco went to speak, but Enzo said "I'll give him the short version Dad."

It transpired that the girls turned up a couple of years ago looking for digs and a place to work. They were penniless, document less and desperate. They look much younger than their twenty-four years now, and then looked a lot younger - jail bait. Nobody would touch them regarding employment, they stood out from the crowd. Anybody taking them on would have serious trouble with the authorities. If they were not discovered by spot checks jealous bartenders would ensure they would be bubbled, Marco agreed he would have done that too.

They disappeared as quick as they came but in truth Enzo Snr had taken them under his wing. He had fed them, let them live secretly in his quarters (how nobody knew) and sorted out their papers. By the time Marco discovered them he was furious, but had inherited a loyal, legal, bar team who drew customers like flies.

They respected Enzo more than anything in their lives. Enzo, of course, had told them how Harvey had saved his life and, they realised, if he hadn't been so bold nobody would have saved theirs. They would have probably ended up in Mani Soler's brothel, "So you are top of their list" he concluded.

"But I did nothing, I was pissed and ..." Marco put his hand on Harvey's arm, "Harvey my friend, nobody knows what could have happened that night. My Father would not have backed down. You were there and the right man for the occasion, nobody got hurt. My family, including those two beauties, owe you a debt of gratitude, enough said. I don't want you going all shy when we show our feelings, and don't worry I will not let them eat you alive." "Ow" Harvey feigned disappointment, well mostly feigned. "And the list". "Haha, you old dog, they have a list of people - well let's say it is their Lay List, and I guess you are on the top, maybe under Hugh Grant..." "But above Danny Devito...." they chuckled as the girls came back.

They sat either side of Harvey, the chat was general and enjoyable with plenty of innuendoes. The bar got busy so did the girls and eventually Enzo.

Marco disappeared briefly and returned with a pair of jeans and an old bomber jacket. He yelled something to Enzo and was thrown a T-shirt bearing the Hill Street Blues logo, and a picture of the girls on the front.

"There you go my friend, fishing gear, nip upstairs and change, the door is open, bring your clothes back down. You will need them later. I'll shout up one more before we hit the high seas." "Fishing, why?" Harvey enquired. "Diversification my friend, diversification."

Chapter Thirty

Marco gunned his Ford Escort a short distance along the coast and pulled up in the shadow of the El Puerto. "My hotel is up there, perhaps I should call it a day." "Oh be quiet, you are on holiday."

Harvey was begining to wish he had gone to Butlins, or even Bosnia. There was too much going on here. "What time is it?" he enquired. "Early" "Marco, the last time you said that it was six in the morning." "Yes, and I told you that if your alarm went off at that time you would agree that it was early" "They were only kidding, the girls right?" "Harvey my pal you are an odd one to be sure. There are balls breaking up and down the Costa, just thinking of those two, and you're hoping their crush on you is some kind of a joke. Fill your boots, once they've crossed you off their list, you will be chip paper" "You're incorrigible, time your wife came back." "Easy Tiger" "Ok, sorry, what are we waiting for?" "You'll see soon."

More or less immediately a familiar black face appeared at Harvey's window. "Hey Whitey, got a job already? You'll soon be after that Cartier eh?" "Latiffe give it a rest. Meet Harvey" They shook hands and Harvey counted his fingers. Latiffe laughed "I like you man, showroom closed now, catch you later."

Marco chained the gear stick to the steering wheel and locked the pedals together before putting the radio in the boot. He and Lattiffe engaged in a high-speed conversation that left Harvey gasping for breath, and culminated in high fives all round.

Lattiffe disappeared into the darkness from whence he came. "What was that about?" Harvey asked curiously. "Diversification" "Bloody Hell, you love that word."

They made their way to the bars by the harbour and had a quick drink before climbing into a small dingy with a powerful outboard motor. They chugged past an assortment of other craft on their way past the sea defences.

Marco pointed out Harvey's hotel, it was flying a variety of flags that wafted in the breeze brought up from the narrow streets. Marco said he had never been but had heard that the manager was a bit eccentric. Harvey thought that demented was a better description.

They followed the newly constructed seawall to open water, careful not to snag the lines of anglers high above. A young boy waved to them as they were highlighted by the lights. Harvey waved back and imagined himself a weather-beaten seafarer off to battle the elements, don't mention the Armada!

Clear of the wall, Marco opened up the motor and nearly dumped Harvey over the stern. "Bloody Hell, what do you feed this beast on?" but his voice was lost in the spray. They sped past little fishing boats with strong lights playing on the water. Some larger boats were operating in dimmer surroundings, setting their nets ready for casting.

Suddenly Marco cut the engine and the small dingy sank back level with the water and they drifted towards a marker bouy of multi-coloured plastic bottles.

A fighter jet screamed low overhead and even lower a helicopter scanned the water ahead, Marco waved as they lit up their position, other boats did the same as they passed. "Not exactly a quiet spot Marco, what's all the activity about?" "The chopper is looking for illegals and drug smugglers, the plane is to frighten the shit out of everybody while reminding the Brits in Gib' who owns this bit of water. Here, one rod and one beer, suit you, sir?" "Smashing." "Good, stretch out where you are and I'll do the same here. It won't get any cooler unless you go sleep walking."

Harvey tried conversation but layed back in the boat, and the day caught up with him. He attempted to fight the sinking eyelids but the lapping water, and gentle roll of the craft, fought against him. He succumbed to a nap. The drink, travel and travails of the day, plus the sounds and motions were as good as a ride around the park in your pram, followed by a fill of mother's milk, and a warm rocking cradle.

Harvey slept but, alas, thought of mother were enough to awaken her. She screamed at death-defying speed out of the Summer sky on the back of a large African in traditional dress. A small black woman sat on the heels of the diving African and held a tray of trinkets so hard that her grip had flattened the edges, causing the contents to spill. Gold chains, charms and Cartier watches rained down on the water and lay in a pattern on the surface. His mother produced a mega-spotlight from her day-glow waistcoat and lit up the glistening display on the water - it spelled out her favourite obscenity in four letters. Heading the large African into the cloudless sky she steered him into a steep dive, pulling him up level with the water where he hovered. The downdraft transformed the obscene word into a battered motorbike, that the small black woman mounted and rode to the beach, pursued at speed by the African and his passenger.

Harvey sat up sharply causing the dingy to rock alarmingly. "Easy man," said, Marco. Harvey looked around, lights played on the water around them and port side, but there was no sign of his mother.

A splash on the starboard side caused Harvey to spin around in despair, surely not! A flash of white showed in the darkness, "Hello Whitey, wanna buy a watch?" hissed Lattiffe through his big grin. "What the fu..?" "Shush and sit still!" implored Marco. "Grab this and pull man" Lattiffe instructed.

Harvey was too bemused to question and pulled on the line he had been given. Marco joined him and together they landed a small shrink wrapped bale in oilskin material which Marco quickly pushed under Harvey's seat. Lattiffe disappeared into the deep with a loud splash and a chuckle. "Pull Harvey, pull you got a big one," Marco yelled loudly. Harvey pulled and they landed a large once handsome but now long dead swordfish.

As they became bathed in lights from the other boats, Marco raised the long dead fish above his head and made it wriggle as if still full of life. They received loud shouts of congratulations from the other boats. The helicopter paid a visit and dipped in admiration at the catch, before spinning away.

Harvey had regained his senses, "Don't tell me, let me guess, diversification?" "A hole in one my dear friend. Give that man a Goldfish, blow the expense, give his cat one as well," laughed a breathless Marco.

It was Moroccan Gold, cannabis, of course. He should have guessed the purpose of the trip, and gone home but, he was here now and did not want to be caught - he was already an accomplice. "You prat, why didn't you tell me?" "Would you have com?" "No" "Answered your own question mate." "Prat" he replied, vowing not to help again.

Marco started the engine and tied the controls to chug straight and slow. He produced a stone chopping board that he placed between him and Harvey. He slit the bale and the smell brought back memories of different days. From his pockets, Marco produced small plastic wallets that they stuffed with the drug and in turn stuffed the fish.

When the job was done Marco emptied two cigarettes onto the chopping board, by gently rolling them between his finger and thumb. He placed a small amount of their cargo, which he had held back, in some foil and played his lighter underneath, it smelled strong. He then crumbled the hash into the tobacco and gently refilled the filter-tipped tubes, packing them down with a match. The debris was wrapped in the original oilskin that Marco weighted and slid overboard.

Against his better judgement, Harvey accepted his cigaret and they both lit up, as the boat chugged towards the harbour. Harvey inhaled and held his breath, on exhaling he felt nauseous and very light headed to the point of fainting. He managed to sit back heavily and catch himself from taking a swim. Marco toped away as he took over the controls, he then collected the remains of their indulgence and cast them overboard.

He splashed a little diesel around their feet to disguise any lingering smell and gunned the boat home. This was not Hemmingway, but Marco displayed the fish with all the pride of the Old Man and the Sea.

They tied up and struggled ashore with their 'catch'. They hid the fish between them while showing it off at the same time. Fortunately, there were no fishmongers lingering and the real fishermen were still at sea trying to land a similar trophy. The crew of a yacht offered to buy the fish on their noisy, boozy way down the jetty without close scrutiny. Marco invited them to his restaurant tomorrow where he promised it would be on the menu. He failed to tell them the location, but they staggered off happy.

The duo walked past the parked Escort and down a very dark alley, where they stopped at a door with a small barred window. Marco gave a knock, tap, knock signal, reminding Harvey of old movies and the door opened. Mani Soler peered out a fraction and took the decomposing fish without a word and closed the door.

Marco directed Harvey to a washroom that was hidden in the darkness. He felt around until he located a light switch that turned on the dimmest light either had seen. In the gloom, they could just about make each other out. The hash sampler had kicked in now and they had a fit of the giggles. They scrubbed up in an old flat sink, probably designed for swishing off sea boots. What the light lacked in power was made up by the strength of the soap. Stripped to the waist the smell of rotten fish, and diesel, was replaced by the strong smell of Eau de Carbolic.

Giggling like schoolgirls, they removed their trousers and pants and gave the rest a scrub. The soap proved too strong for their sensitive bits and they roared as they were forced to run them under the briny cold water. Laughing like loons and with tears of mirth they rolled their clothes under their arms and streaked back to the car. They dressed quickly, Marco had settled for lightweight trousers and a Hill Street polo shirt. Harvey was resplendent in his linen suit and powder blue shirt. "Right my friend, let's have some fun." Harvey thought it must be four in the morning but didn't waste his breath asking and tagged along.

They retraced their steps and carried on to the lights where they turned into a small bar. "Harvey, meet Charlie Osmer. Charlie, meet my friend Harvey."

Charlie was possibly in his early fifties, in unreasonable shape and possessed a happy, welcoming face. With a personality to match.

As he went for drinks, Marco explained, that Charlie ran the small bar on his own. He could cook a bit, play all kind of cards or dice games. He knew a whole mass of tricks, was a practical joker and could hold his own in any conversation, or drinking bout.

If Charlie took a day off, which was exceedingly rare, the bar stayed closed. When he was of a mind the bar remained open - regardless of time or duration of the session. Tonight he was not of that mind. Opera was coming from the CD player, "That's a bit unusual" Harvey remarked, "So is Charlie" Marco replied. This was a quiet night so when the few customers drifted away from the bar he shepherded them out The opera helped.

"I presume Señor Marco is going next door?" Charlie inquired and received a nod. "What's next door?" asked Harvey the innocent. "You'll see" they replied together, causing him to involuntary shudder.

"Drink up," said Charlie. An old guy who had been sitting outside made to enter, "feck off, or come with us," he said. The old man chose the former and wandered off without taking offence.

On request, Harvey and Marco brought two tables and a few chairs inside and stacked them by the door. "I am trying to get people used to smoking outside" Charlie explained, as he lit up. "Don't think it will ever catch on though."

Charlie locked, barred, shuttered and finally padlocked the bar against intruders. Presumably they would be in possession of armour piercing munitions. He then amazed the others by depositing the keys through the high letter box, he could just reach through the shutter. They keys hit the floor with a joint clatter. "Best security system going, I have several sets in the safe at home. It's better than losing them or giving them to a mugger," he explained. "I do manage to take all, but one set home occasionally" they nodded an understanding of his logic.

They walked past three doors marked 'Fire Exit'. One door opened out and a rather drunken man was deposited on the pavement by a large hand-arm combination that slammed the door shut. Past the doors was a flickering neon sign of a female form, badly misshapen by some illumination deficiency. A red arrow pointed down a narrow set of steps.

They descended, the steps widened and at the end was a semi-circle of concrete painted a gaudy red. An intact red neon, above a double in and outward swinging set of doors, announced 'OPEN'. They pushed the doors open against their rubber seals, designed to prevent noise, and fleeing customers, spreading onto the street above. The small sloped floor inside was rubberised and bumpy "For the disabled" volunteered Charlie, after they had been thrown from above thought Harvey.

"I've never been to a brothel before," Harvey said. "Good. They are illegal here" said Marco, as he pushed open another double door and they accessed the brothel. In front of them the small bar area was illuminated by lighting that matched the washroom they had used earlier. The lighting was enhanced by an ultra-violet light that helped adjust one's vision and show up dandruff. Frank Sinatra was singing muted, but beautifully, from a concealed and inadequate music system.

Harvey looked around his first encounter with a brothel, perhaps Marco was right, this did not look like those portrayed in movies.

Behind the horseshoe bar stood a tall lady with unnatural black hair and enormous spectacles. She had the hardened face of one who has seen much. That would explain the glasses.

A small raised platform and a pole were in the centre of a minuscule dance floor. A quick scan revealed that they were possibly the last punters of the night. The tall lady broke off her conversation with a bleach blonde perched on a high bar stool. She wore a white supporting bra and a short mini skirt. The UV lighting made the garments stand out in 3D and distracted one's glance from her face, that had seen a few years hard labour.

Marco murmured that the tall one was the unapproachable girlfriend of the proprietor. Manilito Soler. She went by the inappropriate name of Venus, the other was her sister Cello. Both were smoking long thin Moore cigarettes. Venus took a long final draw and, with smoke issuing from her mouth and nose, approached the trio.

"More like Vesuvius" whispered Harvey. "Shush, that's her unofficial nickname, but because of her volatile nature, right call Buddy" chuckled Marco.

Venus waved a bottle over three shot glasses and pushed them forward. They chinked and swallowed in one. Before Harvey had stopped choking another glass was in his hand. He wiped his tears and sipped, this one was better. The spirit felt warm and he willingly accepted another, three in as many minutes.

"Manilito says, you don't pay tonight and he see you later Marco, OK?" Venus had a surprisingly soft voice. "Thanks, Venus but can we have Martell or Bells please, this stuff is gut rot?" Marco enquired. "No, like I say, you don't pay tonight" slightly harsher. "You can see Sasha tonight. Cello will continue her encounter with Charles, and your smart friend with the big eyes can make the acquaintance of Anastasia. All on the house, a patron, who has just left, made a generous donation".

"The ladies will join you when they have attended to some business." She reached over the bar and squeezed Harvey on the forearm which made him wince, and think of Ellen on the plane. "Nice to see you with a gentleman for once Marco" she smiled, showing crooked, stained teeth, as she nodded her head scornfully at Charlie. "Sorry Venus, this is Harvey, Harvey Venus" they shook hands. "Harvey is English" "My girls don't do anal" she cautioned. Marco laughed, Harvey blushed and Charlie looked guilty.

Cello had left her stool and was standing with Charlie, he had not wasted a second. He cupped his large hands and scooped her right breast from its resting place. He then proceeded to devour her large nipple, Harvey looked around nervously. He prepared to dive in for the matching set but Cello held him back. "Wait, Charles, you'll tear it, undo it nicely." Charlie examined the bra. "I can see it's a front loader, but I prefer the over the shoulder boulder holders, be a mate Harvey will you?"

Harvey ignored the invitation, he signalled to Marco. "I think I'll make tracks, I can find my way, it's only over the road, knackered and all that...." Marco raised a finger to his lips. He pointed with the same fickle finger of fate to the top of a staircase, located in the corner.

Harvey followed the finger and saw two girls had started down towards them. They both had radiant smiles. The first was of the Orient, slim with an attractive oily sheen. She was small, thin and lovely. She had very long black hair and wore a short skirt and black shirt combo. The shirt criss-crossed her small breasts, terminating in a loosely tied knot over her pierced naval. The second girl was Europen, probably Spanish, she dressed in a similar fashion but in yellow, she was a little stockier and wore her skirt longer.

"Marco" Sasha squealed, giving him the hookers equivalent of a flying bear hug. "You ve'y lucky man, you with me tonight fo' flee. You wan good bow lob ye'?" She then looked at him scoldingly, and continued without dropping her voice, "But not bum fluck this time. You want bum fluck you go Cello, right?" Harvey choked on his drink again, Cello looked duly insulted, but Marco just nodded in agreement.

"Hello" a soft voice greeted Harvey and he could barely make her out through his tear filled eyes. He cleared his airways and spluttered an apology. The coarse brandy transferred to the correct route for his gullet. "I like your dresses, my name is Anastasia, you are English like Señor Charles, no?" She spoke like Speedy Gonzales but sexy. "No er Yes, English. My name is Harvey. I am pleased to meet you". "All boys are pleased to meet me Harvey. We shall sit over there" she indicated an area that he presumed contained a seat of some kind. Charlie bashed into him from behind as he wrestled with a submitting Cello. "Good idea may be safer," he said, unsure, allowing himself to be led by the finger.

There were sofas as wide as a bed and they took a seat out of sight of the bar. They could hear the music a bit clearer, it was still Frank Sinatra and he deserved a more attentive audience. The girl did not have a drink so Harvey returned to the bar.

Marco patted him on the back on his way upstairs with Sasha. In the slightly brighter light she looked older. Venus poured two drinks and added a good measure of Sprite to Anastasia's.

Harvey was nearly floored by Charlie again, as he returned with the drinks. Charlie was carrying Cello fireman style to the stairs, any obstacle would be trampled in his wake. In the light, Cello did not look older, just old.

Anastasia was no child, maybe early thirties, but Harvey thought he had the better deal. The he thought, 'What the Hell am I doing here?' She read his thoughts but said nothing. She reached for his hand again and led him like a lamb to the slaughter, up the stairs after the others. Venus shut off Sinatra and started te empty ashtrays.

The sight of Venus clearing up began Harvey's mental clock. Two-hour flight plus baggage claim and the trip from the airport plus the hour ahead. One hour maybe at the hotel, one to take on his walk to Hill Street. Say Eleven by the time they boarded the dingy, maybe twelve. It must be at least four in the morning, no it must be later, no way to tell, he should have bought the Cartier. All these thoughts rushed through his tired, hashed and brandy infused body on the short trip up the stairs. Anything to take his mind of what was happening. 'What am I doing here?'

She opened the door to the room by way of a night latch. When closed the only way back was with a key. The only way out was the crash bar on the fire door and he knew where that led. The room was narrow and dark, the walls were draped with a full-length curtain, she closed the door and it was hidden by the curtains. She sat him on the bed and removed his jacket. Folding it over her arm she bent to retrieve something that had fallen from a pocket. The condoms he had bought in Gatwick gave away that he, at least, had journeyed with intent.

She smiled. "Like you Harvey" "Excuse me?" "Extra Sensitive, you are a wise man Harvey. You protect your wife no?" "No, I'm not married" "Then you protect us, very wise, I like." She laid him back on the bed and put the pack in readiness.

"Sorry Anastasia, I'm not really ..." "Shush" she cooed. She leant over him and undid her shirt, revealing her breasts, and started to undo his zip. He could hear a hiss of a ball clock somewhere filling a cistern, and the drip, drip of a shower from behind the drapes. She got a small reaction which disappeared at the sound of footsteps, laughter and a Police siren.

He remembered they were at street level. He was hopelessly inadequate, should he have taken a portion of his purple pill? Too late now, he didn't want to wait for that to kick in. She removed her skirt and revealed a yellow G-string and a small flabby tummy, with childbearing stretch marks, highlighted in the dim lighting. He thought of the bright lighting in the airport toilet, he thought of everything except his current position, perhaps he was asleep.

He was returned to the present by Sasha's voice from the next room. She sounded so close she could have been laying next to him. Marco was doing ok thus far but,"No come yet" he was being instructed.

Somewhere else he heard the sound of mating Hedgehogs, that must be Charlie and Cello. Harvey's mind was rambling, and not on the job. Harvey went to stand, "No, please for me" she insisted and placed a hand on his chest, he felt a twinge which was not lost on the girl.

She smiled and smoothed his brow, more reaction. As he relaxed, she opened his trousers wide and he felt her caress his erection. She took the condoms and opened the pack with her teeth. She had thought him wise, but he now thought she must be paranoid as she ripped open two Johnnies. She placed them on his upright member, well as upright as a certain tower in Pisa.

His head began to spin as she lowered her mouth over the assorted rubber goods. She started to resemble a nodding donkey in a Texas oilfield.

Drifting in and out of sleep, Harvey was brought to attention by his mother bursting from behind the drapes astride a black Vietnamese pot-bellied pig. She was waving a brandy bottle in one hand and a swordfish in the other, the brandy bottle was making strange gurgling noises. The swordfish disintegrated and fell to the floor with a loud crump.

He came to his senses and found Anastasia gagging on the condoms. They had shot off his rapidly collapsed leaning tower and lodged in her throat. After removing them, with difficulty, he helping her recover her breathing. She had lost all interest in the further activity and disappeared into the shower.

He eased himself into his clothes and out of the Fire Door. He blinked in the slightly brighter dark street, he was sure the sun would be up by now.

A green flashing clock above a pharmacy announced 14C and 3:15. Can't be right, a small cloud flitted over the moon making it wink at him. Lattiffe's dodgy watches were more reliable than his body clock.

Harvey tried to recount his movements again. How long had he been with the girl? Not sure. How long had he slept in the dingy? Not sure. How many Sinatra songs had he heard? Maybe three or four, recorded in the days when three minutes were a long track. The girl had not taken her drink and they had not sat together. He tried to unscramble the time from leaving his car for a few more minutes, impossible, the clock blinked 14C and 3:16. "Liar" he said as the moon winked again.

Two Fire doors crashed open behind him, Marco and Charlie no doubt. Harvey scarpered in the direction of his hotel, and away from the wheezy laughter.

"Sex," Harvey said aloud and shook his head. His thoughts took over again. Why did it always come down to sex? He was not any good at it, didn't like it that much, but it was always there. From now on he would forget about sex and get a platonic female partner. He enjoyed female company and it would be nice without sex. He reached into his coin pocket and took the pills in his hand. He went to put them in the bin by the pharmacy and remembered the Hill Street girls. The pills dropped back in his pocket. "When I get home...." He looked at the sun cream and photography adverts in the pharmacy window, 'must get some more condoms' he thought.

His reflection in the window was much more disheveled than the one that had twirled in Gatwick, but was not beyond repair. Harvey decided that hash, and not sex, was to blame on this occasion.

Now for the hotel, at least that bloody manager would be off duty by now. He hoped the Night Porter was more amiable.

Back at the Hotel El Torro, Ruben had mulled over his position regarding Harvey. He was smartly dressed, well spoken and obviously could make his feelings known. Perhaps that rep had meant something else when she referred to him as 'trouble'. Maybe he was a spy for a tour operator or a Mystery Shopper. Sent to check the hotel for future bookings, or a review.

It was hours since Harvey had stormed out, but he took nothing, so must return. Well Ruben would smooth things out in the morning. Meanwhile his comfy chair was calling. Where that bloody Juan had gone, he was not sure, but he must have sloped away after stirring up the English. He would have it out with him in the morning.

Ruben installed his broken cue between the glass pads. He vowed to doze lightly, in case Señor Bright returned before daylight.

Also dozing, but far from lightly in 217, was Juan. He had taken a few puffs of Mani Soler's finest Moroccan, and was dreaming of a beauty he had held in his arms.

Harvey found himself too easily outside the hotel. The proximity of the brothel bothered him. He was too easily tempted, like Oscar Wilde, he could resist anything but that. Maybe he should request a change of hotel. Still, he reasoned, Marco was off soon, and he would never dare venture down there by himself.

He stood by the door puzzled, it was locked, he searched for a bell or a letter box to holler through, maybe there was an intercom. Nothing of the sort existed. The owners never intended the doors to be locked, so any means of assisting access were not necessary. Peering through the doors Harvey noticed the improvised bolt between the pads. He looked around and found an old bike spoke in the gutter. He bent it double for strength and easily dislodged the cue, it fell soundlessly onto the thick doormat.

Once inside Harvey reinstated the cue and looked for his room key. It was not with the others, it was not behind the desk, then from behind the desk he spotted it. There it was still hanging from the lock of 217, some bloody security. All his possessions were inside and available to all and sundry. Ah well, it would do for tonight. He determined himself to see that rep tomorrow - err later today, and sort things out.

Hearing Ruben's light snoring Harvey could not resist the opportunity. He crept over and tied Ruben's shoelaces together before he retired to 217.

Harvey did not need any powers of navigation, or light, to find his bed. He sat on the edge and kicked off his shoes. He sniffed a familiar smell and thought it must be lingering in his hair. This was his last immediate thought. He lay back, asleep before he was horizontal, and straight into the arms of Juan.

Harvey jolted awake but where was he? It was sweltering, of course. He was on holiday and fully dressed, hang on. He was in bed and somebody was hugging him, not Anastasia, no, he remembered entering the hotel. Not his mother undoubtedly, she never got that close. Not the wrong room, surely.

Harvey eased himself off the bed and found the light switch. It was darker in the room now, and the door was closed, so the small lamp shone brighter and he could make out Juan. Thinking he was at home, and being burgled, Juan lept from the bed and attacked.

He head butted Harvey in the stomach, winding him before he realised where he was, and what he had done. Juan tried to get out of the door. He was prevented by a doubled over Harvey, who was gradually growing in height. Harvey yelled through bruised lungs, "You bastard, you're all fucking mad, come here I'll kill you." Not being THAT mad, Juan slipped past Harvey, and on to the quarter landing.

At the first shout Ruben came to life in time to see Harvey's large bare foot land on Juan's backside, and send him crashing into the foyer. Ruben assessed that his staff were undergoing a murderous onslaught by this English warmonger and jumped up to intervene.

Attempting to take a mighty stride to the fray, Ruben tripped and fell forward and smashed his nose on a plant pot, that housed an enormous cheese plant.

Feeling a bit responsible for Ruben's predicament, Harvey applied a towel, and some ice, from the reception area, and staunched the bleeding, It also gave him the opportunity to untie Ruben's laces.

Sitting Ruben back in his chair, and with Juan prone on the floor, Harvey retired to his room. Leaving the staff of Hotel El Torro incapacitated.

Chapter Thirty-One

Harvey slept so well he missed breakfast and his welcome visit. This, in fact, was just a quick look in by the rep' as Harvey was her only customer at the hotel. After being informed by the management that her client was a homicidal lunatic, who had already attacked two members of staff, she rushed off to her next 'meeting'. She decided to communicate with Mr Bright via notes as, and when only, necessary. He did not sound like a good earner for her.

"Blimey, what did you do wrong in a previous life?" asked Lenny as she peered into the gloom of 217.

She had been sent by Hill Street to check on his well-being. Harvey peered cautiously at reception which was unattended. "Good morning, I think. Please come in, if you can manage to squeeze in." He managed a smile, he looked and felt crumpled.

Lenny sat on the bed, as he manoeuvred around her, watching him like a dog watches his master. "The bikes ready when you are, no hurry. Bloody hell, are you paying for this room? Here, give me your suit, it's not dirty I'll get it pressed for you."

"How did you find me?" he asked. "There is no one about." "No one about?" Lenny nodded,"I just span the register around and looked. There are not many guests and yours was the last name, with 217 penciled in. Here, your passport was on the desk so I brought it. Not very smart, leaving that hanging about, if you look it has a different room number stuck on it. Perhaps they are going to move you." she added optimisyically. "We'll see, chuck me out more likely, can you give me five minutes?" "No worries, it's all I need to get your suit pressed." Harvey blew her a kiss as she squeezed out, she smiled.

Lenny returned with the suit on a hanger and clad in cellophane. He was dressed in light chinos and a pink polo shirt. "Ralph Loren, mmmm nice. That smell him too?" Harvey nodded and hung the suit on the outside of the wardrobe. "Anybody about?" She shook her head. "Good, I think I need a coffee before meeting those maniacs, come on."

They crept down to the desk and deposited the room key in a key shape cut out in the desk. It crashed noisily as hit the bottom of the box and they ran to the front door. Pedro, the Head Waiter, was entering and was unceremoniously dumped on his bottom, as they rushed out. As was his want, Pedro let out a large hiss as he hit the floor and was still hissing as Harvey helped him to his feet and Lenny brushed him off.

They thought that they had punctured something as Pedro continued to hiss, but realised it was either an affliction or a peculiar mannerism. Harvey recalled an old joke about an African learning English from a short-wave radio. He had little time to reflect on this as a loud noise erupted behind them.

Ruben had heard the key hit the collection pot. He peered out of the small window in the wall behind the reception desk, in time to see Pedro hitting the floor. Much as he despised the man and his bits of paper he was staff and must be protected. With no thought for his own safety, he picked up the broken pool cue and charged the assailants with a roar.

Harvey spotted the ungainly soul advancing and grabbed Lenny's hand. "Quick, I told you he was bloody mad, let's get out of here, like now!" With a white plaster across his nose Ruben looked dangerously ready for action, they fled.

Lenny vaulted onto the bike and kicked it into action. Harvey tried to copy and she nearly unseated him as she urged the machine forward with all the horsepower of an unemployed donkey. But at least they made air between them and the charging Ruben.

"Come back you murdering assassins" he shouted after them. A Police Officer was having a casual smoke against his car as the bike flew past with Ruben in hot pursuit. He jumped behind the wheel when the word 'assassins' screamed forth from Ruben, no time to question him, the bike was still in view. He urged his partner to flick on the siren and radio in. His partner sat unimpressed with his arms folded until the driver remembered and flicked his cigarette out of the window. "Bloody Gay," he muttered in Spanish and screamed off in pursuit. His partner entered the fray with gusto, he flicked on the flashing lights and siren. He then proceeded to inform control of a possible fatality from a political assassination, or gangster execution, at Hotel El Torro.

The noise of the motorbike drowned out any other sound so they did not hear the approaching Police car. In any case, Harvey was thinking more about Ambulances than Police cars, as he struggled to stay on the bike. This was nearly impossible, without grabbing any of Lenny's personal bits, so he was surprised when the car pulled alongside bearing gun-toting officers.

Lenny's riding technique was to sit hunched up with her hands level with her ears, as she looked through the centre of the raised handlebars. Consequently she never heard Harvey yelling at her, or saw the police car. It was only when Harvey relented, and touched some personal bits, that she looked round and saw a shotgun aimed at her. The sudden movement and her shock at seeing the gun set the bike in an almost uncontrollable wobble. This sent holidaymakers. and Lookey Lookey men, scampering in all directions, until she brought the beast to a halt.

The policemen immediately recognised her as one of the stunners from Hill Street. The partner proved not to be gay in any language, as they argued over who should frisk her. In the event, they opted for one side each and completely ignored Harvey. He thought the whole episode a bit extreme for a case of speeding, what a country. They finally turned their attention to him as their radio instructed them to return to the hotel immediately. They ignored Harvey again and gave Lenny one more frisk, for good measure, before bundling them into the back of their car.

Back at the Hotel El Torro there was a massive Police presence and a departing ambulance. A large crowd gathered outside a taped off area at the front.

Inside, Ruben, Juan and Pedro were perched uncomfortably on what should have been a comfortable settee. A senior police officer paced the marble floor in front of them. Each time he looked their way they looked at the ground like naughty schoolboys. Harvey and Lenny were instructed to sit together and chose Ruben's favourite chair.

The whole story unfolded, starting with the room allocation, through to flooring of Pedro, leaving Harvey and Ruben feeling pretty foolish. Juan eventually owned up to his part in the debacle and received an 'I'll deal with you later' look from Ruben.

Pedro hissed his part as an unfortunate innocent. He received a glare from Ruben, who had been prepared to risk his life for the worm, or was it a snake? They received a lecture in a mixture of Spanish and English about wasting valuable Police time and resources.

Harvey and Ruben were instructed to shake hands and apologise to each other. The crowd dispersed through boredom and lack of blood. The police withdrew to 'continue their fight against terrorism, illegal immigrants, drug smugglers and prostitution' Harvey was thankful to have received the lecture and not the Inquisition, which would have associated him with. 50 - 75% of the police objectives.

The only draw back now was a sudden rush at the hotel, due to delayed flights, meant Harvey was stuck with 217. He sighed in resigned acceptance but determined to see his rep' at the earliest opportunity. This was not going to happen, she had heard of a mass murder at Hotel El Torro and had taken sick leave, without organising a replacement.

The original police officers drove them back to the bike, which they decided to walk the two hundred or so metres to Hill Street. It gave them a chance to talk.

Harvey gave a brief account of the previous night, after selectively leaving out large chunks to protect her innocent youth. "Oh, you didn't go to the brothel then, they usually do?" Harvey wondered if this youth had ever been innocent. "I see" she laughed as he blushed.

It was the middle of the afternoon as they made The Hill. The pool lads were at the table still, a smattering of imbibers sat in the sun or shade relaxing. Neta waved a greeting, Harvey waved back, "Coffee please" he said and accepted the San Miguel in a frosted glass that he was handed.

Lenny slipped under the bar flap, without difficulty, but was not greeted warmly. After a short conversation and things had mellowed, she shouted, "Hey Harvey, she thought we had it off love, chance would be a fine thing eh?" Neta shoved her unkindly, "My turn to spend time with you next," she said, "you might need that ambulance after."

Harvey decided to take the initiative. "Right, I'll have you both now, on the pool table," he said forcefully. The pool lads gawped and Harvey backed down immediately, as the girls rushed him. "Well let them finish their game eh?" Harvey was losing this contest game, set and match. "Oh Harvey, these were in your suit, sorry I forgot." Lenny threw him his little purple pills. "What are they for?" "Err, my heart" "You didn't bring enough" Neta laughed. 'New balls please' thought Harvey.

"Heart, what's that all about mate?" Marco emerged from somewhere. "Nothing, just a travel precaution" lied, Harvey. "I don't know what you did to Anna last night, she was nearly speechless. Sasha was most intrigued, that by the way is a warning". The pool lads lifted their cues in respect.

Harvey changed the subject and related the goings on at the hotel. Marco found it all amusing but Charlie had been pissed off, as he couldn't get to his bar for Police.

Lattiffe appeared counting some notes and replenishing his display of watches, from a large pouch he wore under his robe. "Hey Whitey, wanna buy a watch, new supply today? I sees you still going, timeless man." "Maybe later Lattife" the big African Drew nearer, he whispered, "Wrong answer man, most people says piss of darky but I see I'm getting you interested" he laughed.

He dropped a bundle of notes in Marco's lap. "From Mani, you wanna buy a watch Marco, mister business man?" "No, fuck off you black bastard." "Wrong answer man, doesn't you ever listen?" he laughed, feigning deep hurt. He loped out of the bar and broke into a beautiful rendition of Vesti La Giubba, from Mozart's Cosi Fan Tutte. "That man never ceases to amaze me," Marco said in appreciation as he eyed his roll of notes.

Harvey nodded, "Where's he from?" "Nigeria, the north I think, they all are, well most anyway." "That's a long way, why here?" "Says he likes to see women in bikinis, not potato sacks that make them look like letter boxes. Said he went to a strip club there once and everybody was shouting 'Show us your face'"

"Marco you are incorrigible, anyway, I thought they were Christian there." "I don't know enough about it mate, but what's showing your tits got to do with Christianity, funny church you went to my friend." "Marco, stop it."

Marco suddenly became serious. "You know that business with young Enzo last night and me?" Harvey nodded. "Well he was right of course but Dad was given the last rites the day before I was going out, not the first time I add, so I rescheduled. I di na want to upset everybody, and I was right he's still hanging in there. So I sorted a few things out just in case. You being here could be a help too. Only, don't poke the payroll." "I've heard that before..." "And did you?" "Yes, married her in fact" "You have the nerve to call me incorrigible" he laughed. Marco was happy to lighten the mood again, as it was to be their last night together, until he got back.

He explained that Charlie had agreed to help out, young Enzo was more than capable but if the shit hit the fan.... Of course Harvey would do his bit.

The ringing phone called Marco away. "Bloody typical, that was the phone company. Some mix up over the last payment. Now we are on incoming calls only, until it is sorted. If you need a phone mate, don't use your hotel, they're notorious for admin charges and the like, not just yours, all of them."

"Don't use them fancy air conditioned booths on the front either" Marco continued. "They give you a coffee and charge you an arm and a leg into the bargain." "I don't think I'll need one, they have this number if I'm needed." Harvey replied. " Anyway there are plenty of pay phones along the strip". "Ha, ha, you'll have to go two streets back to find one that works mate." Marco chuckled. "Why?" "Our black friend is in cahoots with the booth people," Marco explained, "he hammers bent washers into the coin slots, so people have to use the booths."

Harvey went to the bar to replenish the drinks, and for once was nearly ignored, as both girls were engaged in scribbling notes to Enzo. "That's what I should be doing," said Harvey. "No, this is what we should be doing," Neta said, waving a Polaroid camera at him.

They posed in singles, groups. Neta chatted up the pool boys to take one of all them, in exchange for one with them, and both girls.

Young Enzo set up a table and they chatted, argued over snaps and completed their notes as they ate.

The phone rang again, proving at least that incoming calls were getting through, Marco went. He returned stating, "That was Charlie Harvey. He's invited you up later while I get a few zzzs in before the airport." "Do you think that is wise?" he asked. "He'll only come and kidnap you if you don't" Neta advised. Marco nodded "It's because you are the new kid on the block, he's a good bloke, he just wants you to feel like shite in the morning too" Marco explained.

Lenny gripped his much-gripped forearm. "Don't worry Harvey we won't let anything happen to you" Harvey was not convinced. Neta grabbed his good arm, "We will meet you at Charlie's when we finish here, aye slave driver?" Marco nodded, "Best not make it too late or Charlie will have him in Mani's.." He stopped himself from adding 'again'. "Oh good, they never let us buy a drink in there ......what, what?

Young Enzo started to clear away the brunch. "Harvey, have you had any non-alcoholic drinks since you landed?" "I tried." For the next hour or so he and Marco were on a detox of mineral water, sin gas, "Good for the digestion, liver and rehydration" Enzo advised.

With ice and lemon, it was not bad. Harvey drank about a litre of the stuff before being permitted 'one last Sanny' then Marco retired. Marco said he would try to catch him later but, if not, he would be back before Harvey went home.

Enzo drove him back to the El Torro. Both had the windows wide open, as they gagged on the smell of rotten fish and diesel from the clothing in the boot.

Harvey got out promising to call in tomorrow to prove he could be a good boy, and Enzo promising to burn that crap in the boot. As he waved him off, Harvey was aware of a hiss behind him. It was Pedro.

"Señor, you come to the table soon please. I have lemon sole for you and Señor Del Taurino has selected the wine for you personally. Come in an hour before the rush" Harvey thanked him, although he had not long eaten, it was a beautiful gesture. This was more like it. He collected his key from Juan, who rubbed his backside in jest and smiled. Harvey returned the smile and it remained until he opened the door to 217. It really was a shocker, but he had slept well eventually, a quick shower and he could shut it from his mind, until ready for sleep.

The bathroom was a nightmare to negotiate. A notice above the bath advised that the water would be discoloured. Due to water economy measures they used treated sea water, but it was not to be drunk or used in cleaning teeth. The water that eventually spluttered from the combination tap was near pure salt and sand. It had blasted off the surface of the bath and it's non-slip qualities. Harvey stood on a safe island and when the water ran clearer changed the tap to the shower function and stood under the urine coloured flow. It was sufficient to revive and refresh him.

"I am too placid," he thought as he clambered over the furniture to dress. As he folded his chinos his little purple friends fell onto the bed. Harvey broke off one triangle and popped it in his mouth and went to the restaurant.

Chapter Thirty-Two

Pedro met him at the door and hissed a warm welcome. He escorted him to a window seat that looked down slightly on the passers-by. The restaurant was very pleasant and most certainly Pedro's domain. He hissed pleasantries to the diners, some of whom were not hotel guests, the sign of good food thought Harvey. He was not disappointed by the food or wine and did them both justice. Pedro was very attentive and nodded appreciatively at the clean plate and called over the dessert trolley which Harvey declined.

Pedro then did a fierce raspy hiss as a waiter was making a hash of clearing and resetting a table. He pushed the lad aside and with a flourish he wafted a fresh cloth onto the table, he then miraculously appeared to lay four places before the cloth had settled. His attention was then drawn to the feeder bar where a party of Germans were demanding to sit together and giving the waiters a hard time.

Looking around the room Harvey observed that they could have a long wait, as most diners were on their starters. The gentleman in him took over as he gulped the last of his wine and made his table available, thanking Pedro on his way out. Pedro dispatched one waiter to clear Harvey's table. Another waiter led the party of Germans in a circuitry route that ensured the table was ready by the time they arrived. Harvey looked up from the street and saw them being seated, as one of them dropped a cigaret end on his head.

Luckily he had seen the missile coming and was able to brush it away without enduring any harm. He decided that his last gulp of wine had been too quick. He would walk off the food and drink effects before going to Charlie's bar.

Flicking ash from his jacket he heard quickening small footsteps behind him.

"Hal vey, wha' you do Anna? She slick, she ve'y bad float, you bad man" it was Sasha rushing to catch him up. He was not sure if he was being greeted or if he should run, but she linked arms when she reached him. She jigged alongside like a child with her favourite uncle. "I hav' wok ve'y haaa tonight wiv no Anastasia, she no speak. She wight me what you did but she no Wight good and me no weed good. Then she d,waw but she no dwa good, you have long ve 'y fin cock Hal vey?" "No certainly not, I didn't do anything" he sort of lied. Then a little more truthfully "I couldn't ...."

He didn't believe he was having this conversation. "Ah" she made a downward motion with her index finger and he nodded sheepishly. " Ah she t lied too har and fluck tonsils, ah I see. You come me tonight, I salt you out, you pay, no flee tonight, five mill and no bum Fluck wight? That Chaly love bum Fluck" Harvey nodded without really listening. He was too busy trying to convert five million pesetas to pounds - surely not!

They reached Charlie's bar, the old fellow was seated in the 'smoking zone' and winked at Harvey. Sasha tried to pull him to Mani's, but he dug his heels in. "Ok see you lata." She then reached up and popped something in the back of his throat. As he was about to speak and he swallowed it before he realised, she then kissed him and skipped away. This holiday was taking control of him, he was visiting brothels, consorting openly with the girls, drug running, drug taking and who knows what other misdemeanours and this was only the second day.

Charlie greeted him with an open Holsten Pils, without asking. "What's five mill?" Harvey asked. "They call a thousand a mill, so that's about twenty-five quid. Is that what she charged you?" "No...." "Not another freebie, jammy git."

Harvey was in need of sanity in this mad world and walked past Charlie, to use his pay phone, and phoned Amber. He was reassured by her voice, all was well there and he gave her a highly edited account of things thus far. Charlie's rigged phone gobbled up all his change but he felt a bit more normal after the call.

"What's with the music?" Harvey asked. He hadn't put Charlie down as a Prince fan. Charlie gave him another Holsten. "I just lost a bet to him" he pointed at a Prince look-a-like who smiled coyly back. "And now I have to play this Prince Symbol guy for the rest of the night." "What was the bet?" "You don't want to know" Charlie was right about that. "Don't worry, he did some good stuff, I don't think he made too many." "You wanna bet?" Charlie pointed at a pile of tapes and CDs behind the bar "No."

Charlie told him the girls had rung and would catch them here, TNT or Mani's. This reminded Harvey of his encounter with Sasha and the pill she had pushed down his throat. "No worries, it's a cock riser made out of rhino horn and tiger prick or something like that. She must have plans for you later. It takes about four hours to kick in, lucky boy, five mills eh?"

Harvey remembered that he had already taken a pill of his own, he gulped down the Holsten, which Charlie replaced. They had a few beers as customers drifted in and out, and Symbol worked his way through number after number. In the middle of one song, he called upon the figure of his desire to "get your fat ass round her so I can work on that zipper baby". "Oh, whilst we are on the subject, your zipper is open" Charlie advised Harvey. "Since when?" "Don't know, it was like that when you came in." "Thanks, Buddy" "Don't mention it."

More beers followed then a decent Rioja. They were both feeling lively and Charlie decided he'd had enough Symbol for one night. "Coming to Mani'?" he asked. "May as well, the girls aren't here yet, but only for a drink." "Yea, yea, I believe you, but Mani won't like it unless you treat the bar." "Why?" " He's a businessman, idiot, if you are not spending on the girls you gotta buy drinks - lots, he'll see to that. He ain't a bad guy, but you'd need a sniffer dog to find his sense of humour."

Harvey confessed that his trip to Mani's had been his first time in that kind of establishment. Charlie divulged that Marco virtually lived there since his wife went. Charlie then confessed that he wasn't really into the women but found Cello accommodating. He also confessed that he had heart problems so he lived each day as if it was his last. "That way, one day I'll be right." "I can't work out if that's being optimistic or pessimistic" Harvey mused. Charlie leant forward over the bar, "The thing that pisses me off is that a pessimist is never disappointed." "That's very profound, did you just think of that?" "No, it's on that poster behind you, Mr Observant."

Charlie gathered up the evenings entertainment and shoved it all in a crisp box. "Here Doris, one bet sorted, now fuck off." Doris minced over and collected his music, "Thank you" he purred and left. "I worry for that one," Charlie said."I think that Prince would not like being aped by a street queen, sort of ruins the stud image eh?" Harvey nodded. "No I mean I do worry for him," Harvey said nothing but gave a quizzical look.

They cleared up the smoking area and sent the old drinker on his way. Charlie had gone through his lock up routine as they heard the phone ringing inside. "Bloody typical," said Charlie, they could do nothing so shrugged and left.

Venus was not totally enamoured when they half fell down the stairs. But she had a quiet evening and business was business. Charlie ordered gins and tonic without referring to Harvey, 'local custom, you drink what you're given' thought Harvey.

"You pay tonight so you can have Gordon's" Venus declared. They nodded. Harvey spied Pedro and Juan drinking beer at the end of the bar so he sent them a whiskey each. They raised their glasses to him in appreciation.

Above them, a Fire Door crashed open and Sasha could be heard lambasting a punter for attempting an unnatural act. Her not so dulcet tones traveled down to the bar. "I toll you no bum Fluck, you du'ty bubba, how you like it?" The thud and groan that followed indicated a kick to the nether regions had been delivered.

As the door was slammed shut, Venus remarked, "I always tell them no anal but they want to try. I don't know why, never heard of it in my day. Now all the time, maybe it comes from Russians. You Russian Charles?" She looked accusingly at Charlie who submerged himself in his gin, he waved over two more.

Minutes later Sasha and Cello appeared on the small landing. Sasha was dressed as per the previous evening but Cello had changed to an oriental style outfit. It neither suited her or left anything to the imagination, or to desire. They walked down to Pedro and Juan, who had been expecting Anastasia. The site of Cello caused much consternation, but Pedro pulled rank and claimed Sasha.

"Ah that good, he no take long, sometimes don't use pussy" she squawked to the ensemble. Pedro hissed her to be silent. Juan considered that justice had been done and reluctantly followed Cello.

Sasha shot over to see Harvey. She noticed he was tipsy and tried to force more animal unmentionables on him, but this time, he was ready and ducked away.

When she had escorted Pedro upstairs, Harvey stood and gulped his drink. He was ready to leave, until Charlie indicated that another drink was heading his way. "Your an odd bird Harvey, you go along with everything but, with reluctance, as if your mother is watching." "She probably is" he groaned. "Froide would have had fun with you." remarked Charlie.

Before he had touched the fresh drink, Sasha was at his side. "What happened?" he didn't really mean to ask. "Nuffing we-ally, I only touch dick and he split" she told the bar. She then whispered "mo fo you Hal vey." He was beyond the pain barrier, and meekly followed her upstairs.

The room had the same draped walls as the one he had been entertained in by Anastasia. There was a mirrored ceiling, maybe there was one next door he hadn't noticed. The fire door was also concealed, but the running figure could be picked out through the drape, I wonder if he tried anal?' thought Harvey. He lay back on the bed at the aged character, looking down at him and made a decision.

He gave Sasha the five thousand she requested and another thousand. She deposited all in what looked like an armoured ballot box, bolted to the floor.

Farmyard noises from the next room suggested Charlie and Cello were resuming battle. This served to dim his ardour further. She touched him and offered him another pill for luck.

He didn't know the time but guessed it must be nearly morning, at this rate he would need a good holiday after his two weeks were up. "You give me six mill, you want special Hal vey?" "Yes very special" "OK but no ....." "I know, except that, can I really have what I want" "Yes, yes, of cause, what you want?" "To sleep, is that ok?" "Ok, but not all night, I have to go bizi again, you want me naked?" "No, that's ok" "You good man Beibi" she squezed his much squeezed arm.

They slept entwined like babes, but not for long. How long he was not sure. A loud buzzer communicated that Venus had more bizi for Sasha. She laughed and pointed at the mirror, he had a rather large erection sticking out of his open fly. "No time fo' that, next time I Fluck you when you sleep" she laughed, a real laugh. He stood and fought the beast back into his trousers, vowing to get a new zip fitted.

The sleep had revitalised him so he asked her how to find TNT. "Tun wight and follow you'w dick" she laughed. She let him out with a nice kiss.

Unknown to Harvey, Sasha had gone back to the bar and stated he had been so good they had overrun.

Juan re-entered, hoping for a better encounter and she led him upstairs " You lucky man tonight, but no...." "I know, I know, bloody Russians!" Juan was happy with normal fickey-fickey.

The sleep had revitalised Harvey. In fact, he had found it very comforting. He would have been happy to have stayed in the embrace all night, without indulging in any sport requiring purple pills or wild animals' unmentionables.

There were not many in TNT and he spotted Lenny and Neta going through a practiced routine on the small raised dance floor. With much gyrating and booty bumping. They waved and broke off when they saw him, much to the disappointment of the small ensemble of spectators. They joined him at the bar and pulled a face at the raised temperature of their earlier abandoned drinks.

"Don't worry, I got you these, sorry I was late." He handed them a Hooch each and noted that they had been drinking Holsten Pils. He offered his untouched pilsner but they waved him away. He also passed them a small bottle of mineral water each ,and gulped his own straight down.

With the girls no longer dancing, the music changed back to music of the seventies, at a volume that allowed conversation. They had explained that they had phoned Charlie's again to say they would be late but had missed him. The pool boys had got into a tournament with some big spending Germans, and the girls felt that Marco would appreciate the extra cash. They had played their part well ensuring the cash and drink flow were way above the norm and flirted themselveses a good German tip. They intentionally distracted them, to enable a home win for the pool boys to boot. They indicated the boys who were gawping at Harvey in awe.

Harvey explained they had probably heard the call, but it was too late after Charlie had engaged his security system. They nodded in understanding, "I'm sure he is going to get it wrong one day" Neta remarked and they laughed.

The pool boys came closer to try and hear snippets of the conversation. They overheard Harvey explain his visit to Mani's. Harvey himself was a bit surprised he told them that he had slept, not SLEPT, with Sasha. They believed him, they even thought it was 'cool'. The pool boys gave up.

Because they both had to work early, in a few hours, the girls said they would have one dance each with him and go. He felt guilty about keeping them waiting while he was sleeping. They explained that no matter how late, they never went straight home from work.

"You coming in probably cut us some time, I think the boys wanted a dance each - you know. Then we would have been late!" Lenny assured him.

"I don't dance, white men can't dance - didn't you see the movie? Neta ignored his protests and dragged him from the bar. "Really, I can't, especially when I'm half pis... had a drink. I have restricted body movement." "That's all right then, you hardly need move to this one." The Three Degrees had already emitted their "hoo-oo, haa-aa" and "Precious Moments" on the way to to the raised floor, which Harvey nearly tripped up. "You see? I am a clumsy bugger." Lenny called up three more Hooch's of different flavours. She watched as Neta held him tight, presumably singing meaningful bits from the song in his ear - bitch.

"Have you always been so good looking?" Neta asked. "Err, I don't think I am. I'm really not good at boyfriend-girlfriend things. Despite my form book, my life has been one big bluff - really" He thought it best to be honest.

"Liar, we know you are Hugh Grant really" she laughed and pulled him closer. He felt as if the Rhino horn had reformed between his legs and was trying to impale her as she cooed "When will I see you again?" She knew what was going on below and responded accordingly. When the song faded away, she whispered "I really want you, not for life - just an early Christmas present."

Harvey half walked Neta back to the bar with difficulty. He veered off to the toilet before he hit the illuminated area, that would expose his predicament. The toilet was true to form inasmuch that it was dark and stank, reminiscent of the late lamented Whispers. It was empty so he went straight to the basin. There was no need to open the self-opening fly, he removed his inflated member. Even in the dark he could make out every detail of his erection and he had to admit it was a beauty. He could not remember ever having one so good before but it had to go. He stood on tip toe, plunged what he could into the basin and turned the cold tap on full.

He recoiled in pain as red hot liquified sand blasted his member. "Bloody Spaniards, trust them to plumb everything ass about face" he raged. He tentatively tried the other tap, which was a lot cooler, and ran the stream over his swollen organ. He sighed with relief then realised he was not alone. Doris had entered unnoticed, while Harvey was berating the plumbing, and had spent a happy moment observing. "Nice one man" he purred, those three little words did more to dispel the erection than the entire water reserves of the Sierra Nevada could have managed. "Thank you" he replied and left Doris rushing towards a cubicle, while the memory was still fresh.

Back at the bar he took a swig from the offered bottle and looked at the label curiously, "Raspberry, unusual" he smiled.

A Stylistics medley was playing and Lenny jumped off her stool, "My turn, this won't kill you either - well I'll try" she grabbed his arm. On the dance floor, she rested her head on Harvey's chest as the song died away, she thought that was it, "Oh, that's not fair..." She broke off as the twangs of 'Brand New" rang out and she perked up. So did he, she took full advantage of her size to touch his sensitive areas.

The conversation was awkward, without him bending or her standing on tip toe. He tried to think of Doris banging off in the toilet, but Lenny was very persistent. Neta approached as the songsters disappeared down the hole in the middle of the record.

Before she reached them, Lenny pulled his head gently down and said "I really want you, not forever, but for fun and first." He was gob-smacked.

Neta joined them, and they circled in a sensuous threesome huddle to another slow one. There were not many left to witness the event but the pool boys, and all other males who did, just ached with envy. All except one - Doris hoped the bitches would die of something horrible, as he rubbed his scolded and abused bits.

Chapter Thirty-Three

For the second time, and in consecutive nights, it was light as Harvey made it back to the Hotel El Torro. The security system was in place so he rummaged around and found his 'key.'

He dislodged the cue which again fell soundlessly onto the mat. He resisted Ruben's shoelaces and satisfied himself by placing a long-stemmed flower, from the foyer display, on his chest. This transformed the slumbering Ruben to the form of an Eastern European political leader lying in state. His nose was a multitude of colours and one nostril was packed with cotton wool tinged with dried blood. The swelling extended to below the eyes. Harvey felt sorry for the outcome of the misunderstandings as he crept over and took his key.

Ruben had been dreaming of his prestigious French visitors who would soon be arriving, but he viewed Harvey's attempts not to wake him with a smile, especially as he took Fawlty style footsteps to 217.

Room 217 was stifling and Harvey left the main door open while he used the toilet. This was an uncomfortable manoeuvre, and he was pleased that his legs were not as long as Ruben's or Neta. He noticed too late that there was no toilet tissue so he transferred to the bidet and sandblasted himself clean. Still hot, he took a short cool shower, nearly sand free. as the filling toilet and use of the bidet had cleared the pipes a bit. He wrapped a towel around him and lay on the bed with the cool air from reception wafting over his drying torso.

He lay with his body calling for sleep, but his mind racing wildly. It could have only been eight hours since he had spoken to Amber. In that time, he had taken part in a drinking session. Slept, however long, with Sasha and danced away the remainder of the night, with two stunning girls. Each of whom staked a claim on him, like ancient prospectors. Six lots of eight hours earlier, he had been rising to prepare for his journey, and in that time........The Spanish must have a different time system to the rest of the world, he thought, as sleep wafted over him.

Deep in sleep he suddenly felt the presence of others in the room. He remembered the door, no room for robbers he thought. Then he thought Charlie and Cello had followed him for some reason. As he started to sit up, he realised it was Charlie alright, but in Cello's robe was his mother. The pair had an arm around each other's waist, in the classic pose of lovers around the world,

Harvey raised himself up on one arm, they were at the foot of the bed, but he had not felt them climb over him. Charlie made a circle with his thumb and forefinger, smirking like a cat with the cream, in the part light filtering from reception.

"Ronald, I shall be leaving you now," said his mother. It was in a much softer version of the clipped tones, that had been her normal voice, before she took up haunting. "I want you to know that I have now forgiven you and thank you for bringing this wonderful man to me." She gazed lovingly at Charlie Osmer, who looked longingly back. She continued, "Your father is also happy, he's gay don't you know? Well he is a changed man now he has come out, and he has found somebody too, he sends his regards. No more haunting for us, you're not allowed once you are happy."

"Am I dreaming?" Harvey asked, but thinking the opposite. "No, not this time dear. We are going now Ronald, you are about to experience a memorable week, so enjoy it while it last. It is not allowed to last forever. Goodbye my Darling, I love you." "I love you too Mother" he sobbed as she held her nose and faded through the wall into the bathroom. Charlie lingered long enough to hand him an ice cold Holsten and said "Nice horn Harvey" he looked down at his member and up quickly. He was again alone. He sipped the beer and sobbed himself to sleep.

Harvey woke with a jolt as something spilled on his bare chest. He gazed at disbelief at the bottle in his hand. He remembered his mother visiting with Charlie but dismissed it. 'May have been Charlie and Cello' he thought, but why? "I must have brought it back from TNT," he said allowed but was not convinced. He recalled placing the flower on Ruben's chest and also getting into the hotel, collecting his key, everything.

He certainly never had the bottle, unless he was putting it down and picking it up subconsciously, but his last drink was raspberry - or not. He felt hungover and had a claggy mouth. Roy Plummer had always advocated sex as the best cure, but he had never tried that. He settled for an Alkaseltzer mixed with the warm pilsner.

A knock at the door disturbed his thoughts. He tightened the towel and looked up to see Neta looking down at him. "Hi, I've just finished for a bit. Lenny's working through until I get back, coming for Brunch?" she asked cheerily. After peering into the gloom of 217, "Who have you upset?" "Lenny said the same thing yesterday. Come in if you can get in, I'll not be long." She squeezed in and he brushed against her as he manoeuvred into the bathroom, it stank but hoped she put it down to the drains.

"What were you doing this morning, not that you can do much in here?" "Just dreaming really, or daydreaming, not sure." "Dreaming, really? About what? Was I in it? Do tell please." "My Mother actually." He missed out Charlie, didn't want to scare her. "Oh, how sweet." "You don't know my Mother" he muttered. "Early starter?" She waved the bottle at him, he caught a glimpse in the cracked mirror. "Oh that, no, I must have brought it with me last night." "I wondered what you had I in your trousers" she laughed. "You didn't have it in your hand because we three held hands back to the bike - remember?" "Not really, ah whatever, I don't know anymore." "Welcome to Spain!"

When he was in the bathroom, she tidied things into little piles and folded his suit. There were three of the photos from the set that had taken for Enzo on the small chest. She put the one of her and Harvey on top and returned his smile. She could tell from the frantic tooth scrubbing, a metre away, in the next room, that he was nearly ready. She undressed quickly and lay on the bed. She immediately recoiled at the damp patch in the centre of her back until she identified it as Pilsner.

She hoped she did not smell too much of the twenty-three brunches and numerous bacon sandwiches she had served. She had washed quickly at Hill Street. She did not want to raise Lenny's suspicions by overdoing things, or miss the chance of catching Harvey in his room.

Harvey stepped back into the room refreshed. The sight that greeted him was a vision. Neta was more than beautiful, she sat up and patted the bed next to her. "Time to put some fruit on the plate," she said seductively and revealed herself without reservation.

The foreplay was heavenly, he was gentle but firm and she shivered as he hit the right spots. She nibbled and caressed him into a frenzy. When they kissed, it was with the greatest passion, probing and duelling with their tongues. She kissed him all over, taking cheeky nips with her teeth at strategic targets.

His erection was solid and unbending, they moved slowly savouring every moment, this was turning lovemaking into an art form. When they climaxed it was simultaneous and multiple, leaving them both drained but fulfilled.

In days past it would have been cigarette time, but this healthy pair just lay in the afterglow of an unforgettable experience. "Have you ever been to Mijas?" she asked. "Yes, why?" "Good, no reason. You must promise not to tell Lenny, she wanted to be the first and then me. We promised then that would be it or we could end up fighting over you and spoil everything, ok?"

"I thought Lenny had a boyfriend." "She has but he is a prat, he messes her about, chases the tourists and lets her down no end. Still what do you expect from somebody called Ken?"

Harvey was wondering if he should surrender to the Police, there must be laws against such enjoyment. "Of course I won't tell anybody, I couldn't give any description justice anyway. That was too beautiful for words." "It was also the first of two times that it will ever happen, we cannot get involved, right?" "Right," he said, reluctantly. "But when is the last time then?" "Now" she squealed and pounced.

Juan was passing 217 and smiled at the unmistakable noises. This guy was shagging one of the untouchables, just hours after a marathon with Sasha, and they said the English were cold fish in bed. Harvey layed back and made a mental note to consult the Roy Plummer school of medicine a little more often in future, but dope and sex were Roy's answers to most things.

Perched on the bike behind Neta, Harvey was surprised to find his erection returning as firm as before. It was difficult keeping it away from Neta, her riding style was more lay back and lean opposed to Lenny's perch and peer manner. Now Neta had achieved her goal, she was back to her flirtatious self. Enjoying arousing Harvey again, she also admired his stamina.

For his part, Harvey was wondering if his supply of little purple pills would last the course. He though about asking Charlie to get him some pills from Sasha. But he had escaped intact from Sasha last night, he was not going to Mani's again, so there would be no need.

Lenny was wiping the table next to the road as they pulled up. "Good timing," she said. "Where have you been?" "We took a spin up to Mijas" Neta lied. "Oh, how was it?" She looked straight at Harvey, "A bit hairy going up, but beautiful once there" he colluded.

Neta giggled. "Yes the white village is quaint and unspoiled, what's she giggling at?" "We had a close call on the way down" he countered. "Nets is better on that road than me, how do you fancy Torry Morry with me after we eat?" Harvey looked blank.

"Torremolinos, while I'm working," Neta explained as she pulled the bike back on its stand, without difficulty. "Yes fine, I am on holiday after all. What's at Torry Morry then?" "Ken, I haven't seen him for a couple of days. I just need to tell him about the change in hours, so he doesn't waste a trip over here. He works on the beach there, it will be busy, but I'll find him."

Chapter Thirty-Four

The road from Fuengirola to Torremolinos was packed with vehicles of all shapes and sizes traveling at speed. One of the strangest sights that day was Lenny and Harvey on the bike. She perched as usual peering through the handlebars, with him towering over her on the raised pillion. They got many a toot, whistle or cheer. Every time they were passed by a juggernaut Harvey felt as though they were going to be sucked under the wheels. "Are we allowed on this road?" he asked. The intrepid Lenny took no notice and ploughed on regardless.

Harvey gave up trying to hold on the sides of the crumbling seat and opted for putting his arms around Lenny. She responded by moulding herself into his form, it was an extremely comfortable but hairy way to travel. He was beginning to love the bike and the excuse for bodily contact that it provided.

They whined and strained up the last hill to the resort and Torremolinos was laid out in front of them. Lenny cruised to the staff entrance of a large hotel and chained the bike to several others that were parked. They walked to the lobby and took the lift down to the beach. It was packed with beautiful bodies and some that should never be allowed out.

"You go that way and I'll try over here" she instructed and they plodded off on the scorching sand. Some local kids were kicking a ball around in bare feet. They were untroubled by the hot sand, that he could feel through his loafers. He had gone about fifty feet when Lenny caught him up. "You're as daft as I am" she scolded. "Why?" "Ken, what does he look like?" "Oh, I see, good point, we had better stick together then," he laughed.

They continued in the direction Harvey had taken. Although he did not know Ken he sensed, by Lenny's reaction, that the young man ahead was the boy. Kneeling on adjoining towels, Ken was busy rubbing copious amounts of sun cream on to the bare, ample bosom of a giggling blonde. Harvey watched as Lenny stormed over to the couple, in her best Barbara Windsor bustle. Sensing approaching danger, Ken had time to say "It's not what you think Len", before being floored by a crunching uppercut, that was delivered with both speed and accuracy.

She then returned to Harvey before Ken could recover. "Buy me a drink," she said, then added superfluously, " we split up."

They returned over the scorching sand to the hotel. They had chilled Colt 45 beers in the immaculate air conditioned bar. Harvey also consumed nearly a litre of iced water. The conversation was limited as Lenny sobbed quietly to herself and he put his arm around her in an attempt to comfort and console her.

His forehead was burning like mad now due to the sun beating down on him during the ride over. He plucked an ice cube from the pitcher and rubbed his tender skin. He could have done with an application of Ken's cream, but didn't think it appropriate to mention it. "No need for you to join in," she said as small rivulets from the melting cube ran down his face. He gave her a squeeze and she hugged him tight.

Back at the bikes, Lenny unchained the resting machine and leant it against the high kerb. She pulled a long nail file from her pocket and jabbed it into the tyres of the other machines. "What are you doing?" he screamed above the hissing. "One of these is Ken's, but I've never seen it in daylight" she explained.

On the way back Harvey bought some cream and a hat that he held with one hand, as a country Vicar does on a bicycle. It didn't help as it disappeared under the first lorry to pass them. He resumed his position with his hands around her waist and she snuggled back into him. After climbing a really steep hill, she pulled over to show him the fantastic view and they kissed passionately.

They stayed on the hillside for about half an hour in a silent embrace. Juan passed on an errand for the hotel, and nearly crashed the small van he was driving, in disbelief. 'Now he is with the other one, 24 hours and he has claimed the three best girls on the Costa' he thought. 'What a man, a truly modern day El Cid.'

Lenny appeared to have recovered from her let down on the beach and they resumed their journey. They rode back to the apartment the girls shared. She parked the bike under a lean-to, behind a small art gallery. They entered from an enclosed staircase where the parchment smells brought back memories of the flat he and Cass had taken so long ago.

The girls were really into posters and the stairs were lined with all types. In the living room, there was an enormous poster dominating one wall. It was of the girls posing provocatively over a powerful motorcycle. This made their own machine, in the background, look like a very poor cousin. On another wall, a photo of Enzo Snr had been transformed to a larger than life poster that looked down on his protégées, in a pose favoured by Joseph Stalin.

Harvey imagined that Enzo would have been delighted to be held in such esteem. The latest addition was a blow up of the trio Marco had taken at Hill Street. These posters were really good and they must have good connections to get them done so quick he mused. But of course they would.

Harvey put his face against his image and found the latter was a tad bigger than the real thing. From the corner of his eye, he could see the enhanced features of Neta smiling happily and he again admired her beauty. Lenny handed him an iced beer and told him to, stop snogging himself. He withdrew from the wall and sat next to her on a settee. This appeared to be a large bean bag with a padded headboard as the back.

They made love enthusiastically under the gaze of themselves and friends. It had not been instigated by one or the other, it just happened. The settee was not the ideal love bed as the beans moved around, causing small hillocks and uncomfortable hollows. Lenny appeared to be on a mission to please and impress. She either guessed his earlier encounter with Neta and wanted to better it. Or, most likely, she thought she had got him first and wanted to make damn sure she would not be placed second.

Whichever was the driving force it was a hard taskmaster. They both lay back exhausted and wringing wet when all had been expended.

Lenny swore Harvey to secrecy as Neta had done earlier. He felt a pang of guilt and would have confessed, but he could have sworn that Neta winked at him from one wall, and Enzo cracked his features into a large grin from the other. He closed his eyes tightly against the images and they dozed happily for half an hour. Each time he made the slightest move she clung to him like a baby Koala clings to its mother.

They showered together, washed each other and made love under the cool erratic stream that spluttered from the clogged shower head. This was not the stuff movies are made of, their differences in size, his old injury and the previous exertions made it awkward to generate the required enthusiasm. Lenny had given her all in the initial conquest and these extras did nothing to embellish their earlier experience. They ended in a sort of businesslike 'think of somebody nice and let's get it over" manner, adopted by married couples of many years together.

They both regretted their secondary actions, but neither spoke of it. They washed and while Lenny was getting dressed, Harvey busied himself by pricking out the holes in the shower head.

It was time for Lenny to give Neta a short break as both girls were working again all evening. Harvey silently promised not to go near Charlie Osmer's or Mani's. He would have a quiet meal at the hotel and go exploring like a good holiday maker. Back on the pillion he hoped to gain control of this holiday - but if not, what the hell?

"Oh no, she knows!" Lenny gasped as they saw Neta's tear stained face and puffy eyes, evident even from the road. She was standing at the hatch, leaning on the bar, head in hands. "She may have guessed" he agreed. He was suddenly uncomfortable about the whole situation and felt grubby. He would take full blame. Fall on his sword if necessary, check out, go home, whatever, he couldn't bear to break these girls up. Neta was right, it would spoil everything. Perhaps if he had come clean, about Neta, Lenny would have understood. But at the end of the day - he should have known better and acted responsibly.

He composed himself for the awful moment. "How long have we been?" "Well, I'm not late, if anything I'm early. Net, what's wrong? Lenny was concerned. Neta came around the bar and hugged her little friend.

"Enzo has died" she sobbed, shivering despite the heat. She fought to control her breathing and continued. "And that's not all, Charlie died last night in Mani's. They think he had that massive heart attack we have all been expecting. Cello thought it was the drink at first, and lay under him for half an hour, until - well, it wasn't very pleasant for her."

'Well that's anal for you,' thought Harvey. He stifled a giggle and concentrated on grief, but it was difficult.

Enzo came over and they sat in a small silent huddle, each with their own thoughts. Customers who approached could sense the atmosphere was not conducive for holiday spirits and moved on down the Paseo, leaving them in peace. Even the click-clack from the pool boys was subdued. From somewhere Latiffe was singing a dirge, Harvey didn't recognise it, but it seemed appropriate for the mood.

At length, Enzo broke the silence. "Harvey, we are closing up for a few days so we can all go, to the funeral, Granddad's that is. I have arranged flights for me, my brothers and the girls for the day after tomorrow. My Dad wondered if you keep a bit of an eye on the place until we get back." Harvey nodded. "Nothing much, move bits about so the gypsy folk don't think it's deserted. We have a few guests," he gestured towards the pool boys. "We will give them a change of bedding. If we show you how to make coffee they just need the continental breakfast, but that is really easy. Eh?" Harvey said it was the least he could do and wished he could do more.

"Well, you can....if you don't mind doing the same at Charlie's. Charlie and Dad had some sort of agreement and we sort of own that one as well now. When we get back, Mum's coming back here and I'm taking over at Charlie's. Mum and Saz are flying to Italy the same day as we leave here, and we'll all be back here together next week, what do you say?"

Harvey didn't hesitate, "No problem, just show me the ropes - slowly. What about Charlie, his affairs, funeral and all that? " "You don't have to worry about that, Charlie has had, a wife, she is disabled and lives round past Malaga with a Carer/relation. They have been expecting something like this for years and all is in hand. The funeral will be a quick affair and nobody from around here will be invited. Except for the old guy who sits outside - he was Charlie's brother-in-law by the by." "I would have liked to pay my last respects to Enzo, and Charlie for that matter, but if I am to be more use here that is fine." "By the by, Granddad was pleased with your letter, and had the photos you sent with him when he passed."

Chapter Thirty-Five

On the hot, dusty road outside Cadiz, the engine of the coach died in the fast lane. Henri cursed his luck, but skilfully brought the beast to a safe halt on the hard shoulder of the slow lane. Smoke billowing from the coach gave him right of passage that was observed by the otherwise speedy road users.

At first Henri suspected sabotage but the concerned look of his passengers told him it was nothing to do with them. Even ringleader Guy shed his arrogant facade, until the situation was under control, and led the spontaneous applause, directed at Henri, for a job well done.

For Claudette, this was yet another mishap to heap upon the other episodes in this catalogue of disasters. It had been less than two hours since Henri had begged, coaxed and cajoled her into carrying on. With the same ability with which he had brought the stricken coach to a safe halt. He reasoned with her that she had done the hard bit. There would be help around the corner, a short break, then home and payment, for them both - not to mention the promised bonuses. Some of which had already been paid as an inducement.

She had taken some convincing though, the Cadiz stay had been equally as bad as the other places. Although there was plenty to do and see, all the spoiled juveniles were interested in was creating havoc. They got drunk or stoned at every opportunity and tormented the life out of hotel staff, her, and Henri with no remorse.

Their organised trips were a disaster, and spent most of her time just chasing around after them. Her missing underwear had shown up in all kinds of places aimed to cause her maximum embarrassment. Some had been returned soiled, not that she looked too closely as she discarded every item.

The almost final straw appeared under her door that very morning in the guise of a photo strip from one of those booths, used by normal people for passports etc. The subject of this particular photo compilation was obviously male and wearing the last pair of panties she could remember as missing. They were of a lacy design which hid very little and it was pretty apparent what the wearer was up to in the photo. She had nearly vomited, and castigated herself for being stupid enough to look.

After destroying the pictures, Claudette charged into Guy's room and furiously turned out every cupboard, drawer and bag. She even stripped his bed but apart from some filthy magazines she found nothing to link him to the photos. Guy had watched her curiously but had wisely stood back and let her rummage. She had expected some sarcastic comments, but none came.

When she had completed her search, Guy looked at her with a shrug, to enquire what she was about. "I received something unpleasant today and, as you are the eldest, and un-elected leader, I wrongly assumed your involvement, I apologise." She then rushed from the room before her held back tears embarrassed her further. When she had gone, Guy removed the panties, which he had been wearing, and flushed them down the toilet with a grin.

On the side of the road, Claudette stood apart from the group as they waved and cheered at the few French vehicles that passed. Other nationalities were jeered and bombarded with fruit, bread rolls and the like.

She looked at the faces of the group individually but did not get any clues as to the identity of her tormentor. Nobody was looking at her directly, or even slyly. She would have expected something but no, they were just a mob with their only interest being the disruption of everything normal.

She had given up trying to look after them and if one of them got killed by a passing lorry or strayed into the path of a car, ce la vie. It would be too bad and of their own making.

A Police car drew up which quietened the youths, Claudette explained the unscheduled stop and that Henri had gone in pursuit of a telephone. They headed off in pursuit of him but not before giving her a public dressing down, and telling her to exercise more control over her party. She watched them go and spat in the dust which she then ground underfoot.

With the Police gone the idiots started playing up again. Guy started a game of chicken across the busy road, creating mayhem with the traffic. Claudette leant back against the crash barrier and took bets in her head who would be killed first.

She then started to make a mental list of all those she would like to see killed messily, starting with Guy. Before she had completed the order of descent they had tired. They slumped down in the dust - it was not fun if Claudette would not get wound up by their antics.

Henri returned with the Police. They gave Claudette an appreciative nod when they saw the group squatting peacefully. They did not bring good news.

All local firms who were able to undertake the recovery and repair would not deal with Peter Ponting's credit sources. He had the same problem with a locally based coach. A national company would, however, send a replacement and recover their coach for repair but in a few hours.

The Police tried their best to help, in truth they wanted the group off their patch, but their efforts were appreciated. First they got the coach hauled off the main road and had a generator connected so that the air conditioning was working. This should keep them off the road. The hotel they had recently checked out of refused to take them back but did agree to supply and dispatch picnic style lunches, at an inflated price.

The staff enjoyed preparing the food for a party who had driven them all mad for the last few days, and who they would never meet again. God bless their stomachs.

Claudette was having stomach problems long before the food arrived. The gnawing of several rats heralded the beginning of one of her erratic periods. It was an event that she knew must occur. She had hoped her body clock would have waited, until they had reached accommodation for the night.

Now here she was stuck, on this marooned coach full of males, with a stinking toilet the size of a shoe box.

If men had periods, she was sure they would have strove mightily to ensure the matter was treated earnestly - bah men! She tied her sweater around her waist and went to brave the toilet.

While she was away the food was delivered. Henri offered to pay, from his fuel fund, but was advised it was on the house. The youths waded in as if they had not eaten in days. The fresh seafood platters were demolished in minutes. Then they tore at the other food with the ill manners with which they were associated.

Henri declined to join the fray, in disgust. He was happy that not too many had witnessed this serious swerve away from France's legendary appreciation and respect for food. He settled for a glass of milk in the shade. Henri was feeling a bit bilious after the stresses of the day and hoped that all would be resolved soon.

Claudette looked at the remnants of the food and found a pack of smoked meats that had not been opened. She noted the expiry date was long past and a quick sniff put her off trying the contents. She joined Henri in a glass of milk, and sat with him chewing on the hardening bread without enjoyment.

A further three hours elapsed and the replacement coach turned up just as the generator ran out of fuel. Henri and Claudette had unloaded all the bags while the group lounged. But they insisted that the youths help transfer them to the new coach, before they were allowed to board. Henri had to wait for the recovery vehicle which the new driver assured him was on the way.

Claudette viewed the journey to Fuengirola without Henri, with trepidation. But she had to admit the group were quieter now than they had ever been. Half an hour down the road the driver hooted and waved to a large breakdown truck coming towards them. A quick exchange between drivers confirmed he was the recovery vehicle, good, Henri would not be far behind.

As the coached continued Guy stood at the back and spewed a vile smelling mixture down the aisle before doubling over in agony. Two other boys rushed down the small steps to the toilet in the bowels of the coach. They squabbled about who had got the privilege to use the facility first. Neither won as they vomited heavily on each other adding, to the overbearing stench. The driver was livid and pulled over to survey the scene. There was a clamour to exit the door which he was slow to open, and several more boys emptied their stomachs before they could get off.

Claudette spied Georges by the roadside. It was obvious, by the way he was walking, that his food had gone a little further down the digestive track and he had soiled his pants. The smell and sounds over her shoulder indicated that Georges was not alone in his actions.

For once Claudette could do nothing, she buried her head in her hands and laughed hysterically. This was just too much to take in, she said a silent prayer of gratitude and asked for guidance. The driver was hopping mad and screamed continually at Claudette in a style of Spanish she had never encountered. She tried to pacify the demented soul but only made matters worse by having a fit of the giggles. The driver started to believe she may in some way have instigated the apocalypse. When they were joined by the recovery vehicle and Henri, the driver was convinced that he was in the presence of a mass poisoner.

Fortunately, the recovery vehicle was equipped with a jet wash and they managed to hose out most of the foul waste. The driver had now calmed enough to think straight and those thoughts were not charitable. He outright refused to let them back on his coach which he threw into gear and absconded leaving the group behind in the road.

The truck driver was a native of the area and directed them to a cafe/bar a short distance down the road. The group shambled along behind Claudette and she was pleased to see a pile of bags and suitcases in the front of the bar, hastily left by the relief coach.

Claudette spoke to the owner who was very sympathetic and brought pales of hot water and towels to the group. They cleaned themselves and then used the owner's shower to complete their ablutions. The owner also took it upon himself to launder the soiled clothing, in between dispensing coffee and a superb paella, for Claudette that she ate with relish.

After a few hours, the stomach problems stopped. With dry clean clothes the boys started to look and act normal, albeit a bit dejected. When Henri arrived back, with the coach now repaired, he was amazed by the transformation but knew it would not last long. He indicated this to Claudette in a very French hunch of the shoulders, a widespread of the arms with his palms upwards, and his lips drawn down. She understood perfectly and returned a similar gesture with an added nod.

The owner helped Henri with the bags as the group filed quietly aboard. He then presented Claudette with the bill, which was incredibly cheap given the service he had provided. She paid from her emergency fund and ensured that Peter Ponting paid a bit more than had been requested.

At the Hotel El Torro, Ruben was beginning to enter the phase that follows concern and precedes blind panic. The restaurant staff had been sitting around for hours, since serving the last meal, and there was still no word from his esteemed French visitors. At twelve-thirty he conceded to Pedro's hissing requests and stood the staff down. This was the sign for Juan and his colleagues to start belly aching, so after another hour Ruben reluctantly let them go. He sat miserably alone behind his desk. What a catastrophe, he had turned away good guests on the strength of this booking and now they were defaulting.

The loud spitting and spluttering of the old mongrel motorbike pulling up outside caught Ruben's attention. Harvey had been sitting on the pillion with Lenny on his knees behind Neta. Harvey should have been elated to have been in such company, but when he dismounted they had a somber group hug. As the bike chugged off, Harvey turned slowly to return their wave. He entred reception and took the key from Ruben's outstretched hand. "Pleasant evening Signor?" "No, not really. How about you?" "Terrible" "That about says it all, goodnight." "Goodnight Signor."

Harvey did not need to enter 217, he could feel the sweltering heat from the stoop. He left the door ajar and returned to Ruben. "Fancy a drink?" "Si Signor". Ruben tossed him the keys to the small night bar by the restaurant. "Cold beer for me please and you take what you like, on the house Signor" Harvey returned with two beers and they sat in the comfortable chairs by the door, thankful for the small breeze.

It was after 3 am when Henri finally brought the coach to rest by the lights adjacent to the Hotel El Torro. He rubbed his red eyes and prayed a vigilant Police Officer would not happen upon him and check his log sheet or tachograph. How long he had been operating since signing on was way over any legal duration for a coach carrying passengers or any other commercial vehicle. True a lot of time was spent incapacitated and inactive but it still made a long day. He could amend the sheet when given time. He believed that the tachograph was probably disabled by the lack of power, but was not sure. At the moment he hoped he would be taken for just another airport transfer, at the start of his day.

Henri glanced over at Claudette sleeping in the courier seat and could not think when it had been occupied by anybody quite so beautiful. He glanced in the mirror and saw that all his passengers were also sleeping. They were a bad bunch to be sure, but she had given her all to try and control them. He was pleased he had talked her into staying for this last leg. They would not be fun, but she had earned all that was owed to her and more. He knew Ponting would be good for the money, if they got back intact. But she may have struggled for payment if she had jumped ship. It was a shame to wake her, but needs must and he gently tapped her on the shoulder.

Claudette woke slowly, first seeing the flashing pedestrian green man and the traffic light above. She turned and saw Henri's kindly face and smiled, he put a finger to his lips and then pointed behind them. "The hotel is there," he whispered. "The reception is lit up, go and get help and I will start unloading the bags. I need to get the coach off the road as soon as possible." She smiled again and patted his large hand thinking, he must be exhausted.

Harvey and Ruben had consumed a few Heineken, chatting over their relative lives and current affairs. Harvey had not been too revealing about his recent conquests, and Ruben had not pressed him on the matter. Dispite his own observations and Juan's gossip.

They talked like best mates blaming themselves for the misadventures. and their respective behaviours. Harvey neglected to mention that he had tied Ruben's shoelaces together but did apologise, for the state of his nose. and said he felt responsible. Ruben had assured him there were no hard feelings and vowed to relocate him as soon as he was able. This may be sooner than later, if the bloody French did not turn up.

They were interrupted in their bonding by the throb of a large Diesel engine idling outside, and the entrance of a more than a pretty girl with a clipboard.

Harvey immediately thought of a Richard Gere film involving a love match on a kitchen work top, a flying answer-phone and a passionate shower scene. But the name of the movie escaped him.

Before she spoke he knew she was French, and the way she would speak. When she spoke, it was in Spanish, not what he had expected, but the hairs stood up all over his body. He glanced at Ruben and wished he had asked him if he was gay, or very happily married, because the manager paid no attention to her beauty as he stood to his full height.

The girl was speaking again, now in English, Harvey's toes curled. "Pardon me please, you speak English yes?" "Of course, but why English?" Ruben replied testily. "Are you not French, and have you not kept me waiting all night, with not so much as a telephone call?" "I am sorry, we have been marooned on the roadside for several hours, did you not contact our office? Monsieur Ponting was fully aware of the situation. I would have...."

Ruben cleared his throat and mellowed a little, why had he not contacted Ponting, or he them for that matter? "It is enough that you have arrived. I was concerned for your safety and apologise for being sharp with you. I further regret that my staff have now retired for the night and it will be three to four hours before we can feed you, I hope you understand."

Harvey stood back and admired the girl, Neta was beautiful without question, but this young lady was a degree past that, maybe even a Goddess. He looked at his Heineken and stifled a belch. He could not believe his new best friend was being such a prat. He really was more like Basil Fawlty than the real thing, with new guests. He noted Ruben's apology and change of tone that indicated a break in hostilities.

"No matter Signor, my party has experienced a bout of food poisoning en route and are far from hungry. They are all currently sleeping and I will awaken them when you are ready. With the regard to the English, I observed you and your friend communicating as I entered. I obviously speak my native tongue as well as English and Italian. My Spanish is passable, but not credible, so after my initial salutation I opted for English, I was correct no?" "No umm yes, quite correct. Your party Signorina, you are in charge? I believed it was a cultural trip and thought you would be .... older?"

"Golan, Monsieur, Je m'appelle Claudette Golan, and I am very much in charge, certainly when it comes to blaming somebody." She smiled, but Ruben missed it as he turned to man the desk.

Harvey smiled at her and poked his tongue out at Ruben's retreating back. She smiled back, copied his action, and added a thumb in each ear with her fingers wiggling as her own gesture. before returning to the coach with a giggle.

Claudette stood in the coach doorway and clapped her hands loudly. "Attention! Ecoutez. Ecoutez s'il vous plait." When all were awake, she explained that they had arrived and must carry their own bags, which was greeted by the expected grumbles. The fact that there was also no food met with less dissent and they trouped off wearily and drowsy to get their bags.

Remarkably in the hotel they all handed over their passports as required, and retired to their rooms without further comment or histrionics. Ruben was surprised at the age of the party and scanned the passports still hoping for somebody remotely famous, or of note.

"I was expecting a party of somewhat older and more refined guests" he grunted at Claudette. "I am unable to keep apologising for things out of my control Signor. These are your guests as arranged, most are indeed of good breeding, but you would never guess. All are from wealthy families and when they are awake, you will notice their refined arrogance. Now if you will excuse me, I am experiencing my period and wish to retire. If you would please instruct our driver as to the whereabouts of the secure parking, he too is extremely tired and needs to rest, here is his passport so he is not inconvenienced when he returns. Monsieur Ponting has arranged a relief to look after the party for the next few days and I hope they meet with your approval. So I beg you, no early calls for Henri or me, if he is required he will not be available to drive until the afternoon, good night!"

She turned on her heels and did a silent 'phew' to Harvey followed by a big smile and was gone.

"Nice girl, pretty too." Harvey broke the silence. "She has the manners of a fascist pig Signor - another beer?" "Top Man, throw me the keys."

Chapter Thirty-Six

Again Harvey had no idea of the time as he woke. His travel alarm had died and he still had no watch. It was impossible to tell by the natural light if it was day or night, but it was roasting hot and he felt dreadful. He and Ruben had stayed drinking until nearly six in the morning. There was a clue, and they had played spoof for beers, ensuring that Freddie Heineken would have a prosperous year. He groped for the TV remote under the bed causing a belch. Yuk, he tasted the gin and remembered the last few drinks were not beer.

The TV burst into life and from Sky News he determined it was 20:18. "Bloody hell, twenty past eight at night, what was I supposed to be doing today?" he asked the Sky sports correspondent, then he realised it was ok. Providing he had only slept the one day away he was not expected at Hill Street until after 10 pm. "Time for a shower," he told himself and willed himself to undertake the torturous preparation for such a simple deed.

He stood under the spitting shower and scolded himself in urine coloured water. "Fucking solar panels" he screamed and almost fell from the bath. It took a while to adjust the flow and temperature to anything close to comfortable, but it gave the water time to clear a bit. He thought of the last shower he had taken with Lenny, it was not a comfortable memory. He quickly changed his thoughts to the bean bag settee encounter with which he was happier. But he was not able to shake the hangover. He remembered the last one cleared with Neta assisting in the Roy Plummer cure all method. The thoughts of the bean bag, Neta and some vigorous soaping brought an erection and he wondered if a wank would help. This change of tract brought on nausea so he decided against anything along this lines. He arched his back with his hands on his hips, enjoying the experience of a hands-free pee. He derived juvenile satisfaction in hitting the plug hole and watching his darker yellow fluid mix with the shower water. 'Looks like I'm a bit dehydrated, mental note: drink more water.' he thought.

Harvey stepped straight from the shower into the bedroom, rubbing his hair on the sandpaper towel as he went. He remembered again the joyful experience of seeing Neta sitting up in his bed, naked the previous morning.

"Hello darling, come to Mummy," she said softly. He blinked to make sure he was not imagining things.

This was no mirage. He scrambled in next to her and they kissed passionately. She reached for him and squealed, as he lost control in her hand. "Dirty boy, I hope there is more where that came from." She moved him on top of her and another Olympic Marathon ensued, leaving them collapsed in a sweaty tangle.

His hangover had disappeared, he felt invigorated and twenty years younger. Sky News told them it was 21:18 and he had enjoyed one of the best hours in his life.

He silenced the TV. 'Had it really been chatting away all this time or had the presenters just watched proceedings from their front row seats? Anything is possible on this holiday' he thought.

Eventually, Harvey was able to speak. 'I'm confused, you said...." "Yesterday was for you, this was for us" she interjected. He was not sure if he fully understood, but if he did then perhaps it explained his second dismal attempt with Lenny. The first was for him, but there was no us and, therefore, no purpose in seconds. "Who knows? Anything is possible on this holiday" he said unintentionally aloud. "What?" "Just mumbling".

"Well mumble some truth, you fucked Lenny yesterday didn't you." It was not a question. "Yes" "I knew, you had a shower after and fixed it didn't you?" "Yes" She laughed heartily, "You're so English, you shouldn't do things like that if you don't want to get caught." "Perhaps I did, do you mind?" "No, she's my friend, but don't tell her about me ok? She honestly has no idea and when she asked me I said no, and she knows I would never lie to her, so it would break her heart if ... promise?" "But you did lie to her" "Yes, but only to protect her, promise?" "Promise, but won't she guess?" "Of course not, I would never lie to her and she knows that. I want this to go on but slowly and forever, without hurting anybody."

Harvey laid back and considered the logic but it was beyond his comprehension, he had one burning question. "What happens now?" "Nothing Harvey, not yet my darling, we may get another couple of moments like this if it is not too obvious or risky, but I doubt that we have the time. Like I said before - yesterday was for you, even if you had looked like poor old Charlie. It would have happened. But you weren't like him my darling, I enjoyed it, I was not supposed to but I did. You have to have more of what you enjoy, don't you?" "Err, I'm not sure I like being treated like some object of desire..."

She could not contain the raucous laugh, it came from the belly and resounded around 217 like an echo in The Grand Canyon. "Liar" she managed to say, "anyway, what is all this about fucking solar panels? I can't have that, I'd get jealous." "Oh no, you heard that" "Darling, most of the hotel heard that."

She went on to explain that they had been concerned, but not completely surprised, by his absence. Enzo had phoned and been told that he and Ruben had been up most of the night and you Harvey, had not surfaced all day. Your door was ajar, but no key had been handed in. The man Enzo spoke to came to take a peep and you were sleeping soundly. At the end of her shift, the packing, that would normally have taken her half a day, was done in seconds, and gave her time to spend with him, without raising suspicion.

She had left a 'Gone for Harvey' note and pushed the bike until out of earshot before starting it. Lenny would find the note after a couple of hours, by which time they would be nearly on the return trip.

When she arrived, the man with the battered nose indicated the door was open, and Harvey had been swearing in the shower. She omitted the bit about spying on him and nearly dying when she thought he was going to masturbate. That would have been too much information, and she would probably have left if he had. That sort of thing reminded her of a time best forgotten. She had stifled a laugh as he first peed in the air and then, attained a level of accuracy, in the direction of the plug. She would have liked to have been on the receiving end of that deluge, and it made her horny to think of it.

"You know the rest" she concluded. "No, I don't." "What then?" "Do you love me?" "Of course, do you think I do this with everybody?" "Well then?" She sighed, "Well nothing, I told you, I want this to go on but not now, maybe a year maybe ten, maybe never, it does not matter. Don't wait for me, I will not wait for you. It must not matter to you or me. If we meet and make love it will good every time, if never again ok. Nobody can take away these memories - we are the lucky ones." "You speak with youth on your side," he said, a little gloomily, "honest and with all the time in the world."

She made as if to strangle him. "Would you ever marry me?" It was not really a proposal, but he was interested to know. "No, of course not." "Why?" he attempted a whine. "It would upset Lenny, we would have to invite all our friends and then she would know we had deceived her and I had lied." "But I need someone to take over my pension or it will die with me, and I owe it to myself to draw it for at least fifty years." He had his answer and it suited, so now they could play it for laughs or whatever, if it could be that simple.

She looked at him seriously and frowned slightly. "We can either try this, or you must marry a young virgin when you are very old. I don't expect a pension so I will not do that." She looked at him and wondered if he was teasing. "Seriously Harvey, don't wait for me, I'm even more certain now it would spoil things and us. I know Lenny and I will not travel around together forever, but at present we are inseparable, and I like it. You and I could marry others or not, who knows? Regardless we can meet somewhere each year and make love all day and night - it would be perfect. Even if we had partners, we would never get caught. No contact all year. No letters or phone calls, not the same place or time. Just a prearranged rendezvous we make in bed each year for the next, until we are too old to travel or one year one of us does not turn up. Voila, good eh?"

He laughed and made a mental note to find out what Sasha put in those pills, in case his supply of little purple friends dried up. They washed quickly, aware that time was beating them. He kept looking at her and wondered if he would ever encounter such beauty again.

"Hello." Claudette greeted them on the quarter landing as they left 217. The girls smiled at each other and he was caught for a micro-second sandwiched between them. Definitely a case of the bread being better than the filling. "Oh hello, have you settled in ok?" "Sort of, are you eating here?" "No, not tonight, it is very good but they do like to close early." "Oh thank you, I had better hurry then. How is your miserable friend?" Neta dropped her smile and looked a little hurt. Claudette spotted the change, "Oh no please, not you, you ...."

Harvey intervened and explained Ruben's attitude from the previous night. "He was very crabby. I am sorry how rude, may I introduce my friend Neta. Neta this is Mademoiselle Golan, that is right?" "So formal, Claudette please, and you?" she looked at Harvey. The three laughed, "Oh yes sorry, I am ..." "Call him Harvey, don't listen to anything else" Neta broke in chirpily.

A rumpus broke out in the foyer, Claudette made her apologies and shot off towards the restaurant. Harvey watched her go with an appreciative look that Neta spotted. "Harvey" she laughed. "Yes?" "When I said not to wait for me I had hoped it would last a little longer than one step outside your room." "No problem" he smiled, and again they exchanged knowing laughs. They pushed through the crush at the desk and deposited the room key. Ruben was shouting and waving his arms about for all he was worth to no avail. A gang of the French youngsters were running riot over the furniture in an improvised steeplechase, completely ignoring Ruben and the protests of a few guests. Harvey raised his shoulders in a gesture of solidarity and they slipped out to the bike.

"She's nice Harvey, she looks familiar." "She has something to do with that rabble, I think she looks like a French girl in a Richard Gere movie." "Breathless." "No, should I be?" "Idiot, that's the name of the movie, we had it out on video last month," she laughed. "Don't forget, if I find her shower head cleaned out, I'll know what you have been up to." They laughed, she gave him a peck as they climbed on the bike, and headed for Hill Street.

In the crammed holding bar to the restaurant, Claudette was trying to blend into the surroundings. She did not want to be called in to sort out the goings on in the foyer. She looked out of the window and observed Harvey and Neta. She watched them hug and laugh, noted the affectionate peck, as they climbed on the beaten up bike and headed towards the sea. They looked nice together, how lucky she thought, to be so happy, why could she not find somebody like that? He was her preferred age, type and quite good looking.

Enzo was cursing everybody's luck when they arrived at Hill Street, some Air Trafic Control dispute was creating havoc with European flights and they had been put on hold for at least 24 hours. Malaga was jammed with homeward bound tourists. Those travelers with local addresses had been told not to come near, and to check back the next day. Harvey was also put on hold as there was no point closing the bar until their flight was confirmed ok.

Neta began work immediately and Lenny took her break with Harvey. At her suggestion, they crossed the Paseo and walked on the beach. It was a pleasant evening, not as oppressively hot due to a drop of rain earlier. Although now completely dried up, everything felt fresher.

Room 217 had ensured that Harvey and Neta were the only ones on the Costa, who had not realised it had been raining. They stopped at a small beach bar that was selling sardines straight from a homemade griddle, over a small fire of driftwood. The wood smoke mixed pungently with the cooking fish and made them irresistible. Coupled with ice cold beers the small fish on their wooden splinters made the perfect meal - breakfast for Harvey and supper for Lenny.

From the bar they could observe Hill Street and the other bars on the strip filling up. Delayed flights were giving a much-needed bonus to the bar owners. Neta came into view carrying some plates to one of the front tables. Lenny began to fidget. "I had better go in a minute, looks like Net's busy. We should have gone round the corner where I wouldn't be able to see and feel guilty," she laughed. "Are you coming back?" "I'm not sure, if you guys are busy I'll probably get in the way, unless I can be of help?" "Na, you're alright, take a slow walk back to TNT, have one or two on the way and we'll catch up with you there. We decided, Enzo too, no good moping about. This delay is probably for the best. Give us a chance to think straight, as long as we don't miss the funeral. They do them quick here and there you know" "Yes, I know, normally a quick funeral but then they have a proper service when distant friends and relatives arrive. I'm not sure it is because of the religious side of things or a knock on from the days when there was a lack of refrigeration." "Ooh Harvey, that's an horrible thought, change the subject quick."

He was happy with the opportunity as there was something he wanted to sort out. "Lenny, yesterday, are we alright? It's just that the shower..... I'm sorry, it should never have happened." "Was a bit of a disaster eh? You didn't tell Net anything did you? I think she knows, you fixed the shower you dick. She knows I can't reach it." He didn't answer her question, but replied "She doesn't know?" "Probably, but who knows?" "Then she doesn't know." "How can you be sure, did you and Net....?" He again avoided the direct question, "I asked her to marry me, but she refused because she didn't want to upset you." "Why did you ask her that?" "Because she is gorgeous." "Oh Harvey, you are priceless, honest and gorgeous too and I love you for it." "So are you, will you marry me?" "No, I don't want to upset Neta."

They laughed and hugged, he liked her very much, she was a busty beauty but not for him, or he, her. She reached up and kissed him as a friend. "The bars on the way to TNT are Spanish. Don't drink too many, they don't understand people getting hammered, wait til we get there.

It had been a good idea to walk back. Except for the omnipresent Lookey, Lookey Men, offering him everything from 'real gold' 'original' watches to 'a bit o' good shit man'. All of which he declined.

Leaving one of the small beach bars, Harvey came upon the unmistakable shape of Lattiffe hammering a bent coin into the slot of a pay phone. "Encourages Whitey to use the da air conditioned facilities of a friend," he explained. "Hey, you ain't bought nuthin yet man. How's a guys 'posed to earn an honest livin?" Harvey nodded towards the mangled telephone. "Touché" nodded Lattiffe with a laugh.

By the time, he reached TNT Harvey was rested and relaxed. He had taken Lenny's advise and had taken only a couple of small beers en route, if only to give his liver a break. He had a small debate with himself about going in but reasoned that he had agreed to meet the others and he had not actually been awake very long. Sleep in 217 would be impossible while he was in control of all his faculties.

It was another quiet night at TNT and there were more people trying to get out than go in. Harvey settled at the bar and ordered a pilsner. There were some of the rowdy French kids hanging around the few girls in the place, but no sight of Mademoiselle Golan. A small figure minced from the toilet to join the group but kept his distance from the girls.

The Barman gave Harvey another beer 'on the house' and explained that the few customers he had attracted that evening had been driven off by the antics of the French kids.

Only the drag queen, formerly known as Doris, was happy to be surrounded by the youths and seemed genuinely disappointed as they made to leave. The Barman shrugged, "I will close Signor unless you would like to be alone with......? He indicated Doris, who was starting to pout.

"Promise not to poison me or make me useless in the morning and I will earn you some money. Also my friends are coming from. Hill Street soon Harvey said." "Promise," the Barman replied. A little confused but hopeful of putting some cash in the till and seeing Lenny and Neta, he nodded in Spanish.

Harvey jumped from his stool and rushed to the door and barred the exit. "I challenge you to a drinking competition or are you scared to be beaten by an Englishman?" They turned towards Guy. "We are French Mister Roast Beof" spat Guy indignantly. "We are not scared of a little competition. We are getting bored so you had better be careful where you throw your gauntlet."

"Game on then" Harvey replied and they went back to the bar to discuss rules of engagement. They, of course, were not frightened by the prospect of a drinking bout, had they not been on one long one for three weeks? Guy in particular relished the thought of drinking this Anglaise into oblivion and taking his holiday money. Doris twitched with this influx of testosterone and hovered on the fringe.

They stood in a circle around one of the larger round tables, placed a bottle in the centre and spoofed to see who was to take the first spin. In this game once the bottle stopped spinning whoever it was pointing at had to drink whatever the person to his right ordered. The person on the left paid and the drinker span the bottle and so on.

Fate called it that the main participants were Harvey and Guy who were rooted to their positions. The other lads swapped places so they could invent more concoctions from the bar and sharing the burden of paying. After several losses, and a particular weird mixture of Creme de Menthe, Jack Daniels, local Sherry and Quantro, Guy reluctantly admitted defeat and rushed to the toilet hotly pursued by Doris.

Harvey was acknowledged by the crowd, who were quite pleased to see Guy the loser for once. What they did not know was that

Harvey had been drinking mixtures of various food colourings with small amounts of whatever spirits he had been sentenced to drink, Guy, of course, had suffered the full onslaught and the till had benefited greatly. All the same, it had been a long game. Guy had been a worthy opponent, so Harvey had consumed quite a bit, dispite the Barman's best efforts. Nobody else wished to experience the same fate as Guy so the game wound up, as the girls arrived with Enzo.

The French boys stood and gawped at the girls who completely ignored them. The pool boys also turned up to swell the numbers. Their radar was well and truly tuned to the movements of Lenny and especially Neta.

Silhouetted in the doorway Harvey noticed Claudette was peering into the gloom and peeled away to invite her to join them. She baulked a bit when she saw her group but accepted the invitation. Drinks and a table were organised while Harvey completed introductions.

Enzo felt his toes curl as Claudette shook his hand, she was impressed that he and Harvey stood until all were seated.

"And what were you up to as we arrived, all that cheering?" Neta asked Harvey with an accusing grin. Before he could reply a rumpus from the toilets drowned out the music.

Enzo jumped as Doris collided with his chair. He was pursued by a non-to steady Guy. "More to the point what has HE been up to?" Whatever Doris had been up to it was obviously not to Guy's liking, it was also obvious if he caught Doris there would be a murder.

Doris had other ideas, a veteran of similar toilet encounters had given him a flight of foot and the speed of a Greyhound. He weaved through tables to the door, running circles around his unfortunate pursuer. The cheers of delight and derision from his chums only served to enrage Guy more. He was literally crying, like a temperamental child, as he crashed through the Fire Exit in the hopes of catching Doris.

Claudette was delighted to see Guy so publicly humiliated and was pleased her new found friend had contributed to his downfall. She did not expand on her reason for being so pleased, only to say that Guy was 'difficult in a group situation'. She also warned Harvey to watch out for revenge.

Claudette was pleased to find Enzo was part Italian and they spent a while rattling away in their shared second language. She also made allies of the girls by announcing that she had a motorbike of the same hybrid as theirs at home, but not in as good condition.

When Claudette was talking to Enzo and Harvey was distracted, Lenny spoke to Neta. "Nets, he's a lovely bloke but we don't want to fued over him do we? He'll be gone soon, after we get back from Italy, then it will be us again against the world. What ya say we fix him up with Frenchie?" "Your right Len, he's only a man, I'm with you" she lied, 'No! Why did she have to turn up?' she asked herself but smiled and nodded agreement.

They all got on well and the girls invited Claudette to join them at Hill Street. It was agreed that Harvey would bring her during the day. Neta shot him a disappointed glance, she would not be picking him up if he was bringing Claudette.

Harvey escorted Claudette to the hotel as the others departed on the bike, Neta at the helm with Lenny sandwiched in the middle.

They hardly had a chance to speak and Harvey's contest with Guy had started a churning feeling that was catching up with him. Ruben had not bolted the door and was a bit abrupt as they received their keys, Harvey didn't notice and Claudette thought it was just normal. They parted at Harvey's door with the briefest good nights as he fell into 217 and lurched to the bathroom. After about an hour of being sick Harvey went and asked Ruben for water. Ruben apologised for being abrupt earlier and blamed it on his nose that was hurting and those French imbeciles.

He explained that he had tried to offload them, but the owners would not hear of it as they were a good source of income, it was going to be a long week.

Harvey returned to his room and sipped the fizzy water Ruben had given him. He was sick again but by the time he reached the sardines he reasoned that most of the booze was out of his system. He took a couple of Annadin Extra and finished the water. The room was a smidgin cooler than oven temperature and he was able to sleep the next few hours as he sweated out the rest of his toxins.

He woke in the morning in readiness for breakfast. After he had showered he realised he did not have a hangover and, as he peered enquiringly at his bed, or Neta.

Breakfast was a disappointing affair. A buffet of hard bread rolls, ice cold boiled eggs, slices of plastic cheese and transparent cold meats. No wonder the Full English was alive and well at Hill Street.

The Germans seemed to favour the offerings as they filled their plates and pockets as they barged their way to the tables. The coffee was excellent, after a taster, Harvey poured himself a large black one and went in search of a table. This was easier said than done as Herman The German and his Frau were aplenty. In the morning, they appeared to want a table each and were oblivious to other people hovering with balanced plates and cups. Surrounded by breakfast offerings and with a large broadsheet covering their table the occupants would only acknowledge fellow diners with a snarl if they dare approach. It reminded Harvey of a dog with a bone.

Waiters were purely on clearing duty and would not get involved with seating disputes, so Harvey took the initiative. From the corner of his eye he noted a movement as an oversized specimen started to stand. Harvey pounced, he was seated before the chap had completed his manoeuvre.

Sitting amongst the departing Germans breakfast debris, Harvey brushed flakes of bread and eggshells into a small pile. He looked up to see Claudette standing over him, "Not my mess" he said defensively as he stood to greet her. "I know, I was impressed with your speed, especially after last night. You must have a good constitution as they say (I think), and you just beat me by a second." "Oh please you are welcome to join me, I would have waited but we never said a time. To be honest, I was quite hungry until I saw what there was." "I have just seen my relief, none of the group has risen yet and she has the coach and everything waiting, they really are impossible." "Tell her to take the Germans instead, they seem to like whatever is on offer. Will you join me?" "Only if you beg." "Pleeeease, how's that?"

They sat and exchanged smiles. "You are soapy," she said. "Really, well I've just had a shower but, to be honest, it is hard work to get a lather." "What are you talking about? I mean you are silly in that English way." "Ah you mean soppy" and they laughed again.

Juan was on table clearing duty, he had complained to Pedro that the Germans made at least twice as much work. Pedro cut off his protests with a hiss and pointed to Claudette, who was about to sit. Juan rushed over and whisked their table cloth away as Harvey lifted his cup. Juan had his eyes on Claudette but then realised she was not alone, he stood with the table cloth and just gawped, Signor Bright, again!

"He gave you a strange look," Claudette remarked. "They're all a bit strange if you ask me" Harvey replied and she nodded in agreement. "Can I get you some breakfast - petite dejeuner?" "That's close enough but keep to the English. Just coffee, oh look that boy has brought a tray of....." Harvey beat the Germans to the fresh croissants and grabbed two each. He took them in each hand an placed them on the fresh cloth then returned with plates, coffee and jams.

"Now everybody is looking at you strange," she laughed. "You even got one last night from Neta" "When?" "At the end of the evening and don't pretend you didn't notice, what was that about?" "I don't know, I didn't notice really, why?" he semi-lied. "Oh nothing, do you have something going?" "No" he lied. "What about all that laughing and hugging last evening outside?" "We are good friends already, but I only met her a couple of days ago. She is lovely, though." "She is and it looked more than friends really - from the outside. There would be no shame if you were seeing her, you get on well" she was probing. "It's not that simple, nothing is, anyway I'm old enough to be her father." Claudette looked him straight in the eyes and said "That should not matter a jot, and certainly would not matter to me."

He felt his toes involuntary curl and he shivered. She noted the effect for future reference and changed the subject subtly, to one closer to home. She had experienced great difficulty getting a table for diner the previous night because of the other guests unwillingness to share. They made a pact to dine together whenever possible and Harvey promised to bully them onto an under occupied table or use his skills to preempt departing diners. They clinked coffee cups to seal the deal, Pedro crossed himself at this act of sacrilege and hissed.

They walked to the seafront and headed along the Paseo. He listened intently to her stories of childhood and the circumstances that had brought her to the Hotel El Torro. She again skirted around

310

the not so nice bits, but she was enjoying being the centre of attention. He was a good audience. When they got to Hill Street, he knew more about her than anyone she knew. She learned nothing new about him, other than he was a good listener, who she would like to share the rest of her life with. 'Must be the relief of being away from the rabble' she thought.

Neta and Lenny were sitting at the roadside table having a cup of tea as they crossed from the beach. They were not holding hands, linking arms, or walking exceptionally close, but both girls noted a certain body language between them. As they approached the table, the girls looked at each other with their heads tilted and forefingers placed exaggeratedly on their chins "Oooooh!" they said in unison.

"What's the matter you with you two?" Harvey asked. "Nothing" they replied innocently, again in harmony. "Tea?" Neta asked, they both nodded. "Then I shall be Mummy" she quipped, looking directly at Harvey. "Err thank you" he coughed.

Enzo intervened, much to Harvey's relief. He jerkedd his thumb at a vacating table and Lenny scampered off to clear it. "Thank you, ooh thank you very much," she called after the departing backs and put the cash in the till and the large tip in their jar.

Enzo welcomed Claudette and then told Harvey that they had received confirmation from Malaga and would be flying out in the morning. As they had not required hospitality their return flights would be on the airline. He then asked Claudette to excuse them and took Harvey to the bar. He explained all the keys and the coffee machine to him. The pool boys would be there for three more days and had settled up already. He had made an arrangement with a nearby bar for their meals if they wanted them, but usually they just snacked. He told Harvey they were no trouble and would leave their keys on the bar if they didn't see him.

Charlie's keys were more plentiful. Enzo explained he would not need to go there unless something cropped up. He had been that morning and Mani Soler would keep an eye on the place, but would contact Harvey if access was required. Enzo was not keen on Mani having the keys to himself.

"One more favour Harvey, if you don't mind." "Name it." "If you don't get pissed tonight and if you can get up in the morning...." "Ouch!" "Sorry mate, if it's no trouble can you bring Bessie back from the airport for us?" "Who's Bessie?" Harvey was dreading another beauty hiding in the wings. "Not a who. It's our old camper van, my brothers named it. A cross between Beast and Nessie. I'll drive it out there if you can bring it back, she stays in the garage under your old mate's apartments." "I should be able to manage that, it's a busy road but no diversions, just stick to the sea - right? It is insured?" "Great, you're a star, err best to say don't drive it round too much - it err, is not strictly legal." Harvey sighed. "Is anything to do with your Dad strictly legal, or even barely legal?" "Well, some of the girls he hangs out with are barely l........" Harvey launched a cushion at him.

"You look nice." Neta had returned from the table clearing and was making small talk with Claudette. "Thank you, I know you didn't say it for a return compliment, but you look great. No wonder those boys will not take their eyes off you." "They won't will they? Watch this!" Neta went through the finger in the mouth, only dreaming, routine as Claudette hid her head in her hands and shook with laughter. One of the boys nearly fainted.

"They are only boys," said Neta, "and I like men." She observed Harvey lobbing a cushion at Enzo and added "Even if they don't act like it." The point was missed by Claudette as the action had happened behind her. She looked in the direction Neta had glanced, on cue Harvey looked over and smiled. "He's nice, I didn't realise your bar was on the beach. Well nearly, or I would have come to sun bathe." "Don't you swim?" Net asked. "Yes, but I have a heavy one." This was good news to Neta. "What a shame" she lied.

"Listen, why don't you take the bike and pick up something for the beach. We have to work till six, but it will be great if you chill out there and pop over for drinks and stuff. We have some stuff here, but Lenny's will be too small and mine too big." "I will if you don't mind, do you think Harvey would like to change?" "I hope so, I can't wait to see him in something more revealing," Neta lied again. "He's having instruction at the moment but ask him."

Harvey asked her to pick up something appropriate from his room, if Ruben would giver her access. He watched as she swung the bike round in a wide arc and shot off like an angry hornet. "I want to come back as that bike seat," said Enzo. "And I want to tell Saz you're a dirty little git." said Harvey. He received a jet of steam in the ear as a reward. "Always watch the machine when you are using it, Harvey, you might miss the view, but it's less painful." Enzo laughed.

The jet of steam had served to bring Harvey down to earth. He had been feeling rather smug. He had the affections of Neta and now could look forward to a few days in the company of Claudette. He felt drawn to her from their first encounter and he could feel the chemistry between them. He hadn't contemplated getting her into bed, but enjoyed her company. Being surrounded by such beauty and getting so much attention was turning his head. He could understand Sasha and Anastasia, it was their work to turn on the charm to order, but he secretly hoped they liked him too. Lenny had been a strange liaison. He had achieved the ambitions of many a boy on the Costa, but somehow felt uncomfortable with it. Still for sure that would not happen again. Neta had spoken openly about her feelings and if she had asked him to back pack around the world with her, he would have accepted.

Now he detected a small rivalry between Claudette and Neta for his attention. This added to his confusion but boosted his ego a few notches past 'big head'. Enzo was staring at him, "Don't worry Harvey, there will only be one left tomorrow, mind you, carry on the way you're going and another coach could appear later." He tossed a styrofoam cup at him.

He told himself he was a middle-aged grandfather, with very little to offer those with whom he was consorting. These were holiday dalliances that were to be enjoyed, stored in the back of one's mind and only referred to when there was a need to be cheered up, a bit like rereading a favourite book.

The angry hornet returned and for once the pool boys' eyes drifted off Neta. The glance towards the bike were pure instinct but the sight they observed dispelled all other thoughts from their minds. Claudette had chosen a belted pair of dark shorts and a cream cheesecloth shirt. There was more material in the belt than the shorts and the shirt was tied in a knot above her flat tummy. The activity underneath the shirt suggested no bra and a stride through the bright sunshine proved it. She wore sneakers and a cream Amelia hat with a blue and white gingham band, combining school girl innocence with Parisienne chic.

"Claudette looks nice." Neta understated to nobody in particular. "Doesn't have your legs, though" Lenny replied loyally. "Thank you sweety, got the rest though hasn't she?" Any reply would have been superfluous.

Claudette handed Neta the bike key and threw Harvey a small bag. He caught it and charged for the stairs to change. He looked back to watch them smile at his antics and bumped into Enzo. "School out?" he asked.

They spent a pleasant day on the hot beach. They took full advantage of the matted palm leaf umbrellas and the slatted wooden boardwalk, that made the boiling sand negotiable. Over towards Fuengirola, they spotted a speedboat towing a parachute high above it and vowed to have a go later in the week. They talked and dozed, took the occasional beer and had a paddle, comfortable with each other. Soon it was six and the others joined them.

"Hello lobsters'" Neta called. They had caught the sun but were not burnt, only Harvey's forehead shone out. He enjoyed letting Neta rub cream into his scalp. She sat astride the bed with her back to the others, she popped a couple of shirt buttons to let him know what he was missing, as she massaged his temple. She pulled his head gently forward and could feel his breath. He fought the urge to kiss her, Neta sensed this and let his head go back. She looked him straight in the eyes, the look confirmed everything she had said the previous day. He knew he would see her again, if it was to be on her terms then amen, for as long as it lasted.

They adjourned to a small Chinese restaurant where the food was excellent and the service friendly. With an order to 'please bring what you recommend' they were treated to dish after dish of delights, and, Harvey noted, not all the expensive ones.

Latiffe tried to put in an appearance but was shooed away by their little hosts. He shrugged and gave that mischievous grin that lit up his eyes, "See you still need a watch Whitey, get you soon," he promised, Harvey waved and laughed.

They broke off early and Enzo promised to bring Bessie round at six in the morning for the airport run. The girls buzzed off into the night on the bike blowing kisses to all and sundry in their wake. Neta was in charge with Lenny perched behind her, for some reason Harvey was reminded of the Paddington Bear rucksacks he had recently bought his granddaughters for school.

They declined Enzo's offer of a lift back to the hotel in favour of a walk, and meandered off, but did not go straight back. They took a cold drink from a kiosk and sat on the wide sea wall watching the twinkling lights of the fishing boats. They sat quietly immersed in thought. Harvey recalled his antics with Marco when last at sea but did not divulge any of it to Claudette.

She was on a different track entirely as she suddenly snuggled up to him and said "Oh Harvey, this is so romantic." She noted a look of surprise on his face as she brought him back to the moment. "What? Please don't start that age thing, Neta said it is just a number, people count, not fucking numbers." "Your English is really very good" he laughed.

"Please Harvey, tell me about yourself, you can leave out any bad bits, but I don't think you will have caused any." She listened as he told her some tales of his Hippy Days, and he was impressed by her knowledge of the era. She was more in tune with the music than he had been. Not surprising really as he had been stoned most of the time.

"You surprise me, Harvey." "Why?" She laughed "Well I got the impression that you were an instigator, is that the correct term? But you are modest and make it sound like you just happen to be in places where things happen."

He was about to tell her about the Korean at the airport but was interrupted by a loud blaring of sirens and screeching of tires. They watched as a large four by four left the road to avoid traffic waiting at the red light, and sped along the Paseo towards them. Behind the jeep was a speeding Police car and Land Rover. They too mounted the pedestrian way and pulled up behind the jeep that had been forced to stop by some newly placed bollards.

The Police jumped from their vehicles and surrounded the jeep, guns drawn. The occupants were orderedout, one at a time. They had front row seats as the occupants were laid face down and spread-eagled on the Paseo. Thankful that the weapons had not been used.

Harvey swallowed hard as the back seat passengers half climbed and were half pulled from the jeep. He immediately recognised the large forms of Lattife and, he believed, Mani Soler emerging to join the others.

His heart missed a few beats as the tailgate was opened and a rather smelly swordfish was removed. "See what I mean Harvey, you are incredible" she managed to whisper and squeezed his arm.

While the others were being frisked, Mani and Lattife were hustled to the Police Land Rover for the same treatment, neither man showed any sign of recognition towards Harvey. As they passed, Harvey felt two large thuds in his chest and thought he had been shot. He realised that by slight of hand Lattiffe had landed two huge rolls of bank notes in his lap. At the vehicle, they were comprehensively searched before being loaded aboard and driven away.

The other pair were placed in the Police car, an officer reversed their jeep and followed the procession.

Harvey was left holding several thousand, or possibly a real million, pesetas. He quickly concealed them from Claudette, who was wrapped up in the proceedings. He did not owe Lattiffe or Mani a dime or any loyalty come to that, but could not bring himself to alert the Police to his windfall.

"I think that's enough excitement for tonight Mademoiselle" he said calmly. More than a little disappointed at the abrupt ending to their evening. "I have to be up early for the airport." "Harvey, you are incredible, never in my life have I experienced such a thing and you are not even bristling a hair. I am thinking I am going to be shot and you are planning tomorrow, you are incredible no?" "No." "Marry me Harvey" "No." "No? why?" "You would get bored" "Never!"

They walked back to the hotel, he sensed she was shaking a little from the experience. He put his arm around her and she snuggled into him. "Are you cold?" he asked. "Idiot" she replied. It was still early in comparison to his previous nights out and Juan was at the desk. He looked admiringly at the girl and enviously at Harvey as he handed over their keys. Still within earshot he heard Claudette say "Come to my room" but Harvey politely declined and she gave him a big kiss.

As Harvey opened his door the heat-blasted out and she peered into the gloom, "You are sure?" "Go before I change my mind," he said. They arranged to meat for breakfast and she kissed him again before skipping up the stairs. When he was sure, she had gone

Harvey doubled back and amazed Juan by returning his key and went out.

The Spaniard peered from the main door and slipped into the shadows behind Harvey. He watched in disbelief as Harvey descended into the establishment of Mani Soler. "What a man" he declared to the blinking traffic lights and returned in time to be relieved by Ruben.

Claudette thought he was a bit special too and impressed that he had declined her offer. This was different from the treatment to which she had become accustomed. "Special," she said aloud as she climbed into bed.

Harvey was relieved that two girls he did not know were at the bar. Venus rose to her full height and reached for the brandy. He stopped her midway and beckoned her to the unoccupied end of the bar. He did not know if he was doing the right thing, but he gave Venus a brief account of the incident and the large wads of notes. She showed little concern for Mani and Lattiffe, probably confident that they would secure their release without delay. She was however very pleased that he had brought her the money. An amount such as this would indeed have raised questions and probably have got 'lost' in transit. "Mani will not forget this Harvey. Sasha will be down soon, you may have her company for the rest of the night, or the new Romanians if you would like" she indicated the two new girls. It was like asking if he wanted one lump or two in his tea. "They have to stay here, but you can take Sasha to your hotel if you prefer."

In the distance, Harvey could hear the oriental tones of a certain lady bidding a fond farewell to a satisfied customer. "No, err not tonight thank you, I have to do something early but thank you" he spluttered in panic.

The thought of Sasha in Room 217, he retreated quickly and left by the way he'd had come in - not many had done that.

Back at the hotel Ruben told him that the French kids were driving everybody nuts. The new help had confided that they would not put up with much more.

Harvey made a mental note to tell Claudette to keep her head down and went to his room. 217 was sweltering and he nearly fell back on the landing, he ignored Ruben's drinking mime and entered. He considered demanding a replacement but dismissed the thought. Firstly they may move him away from Claudette and secondly he had survived the first week.

He left the door ajar to try and encourage some cooler air in while he took a shower, but failed dismally on both counts. Nothing was circulating round this dead hole tonight and the shower refused to deliver anything more than a sandy gurgle. He settled for a smelly shit which he wafted on to the landing with satisfaction and the aid of a hotel leaflet.

They still had not provided any toilet paper, but he managed with a steady cold dribble from the bidet to clean himself. He sat with his bits immersed for some time. He revelled in the comments of late guests passing by, concerning strange but serious smells and Spanish drains in particular.

He resorted to a tried and tested remedy for sleep. With only a towel around his waist he obtained a large gin and a cold Heineken from Ruben. He consumed these in his room with two Piriton tablets. He then lay on his bed where he finally felt a small draught from the still open door and drifted into sleep.

Deeply asleep Harvey did not stir as the door clicked shut. He only moved slightly as he felt a warm presence next to him. He became fully awake inside Neta as she rode astride him, with more than a degree of urgency. "What are you doing?" he stupidly asked. "Not now my Darling, there are only minutes, and it may be a year before we are together again. I was worried you would be with Frenchy."

He started to get the sex object complex again but put it to the back of his mind. A year was a long time between such experiences. Her urgent groping at his buttocks brought back memories of long fingernails and a painful rectum. They climaxed quickly as she demanded. Almost immediately Neta jumped from the bed causing a loud slurping sound that took Harvey by surprise. He reached to kiss her, but she dodged him and started to sluice herself in the inadequate bidet. "No time my dear Harvey" she called above the splurging bidet, "Enzo is parking as we speak." She emerged looking hurried but calm, she pulled him to his feet and they wobbled in the centre of the bed as she gave him a final kiss. "Now bathroom, go, see you in five in the reception." He presumed she meant minutes, but you never know.

"Jeez Harvey, who have, you upset?" Enzo was in the doorway as Harvey stepped from the bathroom. "Everybody asks that, how did you get in, if 'in' is the correct term for where you are standing?" "Lanky gave me the key, Neta said she couldn't rouse you, you must have been under the shower. We're a shade close to time" he urged. Harvey grinned to himself, Neta could rouse the dead if she wanted.

"Must have been, that bloody shower sounds like a jet..." "I hate ta interrupt - but talking of jets..." "Yes, of course, two minutes, err there is not really room for you if I am to get dressed" "Two minutes and counting."

Ninety seconds later Harvey was in reception. Enzo was at the desk sharing a coffee with Ruben as he descended from 217. Neta was looking nonchalant in the comfy chair and Lenny was perched on the large arm. "Ah there you are" she smiled. "We thought you had a woman with you when Neta couldn't get you up." Lenny had a way with words. "Sorry. shower. Any more coffee going, Ruben?" "I can make more Señor." "No time sorry mate, you can finish this if you want" Enzo offered his cup apologetically. Harvey waved it away and took a mineral water from the stand which he waved at Ruben, who nodded. "Come on then," he said, "I thought you were in a hurry. Neta squeezed his hand as she brushed against him, "Nice work Cowboy" she whispered.

Chapter Thirty-Seven

Outside, in the bright sunshine, Bessie looked worse than Harvey imagined. He fully expected to see his mother at the wheel. She was a VW of the much loved Australian vintage, but made Troy's machine look like a Rolls Royce in comparison. She was not equipped with anything, but some rickety mismatched seats. These did not appear secured to anything. She had been hand painted purple which was peeling, to reveal her original cream and deep rust colour. She resembled something that Monty would take into battle against Erwin Rommel. The sliding midway door was secured open with plastic coated wire that any self-respecting chicken would have shunned and the high rear window above the engine was completely missing.

The two younger brothers sat sweltering in the back and Harvey noticed a hurriedly dismissed cigarett fly from the missing window. Enzo started her up "Deja Vous" Harvey said to no one in particular, as he climbed into a loosely tied down garden chair. "That's for tourists Harvey, come up front." Enzo laughed. He waited for a bit of smoke to clear and slid alongside Enzo on the front bench seat, which was secure. After a few failed attempts to close his door, Lenny shoulder charged it from the kerb, and it reluctantly ground into place. When they set off the VW engine sounded normal but everything else shook. It soundeded like a milk float full of empty bottles rattling in their crates. Harvey was tempted to break into a rendition of Ernie (the fastest Milkman in the west), but that would have been lost on his young audience.

Harvey looked over his shoulder. The girls were unconcerned in their chairs, as they clung on. The boys were perched on upturned Coca Cola crates and were sliding around with the motion. Great fun - barely legal!

As they passed under the watchful eye of the large black bull on the hillside, Enzo started to rummage in the side pocket of Bessie. Enzo drove without concern, as he entered the main highway. He handed Harvey two bunches of keys. "Here are the keys to ours and

Charlie's. I've put a note on them for you, please don't lose them, he half-joked with a sideways glance. Harvey took them without taking his eyes off the road and placed them on the seat between them. He found it hard to concentrate as he watched the serious amount of play in the steering. Bessie responded to half revolutions of the steering wheel, but Enzo handled her like a fairground hand with a dodgem car.

Harvey looked up at the bull and could have sworn it had its eyes closed. "Trouble wi Bessie is that she has nay horn and that can be a disadvantage on these roads." On cue a small Fiat, that resembled a Disco Roller-boot, shot between them tooting wildly at a Sprite delivery van. This making a three lane carriageway out of the legal two, and an old man out of Harvey. He said a silent prayer and vowed that if he got back safely he would not move the beast again.

At Malaga International Airport, Enzo pulled up in the lane reserved for taxis and they began to disembark. The young brothers waved to Harvey and made their way to the toilets for a pre-flight fag. Lenny reached up and kissed Harvey in a friendly way, and then collected up all the travel documents before bustling off to the check-in desks. While Enzo was collecting a luggage trolley Neta pulled Harvey on to the blind side of Bessie.

"I'm not coming back next week. Marco has asked me to stay on and help Mario sort things out. You know Mario's a sweet old queen, but he couldn't sort out squat." "You have unusual terminology for a non-Brit." Harvey teased. "Must be Lenny's influence, anyway shut up and listen. I'll not see you before you leave..." "Ow.." "Will you shut up, anyway the painters will be in." "Eh?" "A spot of colour down below" Before he could speak she continued, "Len says that all the time, either that or something about visitors. Anyway...." "You don't half say 'Anyway' a lot, have you noticed?" "Will you shut up, anyw... Oh fuck it, anyway next week I'm not coming back and you will be gone, but just remember what I said about next year." She put a finger on his lips to stop him speaking so he just nodded. "Good, I have your number, don't change it and I will ring just this one time ok? Kos sounds good to me, Greece. A little difficult from here but good from the UK, OK?" He nodded eagerly, she could have said the dark side of the moon and got the same response. "Good, don't forget, even if we have partners ok?" She looked at him carefully, "Tell her to visit her relations in France" she added with a curious look, but softened and gave him a firm and more than a friendly kiss.

"Come on Net, he won't fit in your bag" Lenny called from the door to Departures. The doors were going mad as she stood in the catchment area of the sensor, "Leave some for the French contingent." Harvey blushed bright red, but Neta grinned and said "Next year, no frogs allowed." She squeezed his bum and yelled back "Coming, just told old Harvey to keep his hands off you next week, and that the shower is fixed now". With that, they were off giggling, and turning the heads of all male travelers in the terminal.

A pile of luggage moved towards him, "You ok mate, you're very red?" "Bit hot." Enzo was also very red as he struggled with the trolley. "Look at this lot I ask ya. One fucking week, it's not as if they wear anything but a belt round their ass and a sash around their tits. You sure they haven't made room for you in here?" He looked accusingly at Harvey, who laughed, "All yours I promise."

He watched them go and jumped behind the wheel of Bessie accompanied by a cacophony of beeping taxis, impatient to use their lane. He left them chewing on exhaust fumes as he made his way towards the exit and the main road back. At least it would be a straight run once he got on that road.

This was worse than he feared, from his observations of Enzo at the wheel. He had made it look easy with his casual fumbling for keys and chat, but Harvey found it a much more difficult prospect. Not only was there nearly a full turn of play on the steering wheel but the column moved up and down as well. For a time, until he had cleared the airport comple, Harvey kept Bessie in second or third gear. He was not sure which. He held the column upright by applying pressure to the bottom of the wheel with his knee. A few speed humps made this a painful experience.

He finally made the Torremolinos road before serious cramp set in. He reasoned at his speed of a steady 40kph he had nearly an hour to endure. At least he was immune to the tailback of frustrated drivers choking on Bessie's exhaust fumes. As the road widened, he was overtaken by vehicles of the large and small variety. They indicated their displeasure in the universal language of a two or one finger salute. Some ambitious souls even used both arms in a bent elbow gesture of unpleasantness.

After a while on the big road he found he could control Bessie by moving the column or wheel up and down, or from side to side, in the way a pilot controls a small aircraft. In this way, he was able to increase his speed but could do little about decreasing the smoke.

The lay-by in which he had stopped with Lenny was in view on the straight road, and Harvey was gaining in confidence. He started to dream that he was a World War II fighter ace, flying his beloved but injured Bessie back to Blighty, after downing a few Hun. He looked forward to viewing the gun camera so he could claim his kills. As his mind wandered, the hills of Southern Spain became the approaching white cliffs of Dover. The trail of smoke behind was where he had been winged by Jerry. He had not seen the blighter but managed to evade him and climbed into the sun. Then he had come around on the bugger, screaming out of nowhere and sent him off to meet his maker. A good job was done, and one more victim to paint on the battered ship. He was on familiar territory now and could almost taste the strong sweet tea back at the base. With luck, Jimmy Caruthers would have a wee drop of Black & White Whiskey to enhance the brew further, before he was debriefed. Then the squadron would have a game of British Bulldog prior to a night around the upright Joanna, singing their hearts out, puffing on their pipes and sinking a few decent ales. Ah good times, war wasn't a bad old game if you played by the rules - BANG!!!

In the rear view mirror, Harvey could make out a small car or van through the smoke. It was dark blue. The official looking dark blue favoured by the Police. He had dreaded meeting them in this infernal contraption, no longer his beloved.

What had happened he did not know, his mind had wandered and perhaps his driving had followed. Whatever had occurred there had been a bump of some kind and the pursuing vehicle was flashing its headlights like mad. The lay-by was now immediately ahead and so there was no alternative than to pull over. No point in making things worse, he certainly couldn't out run them.

The view was spectacular as Harvey blinked in the sunlight with his right eye. He would have liked to blink his right eye too, but it did not want to open. His head throbbed steadily and he could taste blood mixed with dirt in his mouth. "That bugger must have had a friend hiding in the clouds over Dover. Ah well at least I'm on terra firma, and on friendly soil," he told himself. He lay back on the ground and waited for Jimmy Caruthers to come and pick him up, at least he had survived the fall.

The next time he sat up the view, eye, head and mouth were the same. But this time he knew there was no Jimmy Caruthers, no chaps, no beloved Bessie. In fact, no Bessie of any description, and no nicely labelled fucking keys to Hill Street or Charlie's.

He did not know the time, but he knew what had happened, he'd been severely mugged. The official looking vehicle had been equipped with a bull bar and rammed him. When he had pulled over they hauled him to the ground with ease. They gave him a good going over before he could say 'Jack Robinson' (not that he would have). He knew that they were a 'they' but did not know their number.

After a further unnecessary kicking they left him Bessieless in the dirt and made good their escape. His unconsciousness had probably given them more than enough time to do whatever they intended.

Juan recognised Harvey slumped in the dirt and realised that he was not in the lay-by by choice. He helped him into the small van and listened to his tale of woe without comprehending very much. He did ascertain that Harvey had been the victim of a crime and not suffered a beating from a jealous boyfriend as he had first suspected. He was not sure how Harvey would respond to a Police interrogation, so he took him to where he knew he would get all the help he needed.

Chapter Thirty-Eight

Claudette was worried. Harvey had not turned up for breakfast as arranged. The tall grumpy man advised her that he had not returned from the airport since leaving very early that morning. He also advised her that her unruly travel companions were pushing his staff far beyond their level of tolerance. He would not be responsible if a mass murder ensued.

She had pointedly told Ruben that she was officially on leave, and was not responsible for the group until they departed in two days. She further advised him if he had any complaints, he must raise the matter with Monsieur Peter Ponting adding "And please remember that I am also a guest here so, please respect me as one or go fuck yourself."

Ruben was not yet ready to cross swords with Monsuier Ponting, in the hopes that future guests from his company may be of the more luminary types he craved. As for her suggestion, he treated it with the contempt it deserved by giving her one of his best Basil Fawlty glares.

Out in the daylight, Claudette started to recap her last minutes with Harvey. They had been very amicable. He was English through and through, a gentleman, he would not let her down. He surely had not jumped on a plane without a word, no way, something was wrong, seriously wrong. She wandered around aimlessly. To gather her thoughts she walked to the seawall, where they had sat the previous evening, her heart hurt. "Harvey where are you?"

She was distracted by the sight of the jeep from last night pulling onto the kerb by the lights, She didn't actually recognise the vehicle, but the occupants were unforgettable as they disembarked. The big African and the robust looking gypsy type she had last seen being escorted away by the Police were there as large as life. They stood talking by the jeep then did a high five left, high fist right before splitting up. The jeep stood with its hazard lights blinking, but barely visible in the strong sun. The black man had disappeared but she saw the gypsy going into the ground, presumably down some stairs, to a basement, or perhaps an appointment in Hell.

"Lookey Lookey, real gold, nice charms for you lady...." Lattiffe was back on patrol. Claudette waved her arms "Allez, Allez-vous-en!" she instructed and started to walk away, Lattiffe shrugged and chuckled. "No wait" she came back. "Ah you like, maybe a genuine...." "No sorry, last night you were err, busy but did you see my friend?" "Whitey, yes I have made his acquaintance, he really needs a nice watch, you want to..." "No, I've lost him" "Ha ha ha, you and all the other girls lady, he very popular." "Please no, I'm serious, he was meant to meet me for... he was meant to meet me but didn't show up." "Ow that's serious lady, Whitey is very reliable, he is looking after Hill Street, maybe he is detained on business. I was, ahem, detained on business, but I will ask Mani to phone around ok. You know he really needs a watch. Ok I understand you are worried, go to Hill Street, go, you will find him. He is asbestos you know, indestructible." "Thank you, Merci, I hope you are right and sorry for being rude." "Rude lady, you don't know the meaning of the word, go and good luck." As he turned away, he started to sing 'Walk a mile in my shoes'. "I deserved that," she thought.

With the hot sun playing on her back and burning her neck, Claudette hurried along the Paseo towards Hill Street. The Lookey Lookey Men were out in force and she alternated between French, English and Italian when advising them to piss off. Even then it took her the best part of an hour to get there. As she approached Hill Street Claudette could see all was not well long before she got there. The front door was open, many of the white chairs were scattered around and as she got closer, she could see blood. Real blood, it was spotted on the chairs and a vertical stripe of it was evident on one of the windows.

"Harvey!" she screamed and entered without caution. Inside the bar, the pool room boys sat bruised, bloodied and trussed together on the floor. Around them was carnage, shattered glass, chairs and their beloved pool cues lay discarded. After being used on them. She ran past calling for Harvey but when she found no sign of him she returned and started to remove parcel tape from limp limbs and delicate lips.

The lads had been passing on their way to the station when they noticed three gorillas in dark clothing. They were loading bottles and things into Bessie and a dark blue van, that sported a heavy bullbar. Bravado had got the better of common sense and they challenged the raiders, who proved to be ruthless and efficient in wanton violence.

Any passers-by had more sense than to get involved and they had been trussed for about an hour. From what they had seen there was no sight of Harvey. Bessie had been empty except for the newly acquired cargo and the dodgy seats.

This was terrible beyond belief if they could do this to the boys what had they done to Harvey? "Harvey where are you?" she cried and then started to sob.

"He's behind you," said the boys in true pantomime fashion. "Don't be cruel, please" "Really, he's behind you". She started to turn, "Oh yes he is," said Harvey, as light hearted as he could manage and then "Ouch, careful" as she hugged all the bits that hurt.

A loud backfire and screech of brakes announced the arrival of Bessie and some other vehicles. Suddenly the place was filled with Lookey Men laden with mops and buckets. They stared in amazement at the influx of activity as the bar was being restored before their eyes. Blocking out most of the daylight from the door, Lattiffe was barking out orders, while the gypsy man was outside doing the same to another gang.

Harvey and Claudette squeezed outside where she explained what had happened in the bar and the efforts of the pool boys. They were busy collecting their belongings. They were now quite late for their trip home and were relieved to find their tickets but alas no cash. Harvey went to thank them and had a quick word with Mani Soler.

Minutes later the boys were being driven at high speed to the airport with more money than their stolen cash in their pockets.

Harvey related his tale to Claudette, omitting Caruthers and some finer detail. The gist of his story was that after his attack and rescue by Juan he had been driven to Mani's. Alerted by Lattiffe, Mani had phoned around for any unusual activity and voila, somebody was hawking cheap booze and tobacco from the back of a beat up VW. Mani had let it be known that he was interested in buying. The thieves had duly delivered themselves into a very punishing ambush, before being trussed, and taken to a Police unit who claimed the victory.

Mani had been very pleased with the turn of events. He had been able to repay Harvey's good deed before it accrued any interest. Had re-stamped his authority over the area by flexing some muscle and reminded the Police of how wise they were to free him without charge that morning.

The three villains had conveniently possessed enough illegal substances to satisfy the drug seizure quota recently set by Madrid for the area. The fact that the trio was made up of two Algerians and a Moroccan were an added bonus. It proved to Madrid that drug trafficking was purely a pastime of foreigners.

Nobody questioned why the felons bore the appearance of plane crash survivors or that they were ready to own up to any crime put before them. The local clear up rate soared as the foreigners confessed to crime after crime.

The Police, however, knew it was time to stop the interrogation when the gang confessed to a bank robbery. CCTV footage showed clearly, a red haired man of at least six feet tall as the sole perpetrator and whom witnesses described as having a broad Scottish accent.

Harvey and Claudette watched as Hill Street was restored to its former glory. Mani Soler waved Harvey over and after a few words Harvey nodded and returned. "I think that should be ok, he's going to keep, an eye on the place as well as Charlie's. I believe I can trust him. He is also going to park Bessie, thank goodness." "Good," said Claudette without knowing what he was rambling about. He also was starting to look worse for wear and in need of a shower.

They opted for a slow walk in the hopes that would perk him up. They only made the small restaurant before Harvey needed a rest so after a coffee Claudette hailed a taxi. The young driver was not best pleased with the short trip and made some derogatory remark about brawling English drunks. Claudette advised him in no uncertain terms that Harvey was a hero and had been set upon by local villains. Duly reprimanded, the driver helped Harvey out at the hotel and only took half the fare shown on his meter.

She helped him to his room and felt a bit guilty leaving him in such a place, but he insisted and was asleep before she clicked the door shut.

Harvey woke after a few hours, his head was clear and he was feeling much better. He was also relieved that Mani had taken over his responsibilities. His bruises already looked less angry and were blending with his suntan. Most of the swelling had subsided. Although his eye was bloodshot, he was able to focus and thankfully no double vision. His body and bedclothes were wet with his sweat and the room was as hot as Christmas oven. But this time he felt that the heat had helped his recovery. He rose unsteadily at first. He was pleased there was no dizziness and after a few tentative steps had shuffled up the bed. He stepped confidently into the bath, out the other side and onto the toilet.

The shower felt good in his face, it was not skin peeling hot and was a steady flow that indicated that the other guests were still soaking up the rays. He was not sure what arrangements he had made with Claudette, but he would prefer to meet her outside the range of his toilet smells and busied himself along.

The light blue blob of Head & Shoulders ANTI-DANDRUFF SHAMPOO, Suitable for FREQUENT USE. LARGE SIZE, NEW PERFUME and endorsed Greasy avoided contact with the eyes. It was not swallowed and hit the blown away non-slip surface of the bath with a splat. "I'd better get rid of that before I slip on it," Harvey said to himself. He promptly stood on the blob as he attempted to kick it away. He crashed out of the bath smashing the glass shelf and bringing the curtain down on a poor performance.

Red stained water seeped gently under the door of Room 217 and formed a small pool on the marble quarter-landing. At first sight, Claudette thought that a child may have dropped the remains of an ice lolly but as she knocked on the door, she noticed it was getting larger and was flowing under the door.

She pounded the door so loud it resounded around the foyer and brought Ruben rushing with his master key. He unlocked the door but was unable to open it because of a barrier. The slight give in resistance indicated it was not a solid barricade but a prostrate Harvey that was causing the obstruction.

Juan was wiry and strong, he helped Ruben gently inch the door open and slid through the gap when he could fit. The bed and floor were sopping wet and the shower was playing directly on him so he climbed in and turned the thing off. He then turned Harvey gently and just enough to open the door to an accessible width.

"Is he dead?" Ruben asked coldly. He had not meant it to sound so callous, but his concern had drained the compassion from his command of English. Claudette did not wait for Juan to figure out what he had been asked and pushed herself into the room. She felt Harvey's pulse and listened to his chest, all seemed normal. Reassured she looked at the rest of him, for some strange reason he had a smile on his face and lower down an erection. She looked at his face again then noticed with concern a dark pool of blood that had run thick from his ear. It was not pumping but was a definite trickle. Harvey made a small noise and she realised he was sleeping and not unconscious.

"Harvey, Harvey, wake up please, Harvey Cheri wake up, please." She was whispering in his ear and Juan was gazing at the man and wondering for the millionth time what it was about him that attracted all these beautiful women. It certainly couldn't be his lower regions, as he looked scornfully at the shrinking erection. "Must be the way he uses it?" he said allowed in Spanish and received curious looks from Ruben and the girl. "The shower" he explained, but they ignored him as Harvey began to stir.

"What is it? Where am I?" he began groggily, then he touched the side of his head and winced. "Ouch, I fell out of the bath right?" He tried to sit up, but they wouldn't let him. Juan dropped a towel over his groin and smiled as the small pyramid flattened out.

"Señor, you have had a bad fall and have lost some blood. You are still bleeding from the ear and I must insist, on behalf of the owners, that you obtain medical attention without delay." Ruben was in full functional damage limitation mode, lawsuits were paramount in his mind, but a tinge of compassion returned as he realised Harvey appeared ok. "We can call a doctor or an ambulance here if you wish Señor Harvey, I mean Bright, or, and I make it clear, this is your decision. I can take you to a very good clinic and the hospital, not 100 metres from here, behind the hotel." "If it's alright with you I'll go to the local, I don't feel too bad and I don't fancy laying here much longer. I bet you will not let me move until I sign something, right?" He looked at Ruben, who nodded sheepishly, "I will get the form Señor," He turned to Juan, "If he moves before I get back - shoot him." Harvey reached up and squeezed his hand in appreciation of the humour.

The Clinic of the Sacred Madonna was truly less than 100 metres and could be seen from the back door of the hotel, so Harvey declined the ride. He walked with Claudette on his left and Ruben on his right. Both supporting him as a frail and elderly relative, which he found more than a little embarrassing.

The clinic was small and business like, it was sparkling clean and all the staff wore whiter than crisp white uniforms and sported name badges, depicting first names only.

Maria checked him into a screened area and Jesus checked him over. After his examination Jesus looked deeply into his ear and equally as deeply into his eyes. He had a look of unmistakable concern in his jet black eyes as he shook his head solemnly and repeatedly.

"What? What is it?" Harvey was actually feeling better before the head shaking began. "I don't like it Señor, I don't like it at all, how long were you unconscious?" "You can't tell if it is day or night in that hell hole" Ruben looked away, "so I have no idea, are you going to tell me what's wrong?" "He was asleep when we found him and he was alone for two and a half hours. We don't know how long he slept or when he took the shower." Claudette volunteered helpfully. "That's it then" Jesus exclaimed jubilantly, "when was 1066?" "What are you babbling about" "Every English schoolboy is taught when 1066 was," said Jesus "brain damage, no doubt."

"What? No way" squealed Harvey hopelessly.

"No, that's not possible" croaked Ruben haplessly.

"No, please no" sobbed Claudette helplessly, but to nobody in authority as Jesus had shot off and could be heard issuing instructions to Maria.

The trio looked miserably at each other but before they could put any feelings into words, Maria appeared. She brought some stainless steel instruments in a kidney dish, and Jesus. She was wearing a large green apron over her uniform and looked like a plump school dinner lady. Jesus was still wearing his crisp whites which hugged his slim body and flattered his half-hearted workouts in the hospital physiotherapy unit. He indicated Harvey should turn his head and inserted a small pair of tweezers in his patient's ear.

He winked at Claudette and pulled a shard of glass from Harvey's ear."My mistake Señor, it was not your brain at all" he laughed. Claudette giggled. "You bastard, I should get you struck off" Harvey complained. "You English Señor, you think you invented comedy but when it is tried on you there is no sense of humour - pah". "I'm not used to being told I'm about to become a fucking cabbage from a doctor with whom I had full confidence" But it was no use. The more he raged, the more everybody laughed, mostly with relief, and he too had to join in.

Jesus brought the proceedings to and end like an orchestra conductor, except he flourished his fountain pen, not a baton. Ruben had to sign a pile of forms.

A good night of sleep is what the doctor ordered and to ensure Harvey got one Jesus insisted he spend one night under observation. Just to be sure.

Claudette sat with him for a while. He was in a comfortable bed, in pleasant surroundings and in a comfortable temperature. His eyes started to droop. The lifestyle he had been living for the last week, coupled with a beating, and a bang on the head, were taking their toll. They agreed to meet for breakfast at the hotel once he had seen Jesus.

"Harvey, in the last 24 hours you have been the centre of a dramatic Police incident, been beaten up and had an accident, you really do need looking after..." It was wasted, he was fast asleep, she kissed him on the forehead and went back to the hotel.

She found Ruben in the middle of huge activity as she entered Hotel El Torro. He had telephoned the Delgato brothers explained what had happened and insisted on some immediate renovations. He was stood on the landing by 217 and ushered out the old bath with its accompaniments while other workmen hovered in the foyer - not bad for the early evening in Spain.

Ruben lurched to the desk when he saw Claudette and gave her a crinkled smile as he handed over her key. He even patted her hand in some kind of a gesture and she in return gave him a smile that made his knees knock.

Harvey felt much refreshed by his sleep in a proper bed and controlled conditions. He would have happily spent the rest of his holiday there, but he saw Claudette enter and immediately prepared to leave.

Jesus advised her he was fit to leave, but not ready for any more bumps on the head. She promised to take care of him and Harvey liked the sound of that. Even if it was for only one or two more days.

Back at the hotel Harvey was amazed at the transformation of Room 217. Ruben hovered like a mother hen as Harvey examined his new shower cubicle, thermostatic shower and furnishings. His room was also equipped with a ceiling fan and a mobile air conditioning unit. The dimensions of the room were no bigger but compared to before it was now luxurious. He smiled his thanks to Ruben, who returned to Reception a very happy hen.

After a late breakfast, devoid of Germans, Harvey and Claudette decided, that as they were both free of responsibilities, a day in Malaga was in order.

Sauntering around the castle and sampling the delights of the tapas bars would be a very pleasant way to pass the time.

Chapter Thirty-Nine

The rickety old train that Harvey remembered from before had been replaced by a swish piece of rolling stock. It had automatic doors, air conditioning and announced approaching stations in English, German and Spanish. The track was still single like before and there were passing places at stations along the way.

As the train hurtled along Harvey hoped the signal system was as efficient as the announcements. It was a nice way to view the Costa del Sol with picturesque scenes that adorn every travel brochure.

This was better than being hunched on the back of a motorbike while great lorries flew past, nearly stripping the skin from your back. Ok the bike had compensations but sitting next to Claudette was equally as nice. This was definitely better than driving a beaten up old VW bus that should have been put out to pasture years ago. Sitting with Claudette so close was nearly as good as travel got.

Malaga was beautiful but searing in the noon sun. The green flashing temperature guides outside pharmacies read anywhere between 30 - 40 depending on their relevance to the sun. It could have been twice that with the heat jumping up from the pavement, roads and buildings. Not only was it hot but it was buzzing with people everywhere. Some sensible ones used umbrellas as sunshades but were a nuisance to negotiate when trying to walk as a couple.

A small market was set up on the river bridge and the movement of air was a welcome relief while they viewed what was on offer. This appeared to be anything from food to jet engines. Beggars were everywhere, some had sad-eyed children, some were disabled and many sat with a baby in arms, Some sat pitifully alone in a state of confusion. This was sad to see, hard to ignore but impossible to solve.

Everywhere lottery ticket vendors paraded up and down, criss-crossing the bridge. Their wares were pinned to their jackets, held on boards, like protesting students, some were on bicycles, most were walking and one was even on a skateboard.

At the end of the bridge they approached two English girls Harvey thought he recognised, possibly from the plane or the airport. One was speaking softly, without a discernible accent while the other girl was 'Our Cilla' Liverpudlian. The soft-spoken girl was neatly dressed in a loose fitting cream dress and had bobbed mousey hair over which she wore a floppy hat. Cilla girl wore hippy flares of blue denim adorned with flowers, and a tie-dye cheesecloth shirt tied in Neta fashion. She was a little taller than her friend and had cropped hair that may have one time been green. The smaller girl was attempting to remove something from her friend's eye without much luck. "C'mon Chuck, it's gorra be in there somewhere. It don't half frigging hurt" complained Cilla girl.

As the levelled the pair, Harvey removed his handkerchief and offered it to the smaller girl. She took it with a smile and in a trice had removed whatever had been causing her friend discomfort, they both smiled a thank you as Harvey and Claudette walked on. "That's fucking class that is," said Cilla girl admiringly, "a real gent, and a real hanky, none of your Castle Street rags, that ain't, an' he didn't even want it back!" Claudette held Harvey's arm proudly.

Their next encounter were two student girls collecting cash and distributing pink pinned ribbons with the distinctive loop of the symbol associated with AIDS. Claudette dropped some coins in the tin and pinned a ribbon on each of their tops. They had not walked more than two paces when an elderly cyclist spat full force at Harvey hitting him on his shirt above the ribbon. As the cyclist came to the Liverpool girls, he was showered with abuse, a more than generous helping of spit and a good place kick above the crossbar.

"Here Chuck, have your hanky back, careful on the one side there is a bit of mascara but the rest is clean. More than can be said for that dirty bastard." Cilla girl was angry. "It's definitely the ribbon, we've seen it happen before," the other girl said, "it's ignorance really, it's not been very well explained here..." She didn't continue, but they knew what she meant, there was a lot of work to be done in that area and not only in Spain.

Harvey thanked them and they wandered off as Claudette wiped the tobacco stained spit from his shirt. A quick dab or two from her water bottle and the hot sun did the rest. "Poor Harvey, you can't even walk in a street without incident' she said. She put the ribbons in her bag to be safe, but swore to wear them again.

The rest of the day was perfect without any more unpleasantness. They wandered in and out of tapas bars that were as welcome as an oasis in the desert. Despite being busy, the proprietor's delighted in explaining their offerings of savoury titbits and the odd surprise of sweetness. Each bar appeared to have their own speciality and they marvelled at the slim Spaniards who appeared to be constantly eating. They visited the old fort or castle and rested in the shadows of the thick defensive walls then spent a couple of hours in the air-conditioned sanctuary of the Picasso Centre. All too soon the sun sank into the sea and they headed for the train.

It had been a nice, really nice, day and they were happy together. Claudette had found what she had wanted for a long time, an intelligent older man with charm and manners. It was a shame it was at the end of her trip and her pending American adventure. She would go, of course, days like these were as welcome as the tapas bars had been but for how long?

They were both a bit downbeat on the train as the realisation hit home. Future meetings were discussed and could be possible. Harvey was flattered by her attention and was keen to keep all options open. He had no delusions regarding her future, she would go to America and meet somebody for sure, but ...

He would soon return home, his role in bringing up the children was diminishing and Oli would probably want to rest a bit more soon. Amber was keen to let the girls grow up together so he could be free to travel ..... Neta may or may not feature .... His mind rambled and he decided to concentrate on the moment. She sensed this and squeezed his hand. "Let the train take the strain," he said and squeezed back.

The return journey seemed a lot quicker but probably was not. At the resorts, pink and red holidaymakers climbed wearily aboard after a hard day enjoying themselves. They chatted away, mostly in English, planning their next few days and filling the carriage with enthusiasm. Claudette had not spoken for some time but kept squeezing Harvey's hand like a stress ball.

Harvey felt the squeezes which told him they had only the remains of tonight and who knew what little of tomorrow. They came like Morse Code. Squeeze, tomorrow she would be leaving. Squeeze she would be taking the coach with Henri and that rabble. Squeeze, every minute she would be a further kilometre away. Squeeze, he would soon be home. Squeeze, she would soon be in America. Squeeze, she loved him, he squeezed back.

They got off the train, and Harvey looked over the elevated platform, and could make out two large men sitting with their backs to the door to Hill Street. Their swarthy appearance denoted that they were there at Mani's behest and he was reassured.

They walked arm in arm along the warm Paseo back to the Hotel El Torro. As the entered, Pedro hissed his way past a queue awaiting service. "Señor, your table is waiting as requested. Señor Del Taurino arranged it personally. Follow me please." They were glad of the bodyguard as they felt many eyes burning into their backs from hungry couples who muttered disapprovingly. Pedro returned to the waiting guests and explained that the couple were on honeymoon which lightened the mood.

The food was delicious and the selected wine by Ruben was ideal. A near perfect end to a near-perfect day. Harvey was not so sure why absolute strangers kept wishing him well, but it was better than the earlier reception so they both smiled.

All was well until the impromptu floor show. Guy came flying into the restaurant hotly pursued by Ruben, maybe not 'hotly' as he was quite wet. Guy dodged round tables, over tables and even under tables in an attempt to avoid Ruben's long arms. Ruben had a very high strike rate in battering the youth about the head, but he couldn't stop his charging around. Guy's downfall was running into the solid frame of Pedro where he stayed long enough for a giant stride and those gangling arms to reach him.

Once on his quarry, Ruben latched onto Guy's left ear and steered him back through the restaurant. He greeted diners as if this was an ordinary happening despite the cries from the boy and his spreading drops of water like a wet dog fresh from a swim.

"I think I had better sort this out," Claudette said reluctantly. "Are you alright?" It was no use talking to Harvey, he had collapsed onto the table, tears were streaming down his face as he gasped for breath. He banged his fist Crowe like on the table while grabbing his aching ribs with the other. "Well I'm glad you find it funny," she said, but without humour "serves you right, I hope you are sick." He was trying to say something, she leaned forward, "Classic, bloody classic" he wheezed.

By the time Harvey had composed himself and settled up Claudette was stood with Guy outside. Ruben was nowhere to be seen.

"TNT?" Harvey asked. "Please" she replied and they set off towards the club. Guy tagged along silently rubbing his ear. He had played a water trick on Ruben but had not made good his escape and was now paying the consequences. Ruben had advised him that his escapades had added considerably to his personal account and if this was not settled he would make sure it would be a long time before he would be free to return to France.

As Ruben totted up Guy's Bill Guy may have appeared remorseful, but it was his last night here too, and he hadn't finished yet!

TNT had a sprinkling of tourists, and some diehard expats, hoping there would be another Happy Hour soon. Some bump, bump, bumps and strangled yelps indicated Doris was on the decks and a former Prince was on the turntable or CD Player. Guy had not noticed him and vice-versa, Harvey smiled at the Barman who indicated towards the Holsteins and Harvey hell up three fingers. He handed out the bottles that were already dripping condensation. "I wanted Pernod" Guy complained. "I know, cheers," said Harvey as he clinked bottles with Claudette. "Sal-loo" she laughed. "A la votre" Guy responded moodily. "Should you be drinking anymore after your bumps Harvey?" "To be honest I never thought about it, but I feel fine and I know I will take it easy with you around." Guy gave a fingers down the throat motion.

They sat around the table where a few of Harvey's holiday adventures had begun. Ideally he would be wooing Claudette in an air conditioned Room 217 but he had to contend with Guy's company as well. He was starting to feel the anticlimax to a near perfect day, straddled with this moody adolescent.

Above the music, he heard Guy addressing Claudette in French. "What's the matter with him now?" Harvey asked. "He wants me to dance," she replied and pulled a face. "I am here, I do understand," complained Guy, they ignored him. "Why don't you?"

Harvey thought that once on the floor Guy may spot Doris, and whatever followed should give him time with Claudette. "Harvey, to this? With him?" she gave Harvey the look of a naughty puppy caught eating a slipper. "I am here, I do understand." Harvey whispered in his bad ear "You can always piss off you know, we are not being paid to babysit." Guy pulled back quickly.

"What did you say, Harvey?" "I reminded him that a certain hotel manager may not yet be sleeping. Don't you like this one? Even I like this one." "Then you dance with him." Harvey went to stand but was cut short by Claudette pulling him back and Guy's look of astonishment. "Please yourself" Harvey teased.

The arrival of the DJ proper cut short Doris's session of unrelenting Prince. He gathered up his beloved tracks and stuffed them into the shoe box. Crossing the floor close to their table he failed to notice Guy's outstretched leg. He crashed to the ground spilling his recordings on the floor and watched in despair as they were about to be trampled by new arrivals. Guy's foot sprang out again. Doris's lunge to gather up his music made the boot fly harmlessly by his head. A flash of light from Doris's belt indicated that something more serious was about to happen. Fortunately, Harvey was able to grab Guy by the neck hair and give Doris a 'back off' look that prevented it getting ugly. Claudette helped gather up the rest of the tracks and Doris departed.

"You are a prat of the first order Guy and I do not know how you have lived this long" Harvey grunted, as he pulled Guy painfully back to his seat.

Three beers appeared, courtesy of the bar, for a situation avoided and Guy's pals arrived "Phew, that was a close thing" Harvey whispered as Guy left to join them. "Harvey, your whole life is a close thing, please be careful, think Number One for a change." "OK" he responded and led her to the dance floor.

Guy arrived with two Pernod, one misty white and one misty red. "Try it with the black currant Monsuier, it may be to your taste." Harvey tried, "Not bad" "In one then" Guy encouraged, and

Harvey drained it. The end was a bit gritty, but he thought that the black currant had crystallised a bit.

"One for the road?" Harvey asked, rubbing his jaw. "Just one, and something civilised this time, please." They settled for a gin and tonic each and when he returned with the drinks Claudette noted a change in him, "Harvey, are you ok?" "Yes, just a bit warm and very thirsty all of a sudden, do you have any of that water left?" She passed the small bottle from her bag and he drained it. "Thanks, I'll get you another, I think a bruise is coming out in my jaw from before, it is very stiff." "I think we should go, you need some fresh air."

He rose, she stood with him and prepared to leave. Without warning he made his way to the dance floor and started to make a complete ass of himself.

Harvey was in the centre of the gang who were now just watching him and encouraging him to new levels of idiocy. He was not doing this for enjoyment - he was possessed. The music finally finished and Claudette tried to get him to leave but he was not on the same planet. He refused to respond, his new best friends were urging him on.

"Harvey, you are drunk and being a fool, please come now."

"Leave me," said the Leader of The Gang."

"Leave him," said the gang - she left.

Back in her room Claudette climbed sadly into bed, this was not how she had wanted the evening to end. She tried to piece together what had happened. Was it the drinks on top of the recent bumps on the head? Perhaps it was being landed with Guy, he had been tense after Guy joined them but surely not jealous. Guy was a pain, but he had bought them a drink ..... Guy had supplied a drink that Harvey had sunk in one. A drink that was unusual to him that Guy had recommended. A drink that tasted gritty, a drink that was possibly drugged, that was it! The tightening of the jaw, the thirst and heat flush - Ecstacy.

She dressed quickly and reluctantly woke Henri, if he minded he did not show it and listened to her suspicions. It was almost light and although he had a long drive ahead Henri accompanied her to TNT.

They crept past a sleeping Ruben and hid his half pool cue behind a large plant, so they could get back without disturbing him. Outside they could hear Guy and his chums laughing and chanting as they made their way back to the hotel. Claudette accused Guy of spiking Harvey's drink, but he shrugged off the suggestion. Henri eyed him with distaste and would have enjoyed giving him a thrashing, but that would not help with the matter in hand.

They found Harvey on all fours in the road looking under a car and shouting something. "Harvey, what are you doing?" "He won't come out" he replied through clenched teeth. She bent but saw no one. "Who, what?" "My shadow, he went under this car and is hiding" "Harvey, this is stupid, nobody has a shadow yet. Harvey, Harvey listen to me. Henri do something, please."

Henri pulled Harvey to his feet and with equal efficiency knocked him out with an uppercut. Claudette gulped "Henry, was that necessary?" "I'm not sure but if I hadn't done it, they would have." He indicated two Policemen who had heard the noise from Guy and were taking an interest in Harvey. "Too much ..." Henri did a drinking motion with his hand as they struggled to get Harvey to walk.

The Police looked on with contempt, they could not understand this British idea of enjoyment. They would have enjoyed locking him up for a day or two but it looked like he was under control now, and they didn't want to upset the pretty girl more than she was.

They got back to the hotel and Harvey seemed groggy but sane as they entered. Ruben was the opposite of sane as he charged around the foyer like a demented loon and was threatening to murder all his French guests or better still, the entire population.

He was not at all pleased at having a fire bucket of sand emptied on his lap as he slept and being woken as the bucket had been thrown noisily down the marble stairs. They retrieved their keys without interrupting Ruben's circumnavigation and got Harvey to his room. Henri raised his eyebrows at the sight of 217. "It's better than it was" Claudette advised, but Henri's eyebrows stayed up.

They got Harvey to bed, gave him a good slug of water. He went to sleep almost immediately and started to snore a little. They were about to squeeze out but heard what may have been the start of Ruben's massacre from outside and stood rooted to the spot until the noise had abated.

They cautiously peered out expecting the worse but there was no sign of anybody, the main door was secured and the foyer devoid of dead bodies. Henri joked that Ruben was probably in the basement chopping up his victims as they waited for the lift. It was taking an impossible time to arrive so they took the stairs suspecting sabotage.

As they passed Harvey's room, they heard the snoring was a bit louder, but not rasping or anything so continued up. On Claudette's floor, they found the lift door bumping against a knee high ashtray familiar to hotels and offices throughout the civilised world. She gave Henri a peck on the cheek and he jumped in the lift. Unfortunately, it headed down to answer their previous calls but he was soon on the way back up to his floor.

As the lift doors opened Henri smelled smoke before he actually saw it. He instinctively punched the fire alarm on the wall, breaking the Perspex and hitting the button in one motion. He could see smoke curling low around the corner ahead and heard heavy footfalls behind that announced Ruben's arrival.

Ruben recalled the lift and locked it off. He then started to direct disheveled guests down the stairs. The smoke was not dense so Henri grabbed a fire extinguisher and headed off in search of the source.

He came on Guy and caught him completely by surprise, outside his room of all places. He had started a small paper fire in another knee high ashtray, but it had been too close to some drapes and they too had ignited. He was desperately trying to put the fires out as Henri sprayed the area with foam until the fire had died.

A loud siren outside indicated that the hotel was linked to the Fire Department and blue flashing reflections were hitting the wall below the burnt out drapes.

Hearing voices approaching Henri grabbed a foam covered Guy and threw him into his room and told him to be quiet and not touch anything. Ruben, two uniformed firefighters and Claudette arrived and surveyed the scene. Henri explained what he had found and done. The senior fireman congratulated him on his actions and Ruben thanked him. A radio crackled and advised that there were no other signs of fire anywhere and that the smoke had been confined to the one corridor which was rapidly clearing. The firemen poked around in the ashtray and examined the drapes, they smelled the drapes and paper for signs of an accelerating agent and looked at all the cigar and cigarette ends.

An old match that was burnt black through its full length caught the attention of both men. It was intact and undamaged by the foam. At length the senior man diagnosed that the bin cum ashtray had been overfilled with old papers and placed too close to the drapes. The drapes were mostly flame retardant, but with the lit bin so close they had caught fire. The number of butts indicated that better housekeeping was in order. The cause was undoubtedly a carelessly discarded match that ignited the papers.

The senior man relieved Henri of the extinguisher and double doused the area until it was empty. He advised Ruben that he should have also had powder extinguishers installed. He then criticised his poor housekeeping, despite no other bin or ashtray being found full. He was told to expect a large bill for their services. He also advised that the dry risers were due to be tested and this would now take place tomorrow at a further cost to the hotel.

Ruben thanked, bowed scraped and grovelled the firefighters all the way to the front door. Here he was met by a throng of guests in their nightwear and Harvey, who was wearing nothing. He was eating a huge bowl of ice cream and completely oblivious to those around him.

Ruben shrugged his large bony shoulders, Señor Bright failed to surprise him anymore. He set about reassuring his guests and ushering them back to bed.

Fortunately with everything under control Ruben faked the Roll Call. Claudette never bothered to venture out so did not see Harvey. Ruben escorted him back to his room.

Back in his room Henri found Guy smoking one of his cheroots, despite being told not to touch anything. He lost his rag when Guy failed to see the error of his ways and referred to him as a 'Salop', a not very nice word about his Mother and a Docker.

Henri unbuckled his belt and gave Guy several stinging swipes before washing his mouth with the foul hotel soap and booting him out, as Ruben was removing the drapes. One look at Guy convinced Ruben that there had been no carelessly discarded match. Henri did not need to confirm or deny anything, Ruben knew and he cursed.

Testing the pipes that were called 'Dry Risers' was a pain at the best of time but during a working day with guests milling around would be torturous. Each pipe would be charged with mains water. The pressure was taken on each floor, to ensure there would be enough water to douse Hell. If Satan it ever checked in to the top floor of Hotel El Torro, oh what joy. This was the Fire Department's punishment for poor housekeeping, and everybody in the business locally would know and take heed.

Chapter Forty

Not for the first time on this holiday did Harvey awake with a muzzy head and acid stomach. Also not for the first time, somebody was at his door. "Go away" he called grumpily.

Now, someone was pounding on his door and inside his head. It stopped briefly and he was able to survey the room from his position of air-conditioned elegance. Maybe a bit too strong to describe Room 217 as elegant but it was much better.

He eyed the ceiling fan suspiciously, he felt as though it was drawing him up from the bed to meet it. He put both hands firmly on his midriff to prevent his genitals from becoming minced offal as the door opened slowly and the illusion disappeared.

For once warm air entered 217 as Ruben slipped in. "Señor you must come quick" "Go away Rubes, that's a good chap." "Señor, I implore you...." "Fuck off" "Señor, this is exactly why your French friend, Mademoiselle Golan, has asked for my assistance. She has tried and tried and will soon be leaving, now all you can be is rude."

Ruben was tired of firefighters, dry risers, pressure tests and unforgiving guests, he had no time for this. "Please come soon or tell me what to say she has also been to the Doctor again." "Pregnant again is she?" "Pardon Señor?" "French you say?" Then the penny dropped, "Oh My God, Claudette, Doctor? Where is she Ruben? Sorry mate bit confused."

"You are fortunate Señor that I did not give her the key as she requested, or I fear she would have been half way to Madrid by now." Ruben was behaving managerial now he had his attention. "She is assembling her party for imminent departure, once all the rooms have been checked by my staff. That young man, Guy, I contacted his parents. They have no control but a lot of money - they are sending me personal reparation for his trouble" he was interrupted by Juan knocking on the door.

"Ok now go Señor, the rooms are clear and I have a message from the Western Union, the coach will leave very soon, so hurry. Oh and don't stand in any group or at the rear of the bus when saying farewell." Harvey looked quizzical, "You will see, and be careful there are firefighters and hoses everywhere."

Harvey emerged from the hotel and saw Claudette, she was checking a long list of names and looking at luggage labels as Juan and Henri loaded the hold of the idling coach. They smiled at Harvey and she turned around to greet him.

He looked better than he felt and received her hug with relish. "I came prepared for you to ignore me and I wouldn't blame you if you did, Ruben explained a bit, I'm sorry." "If that were the real you, you would be really sorry and never see me again. You were drugged, that Guy, bah, he will not admit anything but I discussed it with the Doctor at the Clinique and he wants to see you when I leave. Promise you will go!" "I promise." "Good."

Henri joined them to say all the baggage was on board "Henri gave Guy a hiding for what he did" "Pour Moi?" Henri nodded with a smile, he kissed his fist and went to his seat to wait for her to load the passengers, his last minute of peace.

"There were, how do you say? Extenuating circumstances" she said with difficulty. Then with ease steered Harvey around the coach away from prying eyes. "It was a pity last night ended as it did because I wanted to share your toothbrush before a shower and breakfast together. But now I just have this and hope you want more at another time." He started to say 'oo la la" but failed as she gave him one of the most memorable kisses of his life. And very French, This relationship, however, is one built on disruption. This time it came in the form of shrieks and howls as Ruben and a handful of firefighters disgorged fire hoses from every window that overlooked the coach, and it's assembled passengers.

Ruben's accuracy proved uncanny as he upended Guy several times before he slipped his way onto the coach. His other tormentors got off a little better, but not much. Claudette giggled at their plight then turned serious "Harvey, I have only known you a short time, but I feel I have fallen in love. Please say nothing. I am worried now that you are going to kill yourself or something will happen to you before I can come and take care of you. You're a disaster, the big black guy says your indestructible, but you are not, you get hurt, please be more careful, for me, not you, me!" "It is not always like this, my life is dull really...."

He caught a look, "OK, I will, I promise!" As they pulled away, Henri put the air conditioner on extra cold to add to the discomfort of his wet passengers and hooted a farewell on the very loud horn.

Claudette sat in the Courier's seat and waved tearfully but energetically to Harvey, all too soon they were gone. A sodden and bruised Guy shivered, he slunk down in his seat planning revenge.

Harvey returned to his room to reflect on Claudette's words of wisdom. This holiday had been exceptional in more than personal disasters, and his life was usually so dull or was it? He was saddened by Claudette's departure because he did not really believe he would see her again. Once she got to America a whole new world would open up for her and... In a way he was relieved they had not spent the night together. Now she could look back at their time together without having to think that he may have been an opportunist on holiday.... His thoughts were firing all over the place and he didn't feel so good as Ruben knocked on the door.

"The fire service has finished and is now enjoying a meal in the restaurant, you, my friend look dreadful. Come with me now, you have an appointment with Jesus and hopefully he can prevent you meeting the other one."

At the clinic, Doctor Jesus explained that they still knew little about Ecstacy and all was not the same as it was a man made potion and could be extremely varied. Harvey's heart rate was nearly double normal and then plummeted. They could moderate this. He was dehydrated which they could also treat and an anti-inflammatory would be administered slowly. They dare not mention anything about illicit, experimental or recreational drugs as his insurance would not cover any treatment. For the after effects of a head injury they were ok. He would also have to be issued with a 'safe to travel' note as he would, or should be, homeward bound in the next couple of days.

Ruben left him connected to drips, wires and monitors. In a comfortable bed and it was not long before Harvey was enjoying a peaceful sleep again, under observation. When he awoke, he felt so much better albeit a little warm.

Jesus explained. They had needed to take some readings without the benefit of the air conditioning, but now they had all the results it had been turned back on and he could get dressed in comfort. First though, Jesus explained that Harvey's experience appeared similar to a fever. It was a mixture of everything he had done since being in Spain, there were signs of cannabis in his blood plus a combination of things he didn't or couldn't explain. Harvey thought of Sasha's Rhino mix plus Dr Hope's little purple pills. He kept quiet and let Jesus blame Guy.

The good news was all that was back to normal and if he did not over indulge in anything or even better, under indulge, it would be for the best. Harvey was starving and Jesus said this was a good sign and he should enjoy a meal as soon as he was discharged.

It was early evening when he got back to Hotel El Torro and apart from being ravenous. He felt in better condition entering than he could remember being in for the duration of his stay. Pedro hissed him elegantly to a table by the window and he felt a little like an Admiral being piped aboard. Fortunately it was change over the day at the hotel and the well wishers from his "Honeymoon" were gone. Newcomers were just finding their feet so the restaurant was a bit quiet. He explained that he had better not have a drink tonight,. Pedro insisted that he had a glass of wine that would compliment his meal of oven baked fish, and he was right.

He took a stroll along the Paseo to check that Hill Street was still in good hands. He then amazed Lattiffe by purchasing a genuine Cartier watch for around twelve pounds - after bartering. He declined the extended warranty. Latiffe walked with him a while and puffed on a reefer that Harvey declined every few paces. They parted at the payphone where Lattiffe produced a mallet and some bent washers. "Day say that they bring card machines soon and I best start thinking about that one, man has to live yo know." "You can't stop progress Lattiffe" "No Whitey, but you can introduce a hurdle, ha he he!"

As he wandered, Harvey felt strangely alone for the first time since he had arrived. He peered into the gloom of Charlie's locked and deserted bar. He looked at his reflection and saw that he was being observed by one of Mani's helpers, nodded and strolled on. As he passed Mani's one of the street doors flew open and a spindly little man emerged. He smiled and winked at Harvey who returned the smile. Sasha could be heard urging the man to return soon and

Harvey scooted off before he could be seen. He got back to the hotel at a reasonable hour and retired to his revamped room, where he slept well in comfort.

The next day Ruben received a mixture of good and bad news. First was the bill for Harvey's hospitalisation that he would have to deal with through their insurers. Next the report from the fire service that was highly critical of the housekeeping at the hotel but added that outside elements were suspected. They were complimentary about the evacuation procedure, the dry riser results and the restaurant. Their bill was not as severe as they had indicated and Ruben made a note to thank Pedro for his help in sweetening the pill. Peter Ponting had paid in full and enquired if a more senior group that were heading his way could be accommodated - he was assured that these were a mixture of very elderly with their carers. Ruben made a note to order extra rubber sheets.

Guy's parents had been generous in both settling the hotels costs and a personal thank you to Ruben, even after he charged them with the loss of the hotel TV service. He had wrongly assumed that the blackout of the service was due to the fire damaging something.

He later found out there was a strike that had disabled all television coverage comprehensively across the Costa del Sol. Some sabotage had also ensured that Sky would not fill gaps left in the national network. What did Ruben care? The news was of no interest to him filled with start to end with gloom and doom from wars to the economic crisis. He could manage without, thank you. As for his guests, he could loop back to back movies through the internal system. He made another note to supply a few complimentary newspapers to make up for the usual babble from the TV.

Now he was faced with a surprise visit from the Delgato brothers. This was not a coincidence but a consequence of a conversation they had recently had with their cousin who worked in the Fire Department. After a brief meeting with Ruben, they accepted the hospital bill as being one of those things and decided to settle without consulting the insurers. They had also asked their cousin not to make his report too public, for fear of the insurers making some issue out of it. The way things were going they needed the insurers on board in case something more serious should befall the hotel over the Winter. They were pleased with the Ponting deal, and awarded Ruben an extra two days holiday which they knew he would be unable to take. For the fire service report they deducted him two days pay. After negotiation, Ruben was not financially penalised. He was permitted to take the rest of the current day off, but must resume duties by 10 pm, the start of his night shift.

After being so generous, they sampled some delights from the breakfast table and left. Ruben watched them leave and collared Juan on his way back from a smoke. He appointed him in charge for the day, which pleased Juan as it would relieve him of any work.

Ruben knocked on Room 217 and was pleased to find Señor Bright up, about and ready to partake in breakfast. "Fancy a day out?" Ruben asked. Harvey had no plans and readily agreed. After a non-tourist breakfast of ham and eggs, they set off in Ruben's small Fiat up into the hills.

The little car whined but took the hills in good spirit, Harvey put whatever complaints the car had down to Ruben's driving technique rather than the car's components. They drove up to Rhonda and Ruben showed Harvey where his Father had jumped to his death. There was no plaque and Ruben explained that he was one of many and he lay in good company.

Most, unlike his Father, had not voluntarily taken the leap and the good people of Rhonda would rather their visitors looked at the view from the bridge and not the modern history of it. They walked around the narrow streets where the houses still bore bullet holes in their white painted walls. The air was pure and refreshing, they took coffee on a small terrace immediately under the bridge and over the big drop. This they followed with a beer each, Ruben ceremoniously poured his over the edge, Harvey unsentimentally drank his.

As Spain rested in the heat, they descended to Mijas and spent a pleasant afternoon at a pavement table in a small bar enjoying tasty titbits under a huge sunshade. The only thing moving were a couple of frogs. They may have been looking for their friends who had just had their legs eaten, in a dish Harvey was surprised to find in Spain.

The short trip was a bit scary as Ruben free wheeled most of the way down. Sometimes as he turned the engine off he inadvertently engaged the steering lock, only realising his mistake at a crucial bend. Harvey promised to pay for the fuel if Ruben would use the motor and to throttle him if he didn't. In the event, they made it and back at the hotel a familiar object was leant against the kerb. Another familiar object in the person of Lenny emerged from the foyer as they pulled up.

"I enjoyed our day together Señor Harvey and I am pleased you will not be alone for your last night with us." "I can't believe it, Rubes, are you sure it is my final night?" "Unfortunately si, you will remember - or not that you lost two days or more. On the good side is your insurance will pay you for your time lost and your small friend looks keen to make you happy though I would counsel restraint if you are able." "Don't worry Rubes, this one is purely platonic, well almost." "Pff, don't tell my staff, oh and one more thing Señor." Ruben handed Harvey an envelope. "The owners are agreed, there was no intention for us to use Room 217 for guests. So you have a full refund for your stay with us, and the promise that next time you visit you will be given a proper room at an inflated price." "Sounds like a deal to me Rubes, although I shall miss not being able to touch both walls as I sleep."

"Hello Harvey, have you missed us?" Lenny was as bright and bubbly as usual, she gave him a big hug. "Well did you?" "Of course, fancy a drink?" "Game on"

As they walked to the bar, they spotted a note, advising 'Mr R Bright and the Simmonds family to vacate their rooms by noon the next day, and be ready for collection from the hotel, at 1600 sharp. A rider explained that the coach may be later, but they should be ready on time.

"You're very quiet Harvey, you did miss us didn't you?" "Yes, of course, and, to be honest, I missed quite a lot. It's also my last night and I really don't believe it. Back to normality will mean back to reality and to be honest, I don't know what to expect, it was all a bit of a rush before I came out."

He tried to explain what had happened or not happened but gave up with a shrug and a "well you know" for the rest. She nodded that they had been filled in and were pleased he had not been seriously hurt. "Neta sends her love and lots of kisses. She asked me to get your address so she, er and me of course, can write or send Christmas cards or whatever. Neta said you can expect one at least, ha ha, that girl. What about Claudette? Did you guys get it together?

I know you hit it off, as they said in your day". "Age discriminator" he laughed and tried to explain his time with Claudette, but settled for saying that they had some excellent meals and things.

Lenny told him all about the funeral, it had been well attended and Enzo was given the farewell he duly deserved. She then helped him pack all but what he needed immediately and to travel. The room was better now but still too small for two, even when one was tiny - or extra small, as she preferred.

Lenny came in handy, though, squeezing into places he couldn't reach and retrieve the odd sock, etc. Although she spent a lot of time on and over the bed there was not a hint of anything occurring from either party. They both realised this bit had been done and was not going to be repeated. He was sure it would have been a different story with Neta, and he was sure that he would have gone home with a few socks missing.

After everything was neatly packed or assembled, they jumped on the bike on went to meet the others at The Green Man, a few bars up from Hill Street.

Mollie was delighted to see Harvey again and enjoyed being brought up to date. The meal was excellent but nowhere as good as Pedro's offerings. The company was enjoyable although they were all a bit shattered.

Marco listened to his tale about the mugging and thought it was a hapless coincidence that all the keys had been nicely labelled. Enzo scowled a bit, and said he thought that perhaps the robbers had got wind of their plans. There was no way Bessie could be mistaken for a hire vehicle, which was the usual prey for that kind of scam.

Harvey got the feeling that Enzo and Marco were at that stage when they would disagree about most things. He was pleased to hear that Enzo was going to manage Charlie's old place with a view to taking it over. They broke off quite early and Lenny dropped him back at the hotel where Ruben was taking the night air at the front door.

"You know Señor Harvey, I could be very um naughty with that one." As he admired her departing bottom. "Well Rubes my friend, she is currently without a boyfriend and I could let her know ...."

"No please, I was thinking aloud .... I prefer to dream, gin?" "Good idea."

Harvey was up by 10 am and lodged his belongings in Ruben's office after saying his farewells to 217. Ruben had promised him shower and changing facilities for later and he was about to breakfast when Lenny appeared. "Come on Harvey, Mollie's doing breakfast and you're invited. Do you like deep fried Mars Bars?" "Yuk!" "Good because it's a good old fry up, ready?"

Hill Street was not opening until the evening so Lenny was free for the day. Over a superb, big, breakfast she suggested they take the train to Malaga and chill for the day. They could stop at the airport and deposit his bags en route. This sounded like a good plan or, in fact, an excellent idea. Far better than moping around, drinking too much and waiting in the dust with the Simmonds family for a late coach full of depressed tourists. Not to mention a courier full of attitude and static electricity.

He bade his fond farewells to his friends after being reassured that they did not need his help. Because of Mani's clean up campaign after the break in, Lenny could be spared too. He promised not to leave it so long next time and Mollie suggested he should bring the girls next time. That too sounded like a good plan, and would certainly kerb the excesses of this trip.

Lenny picked up on this vibe and started to giggle, Marco said "Maybe you wouldn't get so bored with your family around eh?" They hugged and he waved unsteadily as they disappeared in the slipstream of the bike's dust and smoke.

Ruben drove them the short distance to the station and watched sadly as the Englishman and his little friend with the firm bottom climbed the stairs to the platform. "He fancies you rotten, did you know that?" "Harvey, Nets and I get used to that all the time, not being big headed, but sometimes it's nice to go steady. I wouldn't mind him cleaning my shower head." Harvey leaned over the railing and shouted loudly to Ruben as he was getting into his car "Hey Rubes, she fancies you too!" Ruben blushed and waved again, back at the hotel he had Juan clean the bike and put it in the shade.

-

My Dearest Harvey,

I write this from the mountains as we weave our way through the beautiful scenery on this last leg of our tour. The only really good thing was meeting you. The soaking delivered by your friend did not keep this rabble quiet for long and I am pleased to be rid of them soon. Harvey, my darling Harvey, I will miss you so much and my next trip is so long. It will be longer because you are not there. When it is over, I hope you will be pleased if I find you. I will contact you first to make sure you feel the same. Harvey, I know I love you so please remember your promise and look after.....

She broke off as the coach lurched violently sideways, that was sharp she thought. She looked at Henri as the coach lurched again. He was sat bolt upright with an iron grip on the wheel. His face was contorted and he was trying to speak but could not force his jaws apart. His eyes began to bulge, as she unbelted and reached him Henri slumped over the wheel.

-

"What about Claudette then, do you think she will be in touch?" "Lenny, I'm over twice her age. I hate to say it but, in my old age I have become more of a realist than a surrealist. If she wants, that is fine, but in the cold light of day or, more to the point, several thousand miles away in a new country I will seem very small beer, unfortunately."

They had spent a lovely day in Malaga and had retraced the steps he had taken with Claudette and almost as enjoyable. "Come off it Harvey. You have been with me all day , and I've run out of fingers and toes counting the times you have mentioned her name. I'm not complaining, it's nice and from what I saw she is probably the same. Don't give me that age thing - you're only here once."

They hugged like friends old and new have done at airports ever since there have been airports. He gave her a peck on her forehead and once through the departure gate he turned, like we all do, for that last wave "Go and unblock your shower' he called. She laughed, "I might just do that" and was gone.

He looked at the clock which told him it was 1645, his new watch proudly announced it was 2301, the same as the last time he looked. "Should have bought the Gucci or the extended warranty" he sighed. After making the security alarm beep he had to remove the watch and go through again. He smiled as the watch read 2302 and he reset it. Maybe it would work after all.

Heading for the bar he spotted Ellen's granddaughter, Janine? at the Duty-Free. "Oh no" he said to himself, he had gained enough bruises over the past two weeks and didn't fancy being squeezed all the way back to Gatwick.

"Hello," she said brightly through her lovely suntan. "I have a window this time, Nana has the end seat and our new friend is in the middle, but I hope you are close so we can do some colouring." "Me too" he replied with a grateful smile.

He had considered asking her their seat numbers so he could change if necessary - pain does that to a person. She bought a huge Toblerone but didn't have enough Spanish money left so he bought it for her. "We had a great time did you" "Yes I really did, oh Hello Ellen, all ok?" " Hello, a bit nervous but I'm ok this time, thanks."

He was surprised to find Guinness Extra Cold at the bar and ordered a pint. The Spanish Barman poured it to perfection. This, of course, should not surprise anybody as slowly flowing, then waiting as the foaming brew settled, then topping up before serving fits in well with the Manyana school of thinking. Harvey ordered his second pint on the delivery of the first and sank into the luscious, creamy top to suck up the cold dark brew beneath.

"Hiya Chuck, enjoying your beer?" It was Cilla girl and friend. Harvey nodded and lifted his face to reveal a Mr Pastry moustache. They laughed as he licked his lips and smiled back. "Do us a favour Chuck," she said as his second pint arrived, "you look like yer here fora bit, can you watch our bags. We need to go to the lav, there's a luv."

They didn't wait for an answer, but they didn't look like terrorists either so he didn't mind. He looked up at the departure screen, their flight was on time. The TV over the bar was blank, ah well, no news is good news. He wondered if the Simmonds family were still waiting in the dust outside Hotel El Torro. He hoped not as the gate was flashed on the screen. A sudden crush at the bar put a third pint out of the question, "Better not" he thought, he had to drive at the other end and fancied a G&T on the plane. He spotted the girls rushing back. "Just in time for me to have a pee" he said to himself, "they look a bit serious."

"Everything alright girls, forget something?" "No Chuck, it's the newspapers over there" she pointed past a hot dog stall. "Your friend, French wasn't she? Well, I don't read Spanish but she's on the front page."

"I hope you are wrong or she has won the lottery, be a love and watch my bag." Harvey said, with more than a little concern, and strode off to get a paper.

THE END

About the Author

David Tarrant spent nearly forty years in public service, was nominated and once reached the final top forty of the Public Servant Of The Year Awards - but no cigar. He is now 'retired', and Harvey is his first publication. Despite being a single parent for many years he has travelled widely in Europe, cycled from Le Havre to Zurich and the length of The Bay Of Biscay - the dry bit. He has done charity work in the UK, Africa and Thailand and believes every able body should do a stint with Habitat For Humanity. David also worked many New Years as a doorman in a friends bar in Amsterdam. He has two grown up children, Darren and Rebecca (Bex). He currently resides in Corfu with his dog, also called David, and girlfriend Elizabet. He can be found helping his friends Giannis & Elena in The Tudor Inn, Gouvia, researching his next book or planning his Desert Island Discs. Elizabet wishes he would calm down a bit and move to Bulgaria, Bex & Darren just wish he would grow up.